DECEPTION

INFIDELITY - BOOK 3

ALEATHA ROMIG

NEW YORK TIMES AND USA TODAY BESTSELLING AUTHOR OF THE CONSEQUENCES SERIES

DECEPTION

Book 3 of the INFIDELITY series

Published by Romig Works, LLC

2016 Edition

Cover art: Kellie Dennis at Book Cover by Design (www.bookcoverbydesign.co.uk)

Editing: Lisa Aurello

Formatting: Angela McLaurin at Fictional Formats

Print ISBN: 978-0-9863080-9-3 (0986308099)

DISCLAIMER

The Infidelity series contains adult content and is intended for mature audiences. While the use of overly descriptive language is infrequent, the subject matter is targeted at readers over the age of eighteen.

Infidelity is a five-book romantic suspense series. Each individual book will end in a way that will hopefully make you want more until we reach the end of the epic journey.

The Infidelity series does not advocate or glorify cheating. This series is about the inner struggle of compromising your beliefs for your heart. It is about cheating on yourself, not someone else.

I hope you enjoy the epic tale of INFIDELITY!

DECEPTION

DECEPTION, book THREE of FIVE in
Aleatha Romig's INFIDELITY series.

"Infidelity - it isn't what you think"

It all began in Del Mar, a chance meeting with a single rule—one week only.

Or did it?

Lennox 'Nox' Demetri and Alexandria 'Charli' Collins had every intention of following their agreement but rules are made to be broken. In CUNNING they are reunited with Nox setting down new rules for the game and Charli having no choice but to follow them.

Now, once again, the game has changed. Nox and Charli's hot sensual encounter has grown into something more but it is threatened with secrets and regrets. Is it their love and intense sexual chemistry that's pushing them together or something darker, a puppetmaster behind the scenes pulling the strings on their love affair?

Shadowy villains lurk around each corner and everyone is suspect as Nox's and Charli's pasts collide with the present and threaten to compel them back to their predestined fates.

Can deals brokered in the past be negated by something as pure as love and as steamy as the attraction shared by Nox and Charli? Or was it all a deception—starting with that very first meeting?

From New York Times and USA Today bestselling author Aleatha Romig comes a sexy, new dominant hero who knows what he wants and a strong-willed heroine who has plans of her own. With classic Aleatha Romig twists and turns, the depth of this epic romantic suspense continues to reach new levels as past and present intertwine. The Infidelity series will have readers swooning one minute and screaming the next.

Have you been Aleatha'd?

DECEPTION is a full-length novel, over 350 pages, and the third of five books in the INFIDELITY series - *It isn't what you think!*
(This series is not about nor does it advocate or condone cheating)

DECEPTION

Is it really cheating if you're doing it to yourself?

ALEATHA ROMIG

PROLOGUE

The end of Cunning, book #2 of the Infidelity series

CHARLI

I SAW THE plain white envelope lying on the middle of my desk. Slowly, I moved forward, confident it hadn't been there earlier in the evening. My feet barely moved as I made my way around the desk. It was like a dream as I floated closer, as if the envelope were a snake and would sense my sudden movement and strike.

Alexandria was scrolled across the front.

My heart did triple time as I reached for it. Blood coursed through my veins and through my ears, muting the world around me. With shaking fingers, I lifted it and opened the flap.

The first page was a picture. I'd never seen the woman before, but she looked familiar. It was because she looked like me. Her hair wasn't auburn but beautiful rich shades of brown, long and flowing about the same length as mine. Her eyes were a soft brown, darker than mine, but with golden flecks. She was smiling at the camera and dressed in something red. It was only a headshot.

I sank to the chair. I didn't want to keep looking, but like gawking at a train wreck, I couldn't look away. My heart knew who she was, but it needed confirmation. I moved the picture to the back of the stack of pages and began to read.

Alexandria,

I'm sure you're mad or even freaked out that I had this put where you'd find it. I'm sorry. I won't say that I'm not trying to scare you. I am.

You won't return my calls. You won't return my text messages even when Adelaide explained how much I need you. Now I need you to listen. Please listen. Please keep reading.

You know who she is, don't you? The woman in the picture?

Her name was Jocelyn Marie Matthews Demetri.

My stomach sank. I needed to stop, to show this to Nox, but I couldn't.

Was, Alexandria, she was. She's dead.

Your boyfriend killed her.

The Demetris are dangerous. I won't go into all the illegal activities, including prostitution, but know that it's there. I just want you to know about the man you're sleeping with. The man she slept with. The man who killed her.

My empty stomach twisted violently.

Stop! Stop! Stop reading!

My heart screamed out, but my eyes continued to roam.

Lennox wouldn't allow her family to see her body. He had her cremated before any evidence could be found.

Evidence. Her parents have both sworn statements about his abuse. On more than one occasion they witnessed bruises on her wrists. They've both testified to that.

I looked to my wrists. There was a faint brown mark from where I'd pulled too hard against the satin. I continued to read.

He was a workaholic. They say she was sad and scared.

Their testimony is available. They have a civil suit pending against him. He bought off the judge for the petition of evidence in a criminal matter, but even the great Lennox Demetri can't stop all the wheels of justice.

Get out. Leave. Come home or at least move back to your apartment.

Alexandria, I'm scared to death.

I also think he's behind framing me with Melissa. He could be the reason she's missing. By getting rid of her, he can remove me from your life.

Lennox is dangerous.

I'm begging you. Your mother is begging you.

Ask him if he's responsible for Jocelyn's death... and get out!

Bryce

Why couldn't he let this go? Why would he think Nox was connected to Melissa? That didn't make sense.

The letter consisted of two pages. Each handwritten page surrounded the picture. I didn't want to move the last page of words. I didn't want to see her again.

I hadn't realized I was crying until a tear splashed against the paper.

When I looked up, my eyes met Nox's. His pallor matched his cold, icy eyes, so different than only minutes earlier.

"You shouldn't have touched it."

I couldn't comprehend. "Touched what?"

"That letter, Charli. You're destroying evidence. Deloris can dust it for fingerprints."

My head moved slowly back and forth as I realized I was holding Jocelyn's picture.

How angry would Nox be?

Before I could think, I was up on my feet, my heels sliding across the wooden floor as I backed away from him. "Where's Deloris?"

"She's on her way up. What's the matter? What did that say?"

"I-I…" I rolled my lips between my teeth. "I need to talk to her."

Nox took a step toward me. His expression morphed from concern to something more intense as I once again took a step back. "What the fuck, Charli? Are you afraid of me?"

"No," I answered too quickly and too loudly.

When he closed the distance, he snatched the papers from my hand. I didn't release them quickly enough. The momentary tug of war allowed them to fall. They fluttered to the floor, Jocelyn's smiling face looking up at us.

Color returned to his face as red covered his cheeks. The vein in his forehead bulged, and the muscles in his neck tensed. "What the fuck is this?"

I blinked, afraid to speak, yet unable to stay silent. I searched his eyes and worked to even my voice. "I think it's nothing. I think it's my family trying to scare me."

"You think?" He lifted her picture from the floor. "Your family broke into our apartment?"

I shook my head. "I doubt it. They probably paid someone."

Nox couldn't pull his eyes away from Jocelyn. The edge of the page crumpled as his grasp tightened.

"Please look at me," I begged.

The muscles in his temples flexed as he clenched and unclenched his jaw.

"Nox!"

Slowly, he looked away from her to me.

"Just tell me that you had nothing to do with her death. Tell me you weren't responsible, and we will go to the hotel, or stay here. There's no threat."

He didn't speak.

"Please, Nox," I begged, reaching for his hands, wanting to help him, to take away the pain this letter caused. "Please. I didn't gather this information. It was thrown at me. It doesn't even make sense. Just tell me you aren't responsible for her death, and I'll ignore everything the letter said."

The floor dropped out from under me as his answer echoed against the freshly painted walls.

"I can't."

CHAPTER 1

CHARLI

"I CAN'T."

Nox's deep voice echoed from the walls of my newly decorated office. Their vibrations amplified within my soul, the meaning lost as I searched his icy blue stare.

I can't.

Indecision and uncertainty rushed through me.

Who was this man?

Did I even know?

Nothing mattered but the one recurring question that, while answered, remained unexplained.

Please, Nox, tell me that you're not responsible for her death.

My heartbeat quickened as I stepped back from the man who had been my lover, from the man whom I'd trusted. Mute and deaf. The words *I can't* were the only ones I heard over the deafening silence. Yet there was more. The world unrelentingly spun, tilting on its axis as life continued beyond my fog.

Nox's large hand reached for me, pulling me from the abyss of my thoughts. Like fur-lined handcuffs, his grip was strong and unbreakable while at the same time gentle and comforting. The expression upon his handsome face changed before my eyes. The anger or defiance I'd seen only seconds before morphed, combining with hurt and concern.

"Charli," Nox said.

My name hung in the air like the clanging of a church bell, the next ring coming before the other disappeared, each time louder than the time before.

My knees gave way as my retreat met with the freshly painted wall. I couldn't back any farther away. Down was my only option. As I descended into a crouching position, so did Nox. Our physical connection severed, though our gaze remained set.

Afraid to look away, from the corner of my eye I saw her face. Not that of Deloris, now holding tightly to the doorjamb, her complexion as pale as the walls, but of Jocelyn. She smiled knowingly up from the floor near my feet, still clad in the Louboutins. The high heels forced my knees toward my breasts. I grabbed onto my own tender wrists, clung to my legs, and willed my invisibility cloak of childhood to cover me.

What would Jocelyn have said if she were here? Would she assure me of my lover's innocence or warn me of his dangerous ways? Would she hate me for being with her husband or thank me for reminding him to live?

"Alex. Alex," Deloris spoke my name in a steadfast tone as she touched Nox's shoulder and moved slowly toward me.

She didn't stare at the beautiful face of the woman in the picture. If I didn't know her well, I'd say she didn't see it, but that wasn't true. Deloris Witt saw everything. She knew everything. In one glance she'd summed up what had happened—how my world had crumbled in a heap of broken dreams.

Her conclusions were always correct.

At Deloris's encouragement, Nox stood and backed away, his distance allowing me to breathe, giving me oxygen and filling my lungs. The much-needed air gave my body what it needed to carry on its involuntary processes. I couldn't comprehend or consciously think as my body shuddered with pent-up sobs, and Deloris reached for my hand.

"Alex, let me help you stand."

The tightness of my own grip around my knees had gone unnoticed until I released my hold and the circulation returned to my hands and arms, pink returning to my stone-cold fingertips. I wobbled as I stood, unsure why the world was on tilt.

Perhaps I was drunk.

No, I'd barely touched the lemon drop martini. One sip, or was it two?

The room spun around me. Lines that had been straight were now curves, ebbing and bowing. My empty stomach reeled before it free-fell from unknown heights. I stumbled toward the plush chaise lounge.

Nox was immediately at my side, his strong arm encircling my waist as he steadied me.

"Don't touch me." It was the first phrase I'd uttered, my first comprehensible thought.

His warmth disappeared as I sank onto the soft chair, still gripping Deloris's hand.

"Alex, may I get you something? Water?"

Is she serious? Water? I shook my head.

My dry tongue darted to my parched lips as I tried to steady not only my voice but also the ricocheting of my heart. Surely they could both hear it bouncing between my spine and ribs. I couldn't look at Nox. I needed space.

"Deloris," I began, searching her eyes for comprehension. "Will you please take me to my apartment?"

"Fuck." Nox's expletive was barely a whisper, yet it filled the room with his displeasure.

"Alex, you're safer here," Deloris offered.

My senses returned. Noises registered—the hum of the air conditioning and the beat of Nox's shoes as he paced against the polished wood floor. The aroma of our uneaten dinner wafted through the air.

"Safer here?" I rebuked. "This apartment was broken into. Your perfect security was breached. I hardly consider that safe." Each statement came with more conviction.

"It was," Deloris admitted. "However, if you two had stayed out a little longer, I would've had this resolved without your knowledge and you'd still feel safe. I guarantee, I'll get to the bottom of this."

I narrowed my glare as indignation grew. "Without my knowledge? Without my knowledge? If we'd stayed out longer, I would never have known about the letter? It was addressed to me!"

I released her hand, her hold no longer comforting. "What else don't I know? What else has been hidden from me?"

"Charli," Nox's velvet timbre reverberated through the cooled air. "It's for your own good."

"My own good?"

"Lennox and I have tried to explain," Deloris said. "There are constant threats. It doesn't do you or anyone any good to know all of the details. It would be—"

"Suffocating?" I offered the appropriate word to complete her sentence as I stood, my bones now solidly capable of supporting my weight.

"Unnecessary," Nox corrected.

Slowly I spun, taking in the office that had been designed for me. I ran my hand over the back of the chaise, the fibers of the plush material bending to the pressure of my touch. I caught the brown-eyed smile of the picture still lying upon the floor. She was young and beautiful and had a life of promise ahead, and now she was dead.

My neck and shoulders straightened. "Answers, Nox. I need answers or I'm leaving."

Nox took a step toward me. My glare stalled his movement, but not his declaration. "You can't leave. I won't allow it."

"What the fuck are going to do? Are you going to lock me in this apartment? Ground me? Tie me up in your bed? That was what you said before. Well, too bad. You can't."

His lips formed a straight line that in only seconds grew increasingly thin. Without speaking he was telling me he could do that and more. Suddenly that thought was no longer erotic but frightening.

My eyes roamed, unable to endure the intensity of Nox's stare. Deloris had gathered the pages of Bryce's letter, using a tissue to pick them from the floor.

"I'll assume you both handled these pages?" she asked.

"Yes," Nox answered.

"I'll have them dusted."

"Why?" I asked. "Bryce signed the letter."

Daggers launched from the icy blueness of Nox's eyes. "Bryce? Edward Spencer? I thought you said your family?"

"What?"

He stepped closer, his chest nearing mine, cologne again clouding my thoughts as I fought to project a sense of calm I truly didn't feel.

"You said you thought it was *your family* trying to scare you. Edward Spencer isn't your *family*." He emphasized the last word.

"My family's complicated. He claims to be speaking for my mother. The point is, there's no reason to dust anything. We know who it came from."

My gaze moved away from Nox, back to Deloris. She was silent as she read the letter, my letter, the one addressed to me.

"Privacy. Is that what I give up if I stay here?"

"If?" Nox repeated.

"Lennox, you should read this," Deloris spoke from the other side of the room.

I slapped my hands against my thighs. "Sure, everyone fucking read *my* letter. Let's get Isaac and Jerrod in here. I know, call Lana. Is there anyone else?" I pursed my lips waiting for a response. Finally, I went on. "All I want is answers; instead, I'm getting more and more questions."

Deloris turned toward me. "There's a plethora of accusations in this letter. Don't you agree that they could be best addressed if Lennox knew what he was supposed to answer?"

"I've already asked the most important one."

Nox's eyes narrowed in a silent warning, telling me to avoid the subject that loomed around us, the figurative elephant prancing around the room, its trunk raised like a trumpet alarming each of us of its path of destruction. A momentary tinge of apprehension infiltrated my righteous anger as the question resurfaced—did Nox kill Jocelyn?

His posture straightened as he tightened his jaw and lifted his hand toward Deloris. When she hesitated, he said, "I've already touched it. What difference does it make if I handle it again?"

She shook her head and pulled another tissue from the box. Handing that first to Nox, she then passed him the letter.

I shook my head dismissively and reached for my backpack. My overnight bag was already packed.

As I stepped toward the doorway, Nox's command stilled my footsteps.

"Stop."

Images of Alton raced through my mind as I spun Nox's direction. "I'm not a child. If you won't talk to me, I'm not staying here."

"You're not going to that apartment. The security isn't complete."

I rolled my eyes as I let out a long sigh. "You're putting security in *my* apartment?"

"Chelsea's," he corrected. "And of course."

Shaking my head, I replied, "You're unbelievable. Did you think to ask me? Ask Chelsea? I mean, she interviewed for that job. If she gets the one in DC she won't even be here that much."

"Alex…"

I lifted my hand to silence Deloris. I was tired of listening to them answer my questions in circles. "Call Jerrod, or I will. I'm leaving."

"No, you're—"

"Yes, I am."

"Jerrod works for me," Nox declared.

Fuck him! This was Alton all over again.

My neck straightened in indignation. "Then I'll take a cab. You want a say in this? That's your choice. This time it's my number in your phone and the ball's in your court. If you're ever ready to talk to me, to be honest with me, call. Otherwise…" I took a deep breath, debating the end of my sentence. "…otherwise, don't."

"Charli, do not leave this apartment."

His order hung in the air, the final word. Nevertheless, I walked into the bedroom seeing the vibrator upon the bed. Its presence mocked me. Ignoring it and the plans that I'd had for this evening, I found my overnight case.

How had our date gone from amazing to shit in record time? The ring of my phone encouraged me forward, moving me toward the living room, where earlier—when this evening had hope—I'd dropped my handbag.

The screen read *JERROD.*

"Hello," I said after pushing the green icon.

"Ma'am, I'll have the car out front in five minutes."

I wasn't sure if it had been Nox or Deloris who'd contacted him, but at least I wouldn't need to get a cab.

A tear slid down my cheek as I closed my eyes. "Thank you, Jerrod. I'll be there."

My destination options came in rapid succession. I could go to my and Chelsea's apartment. If I did, I was not only disobeying Nox by leaving, but also by going where he told me specifically not to go. Then again, until he could be honest with me, I didn't need to listen to his directives. I could go to Patrick and Cy's apartment. Surely it was safe. Or I could do as Bryce's note implored and travel back to Savannah.

With a heavy heart, I stifled a ragged breath and turned back toward the glacial-blue eyes. Though Nox watched my every move, he didn't speak. Silently, I turned toward the door and exited our apartment.

CHAPTER 2

NOX

FUCK!

I pulled my phone from my pocket as the apartment door closed. After two pushes and one ring, Jerrod answered.

"I want to know where you take her."

"Yes, sir."

"Keep both me and Deloris informed. I want round-the-clock surveillance."

"Yes, sir. You'll be constantly informed. She won't make a move that you don't know about."

Damn, that sounded wrong. I wasn't trying to suffocate Charli. That was her word. I was assuring her safety. Why couldn't she see that?

"Safety. That's my number-one objective."

"Yes, sir," Jerrod replied.

I disconnected the call and looked back at Deloris. She was sitting on the sofa hammering out a text message. Briefly her eyes met mine and then with a slight shake of her head, her attention was drawn back to the screen of her phone. My teeth ached with the pressure as I held my jaws together—tighter and tighter. If I didn't find another outlet, surely my teeth would shatter.

As soon as she hit send, Deloris sighed and looked up.

I waited.

The silence continued.

Finally, I spoke. "Tell me how in the fuck someone broke in here."

Her head moved from side to side. "I can't."

What the hell kind of answer was that?

Then, as if delayed, her words hit hard, drying my mouth and weakening my knees as I fell to the sofa. A *swoosh* escaped my lips as if I'd truly been struck, the impact causing the air to exit my lungs. Her words were the same ones I'd given Charli.

"I can't," I said again, confessing my rare inability.

"No, I can't," she said, misinterpreting my statement as a question for her. "It doesn't make sense. You know my security is top-notch. I don't believe Edward Spencer or anyone connected with the Montagues was responsible for this note. They never would've been able to trick the system."

I stared in disbelief. That wasn't what I'd meant by *I can't.* I'd meant that I couldn't tell Charli the truth about Jo. Not yet. I hadn't verbalized it since it happened, not in a concise statement, nor in a long, breathy rambling statement. Until a few weeks ago, I hadn't even looked at the online reports. I didn't think I could say it aloud.

Though Jo's death was almost five years ago, if I closed my eyes it seemed like yesterday. It seemed like today. Adrenaline flooded my system as perspiration moistened my palms. I didn't want to think about it. The anger. The blood. But it was there, in the forefront of my mind.

It had been the day that wouldn't end. Maybe it hadn't. Maybe it was still today.

It was like that movie *Groundhog Day*. I couldn't think of a worse hell.

"Lennox, I'll get to the bottom of this."

I nodded, unsure if the awful images in my mind would come bubbling out if I spoke.

"You read the accusations?" she asked.

I nodded again. The list came together in my mind: murder, abuse, hiding evidence, coercion of a judge, illegal activities including prostitution. Then it hit me. "The letter blamed me for Melissa Summer's disappearance. Who would have any knowledge of that? And prostitution? That has to be referring to Infidelity." I thought some more. "The writer called Charli *Alexandria*. It seems as though only her family uses that name for her."

Deloris looked my way, her shoulders stiff as she contemplated. "It's her name. Anyone who knows the Montagues of Savannah would refer to her that way. That isn't enough for me to immediately jump to her family. I believe that's the direction the writer wanted us to look. It's the direction the person assumed would have the most impact on Alex."

I closed my eyes and inhaled deeply. "I shouldn't have let her go."

Both Deloris's and my phone buzzed.

Text message.

Jerrod: "*I JUST DROPPED MISS COLLINS AT 1214 FIFTH AVENUE. SHE SAID SHE WOULD SPEND THE NIGHT.*"

"That's Patrick's building," I volunteered. "At least she isn't alone."

Deloris nodded as she replied to the text message. When she was done, she said, "I'm glad she didn't go to the apartment."

"Get the surveillance set up there tomorrow. I want it complete. If she decides to move there, I need to know she's safe."

Unable to take the pressure anymore, I stood with an exasperated breath. "Fuck. This isn't the way tonight was supposed to go." I ran my palms over my stubbly cheeks. I should be balls deep in Charli right now, not sitting here with Deloris trying to put together pieces of a puzzle that didn't fit.

"Did he walk her to Patrick's apartment?" I asked.

"I assume he drove her to the building."

Panic flooded my system. "I've been there before. He lives on the forty-sixth floor. Someone… anyone could—"

Deloris raised a finger as she put her phone to her ear. After a moment, she lowered the phone, disconnected the first call, and scrolled the screen. "I have Patrick's number—"

"You tried Charli and she didn't answer?"

What the fuck?

"She could have the ringer off."

I paced back and forth, waiting for Patrick to answer. The anticipation set my already overwrought nerves into overdrive. Each one zinged to life until my skin felt stretched—too small for my bones.

"Mr. Richardson, my name is Deloris Witt. I work for Lennox Demetri." Pause. "Yes, I see." Pause. "Thank you. Please let her know that we wanted to ensure her safe arrival to your apartment." Pause. "Thank you, Mr. Richardson. Goodbye."

My lungs filled to capacity. "She's there?"

"Yes. She wasn't with him at that moment, but she's there, in the apartment."

"Wasn't with him?"

"He said she was changing clothes. Lennox, she's safe."

I tried not to think about the black beaded dress she was no longer wearing or the gorgeous body that was now clad in something no doubt more comfortable. I didn't want to imagine her across town, instead of glistening with perspiration beneath me.

"She was right."

I turned incredulously at Deloris's assessment. "Right? About leaving?"

"Not about leaving, but about stopping her. You couldn't stop her." Deloris shrugged. "I'm not doubting your ability, but legally, you can't make her stay here."

"I could if her Infidelity contract were real."

"If it were…" she said, contemplating her response, "…you could appeal to her commitment to that agreement, but you couldn't use it as justification in a court of law. Don't forget, Infidelity doesn't exist."

For probably the first time, I wanted it to exist. I wanted Alexandria Collins's signature beside mine. I wanted the right to demand her return. When I didn't respond, Deloris spoke again.

"The most important one?"

I narrowed my eyes. "What are you talking about?"

"Alex said that though she'd read an entire laundry list of accusations claiming everything from abuse and extortion to murder, that she only asked you about *the most important one.*"

"Jo." My one-word answer was all I could say.

"And you answered her. You told her you weren't responsible."

I shook my head. "I told her the truth. Didn't you see how fucking frightened she was when you entered her office?"

"Lennox," her tone softened. "Call her. Talk to her. Don't let your guilt over Jocelyn infect what you and Alex have."

I paced the length of the living room and stared out at the lights of New York City. From high above, the streets were filled with taillights, creating red ribbons of moving and stationary cars. Even late into the evening, traffic flowed in fits and starts.

"I can't talk about it. I can't think about it." I spun back around. "If I do, if I try, it's like living it all over again." I shook my head. "Fuck. Make sure Charli's safe. We both know the truth. The best way to ensure Charli's safety is to keep her away from me."

"Lennox."

I hated it. But now that I'd said it, I knew I was right. "Find out who wrote that letter. Find out who knows my secrets."

"Whomever that person is needs to be stopped."

"First, I want to know why." I took a deep breath and tried to look at the letter from a different angle. Not from my perspective, but from the writer's. "What was the objective?"

"It specifically told Alex to get away from you, to leave you."

"So it worked. Who besides Edward Spencer would benefit from that? Who besides him would want us separated?"

"What do you know about her family?" Deloris asked.

"I know she speaks regularly to her mother. I know the calls exasperate her. I know that her stepfather had something to do with taking away her trust fund. And from the business world, I know he's an arrogant ass who, like Oren, believes deals are made with greased palms over Cognac."

I turned back to the lights. If I took a step back, the window became a colorful mirror reflecting my own image. Instead, I stepped closer. The man in that reflection disgusted me. Charli deserved to be with someone who was above reproach, above the accusations in that letter. I didn't want to believe that person was the slimebag Spencer.

My gut twisted as I turned again.

"How is there a connection between Edward Spencer and Melissa Summers?"

Deloris's eyes met mine. "I tried to tell you. You said you didn't want to know."

"I fucking want to know now."

"He's the grad student."

What the fuck?

"How had I not put that together?"

"Because you didn't want to see it. You didn't want to associate Alex with someone like Edward Spencer."

"Where's the letter?"

"Lennox, even with a tissue, fingerprints can be smudged. It's better not to touch it."

"What did it say about Melissa?"

"Just a minute."

Deloris walked into the kitchen. I waited as cupboards opened and closed. When she returned, she had three large plastic bags, the kind that zipped closed at the top. With care and precision, she gently inserted each page into its own bag. Finding the right page, she handed it to me. My eyes searched for the passage.

Alexandria, I'm scared to death.

I also think he's behind framing me with Melissa. He could be the reason she's missing. By getting rid of her, he can remove me from your life.

Lennox is dangerous.

I'm begging you. Your mother is begging you.

"He's saying I'm dangerous but he's the one who raped and beat Melissa Summers?" My mind spun. "If Melissa dated him…" My stomach turned with the revelation. "…couldn't she have told him about Infidelity?"

"She would've had opportunity. But by the letter of the agreement, she wasn't allowed to tell anyone."

"Obviously, she didn't follow the agreement *to the letter* because if she had, she wouldn't have dated someone other than her client." I lifted my brow. "Do you still doubt that this was written by Spencer?"

Deloris pursed her lips. "I don't think he, the Montagues, nor the Fitzgeralds have the ability to circumvent my security. Did he write it? I can't answer that. Did he put it in here? I can answer that unequivocally no. I need to take these and dust them first. I should also dust the apartment… if we haven't already done too much damage."

"You want me to leave?"

"I turned off the stove. Your dinner is a tad overcooked."

I turned in a small circle, taking in the apartment. I'd lived here for years and it'd been fine. I was comfortable and content. Now, without Charli, it seemed empty and too quiet. She'd been gone for less than an hour and I missed… well, everything about her. I walked back to the bedroom to gather a few clothes.

Her damn vibrator was still on the bed. It was bad enough that someone had been in our apartment. I couldn't leave it there for Deloris or her team to dust. I lifted the purple silicone-covered shaft. It was curved and smooth. My thoughts went to the delicious ways I could use it on Charli. I imagined her moans and screams as I pushed the buttons. There was a music option that would allow the device to respond to my voice. She should be in my bed—in our bed—and with words and this stupid toy I should be taking her to new heights.

The room came into focus, but I wasn't seeing what was really there.

I was seeing what wasn't.

Her delicate hands were bound with an intricate winding of satin and secured above her head. Her beautiful hair was piled high, and stray auburn wisps surrounding her face contrasted with her flushed complexion. My chest heaved as her sexy body was displayed—each curve, each angle—for my optimum viewing pleasure. In my imagination she was nude, except for the black shoes she'd worn to Mobar, the same shoes that had adorned the dashboard of the Boxster. Her ankles were untethered, bound only by my instructions. Her legs were spread, slightly bent, with her knees out and the heels of her sexy shoes threatening to perforate the soft Egyptian threaded sheets. As the humming vibrations rippled through the air, her body trembled in anticipation, and she stifled a whimper. I loved the way she squirmed as she fought between maintaining the position I demanded and her body's natural reactions.

My lips quirked as I added a satin blindfold to my fantasy. It was something we'd never done, but then again, we'd never played with her vibrator either. Without sight, her senses would be heightened. The quiet hum would be louder, a roar in the otherwise silence of our room. My words would be amplified, sending shockwaves from her ears to her pussy that clenched and dripped with unmet need.

I'd tease her mercilessly, giving her small tastes of what was to come.

Then I remembered my earlier directives. I'd told her that I'd bring her dinner. The lack of sight would affect that too. Nibbles of the food that Lana had prepared would be just enough to provide the energy she'd need for our night of fun, but never enough to satisfy.

Keeping her wanting and deprived would be my goal, until it wasn't.

It wouldn't be only her swollen clit or glistening silky folds that would tell me of her wonton desires, her fragrance would fill the air until she couldn't take it anymore and submitted to words, asking, begging, and finally demanding relief. The purple shaft would bring her some, but only as much as I allowed. It wouldn't be enough.

"Your cock. Stop being a dick. I want your cock, now!"

A full-on smile graced my lips at the imaginary dialogue. It was as if I almost heard her voice, the way it cracked with urgency and determination.

"Lennox, I have my team on their way."

Deloris's voice from the living room pulled me from my fantasy as reality fell hard upon my shoulders. I hit the switch again, stopping the hum as the erection my thoughts had created quickly faded. By the time I had a few clothes packed and the vibrator stowed within its case in a drawer, my physical response was completely gone.

Just like my dreams.

Just like Charli.

CHAPTER 3

CHARLI

"YOU KNOW YOU can't leave him," Patrick said as he squeezed my knee. "I can tell you're upset. I don't know what he did, but you simply can't. It's not allowed."

I twisted the stem of the wine glass, the red liquid swirling within the globe. Thankfully, Cy wasn't home and it was just Patrick and I. "Thanks for letting me borrow your gym shorts and t-shirt."

He laughed. "Besides the fact that you kind of look like they're swallowing you whole, you look cute. I don't often get to see a beautiful woman wearing my clothes."

I looked up through my damp lashes as his words tugged my lips into a small smile. "Beautiful? Yeah, I feel gorgeous right now."

"Well, you've got the too-big clothes going for you, plus the red blotchy thing and puffy eyes. A little snot as you sniffle. Little cousin, you're dazzling."

I sighed. "Can I just stay here for a day or two and figure things out?"

"You know you can. I don't even need to ask Cy. You're always welcome, but what about your apartment?"

My shoulders moved up and down. "I told Chelsea she could stay there. She's flying from California at the end of this week. I hate to get all settled only to have her displace me. Besides, I feel like I'd be on display there."

"Display?"

"It's a security thing. I'm kind of over it."

Pat leaned back against the couch. "I had a good feeling seeing you with Lennox. Besides, you have that whole one-week history…" He fingered the rim of his wine glass, and I tried to ignore how it reminded me of my martini glass only hours before. "I'm sure you can work through this."

"He has my number."

"If these were normal circumstances, I'd tell you to forget all about him. I mean, who needs someone like Lennox Demetri? I can only imagine it'd be awful to have a boyfriend who redecorates a room for you, practically weeks after you move in. One who cares enough about your dreams to pay for your education and buy you whatever you want or need, one who gives you the ability to tell Uncle Alton and Aunt Adelaide to stick their conditions up their tight asses. And girl, his looks. Damn, nobody wants to put up with those sexy blue eyes. I mean the way they light up when you walk into a room and he looks at you like he'd eat you whole. I can see how that would get old fast." He took a drink of his wine. "Honestly, I'm not sure how you managed to stay for this long." He shrugged. "There's always good ole Bryce."

I sat forward, put my wine glass on the coffee table, and after placing my elbows on my knees, cradled my head. "I don't need Bryce. Why do I need a man?"

"If you don't know the answer to that question, my opinion of Lennox Demetri has just plummeted. I mean, I'm sure you have a vibrator."

I sighed. The thought of the purple shaft tore at my heart. I looked up. "Pat, I should get some sleep. I have class early in the morning, and I'm sure you've got work."

Setting his wine glass next to mine, he reached for my hand and turned it over. With his other hand, he gently touched my wrist. Unknowingly, I gasped and sucked my upper lip between my teeth as his fingers caressed my tender skin.

Suddenly all playfulness was gone from his expression. "Did he hurt you?"

I pulled my hand free. "No."

"Alex, this is something totally different. I mean, the agreement has one out, and if your wrist is bruised." He stood. "If that bastard—"

"Stop, Pat. Nox didn't hurt me."

"You what…" he asked incredulously, "…ran into a wall? Maybe you tripped?"

"No. None of those things. You're wrong."

He shook his head. "When you first got here, I thought you were mad. You weren't mad. You were scared. You're scared of him, aren't you?"

Am I?

"No," I said sitting taller. "I'm not. He didn't hurt me, not physically. It's about trust." I stood, picked up my wine glass, took a long sip, and paced to the windows. With my back toward him, I asked, "How much does Cy know about you?"

I almost heard him shrug. "He knows me better than anyone."

I turned. "Does he know what the girls said about you at academy?"

"That I'm great in bed?" he asked with a smirk.

"That you used them. All you wanted to do was get in their pants and move on."

"It doesn't take your friend Chelsea with a psychology degree to figure out that I was in denial."

"That's what I mean. Does Cy know about you?"

"We've talked. He's older. It was tough for him to come out too." Patrick shrugged. "He doesn't talk about it much, but he was married, to a woman," he added.

"Did they have children?"

"No. It didn't last very long. You don't know what it's like…"

My chest grew tight, listening to him discuss his own struggles both as a teenager and a young adult. We were pretty close in our young teens, yet I didn't know. It was but another shadow that lurked the hallways of Montague Manor, dancing in the darkness around the Fitzgeralds. Despite Patrick's insecurities, he always appeared the opposite: cocky and self-assured.

I settled back onto the sofa.

When he was done, he asked, "Did you never suspect?"

I nodded. "I did. I remember hating the things other girls said about you. With our age difference, I usually heard secondhand rumors, but it never seemed like the Patrick Richardson they described was my Pat."

He smiled a weary smile. "I always loved you."

"Past tense?"

"No. I mean when it was just the two of us, I didn't feel the need to overcompensate. We existed in our own world whether at Montague Manor or at my house." He shrugged. "It wasn't as if our parents gave a rat's ass what we did, as long as we didn't interrupt whatever they were doing." A smile grew on his face, causing his cheeks to rise. "The only one who knew what we were up to was Jane."

The mention of her name loosened the boa constrictor I'd had wrapped around my chest and I grinned.

"The best part of my childhood," I said with a sigh. "She's still at the manor."

"Really? I would've thought after you moved away…"

"I get the feeling she takes care of Momma."

"That's good. Aunt Adelaide needs someone in her corner." His gaze narrowed. "Speaking of running into walls, I remember more than once when she'd been pretty clumsy." He nodded his head toward my wrists. "I don't want the same for you."

Indignation rose. "Neither do I. Don't worry about that. Nox would never—"

"I don't know him that well," he interrupted. "But I do know Spence. I never understood why you dated him for so long."

Maybe it was the wine or my crying, but I didn't understand the connection. "What do you mean? We were young."

"But you've never really liked him."

My shoulders sank. "I did… like him… as a friend. When we were young, other than you, he was the only one I ever saw, the only person close to my age. I was surrounded by stuffy adults. Jane was my nanny and playmate, but it wasn't the same as being around kids. Since Momma and Suzanna were so close, Bryce was there a lot."

He nodded. "I remember being thrilled when we'd go to your place and he wasn't there. I think I even asked my mom once if he lived there."

"See? He was my best friend."

"Until he was your boyfriend."

The thought churned the wine in my stomach. Bryce *was* my best friend. Isn't that what a lover should be? Nox and I had never been friends. Maybe that was why I was able to walk away today, or was it yesterday? I picked up my phone lying upon the table. I swiped the screen to the clock—after midnight—and the icon that displayed missed calls.

I sucked in my breath. I'd had the ringer off. I'd told Nox the ball was in his court, and then I wasn't there when he lobbed it back.

I hit the small icon. Two missed calls—Deloris and Bryce.

The boa squeezed tighter. Nox hadn't tried to call.

A tear escaped my eye as I brushed it away.

I would call Deloris tomorrow… and Bryce?

What should I say? Hey, Bryce, I got your letter and it worked. I left Lennox. According to you, I'm safe. However, that's only true if death by broken heart wasn't possible.

I looked up to Patrick's expectant expression. "Tell me he called. He did, didn't he?"

My head moved from side to side. "Not him, his…" What was Deloris? "…assistant called."

"Oh, yes. A woman—she said her name was Witt—called while you were changing clothes. I'm so sorry I forgot."

"She called you?"

"Yes, she wanted to be sure you were here."

I sighed and leaned back. "It's suffocating, the driver-slash-bodyguard constant surveillance. I hate it."

Ignoring my pleas to retire, Patrick poured more wine into our glasses. "I'd guess it has to do with his wife."

"What?"

"What?" His eyes opened wide as he shifted on the couch. It was like

Christmas-time secrets all over again. "You mean you're assigned to someone like Lennox Demetri and you didn't Google that shit?"

"I… we… we promised we'd learn about each other from each other."

"And so he told you about the hit?"

The hit?

My heartbeat quickened, the rapid rhythm chasing away the constricting snake. "No… I mean… we haven't discussed."

"Oh, there are fascinating theories. See the thing is, no one knows for sure. It was all very hush-hush."

"I'm not sure…"

His countenance fell. "Okay, I won't say any more, but if Mr. Sexy is overly worried about your safety, from what I gathered, he has reason."

"I don't know."

He sucked his bottom lip between his teeth. "I can't believe you've been with him for all this time and you don't know."

"Pat, you're killing me. I want to know. I do. But it's this thing we have. I mean, I wouldn't want him Googling me."

"Little cousin, you're boring."

"Hey!"

"I mean, sure, you're all heiress and shit, but come on… I grew up with you. That house of horrors was real, but you survived. Millions of people have had childhoods not even as bad as yours and not come out nearly as unscathed."

"Do I seem unscathed?"

"No," he replied, "you seem battered and a little bruised."

When his eyes went back to my wrists, I let out an exasperated sigh. "Not abuse, kink, and… well…" I felt the rush of crimson fill my cheeks. "…I like it. Now drop it."

"My! We need more wine."

"No. I need to go to bed."

"Since this heart-to-heart is about to end, let me tell you what I've observed."

My entire body relaxed as I emptied my glass and laid my head back on the top of the couch. "Fine. Hurry because I'm about to pass out."

"Whatever Lennox Demetri did to upset you." I heard his eyebrows wiggle. "And now that I know about some preferences, I'm less concerned and more intrigued. But I digress. Whatever he did to upset you hasn't altered your feelings for him. You've defended him at every turn. I mean, I have heart-stopping information that may or may not be accurate and you'd rather abide by a promise than hear me out.

"Going back to him isn't optional. He owns you for a year. The fact that he allowed you this temper tantrum shows me that he's an all-right guy. He could've refused to allow you to leave."

I opened my eyes and lifted my gaze. "And what, Pat, tie me to the bed?"

"Whoa," he lifted his hand. "I'm still coming to terms with my little cousin and kink. I don't want any more details."

"You know what I mean."

"Literally, no. Figuratively, yes."

Before I could speak, he went on.

"Here's one more observation. For some reason, Spence—Bryce holds a part of your heart. Maybe it's because for a rich, spoiled princess, your childhood was pretty sucky and you associate him with the better-than-awful parts."

I wanted to protest Patrick's description of me as well as a few other parts of his statement, but he lifted his hand again.

"My point is that I was only one year ahead of Spence at the academy. You may not know this, but I threatened his ass when you two started dating."

It was my turn for my eyes to open wide. "You did?"

"I did. He was jacking off his mouth about you, about things I wanted to believe weren't true."

My stomach turned. We never did anything. What the hell was he saying?

"I told him that you deserved respect and gave him a nice, long list of easy lays. I told him that if he ever hurt you, I'd hurt him."

My face scrunched in disbelief. "You told him to screw other girls but not to hurt me? That doesn't make sense."

"It doesn't now, but it did then. My mom told me about the charges pending in Evanston. I know Uncle Alton is throwing money at it left and right, but I wasn't the only one who had a reputation at the academy. From what I heard, Spence liked it rougher than kink. I wouldn't be the least bit surprised that he got carried away and beat the shit out of that girl."

There were too many parts to his statement to dissect each one. "He had a reputation? Before he dated me?"

"While. Little cousin, all those girls were my cover. You were his." He shook his head. "I'm not saying he's gay. I'm saying his preferences don't make for his Carmichael-Spencer reputation. If you ask me, from all you've said, that's what he wants back. The thing is, I never thought of you as a *spoiled princess*, maybe because I saw the inside of your castle. Now him…" Patrick shrugged. "…I never understood it. Spence walked around Montague like the royal son, when in reality, he was nothing more than a pauper."

"The Carmichaels—"

"Weren't the Montagues. Hell, they weren't even the Fitzgeralds."

I shook my head.

"For some reason, Spence had, correction, *has,* entitlement perfected. If you ask me, you or I should be the ones entitled. Instead, we're the ones signing our companionship away for a year at a time and he's back in Savannah crying in his milk, wanting more."

I stood and this time I took my wine glass to the kitchen and set it in the sink. When I returned to the living room, Pat was still sitting on the couch staring into space. I walked close and planted a kiss on his forehead.

"I love you. Thank you for always being there for me. Not just now, but always."

He reached out and secured my hand. Turning it over he gently traced the faint bruise on my wrist. "You trust him."

It wasn't a question, but I nodded anyway.

"I don't know what's going on in that pretty head of yours, but trust is something that should be difficult to earn and way too easy to lose. Once it's lost, regaining it is difficult. Spence may have earned it when he was three, but little cousin, if you knew all I do, you'd never put it in his grasp again."

"But with the rumors about Lennox's wife…" I almost stopped my question. "…you'd let him have it?"

Patrick shrugged. "It's not mine to give. But from the look of your wrist, you've given it. Do you really want to take it away?"

Do I?

The boa was back.

"Good night, Pat."

CHAPTER 4

Thirty years ago

OREN

"MR. DEMETRI," NIKKI, my newest secretary, said as she opened the door to my office. "Daryl Frazier is here to see you."

I glanced at the clock on the corner of my desk. He was five minutes early—as far as I was concerned, a point in his favor.

"Show him in, and bring us both coffee."

"Yes, sir."

I didn't listen as she asked Daryl the obligatory questions—cream? sugar? Life would be much easier if everyone drank coffee the way it was intended, black. What was the point if sugar and cream muted the strong, robust flavor?

"Mr. Demetri," Daryl said as he entered my office, his hand extended.

"Oren," I corrected as he took the seat across my wide desk. "As you can imagine, my schedule is quite busy. I'm glad my girl was able to squeeze you in, but to be honest, I don't have much time."

"Yes, sir, I'll jump right to the point."

The door once again opened. Nikki entered, her tight skirt accentuating her small waist, her high heels defining her shapely legs, but it was the neckline on the silk blouse that demanded Daryl's and my attention. The large scoop fell low enough to showcase her most obvious assets, however, not too low to have them openly on display.

"Your coffee," she said as she bent at the waist and sat two cups of steaming-hot brown liquid on my desk.

"Thank you, sweetheart," I replied. "Hold my calls."

"Yes, Mr. Demetri."

"You were saying?" I encouraged Daryl, as I reclined slightly, rocking my large leather chair and moving my eyes away from Nikki's assets.

"Yes, there's this parcel of land, just south of Danbury."

"Connecticut," I confirmed.

"Yes, sir. It was just made available. As you're probably aware, the population of this area has grown exponentially…"

Being on the receiving line of elevator pitches never got old. For years, ever since I worked to make a name, I was the one delivering the pitch, the one doing what needed to be done.

I wasn't born to money but worked damn hard for it. Born to a longshoreman, I had a respectable example of hard work. I also saw firsthand who really made the money. It wasn't my father or the other men who worked their asses off on the docks or out on the boats. It wasn't their supervisors, because my father made it that far. It was the men who owned the docks.

It was the families that owned the city.

It was the ones who took risks.

My parents wanted me to accomplish something no other Demetri had done. They wanted me to get an education. They believed that would give me the ticket to move beyond the blue-collared world.

I did, but *it* didn't.

Oh, it helped. It opened doors, but the real doors required more than a piece of paper or letters after my name.

I worked hard—night shift on the docks doing the same job my father had done, while I took classes during the day. I not only learned about business, I saw it. I watched who was paid to keep everything running smoothly, heard stories of unlikely alliances, and knew the truth about the unions.

I'd heard my whole life how they took their piece of my father's paycheck.

He never complained because, according to him, the union and its representatives were why he made good money—why a man with an eighth-grade education could support a family. They were also why he had health insurance and a retirement plan. He willingly paid his dues, and they took care of him. It was the way it was done.

There were men and women in my classes at New York University who came from money, those with the proverbial silver spoon. I never conceded to their birthright. Most of them had no idea where I came from or that I worked all night to sit in the same class as them. The more I got to know them, the more I recognized that half of them would be eaten alive in a place like the docks of Brooklyn or New York City.

Business was not learned only in books.

I did what my parents—God rest their souls—wanted and completed my degree. In the long run, it did for me what working the docks did—it gave me connections. I knew not only the men and the families I needed to know but also up-and-coming people in the world of business. Some things had been too good for too long. I heard the rumors of change. With my fingers dipped in both pies, I was prepared to move with it.

When I first graduated from NYU, I played the game. I worked for the man. I applied for legitimate jobs in big glass buildings. I wore the best suit I could afford and perfected my pitch. I knew the recession was hitting everyone hard, but I refused to give up. I knew the sacrifices that my parents had made for me and refused to squander them.

I made my name known working my way through the ranks.

It was there in the glass buildings with the fancy views that I learned that it was the same game. Everyone played it. Just like the dockworkers, everyone paid. It didn't take me long to change my goal. I didn't long to be someone else's best employee. No. To truly succeed, I needed to be the one who received the payouts.

I determined that Oren Demetri would be on the receiving end, not the one paying out.

I renewed alliances. My friends had friends who had family. We knew who deserved their cut and who didn't but got it anyway. It wasn't the same as my education at NYU; however, it was just as valuable.

The economy improved. Energy was no longer in short supply and business was once again booming. And then the FBI began its stings. Feds began questioning and taping and building cases that didn't need to be built.

The well-oiled machines that had controlled the docks, the construction industry—from the materials to the workers—and the city since the early 1900's began to falter. The commission was still strong, but not what it had been. Just last December, Castellano—Big Paulie—was murdered on the streets of Manhattan, and the rumblings stirred something inside me—a drive.

My father didn't have the same option. Not only because he didn't have a degree, but because his timing was wrong, and his dedication was to my mother and me. That's not to say I didn't care about my family. I've always adored Angelina. She's been the love of my life since I heard her laugh in sophomore English.

I still remember her sitting with three other girls looking at a magazine. If I closed my eyes, I could see her—brown hair, big blue eyes, dressed in jeans and a Metallica t-shirt. She was about as far from the type of girl I usually noticed as possible.

My preference had always been women like Nikki, those who dolled themselves up, knew their assets, and didn't mind flaunting them. That wasn't Angelina. It was as if she didn't realize how fucking beautiful she was or the way her laughter brought sunlight to the classroom, even to a tired schmuck who'd worked all night, gone home to shower, and dragged himself to class.

It took me time, years, to finally make my move. I had a name to build. A beautiful intelligent woman like Angelina Costello deserved better than the son of a dockworker. Besides, her family had connections. Her family *was* connections. I knew the name and valued my life. It wasn't until the name Oren Demetri had clout that I could pursue a woman like her.

As Daryl Frazier opened the canister of blueprints and laid the large sheets of paper over my desk, I smirked at how far I'd come. No longer was I the one searching out investors. People were coming to me. I'd taken those lessons and in this new climate, turned them into a reputable business. Demetri Enterprises. It sounded official.

The families taught me something that NYU only confirmed. Never put all your eggs in one basket. That's what my father and all the men like him had done. They'd worked hard, given everything they had, for one thing—a paycheck. People who received paychecks never got rich. It was the ones who wrote the checks who made the real money.

"And you can see how this subdivision will fill a need not met in the city. These lots are half an acre each. The clearance requires twelve feet on each side of every structure. As you can imagine, people who've lived in the city will pay big money for that much space. It'll be like a mile to them."

"Do you have the prospective on utilities?"

"Yes," he said, as he dug in his briefcase for another folder.

OUR BROWNSTONE IN Windsor Terrace wasn't as grand as I wanted, but Angelina never complained. My goal was to move my family—my wife and one-year-old son, Lennox—from Brooklyn one day. It would take time. Currently, the money coming in was mostly going back out. It was the way it worked and I knew it.

I looked at my watch as I parked my car. It was later than I'd promised to return home. I'd told Angelina I'd be home for dinner. I'd planned to be. After the meeting with Frazier, I had multiple more. I was on my way to call it a night, when I got the call.

I'd been invited to Carlisle's, an out-of-the-way little restaurant and bar in Little Italy. The invitation meant two things: my growing success was getting noticed and—since no one refused an invitation—I was going. The meeting went well. I had faith it would. Angelina's cousin Vinnie had been the one to invite me. Family took care of family.

From the porch I saw the faint glow of a lamp in the living room. Quietly, I opened the front door. On the sofa, covered in a blanket, was my wife. Her long hair was mussed as some of it was bound in a low ponytail and some was free with bits over her beautiful face.

I stood mesmerized for a moment or two, unsure if I should wake her or allow her to sleep. On the end table near her head was a small white box with a thick, golden-colored antennae. It was the newest baby monitor, the one she'd wanted. With it, she could hear Lennox from anywhere in the house even though he was upstairs in the nursery.

I'd always told her not to wait up for me.

Since our son was born, she needed sleep. He was a demanding little guy who now, at nearly a year, was finally sleeping through the night. Every now and then, he'd wake just to see if he could get a response.

Angelina turned, her bedroom eyes slowly opening. "You're home?" Her raspy voice sent shivers down my spine. Even now, it was like her laughter from college. It was my sunshine.

"I'm sorry about dinner."

She shook her head as she sat up, the blanket falling and her large t-shirt-type nightgown falling from her bare shoulder. It made me smile. If I'd been asked when I was younger, I would have said my wife would wear silk negligees, not oversized cotton shirts.

"I got your message," she said. "There are leftovers in the refrigerator if you're hungry. I can warm it up." She shrugged. "I made lasagna."

I sat beside her and reached for her hand. "Damn, I love your lasagna. Baby, Vinnie called. I couldn't say no."

"Did it go… okay?"

I leaned forward and covered her lips with mine. She was so damn beautiful.

As the temperature of the room increased, Angelina pulled slightly away while a smile graced her lips. "I'm going to take that as a yes."

"Yes, it went very well. I have a few investment opportunities, and it seems as though the backing is there."

Her smile faded as her hand fidgeted in mine. "Oren, things are going well. I love our home. I miss you. If you take that money you know they'll expect more."

"Yes, baby, and so will I. I'm not keeping the money, I'm paying it forward. The interest I'll collect will more than cover what I'll owe. I was looking at plans today for a new neighborhood just south of Danbury. The houses will be spaced apart with *yards*. Just imagine a real yard for Lennox. "We could have a swing set and a patio."

"We have a yard," she said.

We didn't. We had a postage stamp of grass out our back door. That hardly made a yard.

"These houses will be on half an acre. I was thinking that I might commission two lots. That would be a whole acre. That's more land than we've ever owned."

She stood. "I'm going to check on Lennox. Are you sure you're not hungry?"

I stood and pulled her close. "Not for food."

Angelina playfully shook her head. "Well then, you'd better plan on eating lasagna for breakfast for the next few days."

The corners of my lips moved upward. "The breakfast of champions."

CHAPTER 5

CHARLI

AFTER TOSSING AND turning for most of the night, I woke early and decided that more sleep was not in my immediate future. The cold sheets were my stark reminder that I was alone. In only a short time, I'd grown accustomed to waking beside Nox, basking in the warmth radiating from his hard body. Closing my eyes, I imagined the way I'd often find his muscular arm draped protectively over my waist as our bodies spooned, fitting together as one. As night turned to morning, even in his sleep his erection would probe my back, the best alarm clock I'd ever had.

Sighing in the dark of Patrick's spare room, I concentrated on what had happened to that fairytale. I thought about what I knew or what I thought I knew. I replayed the scene from the night before a hundred times. As I did, I realized that I hadn't asked Nox if he'd *killed* his wife. I'd asked him to tell me that he wasn't responsible for her death.

What would a man like Nox deem as responsible? What did Pat mean about *a hit*? What kind of case and testimony did Jocelyn's family have against Nox? Why hadn't it already been pursued if her death occurred years ago?

More questions swirled.

I recalled weeks ago that Deloris told me Demetri Enterprises was an umbrella, one with some nefarious subsidiaries. Well, she hadn't used that word, but now with Bryce's note, it seemed accurate. Nox had said that Demetri Enterprises was an investor in Infidelity. Was that what Bryce meant by prostitution?

Still lying upon the bed, my shoulders straightened indignantly, my bare feet sliding upon the soft sheets as I wondered how Bryce would feel if he learned that for only a brief time, I'd been an employee of Infidelity. If Pat were right that Bryce needed me for a cover, maybe I wouldn't be his best choice.

I also wondered if Patrick had considered Millie Ashmore, my high school best friend, an easy lay? Was she on the list he'd supplied? The idea of her, the girl claiming to be my friend, sleeping with not only my boyfriend but also my cousin made me physically ill.

I threw back the blankets. The train of thought I was riding had taken a downward spiral. It was time to disembark before it crashed. Willing myself forward, I decided to get my day going. Despite all hell breaking loose around me, I had class this morning, followed by a discussion session. From everything I'd gathered, the discussion was invaluable.

Thirty-five minutes later, showered and dressed for class, I was contemplating my breakfast and raiding the refrigerator of fruit when Pat entered, all debonair and dressed for work. His spicy cologne reached me even before his footsteps stopped.

Turning his direction, like a thief with my hand caught in the cookie jar, I smiled. "You really do clean up well!" As he made his best GQ-worthy pose, I giggled and asked, "How are things at Kassee?"

"Going really well. Are you finding everything you want?"

"Yes," I replied as I laid the food on the counter. "You did say make yourself at home."

"I did," he confirmed. "I don't know if you remember, but on the day of your… interview, I had a presentation at Kassee that I couldn't miss?"

Though that wasn't high on my radar that day, I did remember.

"I do. Did it go well?"

His brown eyes sparkled as he took a piece of my pineapple. "It went so well, later, one of the partners talked to me about employment after my internship is complete."

"Pat, that's fantastic. What does Cy think?"

"Hmm?"

I squinted my eyes his direction. "Why are you humming at me?"

"Because as much as you're fighting it, you're thinking like one of a couple. If you weren't, you'd have said, that's fantastic. What are *you* going to do?"

I shrugged as I hit the button on the coffee machine. It hissed and sputtered filling the kitchen with the delectable aroma of a French roast brew as I recalled my lonely wake-up. "I miss him. I woke up this morning and rolled toward him."

Pat's fingers laced through mine. "Honey, I bet he feels the same. Call him. Do it now, or you'll never be able to concentrate on those boring professors."

I squeezed his hand and then released mine. "Thanks for the advice, but as I said, I left the ball in his court."

"You know, you can't—"

I interrupted, almost telling him I could, but settled for saying, "I know."

Pat glanced at the clock on the microwave. "I didn't think you went to class this early."

It wasn't even seven. Since I was up, leaving early was part of my rebellion against surveillance strategy. "I don't, but since I'm up I thought I'd head to campus and get a little reading done in the library before class."

"You can stay here. I'm heading out. It'll be quiet."

I shrugged. "I know. Thanks, but I need to move."

Patrick kissed my forehead. "Sure thing. You move. Have you called that bodyguard guy to drive you?"

I stood taller, holding my cup of coffee in both hands and gently blew across the steaming molten java. Looking at my cousin through my lashes I replied, "Nope."

"Tsk-tsk. Are you trying to poke the beehive?"

"I haven't had this subject in class yet, but as a law student, I believe pleading the fifth is an acceptable answer."

"Alex…"

"And I promise I'll be in touch, but if my GPS is off on my phone, don't let that worry you. I will still be around."

"Great. That Witt woman will be blowing up my phone. If I don't get that position at the firm due to too many personal—"

I shook my head. "Fine, I'll send *her* a text."

"Thanks, I appreciate that. I need to run."

"Run?"

"To the subway station." He looked down at his clothes. "Run and ruin this look? Never."

I smiled at his words, a little jealous of his ability to choose his own mode of transportation. "See you tonight."

"Are you sure?"

"It's my plan. If it changes, I'll let you know."

"Sure thing, little cousin, have a good day."

I attempted another sip of my coffee as he walked down the hall toward the door. The beep of the buttons upon the keypad and the turning of the tumblers as the door unlocked and opened let me know Patrick's apartment was safe. And then suddenly my lips sputtered coffee as my throat forgot to swallow. Breaths stilled in my chest and the energy of the once-calm apartment crackled like lightning around me. I forced the hot coffee down as I fumbled with the cup, barely settling it upon the counter as the heavy footsteps belonging to the deep velvet voice I'd just heard grew louder, making their way my direction.

Fight or flight?

I assessed my surroundings. If I ran, where could I go? I contemplated dashing behind the breakfast bar, but decided in the nick of time that it was a juvenile thought and meeting those dazzling blue eyes head-on was better than flight.

My neck straightened as I feigned strength. Let the fight begin.

"Charli."

Thunder.

Nox's gaze found me and then scanned the kitchen, momentarily settling upon my coffee and back to me.

"Mr. Demetri," I said. "Would you like a cup of coffee? I know you like it black."

He stepped closer. The cloud of woodsy cologne gently replaced the robust French roast.

In one graceful yet powerful move, I was pinned, my hips against his. With one arm around my waist and the other my shoulders, my breasts rubbed against his chest. Fighting the urge to be swallowed by the embrace I'd feared I'd never experience again, I boldly lifted my chin.

His voice was strong and even. "I can't give you the answer you wanted last night, but not for the obvious reason."

My mind spun as I pushed back against his hold.

"No," he replied. "I can't give you the answer, not because of what it is, but because I'm not ready."

I pulled back to look deeper into the navy swirls. I recalled the night I'd told Nox I was a Montague, the night he told me not to force any answers, to give them when I was ready in my mind and my heart. He was asking for the same consideration.

I nodded. "I understand."

His chest deflated as he released his breath.

"I'm sorry," I said. "I told you that I trusted you, but then I left."

The tips of his lips moved upward as his tone became more demanding. "I'm not letting you go, not now, not ever." His large hands splayed, pulling his grip of me tighter. "I never should've let you leave last night. I should have tied your beautiful body to my bed."

"Nox—"

His warm lips stopped my rebuttal, seizing my words and dominating my thoughts. A surprised whimper escaped before morphing into a moan, as his hand moved to my neck and his kiss deepened. Fierce and proprietary, his hands roamed as his mouth took what was his. Shamelessly seeking, his tongue didn't tease but sought its mate. The world around us disappeared as we tangoed—sigh for sigh and nip for nip.

My feet left the floor as my ass landed upon the edge of the counter. I wished I were wearing a dress as my legs surrounded his waist and my ankles locked him within my grasp.

This wasn't concession but a blatant reassertion of possession, no longer one-sided—Nox wasn't the client nor was I the employee. We were both demanding something of the other we'd never had. Something we'd skirted around, offered in lighthearted declarations, but learned last night we hadn't truly given.

This kiss was about becoming one, melding together in a way that was unbreakable, in a way that wouldn't be threatened by the outside world. Not by accusations or words on a piece of paper. Not by shadows that lurked in my eyes or ghosts in his past. Not even by the devil himself.

As my lips bruised and our ferocity simmered, my eyes fluttered open. Through veiled lashes I sought the blue I desired. Once our gazes met, mine was no longer veiled. My chin rose and chest filled with determination.

"When push came to shove," I admitted, "I failed."

His eyes closed as he shook his head. "You weren't alone. We both did. What else could you have done? I was the one doing the shoving. I didn't try to stop you."

"We can't let them do this to us. I told you that Alton is the devil. He's influenced Bryce all of Bryce's life. We can't let them have that control."

Though my legs slackened and his grip loosened, I was still surrounded by Nox's embrace. The comforting peace of his masculine cologne urged me forward, to hop from the counter, tug on his hand, and pull him toward my room, the room where I'd barely slept, and allow myself to be swallowed up completely. Yet I resisted.

"I'm not sure they do," he said.

"I know. They only have it if we let them."

"No, that's not what I mean. Deloris isn't sure that note was written by Edward Spencer."

I leaned back, furrowing my brow. "Why?"

"It has to do with the content. She's dusting it for prints. She also doesn't believe anyone from your family, or anyone they hired, could breach her security." His brows rose. "That's part of the reason I'm here."

An unswallowable lump formed in my suddenly dry throat. Lowering myself back to the floor, I asked, "What do you mean?"

He stepped back, assessing me at arm's length. "You look ready for class."

"I am," I replied as I sheepishly straightened my blouse. Sometime during the last five minutes it had become seriously misaligned. "I was."

"When were you planning on heading to the campus?"

"Soon."

"And where's your phone?"

"Nox, why the twenty questions?"

"Apparently, during the night your GPS stopped working."

It hadn't. I'd purposely turned it off. I pursed my lips. "Huh. Really? That's curious. I wonder how that happened?" I shrugged. "Perhaps I hit a button by mistake."

"And I checked with Jerrod. He hasn't received your call or text this morning."

Though my heartbeat had increased, I tilted my head casually and sighed. "It's a nice day. I had time to walk across the park."

Nox linked our hands together and lifted my knuckles to his lips. "Well, isn't that convenient?"

"Convenient?"

"Yes. I have a plane to catch to DC I need to be there for a hearing, but since it's the Batplane and I'm Batman, I have time for a stroll through the park."

"Nox…"

"I won't be back from DC until Friday, but I'm warning you. If you decide to do any other strolls or accidentally turn off your GPS, when I get back, not only will I enjoy punishing your sexy ass, I'll seriously look into that GPS implant." He lifted his brow. "I would bet Mrs. Witt would know where that could be done."

I bet she did.

Though I saw the gleam that I loved behind his threat, I also heard his sincerity.

His gaze narrowed. "Please, push me, princess. You see, I didn't sleep well last night and I'd be happy to give you a reminder to behave before I leave."

I gently shook my head. "Mr. Demetri, I do love it when you beg, but I'm afraid that if we did that… reminder thing, I'd miss class and you'd miss your hearing."

As I gathered my things for the day, Nox lifted my backpack, and I asked, "You won't be back until Friday?"

"No. There are a few days of testimony scheduled on a bill in the finance committee."

Did I want to know more about the bill? Not really. What I didn't want to do was be alone. "Then while you're gone, I want to stay here. I don't want to be in our apartment alone."

Nox stopped midstep and scanned Patrick's kitchen and living room.

"Stop," I demanded.

"Stop what?" he asked innocently.

"I see what you're doing. I can see the wheels turning. You're not having additional security added to Cy and Pat's apartment. If you balk, I'll stay at *my* apartment."

"That's where I want you."

"The one I'm letting Chelsea use."

He swatted my behind. "Is that an ultimatum?"

I crossed my arms over my chest. "Only if you make it one."

"Miss Collins, you drive a hard bargain."

I lifted my brow. "Does that mean I won?"

"No, princess. I choose my battles better than that." His gaze narrowed, yet the gleam I loved flickered in the swirls of navy. "And believe me, if we're at battle, you'll know it."

"Is that a threat?"

"Promise. It's a promise."

CHAPTER 6

NOX

THE RIGHT AMOUNT of briskness hung in the morning air to add a chill as we stepped from the lobby of Patrick's apartment building onto Fifth Avenue. Since I'd spent last night in a hotel—alone—I hadn't received my daily weather report from Hudson, the doorman at my building. Undoubtedly, had I been there, he would have greeted me this morning with 'Good morning, Mr. Demetri. There's a hint of autumn in the air. Stay warm.' The thought brought a smile to my face as Charli zipped her jacket before tucking her hand back into mine.

I didn't want to let her go last night, now, or ever.

When it came to Jo and memories of her death, I found myself helpless, just like I'd been that night. I clung tighter to Charli's hand.

Lennox Demetri didn't do helpless. It wasn't in my DNA. I needed to put this behind me.

As we began walking toward the park, I squeezed her warm hand, not because I wanted the beautiful golden eyes to lock with mine—though I did. Not because I needed to know she was here beside me—though I did. I squeezed Charli's hand to feel the warmth that reassured me that she was alive.

Last night, alone in the hotel room, I recalled holding Jo's hand, her cold, pale skin. I remembered her lips, their unnatural color. I'd done it to her. If it weren't for me, she would have been warm and her lips would have been pink.

"Why don't you run?"

Charli's voice brought me back from the edge and loosened my grip, no doubt restoring circulation to her petite hand.

"I do. You know I do."

"You run on a treadmill. That isn't running."

"It most certainly is," I replied, happy to be in a nonsensical discussion about nothing of importance. It was one of Charli's continual gifts. She reminded me that life wasn't always a level-five emergency, threats weren't around every corner. Triviality had a place of importance. It added balance. Deloris saw that in Del Mar long before I did. It was a part of my life I hadn't even realized was missing until I found it again.

"Well..." Her voice came through the city sounds—traffic and the murmurs of other pedestrians—as we made our way west. "...I guess you get the exercise."

I pulled her hand closer causing her to bump into my arm. "Are you saying I'm out of shape?"

She laughed. "I'm saying that we should run in the park in the morning instead of in your gym. I mean, look at this." Her golden eyes scanned the vista before us. Hints of orange, red, and yellow dotted the landscape. The green that had prevailed all summer was giving way to the inevitability of change.

My gym was secure. This park wasn't. But instead, I gave her a different excuse. "I have monitors in my gym and can catch up on the news and overnight turns in the markets. Besides, you don't run every morning."

"You only have one treadmill."

"I'll buy a second treadmill," I offered.

"Stop. You don't need to buy anything." Her smile turned bashful. "Besides, it's okay. I'll settle for our normal morning workout."

My lips twitched as my cheeks rose. "I missed that workout this morning."

"Me too," she replied, her voice merely a breathy whisper, as if she was concerned that the others around us could hear our topic of conversation. And then I caught a glimpse of Charli's pink cheeks and laughed. By the expression on her face, anyone who looked our way could probably figure out what we were talking about.

"Nox." She turned to me in all seriousness. "I'm going to call Bryce and let him know it didn't work."

"No." I didn't want her talking, texting, or fucking sending smoke signals to him. If that letter came from him, then he knew more about Demetri Enterprises than he should—too much.

Her smile and crimson blush disappeared. "I respect your opinion, I really do, but I'm not asking you. I'm telling you. I've thought about it, and I'm calling him."

"Princess, I'm not being a *dick*." I never planned to let her forget the title she'd given me in Del Mar after our standing ovation at the gas station. "Before you call, let Deloris do her thing. Let's be sure he's the one who wrote it. If he didn't, he won't have a clue what you're talking about."

Her brow furrowed as she considered my argument. "I don't understand how she thinks it could be someone else. Who would know that stuff?"

We had plenty of time before her class and testimony wasn't scheduled to start on the hearing until after the lunch recess. I tugged her hand to stop and led us to a park bench. As we stilled and sat, for the first time since we'd left Patrick's apartment, I saw my security. It wasn't Isaac or Jerrod. They were both parked near the library at Columbia. These were men Deloris kept near. I knew names, but our interaction was minimal, or at least that was how it was supposed to be.

"Charli," I searched for the right words.

Her golden eyes widened, sparkling in the sunshine that filtered through the canopy of leaves.

"Last night, you said to call if I was ready to talk."

"Yes."

I sat straighter, never letting go of her hand. "I'm not."

Her gaze moved away before returning. "I guess that's why you didn't call?"

Involuntarily, my cheeks rose. "I didn't, did I?"

"No."

"I suppose I'm more direct."

She nodded. "Yes, Mr. Demetri, I've noticed that about you."

I took a deep breath. "Deloris told you that Demetri Enterprises is connected to some less than savory dealings. Mostly I can blame Oren."

"Mostly?" she asked.

"Mostly," I confirmed. "But Infidelity, for example, that was me. I learned about the company. I'm the one who made the investment. Some of the people we do business with very well could be involved in straight-up prostitution. I don't know. I don't want to know. So whether that letter was referring to Infidelity or a less organized business, the fact is that Demetri Enterprises could more than likely be connected to prostitution. As for the accusations regarding Jocelyn, I've told you, I can't talk about it." I squeezed her hand again and brushed my lips over hers. "Be patient with me. When I'm ready, you're the one I'll share with. I just need to find the right words."

"Have you spoken to anyone?"

I looked away, trying to forget the images that plagued my sleepless night. "I spoke to the police when…"

Her eyes widened as she listened to my words.

"When it happened," I continued. "That letter said I hid things from her family. That's not exactly the truth."

Charli didn't speak, allowing me the freedom to divulge what I could.

"Jocelyn wasn't close to them, not after we got together. They didn't want her with me." I shrugged. "Much like your family."

"Nox, it isn't that my family doesn't want me with *you*. They don't even know you. My mother is fixated on Bryce. She has been for as long as I can remember."

"The Matthewses didn't like me. They were the stereotypical Midwestern family. Jocelyn wasn't as independent as you. She never had lofty career aspirations. We met young and well, they wanted more for their daughter than me."

Charli's head moved slowly from side to side.

"What?"

"I'm trying hard not to interrupt you. Please, keep going."

My lips twitched. "Begging now, are we?"

Her cheeks blushed. "I'm going to ignore that. Fine. I was wondering how they wanted *more* than you?"

I shifted, allowing my knees to fall farther apart as I clenched my own hand and studied the ground near my shoes. "They said I was nothing more than the son of a two-bit swindler from Brooklyn. I was where I was because I rode my father's underworld coattails."

"You don't see yourself that way, do you?"

"I try not to."

Charli reached for my hand and intertwined our fingers. "I don't know what you do," she said. "I know you work hard. I didn't know you were from Brooklyn. So what? You took me to the house in Westchester. But Nox, I didn't even know your last name in Del Mar and I knew you were a man of substance."

I looked up to her beautiful face framed in the auburn waves. Though she'd pulled most of her hair back, small wisps blew gently in the breeze to tease her cheeks and lips. I reached out and tucked a rogue strand behind her ear. "You've spoken to your mother. That letter said that she wants you away from me. No doubt, she doesn't think I'll do for her blue-blood daughter."

Anger flashed in her golden eyes. "Do you have any idea how much I hate that?"

Before I could reply, she went on.

"I'm so sick of the whole blue-blood world. Shit, it's like the Westminster dog show. The breeding pool is getting smaller and smaller. Pretty soon the only way to maintain pedigree will be to marry siblings or cousins!"

"Patrick did give me a suspicious look this morning."

Her anger simmered. "He's not really my cousin. Other than the fact that he's gay, we could marry."

"He's not?" My back straightened. How many fake family members was she going to claim?

"Not by blood. He's Alton's nephew—his sister's son. I tell anyone and everyone that I'm not related to Alton Fitzgerald. I wouldn't want that man's blood in my veins."

"So Patrick is your stepcousin?"

"Yes."

"Back to your earlier question," I said, "after Jo was gone, I didn't talk about it. I never told the Matthewses the whole story. If they'd come to me, I might have, but they didn't. Instead they made accusations. The only one who knows everything is Deloris. She knows because she worked for us then."

"Isaac?"

"Yes, but not all the details. He didn't work as closely with Jo. Deloris filled in as Jo's family when they turned their back on her.

"Were… are her parents well-to-do?"

"No."

Charli shook her head. "I don't understand why they thought you were so bad, why they'd accuse you?"

"Because with me she lived a life they didn't understand. They wanted her to meet a nice lawyer or doctor and settle down in a small town and live the perfect life behind a white picket fence. They never imagined her in New York City in a high-rise apartment, flying here and there. It didn't make sense to them. If she didn't call, they assumed it was because of me. If she didn't attend her great-uncle's eightieth birthday, it was my fault."

Silence hung heavily in the air as I waited for Charli's response. When I didn't say more, she did.

"Thank you." As she spoke, she lifted my left hand and kissed my palm.

"For?" I asked.

"For talking to me. I still don't know what happened, but…" She turned my hand and swiped the pad of her finger over the mostly faded line where my wedding ring had been. "…I believe you loved her."

She looked around the park—Were those tears in her eyes? Why would she be crying?—before she continued, "I wish I could have met her, but then again, if I could, you wouldn't be here with me." She brushed a tear from her cheek. "I told you before that I trusted you. I've tried to show you that, by giving you a part of me, a vulnerable part, and you've never hurt me. This morning, this talk, I feel as if this time you're giving me something. I promise to do my best to care for this sliver of your past as you've cared for me. I'll treasure her memory, as much as you're willing to share.

"She's a part of who you are, Nox. And for helping to make the man who holds my hand and my heart, I thank her."

I let go of her hand and pulled her toward me. This wasn't where I'd intended to go during our walk. I'd said more than I'd ever said and still there was so much to say. As our lips came together, I marveled at Charli's understanding.

She was right. I was the man I am today partially because of Jo. No one lived through that kind of love and loss and walked away without scars. I'd read somewhere that scars served a purpose. They created tougher skin. They became a shield and made a person stronger. Jo had done that. Loving her and losing her had made me strong and unbending.

Not until Charli had I even had a desire to bend.

When our kiss ended, words continued to flow. I rarely spoke without thinking, yet this morning it was as if I had no control. My voice was strong yet quiet. The words didn't come from my lips but my heart. They were words I'd never thought I'd say again, but I wanted to. The need was too great to suppress. She needed to know the truth.

My world dangled on a string as I spoke and waited for her reply. "I love you."

CHAPTER 7

CHARLI

THEY SAY THAT men fall in love faster, but women fall harder. I didn't know if that were true. I didn't know much of anything as leaves swirled and danced about Nox and I in the late summer breeze. Beyond the small world of our park bench, people carried on their daily routines completely oblivious to the declarations being made. Some ran while others walked. Mothers pushed babies in strollers with wheels large enough to be upon a bicycle, and others walked dogs of all sizes, tethered to leashes and unimpressed with the other canines that they passed.

As Nox's words registered, my mother's expectations crashed down around me.

The pressure in my heart and chest was crippling as everything multiplied.

Love.

Duty.

Legacy.

Nox.

Had I ever been loved—*truly* loved?

The unfamiliar emotion lifted me above the colorful trees and my own mayhem. I wanted to believe that his declaration wasn't a whim or the result of being apart for one night. It wasn't how I interpreted it. I didn't believe that a man like Lennox Demetri made casual professions of love.

Love was the way Nox made me feel like his princess, whether we walked the paths of the park or the sidewalks of New York City. It was the trust I had in him to bind me helpless, yet to know without a doubt that he'd never harm me. It was my desire to take away the pain of Jocelyn's death while at the same time leave space for the memories of his first love.

My lips smiled as tears fell from my eyes. Sleep deprivation did that to me—made me emotional—but so did a declaration of love from a man like Lennox Demetri.

"I love you, too."

The words weren't said to pacify him or as an expression of gratitude for his honesty. They were real and with everything inside of me, I wanted to show more than tell him. I leaned closer.

Again our lips united and his hand went to my neck pulling me towards him. The breeze and birds disappeared. The morning chill was replaced with liquid warmth washing through us and melting us together. We were on an island—alone. No other people, birds, or squirrels—nothing and then…

Chaos.

Commotion.

My blood raced in double time while simultaneously my breath stilled in my chest, and my heart, which had just been made whole, crashed to the depths of my stomach. Men I didn't know or recognize ran toward us, yelling Nox's name.

"Mr. Demetri!" It came over and over, hushed in a veil of secrecy as they surrounded us.

The sudden turmoil paralyzed me as people screamed and sirens wailed in the distance.

Thick, strong hands pulled at my arms, lifting me from the bench as Nox's grip of my hand held steady like an iron vise. Together we moved, or more accurately we were moved, from the place where we'd declared our love.

We'd been somewhere within the interior of the park, and yet somehow a large black SUV appeared, and the men in dark suits hurried us inside. One sat in the front by a driver I didn't recognize while the other large man piled in beside me. Sandwiched between Nox and a man I didn't know, I huddled closer to Nox, my mind a whirl of uncertainty.

Outside of the tinted windows, the mothers with strollers, people with dogs, runners and walkers, all stopped and stared, turning and pointing. Some yelled while others stood with their mouths agape as confusion played on their expressions. The same mystification stirred inside of me as my backpack landed at my feet and the vehicle began to move forward.

What happened?

Where are we going?

Are we being kidnapped?

Determination as I'd never seen covered Nox's expression. No longer was he the man that I loved: he was obsessed or possessed—I couldn't tell. Mechanically, he scanned me from head to toe.

"Are you all right?"

I nodded, also giving myself a once-over.

"You're sure? You aren't hurt?"

"N-no." The word came out shakily as I looked at him. "What about you? Are you all right?"

"Fuckers," he mumbled. "I'm fine. Assholes are going to pay…"

"What happened?"

My question lingered in the air. He wasn't talking to me any longer—his brow creased as he pulled his phone from his pocket. Within seconds, words and orders were being barked. The person on the other end of the line couldn't have been responding. He wasn't giving him or her a chance. His questions came rapid-fire, never pausing for answers. Names I didn't recognize—Costello and Bonetti—flew from his lips as accusations abounded.

Out of the park, the car moved through traffic.

"Shots."

It was a word I heard in Nox's tirade.

I tried to remember. I hadn't heard shots nor had I seen them. But then again, could one really *see* a shot or only its end result? It wasn't like real life was a movie that could be slowed for special effects.

"Break-in—shots—attempted murder—testimony."

Though Nox spoke in a language I recognized, one I'd spoken my entire life, I couldn't decipher his meaning.

A chill rushed over my skin, leaving goose bumps in its wake. I pulled my light jacket tighter around my shoulders and pushed my hands, now free of Nox's grasp, deep into the pockets.

Not long into Nox's monologue I realized it was Deloris on the other end of the call.

The SUV eased onto the highway and I recognized the signs: I-95 north. We were headed to Nox's family home in Westchester County.

My class and discussion group would go unattended. And although it upset me that once again I hadn't been consulted, I also understood. I just wasn't sure if being shot at was an acceptable excuse for absence on the second full day of classes.

"WELCOME," SILVIA SAID as she hurriedly ushered us both inside.

By the way she scanned the driveway, undoubtedly she'd been informed of what had occurred.

"Alex," she said, reaching for my hand, "you're ice cold. Let me get you something warm. Coffee? Tea?"

Nox kissed my forehead before disappearing in the other direction and leaving me alone with the kind woman I'd only met once.

"Coffee, thank you." Forming longer sentences was suddenly outside of my repertoire.

I trailed a step behind Silvia as she walked toward the kitchen. The glistening Long Island Sound shone through the large windows with small white caps skirting across the blue water. I opened the glass door and inhaled the warm breeze.

"Dear, are you all right?"

Once again I looked down at my own body, scanning it as if it belonged to someone else. Flat ballet-type shoes peered out from the legs of my tight jeans and my top hung loosely from the edge of my light jacket. I unzipped the jacket, needing to be sure everything was fine underneath. Removing it, I said, "Physically. I-I don't know or understand what just happened."

"You're safe. That's what matters."

She reached for the glass door that I'd opened and pulled it shut.

"Silvia, I think maybe I'd like to go out to the pool, just to feel some sunshine."

She reached for my arm. "Alex, please stay inside until everything is secure."

How did she know about everything?

The cold chill from earlier returned. "You don't think…" I wasn't sure how to ask my question. "…someone would hurt us here?"

"I've been with the Demetris for a long time. I was briefed before your arrival. What just happened was unusually brazen. The two of you were in Central Park, for goodness' sake. If someone wanted to find you, it wouldn't be difficult for that person to connect the dots. It's a matter of public record that this house belongs to Lennox." She released my arm and tended to the coffee. "This house is safe. I know that. However, outside needs to be secured. And there could be someone on a boat or a flyover for that matter. Staying inside is best."

Oh my God!

My eyes widened at the wall of windows. "You're sure we're all right with the windows?"

"I'm sure, dear."

My knees gave out as I sank onto a chair near the kitchen table and tucked my trembling hands between my knees.

Silvia turned my way. "I didn't mean to scare you. Keeping you safe is the objective."

I nodded, overwhelmed and a bit perplexed over her knowledge and level of comfort with this kind of emergency.

"Does this happen? Has it happened?" I asked.

Her eyes softened. "Not every day. Not every year. But the Demetris need to be prepared."

"I-I." Words began to fail me. I wanted Nox. I wanted to be locked in a bunker or perhaps secured on a desert island with him.

Silvia handed me a warm cup. "I have an idea. Let's go to the pool house. It's beautiful and you can enjoy the sunshine without going outdoors. It will help you ward away the chill."

Without speaking, I stood and nodded. I didn't know what else to do.

As we made our way through a breezeway, Silvia turned back toward me, her sparkling eyes bringing life to her expression. "I may have alluded to this before, but I've been around here for a while…" She allowed her words to trail away suggestively.

"Teenage Lennox?" I asked, remembering her words from over a month before.

She lifted her brow and pursed her lips. "Perhaps…"

I smiled, appreciating her willingness to ease my mind and refocus my attention. Nevertheless, her warnings clung to me like a fog, keeping the warming rays of sunshine just out of reach.

Before reaching the pool house, Nox's voice boomed from the depths of the house. Silvia's eyes met mine.

"Can you tell what he said?" I asked.

"No, but sometimes I hear his father in him."

I shook my head. "I don't know much about his family and haven't been around that long, but I'd suspect that wouldn't be a welcomed analogy."

She grinned. "If you asked either of them, they'd say they're oil and water, but my assessment is different."

"It is?" I asked as we entered the pool house.

I stood and turned. The small outbuilding was gorgeous: glass covered three walls with sunshine lighting the interior. The other wall had a beautiful limestone brick fireplace in the center between large windows, and the ceiling was covered in knotty pine. The furnishings were comfortable, done along the lines of a family room, complete with a large round table. For some reason, it reminded me of Christmas displays and what it would be like to have a family gathered near for the holidays. In December the outside would be cold and covered in snow, yet the inside would be as warm as it was today.

Nothing like the cold stuffiness of the manor.

"I love this home," I said. "There's something about it that makes me feel… I'm not sure of the right word. Homey?"

Silvia smiled. "That's what Angelina wanted."

"Angelina?"

"Lennox's mother. All she ever wanted was this house filled with family."

I feigned a smile. "That's sad."

"It doesn't have to be," Silvia replied. "The house is Lennox's. One day he could fulfill his mother's wish."

The skin of my neck prickled. "I don't know, but I hope that someday Lennox fulfills his own dreams. I know what it's like to have other people's dreams thrust on you. I wouldn't want that for him."

Silvia nodded. "How old are you?"

Sitting on the edge of one of the long sofas facing the sound, I grinned. "Twenty-three. Why?"

"You seem older."

"I hope that's a good thing. Or do you recommend that once this is over, I visit my mother's plastic surgeon for emergency intervention?"

"Oh, no!" she replied, aghast.

We both laughed as we settled on the soft cushions. Silvia curled her legs under herself in a position that told me she was comfortable in this home. I slipped my shoes from my feet and did the same, letting my toes warm beneath me.

Taking a deep breath, I prompted, "Oil and water?"

She shrugged. "I see the two of them more like Italian dressing."

I smiled. "Italian would seem appropriate."

"Yes. It needs both oil and water. If you let it settle, it separates, but if you shake it up, the two ingredients blend. They need one another, complement one another, and wouldn't be the same without the other."

"I like that. How do you think Lennox or Oren would feel about your assessment?"

"I know how they'd feel. Both of them would balk."

"Loudly?" I said with a hint of a question.

"It doesn't take being around that long to know that to be true."

I sighed and placed the warm cup on the table. "Silvia, I don't even know what happened this morning. It all happened so fast."

Her head moved up and down. "You're safe here. Inside of this place is a fortress."

"I'm supposed to be in class. I mean, who's to say I couldn't? You don't think that I was the target, do you?" Each word was softer than the one before as my mouth grew increasingly dry.

Silvia stared for a minute. "At this point, with what we know, it's impossible to say for sure."

I stood and paced around the large room. "Who were those men who drove us here? They weren't our normal security."

"Demetris have many layers of security. It is the way it is."

I crossed my arms over my chest and hugged myself tighter. "How? How do they live like that?"

I didn't realize she'd moved yet Silvia was now behind me. "For some people, the transition to this life is difficult. Those people have never experienced anything like a bodyguard or driver or house staff. They think a commercial company's alarm system is security. And then, there are others…" She touched my shoulder. "…like you, who have lived with this their entire lives and are more comfortable."

Tears teetered on my lids as the Long Island Sound blurred. Did everyone know my past? "But this felt different."

"Because the risk was different," she replied.

I turned toward her. "What do you mean?"

"Being a child under the protection of your parents feels suffocating. Lennox fought it for most of his teenage life. However, protecting someone you love, whether it's your child or your soul mate is different. The risk is higher."

I finally understood Nox's obsession. I still didn't like the loss of privacy, but more than that, I was worried about him. "Silvia, someone tried…" A delayed sob formed in my chest. "…to kill him."

She wrapped her arms around my shoulders. "You're both safe."

"I-I love him."

Her hand rubbed circles on my back as my head settled upon her shoulder. "I know. He loves you too. And you have no way of knowing how happy that makes all of us who also love him. He'll keep you safe."

"Charli," Nox's voice echoed against the glass walls.

CHAPTER 8

A week ago

ADELAIDE

I CLOSED THE door to our suite and took one last look at the outer room. How many times had I dreaded entering this room? There was a surprising comfort in knowing I'd never do it again.

I was well aware that from the outside looking in I'd never appeared strong. God knew I wasn't the woman my daughter was, but nevertheless, I'd fought a gallant fight and I was tired.

From the time I was born, I was reminded of my obligation, my duty. No one will ever know how hard I prayed for my mother to have another child. Not another child. I prayed for a son—a brother, an heir. If only that would have happened, my life would have been so incredibly different. I could have been the daughter my mother wanted—refined and regal—and I wouldn't have had to become my father's poor excuse for a son.

I didn't understand it when I was younger, but as my mother aged, she shared more and more of our history. She and my father married when she was young. He'd completed his undergraduate and graduate school at Emory. She, however, had only completed her freshman year of undergraduate school where she'd planned to study art appreciation. I must have gotten my love of art from her. It was nice to think of my mother with some fondness.

I found it difficult to believe, but apparently my mother's parents didn't approve of her marrying the great Charles Montague II. With his being nearly thirteen years older than her, my grandparents saw him more as a predator than a suitor.

Considering that Alton, my father's choice for my husband, was twelve years my senior, I found that tidbit of information borderline hilarious. My mother, of course, never saw the irony.

While the assessment could have been considered appropriate for Alton Fitzgerald, according to my mother, it wasn't for my father. She never faltered in her profession of love for him. She told stories of seeing him around Savannah, the most eligible bachelor. She spoke of his looks, how handsome all the women thought he was. It wasn't his money that drew her to him. The Cains were more than comfortable and well positioned within the Savannah hierarchy. It was his Southern charm and honor.

No matter how hard I tried, I never saw it.

Oh, I saw his persuasiveness—some would call it bullying—with both Mother and me. I also saw the way he dominated every business deal and conversation. But charm and honor? If they were present, they were attributes he never felt warranted displaying for his only child.

In her final days, my mother admitted to their difficulty in having children. I wasn't born until my father was nearly fifty years old. Taking a young wife was supposed to assure his progeny. I had to wonder if his animosity regarding my ability to conceive was misdirected aggression.

Perhaps it was. Maybe he didn't treat my mother the way he'd treated me. Even after his death, my mother claimed to have never felt bullied. She called it willingness to submit. Now, as I reminisce, I see that too as a trait I inherited.

Does one inherit a behavior or is it taught? It was the old nature-versus-nurture debate.

When I was younger, I would have said it was nurture, a learned behavior; however, now I disagree. Alexandria changed my mind.

My daughter didn't contain a submissive bone in her body. Though since three years of age, she was raised without her father, she was Russell through and through. Her independence and self-reliance were honorable. Alton never thought so, but why would he?

To him, anyone who questioned his authority was the enemy. With the power Alexandria held, though she didn't know it, she certainly qualified as a foe. Somehow, she'd been keenly aware of their animosity from the time she was young. I can't recall a time when the two of them hadn't clashed.

A memory from Alexandria's childhood returned. I settled on the sofa as the scene I'd buried came back to life in my mind. She was young, not even a teenager. The thought churned my stomach.

It was all right; the indigestion wouldn't last long.

Alexandria threw her napkin on the table, her golden eyes shooting daggers at not only Alton, but also at me.

I knew what she wanted. Hiding emotions wasn't one of my daughter's strong suits. She wanted me to disagree with her stepfather. She wanted me to speak up and override the verdict to send her to her room without finishing her dinner.

I honestly couldn't remember her offense—only that it once again set him off.

That wasn't hard to do—to light his fuse. Alton Fitzgerald was a bomb with a trigger ignition. He'd been gone for business, a reprieve for all of Montague Manor, but nothing good ever lasted. With his return came the fireworks of re-acclimation. The cycle repeated frequently enough to make it predictable.

I didn't argue as she stomped away. I knew she wouldn't go hungry. Jane would make sure of that.

It wasn't that I didn't care for my own daughter. I did. I was the reason Jane was there. I was the one who, to this day, fought for her employment. Our system worked. Alexandria wasn't the only one who experienced the fireworks and aftershocks of Alton's return to the manor. That was what I did. My reasoning was that if he were busy with me, he'd ignore her. If I were to take food to Alexandria, Alton would see. He would know.

When my father was alive, it was better. As much as I blamed Charles Montague II for my life, he did everything he could for Alexandria. His preoccupation of Alton's time wasn't appreciated until it was gone.

I never knew what happened on Alton's business trips. He didn't share any information regarding Montague Corporation. The amount of alcohol consumed upon his arrival was my barometer of the success of the trip. By that scale, his latest trip hadn't gone well. He was way into his fifth or sixth Cognac by dinner. The fact that Alexandria had remained at the table until the main course was in and of itself remarkable.

What made this evening different than any other in my mind was the conversation that ensued after Alexandria's animated exit. Once she was gone, Alton returned the daggers she'd sent our way to me.

"Your daughter needs to learn a lesson."

I lifted my wine, praying the Montague Private Label had increased its alcohol content. "You sent her to her room. I'm sure that will have an effect."

He scoffed. "Embarrassing. She attends the best school money can buy, and she's still disrespectful. Really, Laide, would your father have ever permitted you to speak like that?"

I lifted my fork, stabbing the meal upon my plate with vigor. If I allowed him to bellow, soon he'd lose steam.

His palm hit the shiny mahogany table.

The maid standing near the door to the kitchen jumped, the water sloshing in the pitcher within her hands.

"I asked you a question, Mrs. Fitzgerald. Are you having difficulty with your hearing? Maybe I should call Dr. Beck. I'm sure he can do more than prescribe you narcotics."

"I heard you. I don't have an answer."

"Why? Are you too drugged out? Does the good doctor know that you pop his pain pills and wash them down with copious amounts of wine?"

I closed my eyes. "I don't believe I would've spoken that way to my father. Alexandria isn't me." And you aren't her father. *I didn't say the last part, though if Alexandria had been present, she would have. "Alton, let's finish dinner. You'll feel better in the morning. Traveling always makes you irritable."*

His volume rose. "You're turning this around on me?"

It was a no-win conversation. "Perhaps we should go upstairs?"

It wasn't a proposal I wanted accepted, but then again, after as much as he'd drunk, I had hope that he'd fall asleep after only a few minutes.

His laugh was an octave higher than normal. I turned his direction while the shrill sound sent chills down my spine. "Sometimes," he said, enunciating each word, "I wonder why I spend my nights with you when there's a spitfire in need of taming down the hall."

Blood no longer flowed through my veins. It stilled, falling to my feet, leaving me dizzy and dazed. The fork I'd been holding fell to the table, the clink going unnoticed as Alton's tormenting grin and gray eyes dared me to respond.

Just briefly, my eyes met the young girl's with the water. Silently, I tipped my head, motioning for her to go into the kitchen. As the door swung shut, I turned back toward my husband. "What did you just say?"

His brows rose, disappearing under his graying hair. "You heard me. Sending Alexandria to her room doesn't seem to work. Spanking her ass doesn't work. Charles wanted me to turn you into an acceptable wife." He shrugged. "I did. Someday Bryce will thank me."

I didn't remember reaching for the steak knife lying beside my plate. I didn't remember standing. Of all the things Alton had said and done to me, I'd never argued. I'd never fought back.

Before his inebriated mind could process it, I was behind his chair, the blade of the knife firmly pressed against his throat.

"You ever touch my daughter like that and I'll kill you. I will kill both of us." The knife grazed his skin as I applied pressure. "You don't even need to be asleep. I'll slit your throat or poison your brandy. You'll never see it coming, but I swear to God, you'll die, and before you do I'll cut off your cock with a dull knife. That, Mr. Fitzgerald, is a promise. I'd willingly spend eternity in prison or in hell. It wouldn't be any different than what I live every day."

Defensively he reached for my hand. With strength I never knew I had, I held tight to the knife and turned it. The tip was now buried a few millimeters in the soft notch at the base of his throat.

"Say it again. Come on, Alton. We'll end this farce right now."

Blood dripped from his skin onto the white shirt, a small trail making a growing stain.

"Laide."

His wits returned as he squeezed my wrist, causing the knife to drop onto the floor, blood still visible on the blade. In less time than I could fathom, he stood. Suddenly, I was bent over the table, glasses and dishes crashing as their contents covered the table and floor. My hands were secured tightly behind me as my cheek smashed into a dish of something soft.

The Montague staff was too well trained, too frightened of Alton, and too well paid. No one would enter the dining room. No one would stop whatever was about to happen to me.

My stomach twisted as Alton's erection probed my backside. Painfully he twisted my wrists, leaned his lips next to my ear, and loudly whispered, "That's what I'm talking about. Maybe she did get some of that spirit from you after all."

With each word he rubbed himself against me and gathered both of my hands in one of his. Pulling my hair, he lifted my face, the sauce that had been my pillow dripped from my cheek. His menacing tone continued and his Cognac breath soured my stomach. "Maybe I have my hands full, after all."

I didn't have a response. All I could think about was that I'd won. He wouldn't see it that way, but I'd fought and kept his attentions on me. My victory came in Alexandria's safety.

"Keep me satisfied, Laide. I like the idea of what I'm going to do to you after your little stunt."

I felt him stand taller, humming as he assessed his wounds. He tugged my arms farther, eliciting a whimper I tried to suppress.

"You made me bleed." He laughed. "Yes, this is going to be fun." With his lips once again near my ear, he whispered, "If I bleed, so do you."

The night was one I'd rather forget, but Alexandria was worth every minute.

I'd made a promise, and on some level, Alton knew I'd keep it.

Though I wasn't plunging the knife into his neck, my plan for this evening would have a similar result. I'd tried everything. Alexandria wouldn't listen, and I didn't blame her. She was happy. I could hear it in her voice.

My daughter wasn't me. She was Russell through and through. She didn't care about Montague. She didn't love Bryce. And with each passing day, Bryce's discontent with her decision was becoming more evident. Instead of getting closer to my goal, as I'd thought we were a few weeks ago, we were farther and farther away.

The realization that Alton had somehow influenced Alexandria and Lennox's meeting was the final straw. No longer wearing rose-colored Montague glasses, I saw the writing on the wall. Hell, I could read it, even the fine print. Alton believed he'd won.

I wasn't sure why I hadn't taken this course of action sooner. Perhaps I wanted to believe in fate. I wanted to believe in the fairytales Alexandria loved as a child. I wanted to believe the promise my mother made—if I did all I could, it would all work out.

The reality wasn't as pretty. The answer had been at my fingertips all along. A few calls to Dr. Beck's office, more complaints about my migraines and the medicine arrived. That combined with the last prescription, the one I'd yet to use, gave me plenty of pills.

I'd fought my best fight. Now the finest thing I could do for Alexandria was to die.

The answer was so simple.

My death was one of the few outs for Charles's will. If I died, the estate automatically reverted to her. Of course, Alton would fight. He'd fight her. But he wouldn't win. She not only had her grandfather's will on her side, she had Lennox Demetri. I didn't know him, but I had faith that if he were anything like his father, he'd help her get what was hers.

Nevertheless, my daughter's finest weapon wasn't a piece of paper or a man. I took great pride in seeing that Alexandria's greatest weapon against Alton and the atrocities of Montague Manor was what she'd always possessed—her own determination.

Spitfire.

I smiled and let my wish go audibly from my lips, "Rain down hell on him, darling."

With my face washed and wearing my favorite nightgown and robe, I opened both bottles of pills, emptying them into a glass. There were more than I expected. But they were small. For twenty years I'd been an expert swallower. These pills would be nothing.

I started to pour myself a glass of water, when something from my memory came back. If I were going to leave this world, the last liquid to pass my lips would be a glass of Montague Private Collection.

I lifted the phone near the bed and called the kitchen.

"Yes, Mrs. Fitzgerald?"

I suddenly wondered if I'd have to keep that name in the afterlife. I supposed it depended where I landed. Surely, God wouldn't make me keep it.

Satan would think it was proper punishment. "Yes, bring a bottle of Montague cabernet to my suite—1986."

"A bottle, ma'am?"

"Did I stutter?"

"No, ma'am. One or two glasses?"

Stupid girl. The entire staff knew that Alton was gone, out of town until Labor Day weekend. "One," I replied, hanging up the receiver and relishing the idea that for once I didn't give a damn when Alton would be home.

As I waited, I paced the sitting room, uncharacteristically giddy over my future, or lack thereof. I couldn't remember ever feeling as certain about a decision. The weight of the years disappeared. If I'd known the serenity I'd feel, I would have decided this course years ago. Then again, Alexandria might not have been able to handle it years ago. Perhaps my calm came in believing that now she could.

A knock.

"Mrs. Fitzgerald?"

I wrapped my robe tighter around my waist. The voice wasn't some faceless maid. It was one I knew, one I recognized. It belonged to Jane. Hearing it brought a slew of emotions I'd successfully buried.

She'd been the best thing to happen to both Alexandria and to me. Years ago, Russell had said that Alexandria wouldn't miss me as long as she had Jane. My eyes filled with tears as she entered, carrying the wine I'd ordered, and I prayed that Russell was right.

"Mrs. Fitzgerald, are you all right?"

I nodded, pressing my lips together.

"Ma'am, you ain't usually upset when Mr. Fitzgerald's gone."

I shook my head. "Jane, I'm not upset. I'm just… nostalgic."

"Let me help you," she volunteered.

Before I could stop her, she opened the door to the bedroom. I followed behind, my heart beating in overtime. *Please don't let her see…*

I didn't get a chance to finish my plea.

Jane picked up the glass from the bedside stand, the lower fourth of which was filled with small white oblong pills.

"Nostalgic?" she asked.

I shook my head and reached for the glass. "Jane, forget you saw this. I promise it's for the better. I just… I-I…"

She wrapped her arms around me, her embrace swallowing my shoulders.

"Ma'am, no. You can't do this. Not to you. Not to Miss Alexandria."

My head continued to move back and forth. "You don't know. You don't understand."

"I do." For the first time since we'd hired her, her voice grew angry. "I do understand."

"No, Jane, you don't."

"Ma'am, I don't know what you thinks we see or what we hears. But we see everything. Ma'am, Miss Alexandria, she needs you."

"She doesn't. I've tried, but this is the answer."

"It ain't."

My neck straightened as I took a step back. "It is *not* your place to argue with me."

"You can't fire me from heaven." Before I could respond, she continued, "And you can't assure Alexandria's future from there, neither."

"I can." My hand fluttered to my throat as I glanced around the master suite bedroom that I hated. "It's the answer I should've seen years ago."

"No, ma'am. There's a codicil."

I turned back toward Jane.

"Mr. Fitzgerald know it," she said. "Mr. Montague, he told him to tell you. He didn't, did he?"

I stared into her dark eyes. "What are you saying?"

"I'm saying…" She stood taller. "…I see. I listen, and, ma'am, I know."

"A codicil? To my father's will?"

"Yes, ma'am. Mr. Montague, he do it, just before he die."

"Do you know what it says?" I asked.

"I never read it." She shook her head. "*That's* not my place, but I do know it made Mr. Fitzgerald mighty angry."

What didn't make Mr. Fitzgerald angry?

I exhaled as my knees gave out and I sank to the edge of the bed. "I-I need to read it." My mind, which only moments ago seemed clear, now muddied with this new information. "W-why didn't you tell me?"

"I didn't know that he didn't tell you." She crouched down, until our eyes met. "And that ain't my place neither."

"He didn't tell me." I reached for her hand. "Thank you, Jane." I had three days before Alton's return. Air filled my lungs, giving me determination I'd thought was gone. Holding tightly to Jane's hand, I started to devise a new plan. "First thing in the morning, I need to go into Savannah. I need to pay a visit to Ralph Porter's office."

Jane smiled and stood. "Yes, ma'am, I tell Bentley to be ready by nine." She picked up the cup of pills again. "You going to need these?"

I shrugged. "It depends on what the codicil says."

"How about I hold on to them, so no one finds them?"

I nodded. "Thank you, Jane. Leave the wine."

"Yes, ma'am."

CHAPTER 9

NOX

CHARLI AND SILVIA both turned at the sound of my voice. Mindlessly, I scanned Charli's beautiful frame—unscathed and unharmed. My mind knew it to be true, but the need to confirm it was almost unstoppable.

"Come here," I commanded.

Charli didn't question the demand as she stepped toward me, her feet bare and her golden eyes wide and swirling with a kaleidoscope of emotion—fear, concern, and anxiety all vied for top billing.

"Silvia, please give us a few minutes," I said as I reached for Charli's hand.

"Anything you need. I can prepare lunch."

I nodded as I led Charli through the house. The pool house had too many windows for my liking. I didn't know what Silvia was thinking by bringing her out here. Yes, the windows throughout the house had been constructed with bulletproof glass. Nevertheless, that didn't make them less transparent. Anyone with the right equipment could see directly into the interior. Hell, they could read the time on a watch if they had the right zooming capability and the desire to do so. We passed through the kitchen, living room, and halfway up the stairs before Charli spoke.

"Where are you taking me?"

Without answering, I opened the doors to the bedroom where I'd slept for the last four years. The interior was crisp, clean, and relatively austere, decorated in muted tones of brown. It wasn't as large or as ornate as the master suite, but that room contained too many ghosts. We had enough to battle without thinking about any of that.

While Charli halted near the door, I silently walked to the windows; like the master suite, they faced the sound. After confirming the lock was secure on the balcony door, I closed the thick wooden blinds. With only slits of light infiltrating our world, I walked back to Charli, or did I float? After the morning we'd shared, having her here, safe and in my arms, felt like a dream.

I cupped her cheek as my normally sure voice cracked with emotion. "I'm so sorry."

Though her face had inclined to my touch, she shook her head. "Don't be sorry. You kept me safe."

The fury I'd unleashed on Deloris, the same rage that refused to stay at bay during my conversation with Oren, bubbled in my gut, the acid burning my throat. "You shouldn't have to live like this."

"Like what? Explain it to me."

Letting go of her, I spun in the darkness, wanting to pounce, needing to attack, and yet trying with all of my might to project a sense of calm. I didn't want to scare my Charli any more than she undoubtedly was. "Someone shot at us this morning."

Even in the dim light I saw her lips pale from the pressure as she held them tightly together. Finally she replied, "I gathered that from the conversation. But I didn't see anything." Her volume rose. "I didn't hear anything. How do we know?"

"You didn't see her?" My chest clenched. How had she missed the carnage?

"Her?" Charli asked as she sank to the edge of the bed. "The shooter was a woman?"

I took a deep breath, wishing I didn't need to tell her, to explain. However, it was her words from last night, her anger at being unaware that propelled me forward. No doubt this wouldn't go well, but if she wanted to know, I needed to be the one to tell her. With a deep breath, I knelt beside her knees, taking her hands in mine. "We don't know who the shooter was, man or woman. Security believes a silencer was used. There was nothing to hear. Our primary objective was to get out of there."

"I don't understand."

Releasing her hands, I reached for my phone. The news app was usually an annoyance, but today it could explain what I couldn't. I touched the screen until the story appeared. Once it did, I handed my phone to Charli. As she read, her expression of confusion turned to horror.

"I-is she dead?"

"She's in surgery."

Charli stood, rushing past me to get to the bathroom. It must have been her first guess since I hadn't yet shown her around. I followed and found her kneeling near the toilet.

"Charli…"

She shook her head before laying it upon her arm, currently draped over the seat. "I thought I was going to be sick. I want to be sick. But I can't. I can't even… That woman, she's a mother. She was pushing a stroller!"

I offered her my hand.

She shook her head dismissively as she asked, "You're telling me that someone tried to shoot *us* and missed, hitting a mother instead?"

"We don't know who they were trying to shoot. It happened so fast. Security saw her fall, but they couldn't stop it. She just happened to move between us and the shooter at the right time."

"Right time? Nox, that woman is a mother! She's in surgery and may never see her child again. Her child may never know her because she was jogging near us…"

Charli's words trailed away as she crumpled onto the tile.

I reached for her shoulders. "It's tragic, but she very well could have unknowingly saved our lives. Saved *your* life. I'll help her and her family as much as I can. But, Charli—God forgive me—I'd sacrifice a hundred mothers, a million people to keep you safe."

Taking my hand, she stood, her body falling into mine.

Scooping her into my arms, I carried her to the bed, pulled back the covers, and lowered her body to the mattress, and then sat beside her. With a few adjustments, I ensured her comfort as I arranged the pillows and blankets, all the while trying not to notice the tears that silently coated her cheeks.

"I'm sorry," I offered again, wiping a tear with the pad of my thumb. I sat straight, suppressing the emotion my decision evoked. I'd wallow in it later. Now was about being strong for Charli. "The best way to keep you safe is to stop whatever this is between us."

Charli's eyes, which had been nearly closed, opened wide. "No." Her voice was resilient and determined.

"I can't let…"

She reached for my chest, her fingers lingering on the small buttons of my shirt. "Can I trust you?"

My gaze narrowed. "Of course."

"So what you tell me is the truth?"

My indignation grew. What the hell was she talking about? "Yes, unequivocally."

"You wouldn't tell me something just to make me feel better?"

"If you're talking about that woman, she's in surgery. As soon as I hear more, I'll—"

"No, Nox," she said, stopping me. "I'm not talking about that woman. I'm talking about what you said to me in the park. What you said moments before all hell broke loose."

Head bowed, my chin collided with my chest as I reached for her beautiful face. Even with the tears and frightful pallor, she was stunning. Her current line of questioning returned a hue of pink to her cheeks. "I told you that I loved you," I said. "I haven't said those words since…"

She reached for my cheeks and pulled me closer. Just before our lips met, she said, "I've never said those words, and Lennox Demetri…" She brushed a soft kiss on me. "…I love you. You're not getting rid of me that easily."

The pressure from everything that had happened came boiling out. Moisture threatened my vision as the scene before me lost focus. I pulled her closer, not wanting her to see my weakness. With a lump in my throat, I said,

"I love you so much. I can't lose you."

"I'm here. I'm safe."

Without thinking I ripped away the blankets I'd only recently used to cover her. As soon as they were gone, I reached for the hem of her shirt and lifted it over her head. "I need to see you."

Charli didn't argue or protest. She lifted her arms and hips, allowing me to remove her clothing, piece by piece, until I'd exposed each and every inch of her beautiful body.

"Stand up."

After only a moment's hesitation, she swallowed and did as I commanded. Totally nude, she stood before me.

"Turn around."

She slowly rotated as my eyes moved up and down her gorgeous body, scrutinizing her sexy curves, and athletic angles.

No holes. Not even a scratch. She was perfect in every way.

With her magnificent body completely bare, I offered her my hand and pulled her to me. Warm and safe, I drank in her presence. Soft, round breasts met me at nearly eye level as I remained seated on the edge of the bed. They fit perfectly in the palm of my hand as my fingers tenderly caressed each one, eliciting soft mews from her lips as her nipples darkened and turned to hard, pebbled peaks.

Reaching for her waist, I pivoted, returning her to the bed, her long red hair fanning around her serene face. Calm and surreal, she lay still, before lifting her arms above her head and giving herself to me, mine for the taking. With only the tips of my fingers I grazed her warm skin. From the inside of her wrists to her shoulders, her collarbone to her breasts, with both hands I circled her waist and hips. Whimpers filled the room as goose bumps appeared in the wake of my exploration.

Whole.

Safe and complete—the mantra repeated until my brain accepted it as fact.

Her eyes that had watched my every move were now closed as she concentrated on my touch. No longer content to allow my hands the thrill of discovery, my lips joined the mission.

"O-oh, Nox."

I spread her legs and lowered myself to her core. Only moments before she'd been distraught. No longer. Now, her entire body shivered with need. I'd found an outlet for the emotion that had been pent up inside of me, and she was delicious.

Charli's fingernails dug into scalp and her knees parted as she encouraged my actions. My first taste was slow and deep, sweet and enticing. Her hips bucked as my tongue lapped and swirled around her clit. I wanted to make her forget, to make her feel safe. I wanted to take her mind to better places. Lick by lick she responded, withering under my command.

And then the dam I'd attempted to construct within myself burst. My self-control dissolved into her chorus of moans and sounds of ecstasy. No longer did I seek only to please; I was starving for the delicacy before me. Like a man deprived of nutrients, I needed more.

Her hips writhed beneath my unrelenting grasp as I sucked her essence. Each drop was but an appetizer, a hors d'oeuvre that only whetted my appetite. My name joined the other sounds filling the air around us as her legs stiffened and body convulsed.

"P-please," she begged breathlessly.

I didn't need to hear more. In seconds my shoes hit the floor. My pants and boxers were below my knees. I released my rock-hard length, now throbbing in my own grasp.

Her veiled eyes stared into mine. When her gaze dropped to my erection, the smile she'd kept tamed beamed in anticipation as her lower lip disappeared between her teeth. We kissed, my teeth tugging her lip free as her tongue sought out her own taste. Though I wasn't sure it was possible, I grew even harder.

Without words, I encouraged her to roll to her stomach and lifted her ass as she settled on her elbows. For only a moment I took the time to appreciate the masterpiece before me. The Mona Lisa or Starry Night couldn't compare to her beauty: poised, ready, and willing. Charli was picturesque with her entrance and thighs glistening. Her body offered no resistance but pushed toward me as she released a loud gasp and my length slid deep inside. The walls of her pussy stretched and accommodated as they tightened around me. Thrust for thrust, I drove deeper and deeper until her arms gave out, leaving her cries of pleasure muffled by the pillows. My fingers blanched as they dug into her hips, choreographing her movements. Harder and harder, I was possessed. The friction was a drug concoction, a mixture of a stimulant to keep going and a tranquilizer to ease my earlier mayhem. The room filled with her wordless screams as again she detonated, her muscles rigid before finally going slack.

I pulled out and rolled her so that I could see her golden stare, no longer fearful, her beautiful eyes were hooded, satiated, and satisfied. She whimpered a protest as I once again plunged into her core. Slowly I teased, in and out, my dick purposely rubbing her sensitive clit. So amazingly responsive, she began to again move with me. Our bodies synced in a rhythm of their own. The urgency from before was gone. My only desire was to linger in its wake. This was somehow different than it had ever been. I wasn't fucking Charli, but loving her. More and slower, her expression morphed, as the realization became clear to us both.

We were making love.

I was in Charli and in heaven. In the eye of the storm, I was making love to the new love of my life.

Again her eyes closed, back arched, and lips formed a circle as we came at the same time. My body trembled violently as a growl tore, not from my throat but from my chest, and I released inside of her. Though she'd fallen slack against the soft sheets, I continued to come, a never-ending fountain as I released more than my seed.

I filled her with *me*.

I was hers.

When I was finally done, I collapsed, covering her with my body, shielding her from the evil that lurked about us. If I could, I'd keep us here forever. But I couldn't. Once again, I had work that I needed to do at Demetri Enterprises, business that couldn't be postponed.

Her breathing slowed to a point that I wondered if she were asleep. I kissed her forehead and her nose as I pulled out of her. Slowly her lids fluttered as a grin covered her bruised pink lips.

"I think I'm about ready to fall into a sex-induced coma."

My cheeks rose. "I'd like to keep you perpetually induced."

"Hmm." She wiggled beneath me.

No longer connected, I rolled to the side and pulled her close. "Charli, I still need to leave. I'll be late for this afternoon's testimony, but I have to be there."

CHAPTER 10

CHARLI

"NO." THE CALM that had settled over me, lulling me into the coma that Chelsea had warned me about, disappeared. "I don't want you to go."

Nox's brow furrowed. "You'll be safe. You're staying here."

Reaching for the sheets, I pulled them up to my breast and sat against the headboard. Indignation rose. "No. You said we don't know who the target was. You can't go to Washington. That's where you're supposed to be. If you go there, you could be walking into a trap."

Lying beside me, Nox lifted his arm and covered his eyes with his bicep. It was then I realized he was still wearing his white silk shirt. His tie was gone and I suspected that his pants were somewhere buried in the mountain of blankets, yet his shirt was pristinely white—albeit wrinkled—in the darkened room.

"That's why you're staying here," he said.

"What? No. I have class. I already missed today." Though the scent of sex lingered, my thighs still wet, and my muscles clenched, the mood of moments before was gone. "You can't go to Washington and expect me to stay hidden in this house."

Nox sat up and in one swift move he was before me, our noses touching.

"I can and I do. This conversation is done."

Common sense told me to let the dust settle, allow him his little show of dominance and then revisit the subject. Then again, if he were in DC there wouldn't be time for renegotiations. "No."

The covers flew as Nox sat, swung his long, muscular legs off the side of the bed, and searched for the rest of his clothes.

"Don't you understand?" he asked.

"Yes. I get it. I get that you're protective. I understand something terrible happened today. I won't walk in the park. I'll let Jerrod drive me everywhere. I have a responsibility to my schooling."

"Fuck, Charli, so do I. I have a responsibility and it's you."

He was now standing, straightening his shirt, pushing it down into his pants, and securing his buttons, zipper, and belt. Before I devised a plausible response, he continued, "I was not supposed to be in Central Park this morning."

"Yes, I know. You were only there because of…" A cold chill covered my skin as it prickled with fear. "…me."

"Deloris has a full team working on this. There was a communication that went out to Jerrod and Isaac about our change in plans. The network is supposed to be secure, but fuck, I'm not sure of anything anymore."

"H-has she learned anything more about the break-in?"

Nox's hand ran through his sex-messed hair. "Her priority shifted when someone decided to use us for target practice."

"But they could be connected?"

He nodded. "They could." He leaned down upon the bed. "Both are connected to you."

"What are you saying?"

"I'm not saying you're involved, though some on her team are insinuating that."

What?

"I'm saying," he went on, "that someone could be trying to get to me through you. First, there was the attack on Chelsea, then the break-in at our apartment, and now this. I'm saying that this house is the safest place for you until we know more. Even Oren agrees."

Oren? He spoke with his father?

"Contact your professors. Claim illness, the flu, I don't give a fuck. Ask to read from home. If you need anything from the apartment, tell Jerrod or Deloris. They'll get it and bring it to you." His blue eyes widened. "Don't they offer teleconferencing of the lectures?"

My gaze narrowed. "How would you know that?"

"You, Miss Collins, left all of your school shit all over the kitchen table for over two weeks. Did you not think I'd at least glance at all the crap?"

I folded my arms over my sheet-covered breasts. "Nox, I don't want to start my career as a law student as the one hearing the recorded lecture. I want to be the one sitting in the front row and asking the pertinent questions. Do you think I graduated with honors by doing the minimum?"

"No, princess, I don't. I think you knocked it out of the park, because believe me, what we just did here, well, let me say, you hit a home run." He planted a kiss on the top of my head. "I fucking hate this. I do. I want you to succeed. I also need to know you're alive and safe. Today's Wednesday. Give Deloris a day or two. Call Columbia. Tell them whatever you need to tell them. I'll be back on the weekend."

"Weekend?" I asked. "You want me to stay here for three days? What about Patrick's apartment?"

Nox's blue stare lowered a degree or two. The temperature was nearing freezing. Ice was not far away. "Alexandria Collins, this conversation is done."

"I only have my laptop."

"My office is your office. Help yourself. I'll leave all the necessary passwords on the desk."

"Deloris?"

"She'll be out here later. Let her or Jerrod know what you need and they'll bring it."

I sighed, laying my head back against the headboard.

"And stay inside," he went on. "I'm not even a fan of the pool house, at least until Deloris is certain of the perimeter."

Perimeter? I'm in a damn war zone.

"I don't have a choice, do I?"

"Princess, you have a choice. If you choose me, then that's your choice."

"Fuck, Nox, of course my choice is you. Just tell me that I'll be able to go back and be the student in the front row."

"As soon as it's safe."

"What about you?" I asked.

"What about me?"

"How will I know you're safe? Are you flying commercial or in your Batplane?"

"Batplane. The super-secret gadgets let me fly under the radar."

I smiled at his grin and the menacing gleam, yet if he could be worried about me, I could be worried about him. "I still haven't seen your cape, and I'd say we're past the third date."

"No, princess, you haven't seen my cape, but you've seen under the mask. You do realize that makes you part of a very elite group."

Though he was joking, I found more than a little bit of truth in his humor. Lennox Demetri had shown me a side of himself that I doubted many people had seen or even knew existed.

I pursed my lips. "Fine. I'll stay here. Just promise me that you'll come back. Promise me that you'll stay safe."

Once again he leaned down on the bed. This time he kissed me, soft and chaste. "I promise. Thank you for not fighting me on this. I need to concentrate on the hearing." He looked down at his phone. "I need to be going."

I nodded. "I'm going to take a quick shower. Will you please ask Silvia to hold my lunch?"

When he looked up, the menacing gleam was gone.

"What?" I asked.

"Look at this." For the second time today, he thrust his phone my direction. "You might want to reconsider what you tell your professors."

My stomach dropped as I secured his phone in my now-shaky grasp. The video queued on the screen needed only for me to push the small triangle in order for it to play. In the still picture I could make out a crowd of people.

I hit the triangle.

The sound was terrible, mostly static and unrecognizable voices. The picture was shaky and unfocused. It had undoubtedly been taken with someone's cell phone. It wasn't until near the end when the photographer zoomed in on a couple being escorted into an SUV that I saw myself. Instead of keeping my head down like Nox had done, I looked up over my shoulder at the crowd. There wasn't a name, but it wouldn't take long before it was figured out.

The small news snippet asked if anyone knew how this couple was involved in the shooting of an innocent woman in Central Park.

I dropped the phone on the bed, my stomach bubbling with acid and dread. "What? What can I do?"

"Stay put. Let me talk to Deloris. Don't call Columbia or talk to anyone until she tells you what to say."

I nodded.

"Princess, I love you. Don't go rogue on me. With all the fucking chaos, please let me have the peace of knowing that you're safe."

The corner of my lips quirked upward as I tilted my head. "Only because you begged, Mr. Demetri. I do love it when you beg."

Nox came closer and reached for my hand, encouraging me to stand.

"No," I shook my head. "I'm… well, I reek."

"Fucking stop saying that," he admonished as he pulled me to my feet. "You smell amazing." He smoothed my hair. "And your hair is perfect. Hot sex is the best hairstyle on you."

My cheeks filled with warmth as they undoubtedly colored with crimson.

He pulled me close, my bare skin against his slacks and shirt. I inhaled as the cold buckle of his belt sent a chill against my stomach. "Alexandria Collins, I meant it when I said I love you. I will beg you every fucking day if it keeps you with me, but…" The gleam returned to his sexy blue eyes. "…I expect to be obeyed." I fidgeted in his grasp. "Princess, I'll be glad to spank your ass, just don't make me do it because of your putting yourself in danger."

"Is that a promise, Mr. Demetri?"

He shook his head. "Are you trying to make me later than I already am?"

I nodded. "Guilty as charged. I'm trying to make you want to stay with me. Maybe you should punish me now?"

He shook his head again. "I should, and I do want to stay." He kissed me, his tongue teasing my lips, urging them to part. Willingly, I opened, taking all that he had to offer. When he pulled away, he continued. "I'll call."

"Nox?"

"Yes, princess?"

"I love you, too. You told me that you're always truthful. You promised you'd come back safe. I'm holding you to that."

"I won't disappoint."

I couldn't stop the grin, though my chest felt as though my heart might break. He was right. He hadn't disappointed me yet.

I stood nude in the darkened room, the evidence of our lovemaking fresh upon my thighs as Nox disappeared through the door, leaving me alone.

I PUSHED THE chicken salad around my plate, separating the grapes from the nuts. I liked them all, but I wasn't hungry. Lifting my gaze from my plate, I stared out of the breakfast-nook windows toward the water. The afternoon sun looked warm as it shone not only on the crystal blue pool, but also beyond the deep green lawn to the sound. The scene was beautiful, calming even.

I needed something to calm me as I waited for Nox's call. How long did it take to fly from New York to DC? Considering the time it took for my shower and now lunch, he'd been gone for nearly an hour. Rationally I knew he'd also need to be driven back to the city, but that didn't stop my heart from aching.

My phone sat beside my plate. If I weren't waiting for his call, I'd turn off the sound. From the clamor of noises—notifications, emails, and tweets—I suspected that my name had been discovered as one of the people leaving the scene of a shooting.

What did that even mean?

We couldn't be suspects, could we?

With a huff, I pushed back the plate, grabbed my phone and the tall glass of iced tea. Even with the shower, I'd like something else to wear. My capris and top seemed jaded by the memories of the scene in the park. As I walked around Nox's lovely home, I didn't notice the elegant furnishings or the stately architecture. My mind was desperately trying to replay the morning scene.

In the photo I was looking beyond the bodyguards, looking out to the crowd. Yet I couldn't recall seeing the victim.

My nearly empty stomach twisted.

The woman's only crime was jogging. I jogged in the park every Saturday. I'd just been talking to Nox, telling him how we should run in the park instead of on a treadmill. That was all she'd been doing—exercising, and with her child no less.

I was an English and political science major. Physics was never my thing. After calculus I went into micro- and macroeconomics. I understood math as a property of finance, not angles and projections. Somehow, a bullet aimed at either Nox or me was shot from a gun with one of us in the sights and by a person who I would venture to guess was good at what he or she did, when at just precisely the right moment, this woman stepped into its trajectory.

How ironic was that?

The shrill ring of my phone pulled me from my thoughts. I recognized the tune. It was my mother. I took a deep breath as I turned the screen toward me and confirmed the name.

I could let it go to voicemail, but eventually I'd need to talk to her. Had she seen my picture? Did she know I was—at the very least—connected to a violent crime in Central Park?

Taking a deep breath, I swiped the screen and held tightly to my midsection. With my phone to my ear, I said, "Hi, Momma."

"Alexandria, I'm sending a plane. Where in the fuck are you? You're coming home today."

The phone didn't need to be at my ear. Silvia, no matter where she was in the house, could probably hear. It wasn't the words that set my nerves into overdrive. It was the voice.

With the small hairs standing at attention on the back of my neck, I sucked in another breath. "Alton, where's my mother?"

CHAPTER 11

Twenty years ago

OREN

"FAMILY," CARMINE COSTELLO said as he hugged Angelina.

"*Zio*," she replied with a smile.

"Oren," he said, his hand extended.

"Sir, we're happy to be here today."

"Yes, yes," Mr. Costello replied as he walked through the house, his arm around my wife, his niece.

What I'd said was partially true. Angelina and I would never decline an invitation to her uncle's home. That wasn't only because he was her family, her father's brother, but because he was the head of her family. No one declined an invitation.

It wasn't as easy as it had been to get to the Costello home. When we'd still lived in Brooklyn, we could walk. Now we had our house in Westchester County. Sometimes it was as though they had forgotten that we'd moved. I couldn't count the number of times I'd received late-night phone calls requesting my presence at a family meeting. Thankfully, late at night, the traffic was more forgiving.

This wasn't late at night. It was a sunny Sunday afternoon and the tree-lined street was filled with cars. We'd practically needed to walk from our old brownstone in order to find a place to park.

Angelina's Uncle Carmine had met us at the top of the tall steps at the threshold of his home. As we made our way down the long hallway toward the beautiful courtyard out back, the other guests came into view. In the world where Angelina was born, this was an honor to be amongst these people. We were on the inside, along with family that was either blood or who'd earned their way to the inner circle. Earning that right came with the same price—blood.

Blood in, blood out.

The backyard was festive with voices and laughter. Angelina made her way over to Vinny's wife, Bella, and offered her congratulations. We weren't celebrating her accomplishment, but that of her daughter. We were all gathered to celebrate the first communion of Carmine's granddaughter and Vincent's daughter, Luisa, the princess.

I turned to talk to Lennox, to remind him to behave, but he was already gone. He'd run off to the area of the yard where the other children were playing. He was with Luca, Vincent's boy, who was the same age as Lennox. The way Luca stood holding court over his siblings and cousins reminded me more of his grandfather than of his father.

"Oren," Vinny said as he patted my shoulder. "Good to have you here. I heard Angel speaking to Rose. That gift, man, you didn't need to do that."

The gift was a silver jewelry box engraved with Luisa's name and a white gold cross necklace. It was expensive, but nothing but the best for Carmine Costello's family.

"You know how it is," I said, watching the ease in which Angelina intermingled with the other wives. "Your cousin was the one who picked it out."

Vinny laughed. "Glad to hear that jewelry box shopping isn't your thing."

"No, but jewelry..." I left the innuendo floating in the wind as a young girl brought us each a beer.

I'd recently inquired about a few upper-end jewelry stores. They were ripe for the picking. The recent housing boom had taken the lion's share of disposable income, leaving the high-end jewelry market in the affluent suburbs strapped for cash. It was a great investment that I was sure would pay off in merchandise, revenue, and real estate. The buildings themselves were in prime locations. Demetri Enterprises would broaden its umbrella, including more reputable businesses.

I had the investors and the backing, and had worked out most of the kinks.

The problem was that only one of the buildings was in the Costello family neighborhood. I couldn't buy just one. The deal was for three and two were in a neighborhood watched over by another family. Personally, I didn't have a problem. I knew the rules. I'd either be paying family for the pleasure of doing business or someone else.

That would've worked if I weren't married to a Costello, but I was. The deal wouldn't nor could it be finalized without Carmine's approval.

"Not today," Vinny said as he tilted his head toward his father. "He knows. He's considering. That's all I've got right now."

I nodded as I brought the brown bottle to my lips and took a swallow.

"This legit thing," he asked, "you really want to make it work?"

"I do, as much as I can." I lowered my voice. "I know it'll never be one hundred percent. I'll take what I can… for her." I looked up to see Angelina looking my way, her blue eyes smiling as our gazes met.

"Yeah, I get it. Things aren't the way they were, but we're family. We look out for one another. And there are rules," he added, as if I needed to be reminded.

My chest expanded with my intake of air, though it suddenly felt tight. Although Vinny had just told me that his daughter's party wasn't the place to talk business, he'd essentially laid it on the line. My quest for legitimate business would always be at the grace of family. They'd decide what I could and couldn't do. As long as I stayed in their good graces, I had options. That meant not only seeking approval, but also allowing anything under the Demetri Enterprises umbrella to be available to the family whenever they wanted it.

"Oren," Carmine's booming voice interrupted our private conversation.

"Sir, nice party."

"Yes, Luisa is a vision. As you know, I never had a daughter of my own." He patted Vinny on the shoulder. "Sons… a man needs his sons, but a girl, a beautiful girl… my Vincent here's been blessed with both. Look at Luisa. I'm sorry you, Angelina, and Lennox didn't make the church service. Her white dress…" He shook his head. "…a princess. She looked like a princess."

"The sparkling tiara added to the effect," Vinny offered with a grin.

"Nothing but the best," Carmine said, tilting his head toward his son, excusing him from the conversation.

I found myself standing taller, wondering if this was my thirty-second elevator pitch. I'd just been told not to bring up the stores here at the party. It was, after all, Luisa's day, but how often did I have a one-on-one with Carmine Costello?

"Daughters, you know what I mean," Carmine asked, "with only a son?"

I nodded. "I do. Our son means everything."

"But Angelina, she'd like a daughter?"

I shrugged. "We've both decided one child is what we want."

With his lips together, he moved his head—actually his entire upper body—up and down, whether in agreement or concentration, I wasn't sure.

"Angelina, she's like my daughter."

This time I agreed. I'd known that since before I got up the nerve to ask her on our first date.

"That's why she means so much to me. She's happy. Tell me she's happy," Carmine implored.

"Sir, I believe she is."

"You believe? A man must be sure. That woman over there is either your world or she's not. There's no in between."

"She is." I meant every word as I followed her with my eyes. We'd had our share of fights. She had her uncle's temper, like a loose cannon, and yet she was also the most loving mother and wife.

The move had been the hardest thing on our marriage. She'd been happy in Brooklyn, but she deserved more. Even though she didn't see it, I wanted to show not only her, but also Carmine and the rest of the Costellos that I could take care of their pride and joy. I could give her more than she'd had.

The house in Rye was everything she'd ever said she wanted.

From vacations where we'd sat near a pool and she told me how much she enjoyed it, to walks along the shore where she'd commented on the water. I'd remembered every word, every time she'd smiled and told me she was happy. I tried to put it all in one package. The house had everything she loved and more. The attached guesthouse would be perfect for someone to help her. I didn't build her a grand home for her to be the one who had to care of it.

Though she'd moved to Rye, getting her to accept domestic help had not yet happened.

"Why spend money on someone to do what I love to do?" she'd ask. "I love caring for my family. Cleaning is part of that."

I explained that she'd have more time for other things. She could go out with her friends, shop, or spend time in the city.

"I want to spend time with you and Lennox." It was her answer to everything. Sometimes I swore I heard her recite it in her sleep.

She'd been raised in the world of Costellos, yet she didn't understand the time commitment her family required of me. Making my way and navigating both worlds was equivalent to two full-time jobs.

The house was built for her, designed with luxury and safety in mind, yet the one amenity she wanted—me—didn't have time to be present. I had a name to build and a reputation to prove.

"Before her father died," Carmine said, "I promised my brother that I'd look after her. If I ever thought she wasn't happy, I would need to say my piece."

I wasn't worried about him *saying* his piece. I was worried about what would come after the verbal lashing.

"*Zio*," Angelina said as she stepped between her uncle and me. "You aren't talking business, are you? I seem to recall a 'no business at family events' rule."

"*Tesoro*, you know I'm the one who made that rule and we don't break rules, do we, Oren?"

"No, sir, we don't."

So this wasn't my opportunity for my elevator pitch. I wouldn't be talking to Carmine Costello about the jewelry stores today.

I took another drink of my beer and grimaced. The liquid had warmed in the summer heat and the warmth of my grasp.

"Sir, a fresh beer?" the young girl who'd given me the first beer asked.

"Yes," I said, nodding and handing her my warm brown bottle.

"Thank you," Angelina called after the girl who'd hurried away to get me another drink.

When Carmine walked away, I pulled my wife close and whispered in her ear. "Wouldn't that be nice?"

"What?"

"Having someone to bring you drinks?"

Her soft blue eyes fluttered in consideration. "Someone who is at your beck and call and does what you say without receiving gratitude?"

My neck straightened.

What the hell?

This wasn't the place to start a fight. "What are you talking about?"

"Just now, you couldn't even say thank you."

"To her? That girl? It's her job. Do you think people thank me for doing my job?"

"No," she said definitively.

"You're right, they don't," I confirmed.

Angelina looked around the room, her expression perfect, her smile big and happy. It was her eyes that told me she was mad. No longer soft, fire burned behind the color, darkening it to a molten pool of navy lava. "Not the question I answered," she explained. "My no was in reference to your earlier question as in, no, I don't think that would be nice. No sense subjecting anyone else to what I endure daily."

What she endures?

"This is hardly—" I began, keeping my voice low.

Her smile was still too large as she kissed my cheek. "Of course it isn't. The only time I ever see you is when we can't talk. Excuse me, *tesoro*, I must help Bella."

I fought the urge to tug her hand and explain that she didn't need to help.

That was why they had that young girl here. It could be that way for her too, but I didn't reach for her hand. In a matter of seconds she was gone and the young girl was back with my beer.

"Here you are, sir."

Taking it, I nodded, but before she walked away, I remembered my wife's reprimand. "Thank you."

The girl's face lit up as if my words had impact. "You're welcome."

CHAPTER 12

A week ago

ADELAIDE

"RALPH, I WANT to see my father's will."

"Adelaide, this is unexpected. I didn't have you scheduled…"

"I won't take much of your time. I'm certain that Montague keeps you and your firm busy enough to warrant me a few minutes alone with the document."

He ran a pen through his fingers, slowly twisting it as it weaved a course above one digit, below the next. More than likely he wasn't even aware he was doing it. My mother detested nervous habits. She pointed out that they were signs of weakness. Something as simple as the bobbing of a knee showed vulnerability.

I sat statuesque, perched on the edge of the red leather chair facing Ralph Porter's desk, my knees together and back straight. If some people thought they could intimidate me after twenty years with Alton Fitzgerald, they were seriously deluding themselves.

"You see," he began, "we don't just keep those kinds of documents sitting around. You can understand their sensitivity. If you'd have let me or Natalie know that you were coming, we could have pulled the will." He feigned looking at his computer screen. "With the holiday coming, we're very busy. I could have it for you on Tuesday."

"No."

His eyes widened. "Excuse me?"

"I said no. I'm here today. My time, too, is valuable. Am I or am I not an heir to Charles Montague II?"

Ralph's shoulders moved back and then forward. "Adelaide, I don't understand what's gotten into you. Perhaps if you just ask me whatever it is that you want to know, I can answer your question. The wording of these documents is legalese and confusing."

Asshole.

He might as well say what Alton's been saying for twenty years. 'You're too stupid to understand.'

"Despite public opinion to the contrary," I replied, "I do know how to read."

He shifted in his chair. "Now, Laide, that isn't what I meant."

"Mrs. Fitzgerald. Adelaide Montague Fitzgerald, and I'll thank you to remember that."

"Yes, of course," Ralph said, his thinning gray hair doing little to hide the crimson now seeping from his skin. "It's just that we've known one another for most of our lives. I helped when Russell died. I worked for your father…"

"Yes, Ralph, you've been a great asset to my family, our company, and to me. Tell me why you don't want me to see my father's will."

"I-it isn't me."

My neck straightened. "Mr. Fitzgerald cannot restrict who sees and doesn't see my father's will."

"He can…"

I narrowed my blue eyes. "Legally, Ralph? Because if I don't see that will and all of the codicils *today*, I will seek new representation. I will see my father's will today or by court order. So if Mr. Fitzgerald's request doesn't have legal backing, I suggest you reconsider your answer to my next question." I paused. "When can you have my father's last will and testament and any and all codicils sitting on a table in front of me?"

"I-I need to at least consult Mr. Fitz—"

"No, you do not."

"You don't understand the position you're putting me in—that you're putting our firm in. If he learned that you—"

My cheeks rose as my head tilted slightly to the left. I may be in my early fifties, but between personal trainers and plastic surgeons, I'd done what my father had told me to do and kept the wrapping on the package appealing. My words dripped with Southern charm. "Then you have you your answer, Ralph."

His eyes opened wide. "My answer?"

"Mr. Fitzgerald doesn't *need* to learn a thing. This…" I motioned between us. "…will be our little secret." I winked. "Isn't that what old friends do for one another? We keep secrets. You see, I don't plan on announcing to anyone that we had this chat, not as long as I get to see what I came to see." My lips pursed. "But then again, if this becomes a big 'ole fight, if I have to involve another law firm…" I contemplated. "There's a new firm, Preston, Madden, and Owen, I believe…"

"Why?" he asked.

Continuing, I oozed charisma. "Now, Ralph, that right there is a question friends don't ask one another. You see, a woman's age, her dress size, and why she does whatever in the hell she sets her mind to do are all off-limits for friends. And we are friends, aren't we?"

Nearly an hour later, clutching my purse, I paced back and forth in the small conference room. There were two windows that looked out to a small parking lot. The September sun shone bright and warm. After all, this was Georgia. Autumn may be on the calendar in less than three weeks, but rarely did we see the cooler temperatures until much closer to the holidays.

It was hard to believe I was thinking holidays when only last night I'd been ready to leave this world behind. As my manicured nails pinched the leather exterior of my handbag, I contemplated what I was about to read. Part of me feared that I might not understand it. I'd been told for so long how stupid I really was.

I tried to recall reading the original document after Alton's and my engagement was announced. That was the last time I'd seen my father's will, and as I recalled, I'd only seen the section and subsection related to our marriage and that of Alexandria and Bryce's. My father was an incredibly wealthy man with many holdings. His entire last will and testament was ridiculously wordy.

My purse vibrated with an incoming call. I glanced toward the door I'd wanted to open for at least the last forty-five minutes. Ralph had told me that I could leave and return, but I refused. I was here and didn't plan to leave without accomplishing my goal.

Another vibration.

Opening my purse, I looked at the screen and sighed. *ALTON*.

I didn't know how to do the thing that the kids did, how they gave each caller their own distinctive ring, but if I could, I'd have some ominous song alert me of my husband's calls. I'd read a book that talked about a dark song called Fatal Lullaby. After reading the book, I listened to the song over and over. It was perfect for the book, and in hindsight, would be the perfect ring for Alton's calls.

Another vibration.

Even just the idea of that song announcing him—such a secret and tiny rebellion—brought a smile to my face as I pulled the phone from my purse. Swiping the screen, I said, "Hello, Alton."

"Where are you?"

I shook my head. If Ralph had called Alton, I'd leave this damn office and head straight for Preston, Madden, and Owen. "I'm in Savannah. Do you need something?"

"Yes, why the hell else would I call?"

I bit my lip. I had so many responses. "What do you need?"

"I'll be back on Friday night. The damn meetings were supposed to only last until…" I listened as he ranted about something that made no difference to me other than to alert me of his impending return. Once the entire conversation was complete, I deciphered that he'd wanted me to check on the caterers for our annual Labor Day barbeque. When I assured him that it was all taken care of, he went on a rampage about someone leaving a message on his cell.

The damn world didn't know how important he was—yada yada yada. He couldn't bother with mundane… blah blah blah. I tuned him out at some point only to come back to the conversation when he said, "…and Brantley said he'd taken you downtown. You don't usually leave the manor on Wednesdays unless you do that luncheon, but it's not this week. What are you doing?"

"Dear, we're having our annual barbeque in a few days. I didn't think you'd want me wearing some old thing I'd worn to other outings all summer long. It just wouldn't do."

"Shopping? You're shopping?"

"Yes. Is there a problem with that?"

"No. Fuck, I don't give a shit. Get me something, too."

"Certainly. We'll be dressed for the occasion."

"I need to go. Wait on me for dinner Friday night."

My teeth ground together, yet my words dripped with sincerity. "Yes, Alton. I'll see you then."

The line went dead just as the door opened. It wasn't Ralph, but some young man, possibly younger than Alexandria.

"Mrs. Fitzgerald," he said as he placed a box on the table. "Your father had many documents. Mr. Porter asked me to help you find whatever it is you want to find." He looked at the box, shook his head, and brushed the dust from his hands. "Would you like a cup of coffee or something? We might need it to get through all of this."

There was something I liked about him. In this world of sharks, he was refreshingly naïve.

"Do you work here?"

"Yes, ma'am, I'm an intern from Savannah Law."

Savannah Law—that was where I wanted Alexandria to go. "Really? My daughter's a first-year law student."

His eyes widened. "She is? I'm second-year." He shook his head. "I haven't met many of the first-years. Maybe she should be here with you?"

"I'd like that very much, but she attends Columbia, in New York."

He let out a low whistle. "I didn't even apply there. Wow. You must be proud."

"I am. Son, what's your name?"

"Stephen."

"Stephen, I'd love some coffee." I took the lid off the box. "We may even need sandwiches before the day is through." I felt the gleam in my eyes. "You weren't planning on doing anything else today, were you?"

His smile turned bashful. "Not after Mr. Porter told me to help you."

I nodded. "Good answer, Stephen. You get the coffee—I'll take mine with cream—and I'll start removing the files."

"Ma'am, they're kind of old. Some of these haven't seen the light of day for nearly fifteen years. You might get dusty."

"My name's Adelaide, and I've been dusty before. Not to worry."

"Yes, ma'am, I mean Miss Adelaide, I'll be right back with coffee."

Some of these?

Stephen's words hit a cord. "Stephen," I called, though he'd already stepped away.

A moment later he was back. "Yes, do you want something else?"

"No, I have a question. What did you mean that *some of these* haven't seen the light of day in nearly fifteen years? Does that mean that some have?"

"Well, yes. We have a content inventory. Usually we don't bring all the records at once. Usually particular documents or even sections are requested. It's all cataloged."

The box only contained files.

"Where is the catalog?"

"I can access it from the server."

"On your computer?"

"Yes, ma'am… I mean, Adelaide."

I waved away his correction. "Stephen, will you please bring us coffee and your laptop. I'd like to see who's accessed these files, which files they've accessed, and when."

His countenance fell. No doubt he'd been hoping to dismiss me before sandwiches became necessary. "Yes, right away."

"Oh, and Stephen?"

"Yes?"

"If Mr. Porter doesn't ask you for particulars, you don't need to share with him what we discover."

"If he does?"

I shrugged. "I'm the heir to Montague Corporation. We're always looking for good men to work and run our legal division. Hiring from local universities is one of my husband's favorite things."

"Yes, Adelaide, coffee, one cream?"

"Thank you."

I POINTED TO the clause. It was the last amendment, the last codicil added to my father's legal last will and testament. On the top of the typed page was a date with my father's initials and those of Ralph Porter.

"What does this date mean?" I asked.

My shoes were now neatly stowed in the corner of the small room. The hem of my silk blouse hung loosely from my skirt. The table was completely covered in papers, including the wrappers of the sandwiches we'd ordered hours ago. The only thing missing from my long morning and afternoon was wine. And while my body craved it, my mind was happy to be alert and awake.

Stephen was just as comfortable. His jacket and tie were gone and his shirt was unbuttoned at the collar. The blinds on the two windows were closed in an attempt to keep the late afternoon sun at bay. Nevertheless, the temperature of the small room had risen, despite our attempts at manipulating the thermostat.

"It's the date this codicil was approved by your father."

I stared as my chest tightened.

"Why?" he asked. "Is it significant?"

My head bobbed, though I couldn't form the words. "I-it's the day he died."

The young man beside me sucked in a breath. "Th-that…" He stammered, "can't be right. Maybe it's a typo?"

"It could be right. He died during the evening, a heart attack after he fell asleep." They say that a quick and painless death is like being kissed by an angel. I always wondered how he warranted a kiss. Maybe this codicil was it?

Stephen's head moved side to side. "Whoa, that's just… weird… coincidental."

Frankly, it seemed suddenly too coincidental.

I pushed further thoughts of my father's death from my mind. "Okay, tell me again about this amendment."

He took a drink from the water bottle. "In effect, it qualifies the provisions in Article XII. The article that deals with the marriage…" His words softened as if he had a difficult time believing that such a thing would be mandated from the afterlife. "…of your daughter, Alexandria Charles Montague Collins, to Edward Bryce Carmichael Spencer."

"Qualifies?"

"Basically it's saying that any manipulation by any of the interested parties alters the provisions."

"If someone involved in this agreement does anything to persuade the outcome—" I tried to paraphrase.

"Sorry, ma'am, it specifically states that if anyone does *anything* to dissuade, to interfere with the natural progression of, or to stop the planned arrangement, then that person null and voids his or her assets or any claim to said assets."

"What about this?" I asked as I pointed.

"In the event that the marriage doesn't go as planned, Montague Corporation will remain a viable entity; however, the current board of trustees will be dissolved, and the entire corporate structure will become a publicly traded company."

"But the original article stated it would be sold and the proceeds would go to Fitzgerald Investments?"

"Adelaide, that's what a codicil does, it allows people to change their minds."

"What about the assets?"

Stephen shook his head. "If the marriage doesn't occur, or either person marries someone else, your father's last will and testament will enter probate again where all interested parties must make a case for their rights. Assuming that the earlier mentioned interference isn't an issue, theoretically, the estate will be equally divided amongst the living heirs."

"This has been present for fifteen years and it's the first time I'm seeing it? Why is that?"

"I don't have an answer for you. I can tell you that after the addition of the codicil and apparently your father's death, there was an attempt to revoke the codicil, to make it null and void. The presiding judge refused to remove it."

I didn't need to ask who had made that attempt.

I removed my phone from my purse and turned on my camera. Page by page, I photographed Article XII as well as the codicils. When I was done, I said, "Stephen, thank you. Let me help you put this all back in the box. Would it be possible to forget to log what we saw into that catalog?"

He shook his head.

"I understand. Then could it simply say that we explored the contents of the documents with no specifics?"

His expression blossomed. "That space for content is too small to describe all that we did."

"And who's made aware of that catalog?" I asked.

"Only people who seek the information. It isn't automatically given to anyone." He shrugged. "If it were, you'd be on that list."

That was true.

"Thank you again," I said. "I'd be happy to buy you a drink. You are old enough to drink, aren't you?"

"Yes, ma'am, and after today, I'd like a drink."

"Me too, Stephen. I feel like celebrating."

CHAPTER 13

CHARLI

"TELL ME WHERE you are," Alton's booming voice demanded.

I wasn't born yesterday. If my GPS worked for Nox, it also worked for Alton. "Let me talk to my mother, or I'm hanging up."

"I didn't realize that Columbia had a satellite campus in *Rye*." He said the word like it was a backwoods Georgia dot on the map, not one of the nicest, most expensive zip codes in New York.

Asshole.

"It doesn't."

"Well, obviously, this law school farce didn't last long. Second day and you're already skipping class."

"Goodbye."

Before I could disconnect the line, my mother's voice came through the cell phone. "Alexandria, are you all right?"

"Yes, Mother, I'm fine."

"Tell us what happened."

Nox had told me not to talk to anyone about this morning until I heard from Deloris. Did that include my family? "I really don't know." It was mostly true. The scene was a blur.

"Bullshit!" Alton's voice boomed from the background, turning my stomach and setting my teeth on edge.

"Speakerphone? Really, Mother?" I wondered if they were in his office at that damn ostentatious conference table. Were we now doing long-distance family discipline sessions? Soon it would be time to talk about how once again I'd disappointed my family and sullied the Montague name.

"Dear, your father is worried sick. You were involved in a shooting! Your face was on the news. Do you have any idea of the repercussions to Montague Corporation?"

Yep, there it is!

So many issues—number one, he's not my father! Number two, I was shot at and Montague Corporation is the biggest concern?

"I wasn't *involved.* It happened. We left. I don't know more."

"But you're not at class?"

"No, I'm not. The shooting interrupted my schedule."

"You're coming home," Alton's voice again demanded. "Why the hell are you in Rye when you should be here?"

I shook my head. "Why should I be there?"

"Dear," my mother tried to explain, "obviously, there's danger. It's that young man."

"Just like his father," Alton added.

Continuing as if Alton hadn't spoken, my mother went on, "You need to be safe. From what I saw on the news, you're not. I love you, Alexandria. I want to know you're safe."

"Momma, when you can call and talk to me without your husband in the background, we can discuss it. You know my number."

"He's right, dear. Why Rye?"

That was it. I was turning off the damn GPS. I'd tell Deloris, Jerrod, and Nox. As long as I was here, I didn't need to broadcast it to the world.

I took a deep breath. "Rye is where…" I stopped talking as Deloris entered the room, her head moving from side to side and her lips puckered in the universal 'shh' sign.

"Who is that?" she whispered.

I covered the mouthpiece of my phone. "My… parents." I hated that description, but it was a shorter explanation. "They saw the video."

"Of course they did. It's had over half a million hits."

"Who are you talking to?" my mother asked.

"Mom, I need to go. I'm fine—completely fine. I'll call you later when *you* can talk."

"Alexandria, your father is insistent about sending the plane. He's looking it up right now. There's a private airport not far from where you are…"

My eyes opened wide toward Deloris. I knew she could hear as she continued to shake her head back and forth.

"Don't send a plane," I said. "I'm fine. I'll be back to class tomorrow. Savannah really doesn't fit into my schedule."

This time it was my mother who covered the mouthpiece. Behind the muffling of her hand, I could hear hers and Alton's voices though I couldn't make out their words.

"Alex, hang up," Deloris said.

I shrugged. "I've tried."

She reached for the phone. Before I realized what she'd done, she hit the disconnect button. "Yes," she confirmed with her ear to the phone. "It wasn't difficult. The button worked."

What the hell?

"That was my mother, and what you just did was rude."

"It may have been rude, but after what I just learned, it was warranted."

"Is it…?" My stomach dropped. Anger at her behavior immediately turned to panic. "…Nox? Oh my God, is he… did something happen?"

She reached for my hand. "Come, let's sit."

My flat shoes that I'd found near the sofa in the pool house held tightly to the wooden floor, keeping me steadfast. "Tell me, Deloris."

She shook her head as she tugged my hand. "It's not Lennox. He's in flight. He's fine. It's about the letter."

I followed her to one of the long sofas. After we sat, I asked, "What about the letter?"

"Think carefully. Who touched it?"

I tried to recall. It seemed like weeks or even months ago, not last night. I remembered going into my new office, seeing it sitting on my desk, and picking it up. Nox took it from my hands, and then Deloris handled it with a tissue. "Me, Nox, and then you."

"What about the envelope?"

I shrugged. "Me. I don't even think Nox touched it. I was the one to open it. He grabbed the pages from me, but the envelope… I don't remember if I threw it away or left it on the desk."

"It was on the desk," she confirmed.

"Why?"

"Because there's a partial print on the envelope. The letter itself has your prints and Lennox's. The other prints are being verified. So far Mr. Spencer's prints have not been detected."

My eyes grew wide. "What?"

"I've alerted Lennox, but I wanted to be the one to tell you."

My head moved from side to side. "Maybe Bryce wore gloves or something."

"Why would he wear gloves and sign his name?"

I don't know.

"D-do you have it, or even a copy?" I asked. "Maybe if I looked at it again, I could tell if it was really his signature."

"I didn't bring it with me, but I have a picture." Deloris reached into her bag and pulled out her tablet. As it came to life, she said, "The only other prints on the paper were not in our system, but I found the possible match in a database of employees."

I didn't understand.

"Demetri Enterprise employees?" I asked.

"No, Infidelity."

I gasped.

"Do you recognize the name Whitney Blessings?" Deloris asked.

I shook my head. "Karen said we wouldn't know any of the other employees."

"You wouldn't know her from Infidelity. You might know her because of where she works—her main job," she qualified.

"Why? Where does she work?"

"Montague Corporation. She's your father's—I mean your *stepfather's*—secretary. Personal assistant. Her job description isn't very specific."

My stomach twisted. What did this mean? Was Alton an Infidelity client?

"That doesn't make sense. I mean I've known forever that he screwed around on my mom, but why would he be a client?"

"Are you saying that he's such a charismatic charmer that paying for companionship would be beneath him?"

I scrunched my nose as bile bubbled from the pits of my empty stomach.

Gross!

"No, that's not what I mean. I-I just never imagined he'd be a client."

"I didn't say he was. I said his assistant is an employee, and I believe she touched the letter—more accurately the paper—possibly long before the words were written and it became a letter. This theory leads me to believe that the paper at the very least came from your stepfather's office."

I tried to process. "Maybe Bryce got the paper from there. He works at Montague in the corporate offices."

"That's a possibility. But wasn't your stepfather on that call?" Deloris asked.

"Yes. He called me on my mother's phone."

"Why would he do that?"

I shrugged. "Because he knew I wouldn't have answered if he'd used his own phone."

"And he wanted…?" she asked.

"He said he was sending a plane. He wants me home… to Savannah," I clarified.

Deloris's expression remained blank, neither concerned nor anxious, as if dealing with threatening letters full of Demetri secrets was an everyday occurrence. She turned her attention to her tablet.

My phone buzzed with a recognizable ring.

The screen read *ALTON.*

Deloris's green eyes met mine. I'd never looked at their color before. With the sunlight from the windows, flakes of gold and brown shone from their depths. Perhaps she was showing more emotion than usual, though she was much better at hiding it. "Alex, I apologize for cutting your call with your mother short. I'm concerned."

My phone rang again.

"Lennox," she continued, "has entrusted me with many tasks. Keeping you safe is one of them, one he holds as my greatest priority."

Another ring.

"And him," I said.

Deloris nodded. "As you know, that *is* my number-one priority. I should be with him in DC right now…"

Ring.

"If I don't answer this, it will go to voicemail."

She hitched a shoulder. "Would that be bad?"

"You saw the screen?"

"I did."

My phone vibrated, indicating the call was sent to voicemail.

Though I had no desire to answer that call or listen to the message, I knew without a doubt I'd pissed Alton off, more than usual. Not only did he think I'd hung up on him but now I'd refused to answer his call.

"Here," Deloris said as she pulled up the picture of the letter I'd found. She scrolled to the final page, the one with the signature. It simply read *Bryce.*

"You know," I said, "he goes by different names."

Deloris's eyes opened wider. "That seems to be a trend I'm noticing with both of you."

I tilted my head to the side. "Touché. But I was never Charli, not until Del Mar. I wasn't even Alex until Stanford. I was always Alexandria. That was the name on the outside of the envelope. My point is that my cousin, Patrick, knew Bryce… well, forever. He calls him Spence. I'd never thought about it until the other night when Pat was talking about him. Over and over, he referred to him as Spence. Nox knows him, somehow, and calls him Edward."

"His first name."

"Yes, Edward Bryce Carmichael Spencer."

"What are you saying?"

"I'm saying that only some of us who have known him forever call him Bryce. According to Nox, in business, he goes by Edward."

"The letter was signed Bryce."

I nodded. "Which is the way he'd sign it if it were from him to me."

"You're saying that others may mistakenly use one of his other names?"

"Yes. For example, if Nox received a letter from me and it was signed Alexandria, you could assume it wasn't written by me."

"What do your parents call him?"

The little bit of chicken salad I'd managed to eat hardened in my stomach. "Bryce. It's what his mother calls him too."

"What do you think of the writing?"

I shrugged. "It's messy. It's barely legible and it could be his. It's been a long time since we passed notes at the academy. I would say it is his writing, but…" My eyes opened wider. "…you could have a handwriting expert look at it."

"I could," Deloris confirmed.

My phone buzzed again.

I didn't need the screen. I knew the tune. "It's my mother."

"Or your stepfather using your mother's phone."

"This is only going to escalate," I warned. "Trust me. I have experience."

Ring.

"My job is to keep you safe," Deloris said. "But you're not a prisoner. Do you want to go to Savannah? Would you feel safer in your home?"

My home?

I knew the answer. I knew where I felt the safest, and it was in the arms of the man in DC. I hadn't considered Montague Manor my home since the day I boarded the plane to Stanford. My home had been with Chelsea, and over the past month, it had been with Nox.

"No. I trust Nox. He trusts you. I know my stepfather and that isn't reassuring. I want to assure my mom I'm all right. But I don't want to leave."

Ring.

She reached toward me. "May I help?"

Uncertainty flooded my system, testing my last statement, pushing me to my limit. If I handed my phone to Deloris, I was making a big leap of faith, trusting her not only where I was concerned, but also my mother, or God forbid, Alton.

Ring.

As I handed her my phone, Deloris nodded, neither appearing happy or discontent with my decision.

"Hello?" she said.

I could hear Alton's voice again.

"This is Mrs. Witt, Mr. Demetri's associate…"

Lifting my glass of iced tea from the table, I stood and paced near the windows, listening to both sides of the conversation as Deloris spoke with Alton. I loved her calm. Nothing rattled her, not even a billowing blowhard threatening legal charges.

"I assure you that Miss Collins, a legal adult, is safe and here of her own free will…"

I looked around for a clock. What time was it? Was Nox in DC?

I jumped as a hand touched my shoulder. I turned to the soft brown eyes of Silvia.

"Alex, Mr. Demetri is on the house line for you."

My heart swelled. "Thank God! He probably tried my cell. My parents have had it monopolized." I tilted my head toward Deloris, still in conversation.

"No, not Lennox, his father, Oren."

CHAPTER 14

CHARLI

"WHAT?" I ASKED Silvia as I tried to comprehend her words. "Nox's father wants to speak to me?"

"Yes," she said. "You can take the call in Lennox's office, if you'd like." She tilted her head toward Deloris. "It would be more private."

More private? I still hadn't been told the story I was supposed to relay about the shooting. I'd pleaded ignorant with my parents, but if I recalled, Nox had mentioned his father's name, as if he'd spoken to him since our return to this house. If he had, then undoubtedly, Mr. Demetri knew what had happened.

I stared for another moment at Deloris, wondering if I should speak to her first.

"Alex, what would you like me to tell him?" Silvia asked.

I straightened my shoulders. I wasn't good at waiting for permission to speak. If Nox had spoken to his father, then I could too. "Please tell him I'll be right there." I looked around. "I don't believe I've been to the office. Can you show me?"

I nodded to Deloris who was still doing her best to reassure my mother of my well-being and followed Silvia from the sitting room. Ironically, I recalled seeing Oren Demetri for the first time in that room, sitting very close to where Deloris now sat.

The office was as beautiful as the rest of the house. It too was walled with windows: one side looked out to a patio, surrounded by greenery that I remembered led to the pool deck. The other wall of windows looked out to the pool itself, with the sound beyond.

"How could anyone get work done in here with that amazing view?" I asked as Silvia lifted the phone on the desk.

She smiled her response before hitting a button and speaking. "Mr. Demetri, Miss Collins is here." She handed me the phone. "I'll ask Mrs. Witt to give you a few minutes."

"Thank you, Silvia," I said, sitting behind the desk. Before I spoke, I saw the piece of paper, folded in half and lying on the ink blotter. On the outside was sprawled *Charli~*.

Unlike Bryce's writing, Nox's script was neat, flowing and legible. I'd asked him about it once, and he'd blamed Catholic school. A smile came to my lips, imagining Lennox Demetri being instructed by mean nuns. Maybe that was where he acquired his delectation for corporal punishment.

Charli~

My office is your office, like my heart. It belongs to you.

The password to access Internet is…

My cheeks warmed as I read. Each little thing that Nox did endeared him more and more to me. Alton would never give anyone, not even my mother, full access to his office or his computer.

Though I can't wait to take you up on your offer and punish your sexy ass for making me hard with just memories of you, I will travel easier knowing you're here and safe.

Don't disappoint me. If you do, I guarantee you will

not be sitting comfortably for a while.

Love~
Your Nox

My Nox.

I shifted in the big leather chair, my backside tingling with phantom repercussions of that threat. At the same time the blush from my cheeks blossomed, warming my entire body as I sat, thankful that he'd folded this note so that Silvia couldn't read his affection or warning.

I suddenly wondered if talking to Nox's father would be considered disappointing him? I didn't have time to consider it before Oren's voice came through the handset.

"Miss Collins." His tone was deep-sounding like Nox's, though Oren's had more of an accent. If Nox sounded like his father, I would have known his roots ran deep in Brooklyn.

"Alex, please call me Alex, Mr. Demetri."

"Likewise, Alex, I believe I've already asked you to call me Oren."

There was something in his tone that put me on alert and made me sit taller. "Yes, Oren. Thank you for calling."

"Now, you don't know why I called. Perhaps you should hold off on the gratitude."

"All right?" I replied.

"I'm happy to hear you sound strong and safe. When I spoke with my son earlier today, he was rather concerned."

"It was a frightening experience," I admitted.

"But you are all right, no injuries?"

I shook my head. "I'm fine. I'm concerned about the woman who was struck."

"That's kind of you, but she really isn't your concern."

"Your son is."

"Excuse me?" he asked.

"Your son is my concern. I'm worried about him. I'm here in your home.

I'm safe. He's not. He's on his way to Washington." As soon as I mentioned Nox's destination, my stomach twisted. What if he didn't want his father to know where he was?

"Yes. He's doing his job for Demetri Enterprises. That's why I called to speak to you."

"I don't understand."

"My son has taken a shine to you. Alex, you may not realize this, but it has been a long time since anyone has distracted Lennox from his responsibilities. Since that time, he's done many beneficial things for our company. I don't want to see his talents wasted."

My neck stiffened. "Perhaps you need to explain yourself. I'm not following you."

"Come now. I've done my research. You're a very intelligent woman. It should be obvious to you that in the short time since the two of you met, Lennox's attention has been less on his work and more on you. There are deals that won't wait. There are responsibilities that we cannot afford to have him neglect."

"If you've done your research, you're aware that I too have responsibilities. I should be in class today, not sitting in Lennox's home."

"My home. And you're a guest. You're welcome as long as my son wants you there. I want you to understand, however, that if being with you puts my son's life in danger, I will do all I can to discourage your association."

I blinked a few times, trying to make sense of his words. "You're blaming me for what happened today?"

"I'm not blaming anyone. I'm simply stating the fact that before his attention was diverted, my son was not being shot at."

"This may come as a shock, but today was my first shooting, too."

Oren's laugh rumbled through the handset. "Bravo, Alexandria."

"Excuse me?"

"You have *forza*! And I like it. It's obvious what Lennox sees in you."

Forza? What the hell was that?

"Strength," Oren answered before I could question.

Maybe it was a Demetri trait—the ability to answer unasked questions.

"I apologize," he went on, "for my insinuations. You aren't like she was. I get the feeling you're not pining away, waiting for him to return. As you said, you have your own responsibilities. You're beautiful like your mother but have your father's *forza d'animo*."

More Italian. I'd need a translator if this conversation was to continue. Instead of asking for the meaning, I replied, "Oren, Alton Fitzgerald isn't my father. He's my stepfather, and saying that I have any of his qualities, in my opinion, is not a compliment."

"Alexandria, I was not speaking of Alton Fitzgerald. That man is a pig. I hope my assessment doesn't offend. I was speaking of your father, Russell Collins."

I stared at the beautiful room, the windows, the furnishings, and the ornate bookcases, but none of it registered. "Did you know my father?"

"I do."

What the hell?

"Oren, my father died when I was three years old."

"You're right. Russell Collins died."

"What does that mean?"

"I only meant that you would make him proud. He would be very pleased with the young woman you have become."

The entire conversation was making me uncomfortable. "Thank you for calling. I have no intentions of hurting your son. His safety and his success are my main priorities."

"Don't let them be."

"What?"

"Don't give up your dreams for my son. He isn't worth it."

Indignation rose. How dare Oren Demetri call, question Nox's and my relationship, and then demean his own son? "I would disagree; however, the point is moot. He has encouraged my dreams as I have his. It's what two people do who love one another."

"Hmm, I do appreciate your *forza*. Goodbye, for now, Alex. This conversation has been enlightening."

I couldn't disagree more. If anything, it left me totally puzzled.

"Goodbye, Oren. I'll be sure to tell Nox you called."

"That's your choice, dear."

The line went dead.

Slowly, I returned the handset to the cradle and stared at the phone.

What the hell had that been about? Was he telling me he didn't want me dating Nox, and then saying he did? What about my father? How did he know both my mother and my father? Maybe he knew them as a couple.

The repeated rapping of a knock upon the door pulled me from my questions.

"Come in," I called.

The door opened as Deloris entered, my phone in her hand. "You missed a call from Lennox."

My heart dropped to the floor. I fought the urge to stand, afraid the wheels of the chair would crush it, tearing it to shreds. "Did you speak to him?"

"No, I was still speaking with Mr. Fitzgerald. By the way, he's an interesting man. I'm guessing that he isn't accustomed to hearing no, especially not from a woman."

My one cheek rose in a lopsided grin. "I'd say that's a pretty accurate assumption."

"Your GPS—"

"I turned it off. I was going to talk to you about that. I'm not doing it to hide from you or Jerrod or Nox. I'm doing it so my location isn't broadcast to everyone, including my family."

Deloris nodded. "I concur. We can give you another tracker. You can keep it in your purse or I could have it put on jewelry? Something that will stay with you, but that others can't access."

Silvia entered with a soft knock to the open door. "Is there anything I can get either of you?"

Since I was still at Nox's desk, I asked. "Do you know what I did with my backpack?" I remembered having it in the SUV on the way here. I hoped I hadn't left it there. "Since I'm here at this desk, I could work on some schoolwork."

"I put it in your room. I also put the things Mrs. Witt brought up there."

My room. I liked the sound of that. Despite what Oren had said, I knew this was Lennox's house. He'd said his mother had left it to him.

"Thanks, Silvia. I can get it."

"Nonsense. I'll bring it down."

I smiled as she left us alone.

"I brought you a few days' worth of clothes," Deloris said. "Lennox should be back Friday night."

I shook my head. "I can't stay here. I have to go to class tomorrow."

Her lips formed a straight line.

"You were the one who said I'm not a prisoner," I reminded her. "I have a responsibility to do the best I can in school."

"Lennox wants—"

"He wants me to be safe. I will be. I'll wear the GPS you devise. I'll not walk in the park or do any unplanned activities or outings. Jerrod can drive me."

"Alex, Jerrod is no longer with us. Isaac is in DC. I think in the meantime, if you must leave this house, I'll have one of the men from this morning assigned to you."

"Why? I was used to Jerrod."

She swallowed before meeting my gaze. "My job requires decisions that most people never want to make, ones most people are unaware even exist. You need to let me do my job. I can't nor will I explain every decision."

"That's a reasonable request, but considering everything that's happened, I should know why you fired Jerrod."

"The partial print on the envelope matches his."

I leaned back, causing the chair to recline as I blew out a puff of air. I was obviously becoming numb to the mortar fire occurring around me. "You think he…"

"I think that it would be difficult to breach my security unless you were familiar with the system and understood the way it worked. I had to look at this from the inside. I don't believe he wrote the letter. I believe Jerrod was involved in placing it."

"Whom did he do it for?"

"We're currently in talks to discover that bit of information."

Talks?

Was that code for something? What lengths would Deloris Witt go to in order to learn valuable information?

She nodded toward my phone. "Call Lennox back. Let him know you've spoken to your parents and his father."

My eyes widened.

"Are you surprised that I knew that?"

I shook my head. "I guess not."

"After you talk with him, you and I will devise your story for this morning. Then, we'll discuss tomorrow."

"I'll call Nox, but as far as our discussion about tomorrow, it will be about what time we need to leave here for me to get to class."

She nodded. "It would make both our lives much easier—yours and mine—if you wouldn't fight Lennox at every turn."

I tilted my head to the side. "I'm not fighting, and for the record, I'm well aware of how he may respond. I'm not fighting that either."

Deloris lifted her hand. "There are some things that are better for me not to know."

"I thought you were like Oz, great, powerful, and all-knowing."

She didn't respond to my statement as she walked to the windows overlooking the pool.

"The perimeter is clear," Deloris said. "I wouldn't recommend going to the shore, but the pool house or even the pool deck is safe."

I suddenly wondered if there were people stationed outside, dressed from head to foot in black, watching for any unusual activity from the bushes, ready to pounce or shoot without hesitation. Maybe I'd watched too many spy movies, but my imagination was running overtime.

"Thank you," I replied. "We can talk after I call Nox."

"I'll give you some privacy," she said, walking toward the door. When she reached the threshold, she was met by Silvia.

"Let me leave this with you," Silvia offered as she walked past Deloris and sat the backpack on the floor near the desk.

"Thank you."

Once I was alone and the door was closed, I hit my incoming calls. Nox answered on the second ring.

"Are you trying to give me a heart attack by not answering? I couldn't reach Jerrod either. Your fucking GPS isn't working. Tell me you're still at my house."

I couldn't help but smile at his loving greeting. "Hi, it's good to hear your voice, too."

CHAPTER 15

NOX

AFTER MY CALL with Charli and another with Deloris, I quietly eased into a chair near the back of the gallery. The room was near capacity with afternoon testimony before the Senate Finance Committee in full swing. From my position, I could see the backs of most of the attendees. According to Oren's rules, I was where I should be—no one seated behind me. In the small space between the chairs and wall, Isaac stood, also watching. While my concentration should be on the proceedings and testimony, his was on the surroundings and occupants.

Rarely did I travel without him. Usually, he would have been with me, regardless of what had happened this morning—it was his job—but now it seemed even more paramount. Isaac had been with me for going on seven years. Next to Deloris, he was my most trusted associate.

I needed to add Charli to that list. Considering the strides we'd made in our relatively new relationship, that shouldn't be hard, but it was. Oren had taught me well. Few people deserved trust. Those who did earned it. I knew if I'd talked to my father about it, he'd tell me that after our short time together, Charli hadn't earned it.

Fuck!

I didn't fucking care if her name was Montague or even Davis—as in Severus Davis, the man testifying—at this point. The way I felt, the overpowering need to protect her, the way she made me feel, like I did deserve a woman like her, negated his warnings. I wasn't being impulsive, nor was I thinking with my *dick*, as he'd said about my impromptu trip to San Francisco. I was thinking with my heart. I'd only ever listened to it once in my life. At thirty-two years old, it was time to give the vital organ one more listen.

After Isaac picked me up at my house in Rye, for the first ten minutes of our drive, he apologized profusely for not being present in Central Park. I told him it was all right. It was.

It wasn't his fault. It was mine.

I was the one who told Isaac to drop me off. I was the one who texted him and told him to meet me at Columbia. I was the one who allowed Charli's desire for fresh air and sunshine to nearly be our demise.

If the shooter hadn't hit that woman, again, I would be responsible.

Me.

Her.

It was what Charli did to me.

I'd thought about the entire scenario from the moment I left Charli at the house. The danger we'd averted consumed my thoughts as Isaac drove and during my flight to DC. The entire time, as I read notes and prepared for the task ahead, Alexandria Collins was on my mind. Sometime during that reflection, I made a decision. I couldn't allow her to do it any longer. This morning, I'd been thinking with my dick or maybe my heart. There was a time for that, but not when I needed to keep my head in the game.

I wouldn't let that happen again.

I wouldn't allow Charli to lower my defenses or lessen my instincts. Those predispositions had protected me throughout my life. They'd kept me safe and alive. If I'd have listened to them instead of concentrating on work, Jo would still be alive.

A new and unaccustomed discomfort filled my chest. For the first time—ever—I wasn't overwhelmed with sadness at the thought of my wife. I loved her. I always would, but Charli said something this morning that I couldn't shake. If Jocelyn were alive, I wouldn't have met Charli. We wouldn't be together. It wasn't like I'd have ever left Jo. I wouldn't.

I was a one-woman man.

A smile graced my lips as I thought about Charli—as I thought about being buried balls deep inside of her earlier today. How in the fuck could I imagine doing what so many men did? How could I imagine indulging in other women when I had the best, most amazing, sexy-as-hell, intelligent, witty, and beautiful woman waiting in my home?

The last words she'd said in the bedroom came back, asking me to punish her, asking me to stay with her.

Fuck!

I needed to think about the testimony and listen to the speaker. If I didn't, I'd grow so uncomfortably hard sitting right here amongst this gallery of finance assholes that I wouldn't be able to stand.

No matter what the future held, I couldn't imagine cheating on, or leaving Charli—or losing her. Thankfully, at this moment, I could divert my attention knowing that she was safe with Deloris and Silvia. Tomorrow was another day. I refused to think about her back in Manhattan or about the possibility of dissension among Deloris's ranks.

I also couldn't think about Jerrod right now, even though Deloris had told me what was happening. Worrying about it was Deloris's job. She'd find out what happened.

"No, sir." The answer of the gentleman behind the microphone refocused my attention to the front of the room and reminded me why I was here instead of beside Charli.

"What can you tell us about the implications of this minimal increase in taxes?"

Minimal? Has he read the same draft I have?

"The revenue will be invaluable to the states involved…"

Fuck.

My fists balled as I listened to Severus Davis. The fact that this paid mouthpiece was testifying in an expert role was laughable.

While Davis waxed eloquently, the committee seemed enthralled with his answers. Step by step, he shared figure after figure, effectively painting a completely inaccurate picture. I pulled my phone from my pocket and quickly took notes.

This was why I needed to be here—to hear exactly what was being said, the lies our side needed to combat.

As Senator Higgins finished his questions, the committee called an end to today's testimony.

Severus stood and turned toward the galley. When he did, his head moved back and forth in rapid succession. As he did a double take, our eyes met.

I nodded, standing with the others in the crowd.

"He looks surprised to see you," Isaac whispered from behind me.

I agreed. Perhaps I'd assumed wrongly earlier. Perhaps the instigator of the hit was standing at the front of the room. Perhaps Davis had anticipated my being in a morgue in New York City, instead of at the hearing.

"I'm going to speak with him," I replied, unwilling to walk away. Rule number twenty-seven of Oren Demetri's decrees to live by—never back down from a challenge. The statute had been good to me during my MMA years.

"Mr. Davis," I said, standing tall and addressing him as soon as he stepped from the well. "I couldn't help but notice that you were looking my direction."

"Mr. Demetri." He nodded. "I suppose I didn't spot you earlier. I thought you might not make it."

I shrugged. "I wouldn't miss it for the world. I found your testimony… what is the right word? Entertaining."

"I don't think that's the right word. Enlightening would be more appropriate."

"To-may-toes, to-mah-toes."

"Hardly."

He sounded less than amused with my assessment. "My father said that the two of you had a nice meeting a month ago. I'm sorry I missed it."

Davis's brows rose. "I'm surprised Oren bothered to mention it. The exchange was rather uninformative. Perhaps the two of us could make more progress?"

With my lips pressed together I nodded. "I'll need to check my schedule. I'm always interested in hearing the plights of others."

"Plights, Mr. Demetri? My clients are hardly enduring plights. As you may have heard during my testimony, the bill will benefit everyone."

"Everyone? I suppose that's a matter of opinion."

"As long as it's the opinion of the committee, that's all that matters."

"Thankfully, today was only the first day of testimony."

He nodded. "And you plan to stay in DC for the remaining testimony?"

"I do."

"Then we should talk…" He looked around the emptying room. "…perhaps in a more private location?"

"I look forward to it," I said as I stepped back, allowing him to pass.

Isaac remained near the back of the room, now closer to the door. As I followed Davis, Isaac waited and exited behind me. Once we were in the hall, he whispered, "Shall I get the car?"

"I'm not in a hurry. I'd like to talk to Carroll."

"Yes, sir."

CHAPTER 16

NOX

MY COSTLY SUITE was filled with all the amenities: a bar, a living room, a scenic view of the Washington Monument, currently lit up against the night sky. Though I couldn't see it from my room high in the sky, I knew that just west of the bright white-illuminated monument, beyond the reflecting pool, sat our sixteenth president. Abraham Lincoln presided over the district in the throne-like chair, day after day, overlooking the ramifications of his decisions.

Over a hundred and fifty years later.

"What do you think, Abe? Are you happy with what you see?" I sneered at my own negativity.

He'd made historic decisions that changed our country forever. Without his insight, America would be a different place. A simple man from the Midwest, born in Kentucky and raised in Indiana, he grew to adulthood in Illinois. It wasn't the résumé of a great leader, yet history said otherwise. And yet after everything President Lincoln accomplished, he'd succumbed to the fate that had tried to take me out just this morning.

He'd been assassinated.

The idea sent a cold chill down my spine.

Assassinated.

Shot.

Killed.

The difference, as I saw it, was that Mrs. Lincoln hadn't been a possible victim.

I needed to know who the intended recipient of the bullet was.

Me or Charli?

After seeing the look on Davis's face, I believed it was me. But it could have just as easily been Charli. She was now my weak link, the one I'd sacrifice anything for. For that reason she needed protection.

This wasn't my first personal brush with death. The grim reaper and I were old friends. Before he took Jo, I had my own near miss with him. The final result of that encounter was much more painful than what Charli and I'd experienced this morning.

It was the night I found myself staring across the octagon at my cousin Luca Costello.

Family.

From the time I was old enough to understand, my parents told me that family was important. Luca was the son of Vincent Costello, my mother's cousin. She and Vincent were close. My grandfather died young, and she and Vincent had been raised like siblings by his parents, Carmine and Rosa. When Luca and I were children, we'd played in backyards and parking lots all over Brooklyn. Together we were little shits who had one another's back. After we moved to Rye, I rarely saw Luca. Nevertheless, kick-the-can in some back alley was a far cry from the MMA octagon.

When that night came, I was "Nox" Demetri, MMA champion. In my short career I was the youngest contender to accumulate so many wins—in points and knock outs—more than anyone else in the Newark area.

The MMA establishment was on my side. The organizers of the fight club in Jersey had made a fortune on me.

The thing about MMA was that it was a crapshoot. I never knew who'd step into the octagon with me. I was listed as the headliner—but not in public record. It wasn't like the fight club had a banner flying behind a plane on the

Jersey shore or even a lighted placard outside the gym that was more of a warehouse.

Word of mouth was the means of broadcast.

Nox Demetri, undefeated MMA champion. It drew the best opponents.

Cocksuckers lined up, begging and pleading with the organizers for a chance to take me down. That was what I did—NYU during the day and then I'd cross the bridge to Newark and fight at night. My parents were done raising me. They were done with one another. Oren was busy screwing everything in a skirt and making backroom deals to *better* the Demetri name. And my mother spent her time in Rye finally coming out of the oppression of twenty years wasted on him. I was happy for her. Him, I didn't give a shit.

MMA started as a pastime and grew into my own rebellion. I knew what I was doing. I knew who I was making money for. It was my own version of Oren Demetri's deals.

I'd heard my parents' warnings. I knew about the neighborhoods and my mother's family name. But I'd never been a part of it. Especially after we moved. That didn't mean I didn't know.

By doing what I was doing, where I was doing it, I was accomplishing two things: I was making the Demetri name known for me, not Oren, and I was screwing Oren's backroom deals at the same time. The underground world of MMA included families and cartels and all kinds of people who my father would rather me not know.

Fuck him.

At twenty I thought I was immune. That was until I saw Luca and Vincent and I knew.

I'd been making my name known and bringing a fortune to the wrong people.

I understood…

Instead of being in college like I was, Luca worked his father's crews, running some and second-in-command on others. At barely twenty, being the son of the head of the family, Luca had a reputation for following orders. I'd heard the rumors and seen the news. Luca was proficient at eliminating problems. Guns, knives, or his hands were all options. He'd already beaten one murder charge and had another one pending.

My cousin had willingly done what I hadn't wanted to do—follow in his father's footsteps.

Vincent, Luca's father, wanted my involvement in the MMA enterprise to stop. That night he was present, ringside, to be sure it came to an end. I just wasn't sure if he was there to watch a warning or a hit.

My father's admonition came back to me, his anger at my pastime. His insistence that I do something else, that I have more respect for my name and where I came from. I hadn't listened.

The moment Luca's eyes met mine a sense of dread washed over me like I'd never before felt—especially, in the octagon. When I turned back to Vincent, I knew there was going to be a beat-down and that Luca had been sent to teach me a lesson.

I was good at fighting, the best at mixed martial arts, but death wasn't my goal.

The hit they had planned wasn't a clean shot from a gun.

What they had planned wouldn't be fast and painless.

Instantly I understood that what I'd done as a purposeful disgrace to my father had farther-reaching repercussions. I was a Demetri, but I was also a Costello. I wasn't sure if Vincent had planned this solely for me, or if it was meant to hurt Oren, too. All I knew with some certainty was that I was about to be bludgeoned to death before hundreds of witnesses.

Three rounds, five minutes per round.

Normally the fight was stopped when the injuries got to be too much. Still, I knew in the pit of my stomach as Vincent stared at the organizer that no one would step in. No one would stop what was about to happen.

Back in my hotel suite, over ten years later, I closed my eyes and pushed away the memory of the blood and gore. The sound of bones crunching beneath my fists, the crumbling as my fist contacted bone and cartilage. The eerie realization that my bones were breaking too.

In a sadistic way, it was addicting to be the perpetrator.

Crunch.

The sound a person made as he expelled the breath he needed to continue his involuntary functions. Somewhere between a 'whoof' and a 'sigh.' During my time in the octagon, I'd become hooked on the pain and anguish.

Receiving it in greater measure wasn't as exhilarating.

I survived. Luca survived.

Oren had appeared sometime during the fight. My memory wasn't clear. But as I recovered, I wisely decided to heed his warnings.

Vincent gave me a choice: I could continue to do what I'd grown to love, the carnage and destruction, but instead of doing it for my own name, I would do it as Luca did it—for family. Or I could disappear from that world and have my freedom.

Everything came with a price.

Though I hated to admit it, I knew that somehow I owed that freedom to my father. I still don't know the price he paid, but in order to maintain it, my duty was to step away from MMA and never look back, and to do my part to make Demetri Enterprises a success—a reputable success.

That incident helped me understand that not everything Oren had told me were lies. I never wanted to admit that he'd actually worked hard to get where he was, but he had. My father had worked both sides of the business world and made Demetri as legitimate as he could. As I healed I vowed that I'd be the one to take it further, seeing for the first time how, in many ways, his hands had been tied.

I pushed the thoughts of my young adulthood away as I made my way back to my computer in my hotel suite. The pristine furnishings in the suite were all part of the life I'd helped to create, the life Oren had begun but I'd continued.

Was today's incident in the park another warning? Or was it intended as more?

Questions still loomed. Could I blame today's incident on Davis and the hearing at hand, or were there old ghosts from past dealings who still believed I should pay?

Was that freedom that I'd been granted years ago still mine to enjoy?

A voice in my head told me to do what I'd done last time and heed the warning. I knew what happened when I didn't listen. The consequences were devastating.

The transcript from today's earlier proceedings sat before me as I tried to concentrate. The dinner that Isaac had brought me sat untouched. I needed to learn what I'd missed while dodging bullets and getting lost in Charli.

Today the hearing had been mostly dominated by testimony from those in favor of the bill's current wording. To listen to the so-called experts, this bill would do everything from saving baby seals to curing childhood cancer—literally. The revenue they claimed would come from the increase in tax was already appropriated to specific destinations, yet the testimony made it sound as if it would be sitting in the form of a great big check, waiting for appropriation into everyone's favorite pork-barrel project.

I dialed Senator Carroll's private cell phone.

"Doyle," I said after he answered. "I'm very concerned about the whales."

"Whales?"

"Seals will benefit from this bill but who's looking out for the whales?"

"Lennox, I'm more concerned about you and that pretty little girlfriend of yours. I've been completely distraught over what you told me following today's testimony."

"We're both safe," I answered, bristling at Senator Carroll's description of Charli.

She was beyond pretty, and hearing the words from his lips made them sound inadequate. I fought the urge to tell him that Charli wasn't just pretty. She was ravishing, a spitfire with a mind of her own, who could tear him and any other condescending man to shreds. I'd warn him to approach with caution, because though she may appear tame, in reality she was almost too hot to handle. In her eyes she held her essence. They glistened with joy and love even when danger and pain surrounded her. Her beauty went further than her gorgeous exterior. She was enthralling and alluring.

Pretty was a disservice to my girlfriend. She was way beyond that, and most importantly, she was mine.

"Should you be here?" Doyle Carroll asked.

"Yes. I don't have proof that the attempted shooting had any connection to this hearing. I'm scheduled to testify tomorrow. Davis not only acted like he was surprised to see me, but also surprised I'd be returning for the next few days."

"He's baiting you. That man knows the schedule backwards and forwards."

"Well, I didn't bite, but I admit he's on my list of suspects."

"He's on many people's lists, and I don't think any of them have him listed as 'good.'"

"I'm reading today's testimony. Tell me what I'm not reading."

"What you're not reading?" Doyle Carroll asked.

"Tell me what I missed that didn't make the transcripts," I clarified.

"Higgins seemed pretty confident. It's as if he knows he has the votes, but that isn't possible by my count. I'm not confident we have them either. It's close, very close."

"Who's on the line?"

"Two minority, Hatchett from Oregon and Kelley from Tennessee and three majority, New York, Michigan, and Wisconsin."

"New York? I thought she was on our side?" I asked.

"She was. Now she's not sure."

"It was the seals, wasn't it?"

"Lennox, I'd like to think the committee is smarter than that, but to the extent possible, you need to emphasize that the appropriations have already been earmarked, that it won't be a pork-barrel smörgåsbord, and that this will cost jobs. Give specifics. Talk about how the increase in tax will cause companies not only to cut employees but quite possibly take business elsewhere."

I sighed. "I have that all planned. I was just wondering if I should mention the obvious whale omission?"

Doyle laughed. "I do appreciate your sense of humor. I'm glad you're here, and I'm glad that son-of-a-bitch missed."

"Thanks. I'm happy about that, too."

A call beeped into my phone and I looked at the screen.

"Doyle," I said, "I have a call. I don't recognize the number, but with the way my day's gone, I'd better answer."

"I'll see you in the morning."

"Yes, I'll be there."

I swiped the screen, hanging up one call and connecting to the next. "Hello."

"Demetri, it's Severus Davis."

"Severus, nice to hear from you."

"Join me for a drink?"

I looked around my suite and down at my comfortable jeans. I would rather stay where I was, but this was the shit that got things done. This was what I did, what Oren had done. "Where?"

"The bar in your hotel."

"My hotel?" He knew where I was staying?

"Yes. I'll be there in fifteen."

"See you there."

I hung up and called Deloris.

CHAPTER 17

Twenty years ago

OREN

"THE PARTY FOR my granddaughter, it was nice?" Carmine Costello asked as he settled against the large chair in his office.

I was back in his home, back in Brooklyn. It didn't matter that I had businesses to run and a wife constantly complaining that I wasn't around. I was replying to a summons that had me trekking from Westchester to New York City, and from the city to Brooklyn. I needed a fucking helicopter to cut down on travel time, or maybe a clone. Then I could be in two places at once.

"Yes, sir," I answered. My face set in its customary expression of full attention and respect, as if saying anything negative about his granddaughter's first communion celebration was an option. "It was lovely, but not as lovely as Luisa. She beamed."

Carmine smiled, his full cheeks lifting in approval, just before he looked about the room at his men and his features changed. "Enough. Tell us about the jewelry stores."

I leaned back casually, attempting to show both my wife's uncle and his minions that I wasn't intimidated. After all, I was family. "There are three," I explained. "I've done my research. They have potential. Their current inventory is valued at nearly as much as the asking price. That doesn't include the property, which as you know is invaluable. Acquiring a storefront on the island is like striking oil."

Carmine leaned back and nodded.

"Of course you're familiar with the one near here. The other two—"

"I know where they're located," Carmine interrupted. "I also know that you've been talking to the other families."

I fought the urge to sit taller. "Yes. I've been in negotiation."

"Have I missed *our* negotiation?" Carmine asked.

"Sir, I've spoken with Vincent multiple times. He's been aware of everything. He told me to wait before I brought it to you."

Carmine leaned forward, placed his elbows on his desk as his fingertips met, one at a time, until both hands came together. I was most certain he wasn't about to pray. If he was, I was the one who needed divine intervention. "I see. So it's Vincent's approval you seek?"

"No, sir."

"You don't seek my son's approval?"

Over the years, everyone knew that Vincent had become Carmine's second-in-command. He was a *made man*, had been for nearly ten years, back when the families wielded more power than they did today.

That said, I was quickly discovering that their loss of power could be more myth than reality.

"I do seek Vincent's approval, but yours is the most vital. Even the other dons are waiting…" My words trailed away as Carmine's hand came up indicating my silence.

When the room was silent, he nodded to Jimmy, the man on his right. The burly hulk was more than a bodyguard: he was known as the enforcer. The last thing anyone wanted to see was Jimmy's mug at his door in the middle of the night. If that ever happened, it would be the *last thing* that person ever saw, as well as the only warning that morning wouldn't come.

Without speaking, Jimmy stepped back and led the parade as the room cleared, leaving Carmine and me alone.

"Oren, you're family. My Angelina, she loves you. Lennox, he's family."

My chest constricted as I tried to breathe. Lennox was only ten years old.

He was the real reason I'd moved Angelina to Westchester County and the reason I wanted to make Demetri Enterprises legitimate. I didn't want him to be sitting in the same position as me. If I had my way, he'd never know the truth behind the business. That was why I worked countless hours. I secretly hoped that with time, the families' powers would be whittled away. By the time my son was old enough, he could truly run legitimate operations.

"Yes, family," I confirmed.

Carmine nodded. "Trust, Oren. I've trusted you with Angelina, but you see, I'm not convinced that you've made her happy. Will you make *me* happy?"

"Sir, our marriage is healthy. I love Angelina, and her happiness is my goal. Sometimes she is… feisty."

Carmine's laugh filled the room, echoing from the bookshelves to the walls. Being an interior room, it lacked windows. I'd never thought that was by accident. "Feisty… good word. She's a Costello. We've been called worse." He lowered his voice. "She confided in my Rosa that she wants a daughter."

I couldn't hide the surprise from my face. "We—we talked about it."

"Sometimes women, they say one thing, they mean another."

"You want me to give my wife a daughter? I-I can't promise a daughter. Even if we were to have another child, it could be a boy."

Carmine nodded. "But you're willing… to try?"

What the fuck?

"Angelina and I should talk."

"Yes, you should." His forehead wrinkled. "But I'm sure I don't have to tell you… talking won't give my girl her daughter."

I was at a loss for words as I simply nodded my head.

"Oren, I have a job for you. You do want me to be happy, don't you?"

He has a job? Impregnating my wife is a job? Or is it more?

"Sir?"

"I want you to accompany Vincent to California."

I clenched my jaw and immediately regretted the knee-jerk reaction. Perhaps if I relaxed it, my tension would go unnoticed.

Carmine's eyes widened. "Or are you too busy to take a trip with my son?"

Of course it didn't go unnoticed. "No, sir, I'd be happy to go to California."

"I've never asked you to help the family before, but, son, I need to know where your loyalties lie. After all, you have been negotiating with others and not with me."

Loyalties?

"I assure you that my loyalties—"

"Words. It's all words until I see evidence with my own eyes."

"May I ask," I began, "what this job will entail?"

Carmine shrugged. "It isn't a family connection. It's a debt—a favor. A man who once helped me asked me for assistance. That's what we do: we help our friends. Right, son?"

"Yes, of course."

"This man," Carmine said, "has a problem and asked that we help him get rid of it."

My pulse raced. His words between the lines were louder than the ones he spoke. I'd lived around it, even before Angelina. After all, my father worked the docks. I knew the score. I knew what was done, but I'd never participated, not in anything of this magnitude. I'd arranged money laundering, even allowing my reputable business to service those needs. I'd collected debts—financial debts—but never had I participated in murder.

"Son, you want *my* help. I'm requiring yours in exchange. After the jewelry stores, there will be other businesses, other endeavors. I'd like to offer my allegiance. I need to know it's reciprocated. Is that a problem?"

The knots in my stomach painfully twisted. "No, sir. No problem."

"Tomorrow."

I looked around the office before my eyes settled again on Carmine. "Tomorrow?"

"Tomorrow, you and Vincent will help my friend. It'll look like an accident—quiet and quick. It needs to happen fast. This *problem* is due back to his home in Savannah in a few days and if he returns, well, let's just say, my friend won't be happy."

"Sir, I've never…"

"But this time, Vincent, he'll teach you. You'll learn. You'll witness and participate." *And then you too will be indebted to the Costellos for their silence.*

Carmine didn't need to say the last part. It was more than implied.

"Yes, sir."

"And," Carmine said, "when you return, I'll not only consider your request for the jewelry stores, but I'll have a gift for my Angelina."

"A gift?"

"Let's not ruin the surprise. Go. Come back when it's done. The future is full of possibilities." Carmine stood and walked to my side of the desk. With his hand upon my shoulder, he smiled. "Because, son, we're family."

I SAT BESIDE Vincent at a table in the hotel bar. Our backs were against the wall as we watched the red-haired Irishman at the bar. He wasn't drinking alcohol, like the other businessmen around him. Instead, I'd heard him order his meal with a sweet tea. Stupid Southerners. Alcohol could plausibly cause an accident. Not so much sweet tea.

"Go talk to him," Vinny said with a tilt of his head.

The knots from yesterday's meeting with Carmine had yet to unwind. If anything they'd grown larger and tighter. My gaze went back to the man. I didn't want to talk to him, get to know him, or even be associated with him. Why? Why would I want to do that?

I had so many fucking questions that I'd never be able to ask.

Too deep. I'm in too fucking deep.

"Talk to him? Why?" I asked.

"Because an accident needs to look like an accident. Falling from a plane, if the person don't fly, looks suspicious. We need to know his likes and dislikes."

"Like a fucking dating service?"

Vincent's eyes narrowed, reminding me of my wife's. "Like a job. You're a negotiator, go talk."

That fucking word—*negotiator*. It was Carmine all over again.

"Find out what he likes," Vincent said, "what will help us. What will work. I'll be here, waiting."

I turned my stare from the man at the bar to my cousin-in-law. "I don't want this for Lennox."

Vincent's brow furrowed. "You have balls. I'll give you that."

"I mean it. I married Angelina. I made my requests and ambitions known. One day it'll be you in the large house with the goons at your side. I don't want this for Lennox."

"This life is an honor. I'm taking after my father, who took after his. It's what Luca will do, what he should do. The honorable thing. You don't want your son to be honorable?"

"I want my son to have choices."

"Family isn't a choice," Vincent said.

"It can be. It'll be your choice."

"Then don't disappoint me or my father. The future isn't written."

It wasn't a written promise, but it was the best I'd get.

Nodding, I took a deep breath and stood. My eyes swept the bar. The barstool to the left of the man was empty. Easing my way across the crowded bar, with an exaggerated breath, I eased onto the stool and nodded in his direction.

When the bartender came close, I flagged him down. "I'll take a tall of whatever you have on draft."

"Yes, sir."

"Rough day?" the red-headed man asked.

"Worse than normal," I replied.

He looked up from his plate to the television above the bar. Brightly painted cars were circling on a track. There were lights and people in large stands. Wherever the race was occurring, it was nighttime. The sound was muted, but the ticker near the top of the screen ran continually with numbers in order of their laps led. I'd never been much into racing, especially NASCAR. I didn't have time for such pastimes.

"Who's leading?" I asked, feigning interest.

"Gordon, but the damn caution just started. I hate when they end under caution."

I looked back at the television. "You like racing?"

"Yeah, the faster the better. How about you?"

I shrugged. "I'm not much of a fan. Kind of busy these days."

The man nodded, turned my direction, and extended his hand. "Russell, Russell Collins. What brings you to LA?"

I shook his hand. "Oren. I'm here on business."

"Yeah, me too. Where's home?"

"New York. You?"

Russell ran his hand over his hair. "Georgia, for now."

"For now?" I asked.

"I'm not looking forward to going back."

"You're not?" I asked casually, sipping my beer.

"No. Fucking shit's going to hit the fan. But it's been a long time in coming."

I took a longer drink before setting the glass in front of me. "I'm not an expert, but you can talk about it. My wife tells me I need to talk more."

Russell chuckled. "So you have one of those too?" He looked down at his left hand and then over to mine, assessing our wedding bands.

"Yes, for now," I confessed. It was the first time I'd said it aloud. It was cathartic and safe. I figured in the grand scheme of life, it wouldn't matter. This man wasn't long for this world. Maybe for once I could be honest and say that my marriage was not getting better; it was falling further and further into misery.

"I told mine that it was over," Russell said. "Let me just say, it was fucking liberating. Saying the words was like loosening a damn vise from my chest."

I wasn't sure what it was about the anonymity of conversing with a stranger, but for the next hour or so, both Russell Collins and I took full advantage. We said things that cleansed and relieved. I wasn't a fucking priest, but maybe, just maybe, I was able to help him, because I knew that come tomorrow, his time for absolution would be over.

CHAPTER 18

NOX

AFTER THROWING A suit coat over my shirt and not bothering to change out of my jeans, I made my way down to the bar. The area was large with clusters of tables and plants surrounding a central circular bar glistening with glass columns illuminated in blue light. As I scanned the room, I didn't see Davis, but many tables were occupied by familiar faces. If Davis had been looking for privacy, this wasn't the place. Then again, maybe that wasn't his objective. Maybe it was to have us seen together.

Well, game on.

I wasn't Oren meeting in a closed office building.

Near a back corner, I found an available table with high-back chairs and settled in. Directly behind me within the far wall of the bar was a giant fish tank holding an array of colorful sea creatures, strangely shaped fish, and bright coral. It was a world within our world, carrying on their lives as if they weren't placed behind glass for the entertainment of others.

From my vantage point, I could survey the growing crowd, which included a good number of the same faces from today's hearing. My gaze settled on the profile of a man I'd never met, but his exploits were well renowned. Though young, he didn't have a problem with standing by his convictions. The junior senator from Oregon could just possibly be the person to help swing the vote our way. Oregon was one state where Demetri wasn't invested. Maybe it was time? As I stood to introduce myself, a waitress approached.

"Hey honey," she purred, "can I get you something?" Her eyes scanned from my face to my feet and back to my eyes as her smile grew even wider. Maybe it was because if someone had looked at Charli the way this woman had just looked at me, I'd lose my shit. Instead of feeling flattered, her attention turned my stomach. I'd much rather be back with Charli.

"Grey goose, straight up."

"Sure thing, honey. I'll be right back." She winked. "If I can do anything else, don't hesitate to ask?"

"Drink's all I need."

"Suit yourself, but the night's young. You can always change your mind."

Her plastic smile never wavered as she walked away, her hips suggestively swaying from side to side.

"Looks like you could have some company tonight, if you're so inclined."

I turned toward the voice of Severus Davis, who now had landed his hand upon my shoulder.

"I'm not so inclined," I replied.

He nodded toward a woman I knew wasn't his wife, Maura, nor was she Chelsea. He puffed his chest. "I'm a little tied up myself." Lifting his brow, he asked, "If you know what I mean?"

I wasn't sure why he felt the need to share or why he thought I'd be interested. It wasn't as if I was about to suggest a three-way with the waitress.

Asshole!

The woman who'd been with him walked away and settled at the blue bar. The way her long bare legs were crossed suggestively at the knee caused her skirt to ride higher on her thighs. Her breasts were covered, but the material of the blouse was tight enough to make out the straps of her bra. Her center of gravity was definitely ill-proportioned. If she wasn't careful, she could topple over into the drink she'd just ordered.

As we both sat and he mumbled something else about his companion, I thought about how hearing the details of Davis's sex life was not on my list of desirable activities.

"Your wife is welcome to join us," I suggested.

Severus laughed. "My wife doesn't travel with me, not if she can avoid it. Catalina does."

Nodding, I pursed my lips. "That's convenient."

He shrugged. "She's new, but so far I like what I've seen." He leaned closer. "And there isn't much I haven't seen." He looked around. "Where's that cute little waitress that's hot for you. Flag her down. I could use a drink."

"New? You recently became involved?" This wasn't any of my business, but I wanted to know what the hell happened to our plant. Why wasn't Chelsea the one with him, learning his secrets?

"Yep." He inclined his head toward the bar. "Real looker. I'd say more, but I plan to have her around for a while."

"I would suspect in your line of work it's difficult to know who you can trust."

"It can be."

"Congratulations on finding someone." I tried to push my questions about Chelsea and Infidelity out of my head. Something had obviously happened and as soon as I got back to the room, I intended to find out what. Changing the subject, I asked, "Now, what progress were you talking about earlier today?"

"I'd say this is an example of knowing who I can trust. Is that someone you?"

The waitress returned with my drink. I swirled the colorless liquor as Davis ordered his own poison and told her to put Catalina's drinks on his bill.

She turned back my way. "Would you like me to put your vodka on your room, sweetie?"

I grinned. *Certainly sweetheart, let me give you that number.* "No." I pulled a hundred-dollar bill from my money clip. "Keep them coming, I've got it covered."

"Sure thing." Her lips teased a smile as she turned and walked away.

"Shame," Davis said. "Look at those legs. There's a lot that could be done—"

"Severus, to answer your question, trust is a two-way street. First, why don't you fill me in on your thoughts about the uninformative meeting with my father?"

"WHO IN THE hell is Catalina? Is she from Infidelity? What happened to Chelsea?" My questions came fast and furious.

"Mr. Demetri, I'll try to explain."

I gripped my phone tighter as I paced back and forth in front of the windows. In my current state I didn't notice that the lights of Washington DC shimmered stories below. "*Mrs. Witt…*" If we were going to play this professional tone, I was ready. "…this was your plan. This was your idea, and now it seems to have been blown to hell. I'm not accustomed to incompetence coming from you. What happened to Chelsea?"

"She interviewed with Infidelity while in California. She was accepted as an employee. Her profile was being assimilated just the other day. I'd kept Severus Davis's request on the back burner, hidden to the Infidelity staff. That was where it all stood the last time I looked, not more than a few days ago. Something must have happened."

"You think?" I felt the vein in my neck throbbing. This fucking day needed to end and the next two along with it, so I could be back with Charli.

"*Mr. Demetri*, for the last thirty hours I've concentrated on you and Miss Collins. You're both alive and safe. That was my prime objective."

"Tell me that Charli is still in Westchester and dear old Dad hasn't made any more calls."

"She is and he hasn't. As she told you, she's demanding to go to class tomorrow."

I ran my free hand through my hair as I collapsed on the sofa. "I'd rather have her safe where she is. That house is a fortress." My chest seized as I started to say that it was the safest place for her to be, but I knew that even in that haven, tragedy could happen.

As I collected my thoughts, Deloris spoke. "It is. Obviously, what happened before won't happen again. Silvia is there. She's making sure."

Silvia had been gone that horrible night. She was never gone—or at least rarely. I hadn't known Jo would be alone for the night. It wasn't like there would have been others in our apartment. I was working. But at least if she'd been in the city there would have been people nearby instead of iron gates and impenetrable perimeters.

"What's the new guy's name?" I asked, changing the subject to Charli's new bodyguard.

"Clayton. He's not new."

"Jerrod wasn't new either." The day had been too long. My filter was gone.

"Jerrod swears he didn't intend any harm. It was simply a *family request* or so he was told."

I was immediately on my feet. "And he fucking thinks that's okay, to deliver secret letters to my girlfriend who's living in my home? The man is fired."

"Yes, sir. That wasn't a question."

"Make sure Clayton is with her. I don't care if he has to sit in her damn class."

"She told you about the GPS on her phone?"

"Yes," I answered with a little less determination.

Earlier today when I'd called Charli, she didn't answer and her GPS was off. Well, when she called back, I was on the verge of blowing a gasket.

My head was about to explode.

My voice alone should have fucking scared the shit out of her. If she'd been next to me, instead of states away, I would have tanned her fine ass and asked questions later. The thought made my lips quirk to a grin. She wasn't the least bit intimidated. Hell, even the threat of a spanking didn't unsettle her.

I had a sudden flashback of how she'd even asked for it.

Before I left she fucking told me to do it.

Instead of backing down or apologizing like anyone else with any sense would have done, when I answered her call with my tirade, my Charli laughed, a sweet harmony rippling through the phone and effectively silencing my slew of accusations.

For a moment, her reaction silenced everything I'd planned to say. The rage and helplessness at not knowing her exact location, of not being sure of her safety, dissipated into the ring of her laughter.

She had no way of knowing how deeply she affected me. In my dark world of secrets and deals, she was the light—a breath of fresh air in a smoke-filled room. She filled me with a promise of something that I'd forgotten existed—a promise of more, of love, laughter, and life.

I shook my head, concentrating on Deloris rather than the images I created in my head by combining memories with desires. After I got off this call, I'd see if I could interest Charli in phone sex. It wouldn't be as good as the real thing, but right now, it would have to do. God knew, I certainly wasn't interested in the waitress downstairs.

"…will have it tomorrow."

"What? Sorry, I was distracted. You'll have *what* tomorrow?"

"The GPS chip."

"Shit," I replied. "I wasn't serious when I told Charli I'd have one implanted."

"That's possible," Deloris said matter-of-factly. "But that wasn't what I just described. The chip I'm talking about is small, charged by solar power. As long as she wears it in the sun or even under most artificial light, it will stay charged."

I tried to imagine what she was saying. "Wear what?"

"Jewelry, Lennox. Maybe our connection is bad?"

Or maybe I was busy daydreaming about Charli's reddened ass and wasn't listening. "That must be it," I said. "What kind of jewelry?"

"Necklace. It's even waterproof. She can shower in it. Though I'd recommend she take it off to swim."

Or bathe?

Deloris went on as I tried to keep at bay the images of Charli submerged in a tub of bubbles, "…and with this, you can pinpoint her location even if the GPS locator on her phone is turned off. As she probably told you, we weren't the only ones who could see the GPS signal on her phone. So could her parents. They know she's here, that she's at your house in Rye."

I took a deep breath. Charli had told me that and about Oren too. Unfortunately, my father's knowledge of our near brush with death wasn't due to a picture on the Internet; it was because of me. I called him and ranted about the shooting, certain there were family ties. During my tirade, I'd told him that Charli and I were in Westchester.

"Yes," I said, "Charli told me. She also said you spoke to her stepfather."

"Yes, interesting man."

"I hear more of a story?"

"Another day perhaps," Deloris said. "My plate is overflowing."

"I like the jewelry idea," I admitted. "Did she agree?"

"In principle. I don't have the necklace yet, but I hope she'll be all right with it."

"Find out about Chelsea. If we blew it and she can't be with Davis, get her out of Infidelity. You got Charli out. Get Chelsea out too. I don't care if she's expecting the job. Get her something else that pays as well. I've been uncomfortable about involving her from the beginning. I can't imagine what Charli would say. Chelsea is her best friend."

"Let me work on it. I'll keep you posted. And tomorrow, after Alex is back in the city, I'll fly to DC and install the GPS software on your phone and Isaac's. With the way things have been going, I'm not even trusting our network to send you the links. After I put the app on your phones, you'll both have access to her whereabouts." She paused. "Are you still okay with Isaac?"

I didn't need to consider my answer. "Yes. Jerrod is one thing, but Isaac's been with me almost as long as you have." I hesitated. "You don't have reason to suspect him?"

"No, I don't, but after Jerrod, I'm watching everyone."

CHAPTER 19

CHARLI

I KNEW IT was my imagination. Nox's home in Rye wasn't Montague Manor. There weren't shadows lurking behind locked doors. And yet after finishing dinner and retiring to the room Silvia referred to as *mine*, the one where Nox had brought me earlier in the day, I had the strange sensation of being surrounded by knowing spirits. They were the ghosts of occupants past.

Not literal ghosts. There weren't white floating figures swirling about the room; nevertheless, I felt a strange combination of safety and danger—a reassuring calm in the interior stillness while an alarm wailed beyond the walls.

All day I'd longed to go outside, to feel the sun on my skin. Now it seemed as if the heavens had opened, purging the sins from the air as the roar of the wind howled beyond the wooden blinds. Though my childish imagination could make it into more, it was simply a late summer storm. Very common as warm days clashed with cooler nights. Winds raged and torrents of rain peppered the windows, the latter's crash loud enough to mimic a spray of ricocheting bullets.

Stop it!

Not a good image.

Washing my face and brushing my teeth, I prepared for bed and contemplated the ups and downs of the day. When I woke this morning, I had no idea what to expect in my relationship with Nox. Was it done or at least paused? I had been nervous and confused, unsure of how I felt or where we stood.

As I changed into something more comfortable, that feeling seemed like it occurred a lifetime ago—before we thwarted death, before we consummated our new declarations of love, and most importantly, before I learned more about my mystery man. He'd been that—a mystery—in Del Mar, and now, the more I knew about him and saw the man behind the mask, the more of an enigma he became.

It was as if every answer was wrapped in a hundred questions.

The best part about being here in his home was getting to know Silvia. She was the only family Nox seemed to claim. Though they weren't related, I remembered the day he'd told me that he understood how Chelsea and I were as close as sisters. He'd said he didn't have siblings, but that some bonds were stronger than blood. I had the feeling that included Silvia.

As the day progressed, Silvia and I became better acquainted. She willingly shared how she'd worked for the Demetris since she was very young. By the way she spoke of Nox's mother, I got the feeling that they had been close. When she spoke of her youth, Silvia said that she began working too young, not even finishing school until Angelina stepped in. After Silvia's father died, earning money was the most important thing to her mother. If that meant selling her teenage daughter off as domestic help, she did it.

The Demetris weren't her first employers. At thirteen she'd gone to work for a wealthy family member of Angelina's. As I listened to her stories, I began to construct a family history, one that Nox had yet to share.

I knew how Nox and I felt about learning one another's private information, but the way I saw it, he was the one to leave me alone with Silvia. The first time I'd met her, she offered to tell me stories of a teenage Lennox. He had to know what would happen.

In our time together, Nox and I had limited what we had shared about our past. All I knew about his family was that his mother passed after she and Oren divorced, how Oren had started Demetri Enterprises, and how Nox didn't believe his father appreciated his dedication to the business.

Silvia commented more than once that Oren and Lennox were more similar than either cared to admit. They were both determined, hardworking, and stubborn. From what I knew, I couldn't help but agree—especially with her last assessment.

In every instance, Silvia spoke fondly of Angelina. Apparently, Silvia had worked for Lennox's mother until the day she died. She even admitted that she'd almost moved away after Angelina passed. She no longer needed the Demetris financially. Angelina had ensured her economic independence. Silvia admitted that she probably would have left were it not for Lennox.

After the support Angelina had given to her, Silvia wanted to fill that role for Lennox. Despite their relative closeness in age, she wanted to be there for him.

I wanted to ask about Oren and why he was absent, but I didn't want to interrupt her memories.

She shared as we sat, cooked, and ate. Intertwined throughout each story were innuendos that there was more than she could say. Though I didn't fully understand exactly what she meant, I'd already learned that it would take more than a couple months with Lennox Demetri to make sense of his world.

I supposed it would be the same for him, if he were at Montague Manor. Perhaps that was one of the elements that drew us together, a shared sadness for childhoods lost.

By the time I retired for the evening, I sensed that Silvia and I were now friends. Since Nox's happiness was one of her priorities, I knew that she was someone I wanted on my side. The only unsettling feeling I had while at Westchester, besides the obvious external threat, was when Silvia and Deloris were together. Maybe it was simply because my day had been too long and too dramatic. Maybe I was seeing clues that weren't there. But I got the feeling they weren't close.

Now as I settled in *my room* with a warm cup of Earl Gray tea, I longed for the reassurance I'd felt sitting with Silvia. Instead, as the wind blew and the rain coming off the sound pounded against the windows, I was tired and uneasy. My mind was a blur with all that had happened, and I wanted nothing more than to rest in Nox's arms and feel his strength around me as he protected me from the ghosts and shadows.

Though I wanted to call him, I hesitated. Nox was working, away doing whatever it was he did. Oren had all but said I was a distraction. Calling Nox would only confirm his father's opinion. I hated comparing Nox to Alton, but I truly had no other reference. I rarely remembered my mother talking, or wanting to talk to Alton when he was away.

So instead of calling Nox, I tried Chelsea.

Her phone rang three times before going to voicemail.

"Hey girl," I said, trying to sound more upbeat than I felt. "Let me know when you're coming in to New York City. I know you have that big secret job in DC." And then the thought occurred to me. "Oh my goodness, Nox is in DC for business. Maybe I'll be able to visit you there when my classes allow. In the meantime, I'm ready for some girl time. Things have been… well, this message isn't long enough to finish that sentence. We need wine. Tell me you're getting to New York before Friday. I miss you! Call me."

I disconnected the call even more uneasy with not being able to reach her. Since leaving Montague over four years ago, after my graduation from the academy, I'd always been with Chelsea and then with Nox. I told myself that it was normal to feel alone. I just needed to face it. After all, I was the one who had planned to live alone in that apartment. Well, I had considered a cat.

As I was about to pull back the covers, it occurred to me that this was the same bed where earlier Nox and I had come back together—literally.

My face flushed as I recalled his passion and hunger. The way he looked at me, needing to assure himself with his eyes and touch that I was whole and unscathed.

My mind couldn't process that someone as possessive and protective as Nox could or would ever hurt his wife.

He wouldn't.

I just wanted to know why he felt responsible. Had something like today happened? Patrick had mentioned a hit.

Then a realization struck that changed my train of thought. The bed was made.

No longer merely flushed, heat filled my cheeks, no doubt turning them redder than my hair. I hadn't made the bed. I was certain Nox didn't.

That meant the entire time I was getting to know Silvia, she already knew me or about Nox and me, about how close we were.

As that embarrassing thought resonated through my consciousness, my phone rang.

My sullen heart leapt, hoping it was Chelsea.

"Hello," I answered, not looking at the screen, but knowing that the tune meant it was a friend versus a foe.

"What the hell, little cousin?"

I grinned, hearing Patrick's voice.

"Yes, sorry for the cryptic message earlier today."

After Deloris and I talked about what I could say, I simply left Pat a message saying I wouldn't be staying there tonight. I didn't mention anything other than that Nox and I were fine. Leaving details of my day on his voicemail didn't seem like a good idea.

"Cryptic?" Pat asked. "Girl, I couldn't have figured that out with a decoder ring. All it told me was that you were well enough to call. At least hearing your voice left me a trail of breadcrumbs to follow. What the hell happened?"

I recalled Deloris's advice—keep it simple. "After you left the apartment, I told Nox I wanted to walk to class. Well, you know him?" I didn't wait for him to respond. "He's not very big on my walking alone."

"Apparently he has reason!"

I ignored Pat's comment and continued, "Nox walked with me and while we were in the park, chaos broke out. It was frightening. I didn't see much. It all happened so fast. Nox has… people."

"A good looking man with people. Jackpot!"

I shrugged. "This time I'm not complaining. The people were a good thing. They whisked in from the commotion and took us away."

"You don't think that what happened—the shot—was meant for one of you, do you?"

"Shot? So you heard about it?"

"Heard? I saw your face pop up on my news app. It scared the shit out of me."

It wasn't until my talks with Silvia that I began to think that maybe the shots could have been meant for one of us. I guess in some ways, Silvia's innuendos scared me more than anything Deloris or Nox had said.

"I have no way of knowing who the person was shooting at," I replied, "but why? Why would anyone want to do that?"

"Little cousin, I don't know. I'm just glad you're both okay. I saw on that news app that the woman who was shot is in stable condition."

A bit of the fog that had begun to settle around me lifted. "That's great news."

"So I imagine you'll be staying wherever Mr. Good-looking has you hidden away for what, the next year?"

I shook my head, now sitting against the headboard, my legs tucked under the blankets. "No, I've got class. I'll be back in the city tomorrow."

"You? What about Mr. Good-looking?"

My cheeks rose. "Why don't you or Chelsea call him by his name?"

"I don't know. I like Mr. Good-looking. If your friend calls him the same, she and I'll get along fine."

"She calls him Mr. Handsome."

"Same difference," Patrick replied.

"Mr. Whatever-You-All-Want-To-Call-Him is working out of town. I was going to call you and ask if maybe I could—"

"If you could shack up with Mr. Sex Appeal himself?"

"So now we all have code names?"

"You're the one living in a spy movie. I want some of the action."

"Okay, so Mr. Sex Appeal? You're saying that Cy will be back? That's his code name, right?" I asked with a grin.

"Oh, little cousin, that hurts. I was referring to me."

"How about I just call you Pat? We can say it's short for Mr. Sex Appeal."

"That works for me, and Cy won't be back until Friday. You're always welcome. You know that."

"Thanks. I'm waiting to hear from Chelsea. She's due in the city tomorrow or Friday. I'm so messed up with everything, I can't remember."

"We can have a slumber party."

"I love that idea," I said, "but if she gets in, she'll want to hang out at the apartment on 112th."

"As long as you're okay. Just so you know, I hesitated leaving you this morning. I may have hung out for a minute or two, but then as things sounded like you and Mr. Good-looking were getting along, I felt a little like a stalker and snuck out."

Memories of Nox telling me that he loved me and my professing the same gave way to thoughts of this bed. I shifted against the soft sheets. "Yes, other than the minor little problem with the shooting, we're doing much better."

"You sure know how to keep life exciting. Your face is everywhere. Even my mother called. I hadn't spoken to her for a few weeks."

I scrunched my nose. "Sorry."

"No, don't be. I wanted you to know that she and my dad were worried. She even said that Aunt Adelaide and Uncle Alton were upset."

"Yes, they called."

"And…?" Patrick encouraged.

"Same old story. Come home to Savan—" An incoming call interrupted my sentence.

I peered at the screen. Talking meant there wasn't a tune to alert me to friend or foe, only a vibration.

NOX PRIVATE NUMBER.

I sucked in a breath. "Hey, Pat, Mr. Good-looking is calling."

"Oh, then girl, you talk to that man. Tell him to hurry up and finish whatever work he's doing and get his fine ass back to you."

Fine ass? Most definitely.

My smile blossomed to full bloom. "I will. See you tomorrow."

"Love you, little cousin."

"Me too." I swiped the screen.

CHAPTER 20

CHARLI

"MR. DEMETRI," I said, connecting to his call. "I didn't want to bother you while you were working."

"You could never bother me." His voice rumbled deeper than the thunder beyond the windows.

The sound of his voice lifted any remaining fog, the rich bass tone resonating through the room, eclipsing the outside winds and rolling to my core.

"I seem to recall some rules," I teased.

Nox cleared his throat. "I do like rules."

"Something about only calling you if I had a question that you needed to answer."

"I believe I've mentioned that the rules have changed."

"So that means I can sext?"

"Only if you want Deloris and quite probably other members of my security to see it."

I wasn't sure what had gotten into me. Well, that wasn't true. I was thinking about what had been inside of me earlier this afternoon, more accurately who. "Only if that's what you want, Mr. Demetri."

"Fuck!" His expletive came out like a growl. "I've told you before what will happen to you for making me uncomfortable. When you say my name that way, it makes me so fucking hard, it hurts."

"I wish I could make it feel better," I purred, pushing my limits on seductress. The power my words wielded was suddenly intoxicating.

"Tell me where you are."

I bristled at the change in his tone. Apparently, Nox wasn't in the mood for my seduction. I answered him, "I'm still in Rye. I told you I'd spend the night."

"Where are you?" Nox asked again. "Exactly."

"I-I'm in the bedroom. What's the matter?"

"No questions," Nox said with an air of dominance that twisted my insides. "That's my job. Yours is to reply appropriately. What are you supposed to say?"

My heartbeat quickened. "Yes, Nox."

"Are you in the same bedroom we were in this morning?"

I fought to breathe and speak as my response came out in a whisper. "Yes."

"Do you remember my lips on you?"

"Yes."

"How about my hands, my fingers?"

My suddenly dry tongue darted to my parched lips. "Yes."

"I know you were sounding all sexy a minute ago, and I like that, but right now, princess, I need to be in control. Do you have a problem with that?"

"No, Nox."

"Listen carefully."

I nodded, though I knew he couldn't see me.

"If I were there, I'd do what I did this morning. I'd unwrap you, like a fucking Christmas present. Each piece of your clothing would find its way to the floor as I exposed your perfect, sexy-as-hell body. I'd run my fingers and tongue over every inch of that soft skin, tasting you and leaving goose bumps as a trail of my exploration."

My eyes closed as his words touched me.

"Princess, I'd punish your ass for your insolence in pushing to go back to the city tomorrow and for scaring the shit out of me by not answering your phone. Then after I turned it fire-engine red, I'd make it feel better, showing you how much I admire your strength and determination."

My neck strained as I sucked in a breath, lifting my behind from the mattress and imagined all he described.

"I'm not there," Nox continued, "but I'm going to take what I can get. Do you have a problem with that?"

"N-no." My voice sounded wonton, even to my own ears.

"Now, princess, tell me what you're wearing."

I hurriedly kicked back the covers, revealing my yoga pants and stocking-covered feet. "A big t-shirt, yoga pants, socks…"

"Stop."

I sucked my lower lip between my teeth, waiting for his next command.

"Tell me what I want you to be wearing."

"Nox?"

"Is the bedroom door locked?" he asked.

"I-I don't remember, but Silvia went back to her part of the house. She gave me her number."

"Lock the door, Charli."

Without thinking, my feet, covered with fuzzy socks, landed on the soft rug that surrounded the big bed. My socks slid as I skated across the wood floor, no longer worried about ghosts or Demetri secrets.

My thoughts were now consumed with everything Nox.

I tested the knob. As I did, it clicked and the small button within the knob popped out. I pushed the button back in and verbally confirmed my mission. "The door's locked."

"Are the blinds shut?"

I turned toward the windows. Was it still raining? I couldn't hear anything but the way Nox's voice reverberated through the phone, sending shockwaves throughout my body, my blood coursing to keep up. "They're shut."

"Keep the lights on."

My hand lingered over the switch. Would he know if I disobeyed?

"Tell me they're on."

With a sigh, I did as he said and moved my hand away from the switch. "They're still on."

"Now, put me on speaker phone. I want you to fix the attire problem we mentioned earlier."

My lower lip disappeared as I hit the speaker button and laid my phone on the bed.

"Charli, you need to respond to me. I can only hear you."

"Yes, Nox." My t-shirt grazed my now-sensitive hard nipples. "I-I promise, I'm responding."

His deep laugh echoed through the room. "Tell me. How?"

I pushed the yoga pants over my hips, stepping out of them. One by one, I kicked off my socks. Though my skin became covered with goose bumps at the timbre of his voice, the chill I'd felt earlier was gone.

"M-my nipples are hard."

"And now you're wearing…?"

"Only my panties."

"The blue ones from earlier?"

I shook my head. "No, these are white."

"White?" A laugh rumbled from his throat. "White is for good girls and what I want to do to you isn't appropriate for good girls. Princess, if I were there, I'd fuck you so dirty you'd never wear white again."

I sucked in a breath. "I wish you were here."

"Me too. I'm so fucking hard. We're going to keep going. Are you still all right with that, my naughty princess?"

"Yes, Nox."

"Before you take off the panties, go to the closet."

The closet?

"I want you to find one of my belts."

"O-oh God…" I murmured, both anxious and excited about his unspoken plans. Reaching for the phone, I carried it into the large closet, switched on the light and began opening drawers.

"Talk, Charli. Tell me you're doing as I said."

"Yes, Nox. I'm looking for your belts."

"On the right," he directed.

I turned that direction and opened another drawer. There, perfectly coiled, were different belts in varying colors. "Do you have a favorite?" I asked.

"Whichever one you use tonight will be my favorite."

The tips of my fingers tingled as I reached in the drawer. Brushing the leather, I imagined each one against my skin. As my breaths became shallower, I pulled one from the drawer. It was black with a small silver buckle that resembled a swirl. "I have a black one."

"Now take my belt back to the bed. But before you climb on the bed, take off those white lace panties."

My head spun around, looking for a camera. "How do you know they're lace?"

"Because all your panties are lace."

My lips quirked to a grin as I eased the white lace down my legs. Even in a sexier-than-hell moment, when Nox was acting all dominant, his intimate knowledge and attention to something as simple as the material of my underwear filled me with warmth.

"They're off," I said with a hint more confidence.

"Now answer my question from before."

"What question?"

"No, princess, that's a question. Remember I told you that asking was my job, not yours? What happens when you disobey?"

My pulse soared as my gaze went to the belt. "I remember what you said, but I don't remember your question."

"Tell me how you're *responding*." Nox drew out the word.

"My nipples." My answer was now only partially true. The walk to the closet and mixed emotions had softened them.

"Put the belt beside you, and since you're using the speaker phone, you have both hands available to cup your breasts."

As soon as I did, my nipples pebbled, back to the hardened nubs from before.

"Harder, princess, pinch your nipples. I want to hear you."

Again, I closed my eyes and obeyed. My caresses that were soft at first took on strength of their own. Nox's commands as well as the tone of his voice encouraged my movements. More than one whimper escaped my lips as I twisted and tugged, each painful tweak sending pulsations of pleasure to my core.

"That's it," he encouraged. "Tell me how it feels."

My hips squirmed against the bed. "Good. And bad."

"Bad?"

"Good, definitely good." I moaned as my nails scraped the tender skin. "It hurts, but it feels good."

"Fuck," he growled. "Tell me about your pussy."

I moaned as my hands left my breasts and trailed down my ribcage, my palms flattening as they spanned over my stomach. Unknowingly, my back arched as my fingers inched lower.

"Spread those sexy legs. Tell me if you're wet."

I knew the answer before confirmation.

"Y-yes," I replied as one finger tentatively searched between my folds.

Though Nox was speaking through the phone, it was as if he were with me, beside me, guiding me. "Say it. Yes, what?"

"I'm wet."

"What do you want?" His question floated in the air, the tenor knowing and the tone demanding response.

"I want you."

"Charli." In one word I'd been reprimanded.

"Your cock," I corrected. "Nox. God, I wish you were here."

"Move the phone so I can hear you."

My stomach twisted as I moved the cell phone to the mattress between my spread legs.

"It's there," I said, my desire heightened while at the same time I felt ashamed that my arousal would be audible.

"Work your fingers, princess, plunge them deep. Let me hear it. I want to imagine that my chin is dripping with you. I want to imagine that slick wetness on my tongue and on my dick. Move those fingers."

To my horror, as I did what he said in the otherwise quiet room, I too could hear the sound of my essence, the wetness echoing through the large room as I thrust my fingers in and out.

"You're so fucking beautiful," he said.

My neck arched against the pillows as my knees fell farther apart. "O-oh, Nox..." I couldn't stop the indecipherable sounds as I concentrated on his voice and did as he said, imagined it was him.

"Not yet, you're not coming yet."

He was wrong. I was. Maybe if I tried to keep it quiet.

"Stop." His command stilled my fingers. "I can hear you. Did you think I couldn't? Princess, you make the most fantastic sounds when you're about to come. Maybe after your punishment, I'll let you come."

"W-what are you talking about?" I asked, lost in the ecstasy his voice and commands induced.

"Another question. Princess, it's time for the belt."

A cold chill blanketed my warm skin. The perspiration that had glistened at the tone of his instructions turned to frost as I stared at the belt beside me. For only a moment, I envisioned a snake, coiled and ready to strike. "W-what do you want me to do?"

"Listen to me. Will you do that?"

I swallowed the lump that had formed in my throat.

"Princess?" he asked. "Are you ready?"

What is it about this man? Is there anything that he could ask me to do that I wouldn't?

"Will I get to come?" I asked.

"Another question. That's three. I also bet you've spent the day learning things I might not be ready for you to know. Tell me, princess, do you need to be punished?"

Fuck! How did he do that, make me want what I shouldn't?

"Mr. Demetri, you're right." I concentrated on the painful pitch in my core. "I've disobeyed."

"Pick up the belt and fold it in half."

My hands trembled as I did as he said. I sat up, mindlessly running the leather across my palm, imagining that it was Nox doing the same.

"I'm ready," I bravely replied.

"Are you still lying back?"

As I moved he undoubtedly heard the rustling of the sheets. "No."

"Lie back, like you were. I want your head and that beautiful hair on a pillow with your legs spread wide. If I were there, I'd be looking at that perfect pink pussy."

My breathing hitched as I moved to the position he described. The cold buckle in my grasp warmed with each second as my anticipation grew.

"Tell me what I'd see if I were there," he demanded.

"Me, I'm ready."

"Would I see how ready you are? How much your pussy wants my cock?"

"Y-yes." I said, losing myself to his commands.

"You're so damn hot. My dick is fucking stone. Each time that belt leaves a stripe on your gorgeous skin, each time you do what I say, I want you to imagine my hand pumping. In my mind, I'm coming all over that freshly pink flesh. Princess, never forget that I fucking love you. With each strike, I'm marking you, again and again."

I could barely breathe as the image of him leaning over me, his length in his grasp, dominated my thoughts.

"Do you have a problem with this?"

"Yes," I bravely replied.

"You do?"

"Fuck, Nox, I wish you were here. I want it all."

"Me too. Close your eyes and do exactly what I say…"

I couldn't concentrate. The room around me was no longer present. I was suspended, floating in the sound of his voice, the deep dominating timbre telling, demanding, and commanding. Though my hands were delivering the punishment, it was all him. My hands were merely an extension of his, lost to his will.

A gasp filled the air and my hips buckled as the first lash landed upon my stomach…

CHAPTER 21

CHARLI

"MISS COLLINS, MISSING one day of class does not usually result in a discussion with your counseling faculty. Your case appears to be unique."

I sat perched on the edge of a chair in my faculty counselor's office, facing her desk as she shuffled through notes. "I don't understand. I called yesterday afternoon and explained the situation."

"Your name is associated with our school. The most recent newscast has you listed as a first-year student."

I nodded. "I was at the wrong place at the wrong time. The situation was traumatic and I…" I wasn't sure how to end the sentence. I was taken away into hiding. I was transported before I realized what happened. I have a boyfriend who is extremely protective and well protected. Before I knew what happened his bodyguards swooped in… I had too many options.

The counselor nodded. "I understand. What you saw would be traumatic for anyone. I've lived in New York for most of my life and have never been that close to a shooting. According to the news report, you were seen being taken away from the scene with a Mr. Demetri."

I didn't respond to confirm or deny her observation, though I found the use of Nox's name interesting or maybe confusing.

As I pondered, she continued, "One of the reasons I called you to my office is because the university has counselors, ones who could help you deal with this. You're about to embark on a very busy semester. If this situation weighs too heavily…"

I sighed as she continued with her recommendation for therapy. If she only knew that in the grand scheme of the last few months of my life, this incident was a minor blip—now that I knew the woman who was shot in our stead was going to survive. That was, until she mentioned a name I never wanted associated with me.

"Our other concern is the call I received yesterday from your stepfather, Alton Fitzgerald."

The relief I'd felt at her concern for my mental health faded as the small hairs on the back of my neck stood to attention and my back straightened. "Why would he call you?"

"At first he was calling to see if you were here, to check on your safety."

Bullshit. He wasn't checking on my safety.

"At first?" I asked.

"He voiced concerns about tuition and about your missing class. He's concerned about your handling the responsibility…"

My teeth ground together as she continued. Finally, unable to take it anymore, I interrupted. "Dr. Renaud, I graduated with honors from Stanford. This is only the first week of classes. I did well on all of my evaluations during orientation. My stepfather has no right to voice his opinions."

"He said that you might say that. He also made it known that he had other ways to influence Columbia. We rely heavily upon donations."

"What are you saying?"

"I'm saying that accepting you into our program was a well-thought-out decision, not one that our admissions committee made lightly. We put a lot of time into our selection process. Please don't give us reason to doubt our decision."

"As far as my tuition is concerned, I'm paying for my classes, not my stepfather or my mother." Okay, it wasn't me, but Nox. "I've secured the remainder of my tuition for the next three years. In the future, I'd like the name Alton Fitzgerald removed from all of my records. Speaking to him about me will be considered a breach of my privacy."

Dr. Renaud sat silently for a moment, studying me, and then her veneer shattered and she smiled. "I like you. Show this same fortitude in your classes and I have no doubt that our decision to admit you as one of our students was a correct one. As a matter of fact, after what I just saw, I'd like to recommend you for an internship with one of your professors."

I tried to keep up. One minute it seemed as though I was fighting for my right to continue as a student and the next she was talking to me about an internship. "Which professor? What would the internship entail?"

My stomach twisted with new nerves as she spoke about the duties required of all the interns. The work would mostly involve research, citing old cases and finding precedents to substantiate the cases in—or preparing to be in—litigation. My counselor joked that computers and databases made the research less exhausting than it had been back in her day; nevertheless, the work would require extensive time and would be unpaid. Despite all of that, she emphasized the benefits. Being accepted for this opportunity would give real-world application to my studies, making it not only an excellent experience but would also look great on a résumé.

"You may not be aware," she said, "but Professor Walters is well known for his work in federal litigation in the fight against legalization of recreational marijuana. His research as well as sources was groundbreaking in its day. Having your name associated with Joseph Walters will open many doors."

My name associated… will open doors?

Bryce's warning of Nox came back to me. Was she speaking of opening doors for me, or would having a Montague, a tobacco giant, working with Professor Walters help him?

Surely that wasn't what she'd meant.

I was just overwrought. It was the perfect ingredient for triggering my overactive imagination.

Dr. Renaud's words brought my focus back to her as she said, "I'd be happy to recommend you to Professor Walters, but my recommendation alone wouldn't guarantee you a spot."

I nodded and, swallowing my concern, I considered the time commitment. Nox had his work and gladly supported me and my time for studies, but how would he feel about my spending more hours on this internship?

Why did I suddenly care?

Was I doing what Patrick said and beginning to think like a part of a couple?

In California, at Stanford, I would have willingly jumped at an opportunity like this.

"Dr. Renaud, is there an application or something I need to complete?"

She hit a few keys on her computer. "Let me email you the link."

My chest rose and fell with the unfamiliar conflict of my future versus my present. Feigning a smile, I said, "Thank you for thinking of me for this opportunity. I'll do some research and take a look at the application."

"Miss Collins, these internships are coveted. Consider that as you're doing your research."

As I left Dr. Renaud's office, I checked my phone and saw that I had fifteen minutes until my next class. Since that meeting with my faculty counselor had been unplanned, I decided to text Clayton, my new driver-slash-bodyguard.

Despite the warm afternoon, as I stepped against a building into the shadow to better see my screen, I thought of Jerrod. I'd grown accustomed to his presence and he'd failed me—us. The idea that the man who'd been assigned to me, who'd accompanied me for nearly the last month, was even partially responsible for the letter in our apartment filled me with a sense of doubt. I wanted to trust all of Deloris's decisions, because I knew Nox did, but how could I be sure about Clayton? Would I be better off with someone from Montague Manor? If I did, who would it be? No matter how eloquently Alton professed his concern over my safety, giving up Brantley, his right-hand man, wouldn't be an option.

My mouth filled with a sour taste. I didn't want Brantley anyway.

If only I were the naïve woman Nox assumed I was when he first told me that I would have a driver, when I first protested. If I were, I wouldn't be familiar with the way the system worked. Yes, the man or woman entrusted with my safety would be *my* bodyguard, but life experience told me that no matter where he or she came from—Deloris or Montague—I wouldn't be the person who the bodyguard ultimately reported to. Supposedly, where I sought security was my choice, but in reality all it did was determine who would receive the reports of my daily activities, Nox or Alton. Knowing which answer I wanted, I shook my head and fingered the new drop-pearl necklace dangling from my neck.

The style looked chic and simple: a large ivory pearl floating freely within a diamond-dusted platinum cage. To the unknowing, it was a beautiful, understated accessory. Only a few people knew that the pearl wasn't real but an iridescent casing around a microchip that broadcast my location via GPS to Deloris. More than that, it recorded my movements, my respiration, and even my heart rate.

Deloris had offered earrings, beautiful pearl-looking ones with a serpentine diamond base. The issue was that she wanted me to wear the jewelry all of the time—twenty-four hours a day, seven days a week. I didn't like sleeping in earrings, but I could in a necklace. According to her, it only needed to be removed when I swam.

When she explained that I should basically not remove it, I narrowed my eyes and asked her to confirm that there wasn't a camera attached to the necklace. She promised me that it was more like the health bracelets everyone wore, with the added benefit of pinpoint-accurate global positioning.

Recalling my telephone conversation with Nox from the night before, my face warmed. More than likely my cheeks were changing to the same color as the markings I'd willingly delivered to my own body as I worried about the heart-rate part of this necklace. I wasn't sure I wanted Nox's security to know that much about me.

I could hear them now. "Her heart rate is too high. Maybe we should call an ambulance?" And then they'd rush in and find me and their boss in some compromising position.

Shaking my head, I sent my text message to Clayton:

"I WILL BE DONE IN AN HOUR AND A HALF. YOU CAN PICK

ME UP THEN, SAME PLACE YOU DROPPED ME OFF."

Almost immediately Clayton's response buzzed on my phone.

"YES, MA'AM. I'LL BE THERE."

I FELT ODD watching Lana cook, but not Pat. I loved seeing how he combined ingredients to create heavenly meals. I sat at the counter overlooking his kitchen. Just beyond the smooth surface and my glass of chardonnay, my cousin was once again preparing magic in a pan—in three pans, to be more exact.

"Did you see the latest about the woman who was shot?" Patrick asked.

I cradled my head in my hands with my elbows on the granite. I had too many things to think about. I wanted her to be safe and spend my time with other concerns. "No. What did it say?"

"Oh! This isn't a hold-your-head kind of thing." His voice was full of animation. "They've changed their mind about her being an innocent bystander."

I lifted my eyes. "What do you mean?"

His brow lengthened, revealing more of his forehead with his thinning hair, and his light brown eyes danced with secrets. "I don't know for sure."

"You lost me."

"I think you should call that Mrs. Witt lady. All I know is that they said the case has been changed to attempted murder."

"Wouldn't it be anyway? I mean, she was shot. It's not like I've been questioned and the police think Nox or I was the intended target."

"That's the thing. In the beginning they were saying that she was a woman in the wrong place at the wrong time. Now there's something about her relationship with her husband, questioning his whereabouts. It all makes it sound as if she was the intended target." He continued to dice and stir, filling the air with the wonderful aroma of onions and peppers. "I could be reading too much into it, but I bet that woman knows more."

"The woman who was shot?" I asked.

"No, that Witt woman."

I shook my head. "Pat, I don't know if I can entertain any more conspiracy theories."

"But don't you get it? If she was the intended target, it wasn't you or Mr. Good-looking."

I took a deep breath and leaned back against the tall stool. "That would be nice."

"By the way, does he know you're here?"

"Yes. My sleepover is Demetri-approved."

"What about Montague? Do they approve?"

I shrugged. "Does it make me a terrible daughter if I say that my fucks are completely used with other concerns? I have no more to give."

Patrick laughed. "No, little cousin, I think you deserve that. Now where were you last night?"

"Nox's house…" If it had been almost anyone else, I wasn't sure if I'd have answered the question so freely, but Patrick made me feel safe, just as he had all of our lives, protecting me in ways I didn't even know.

After dinner, I asked, "Do you know anything about marijuana legislation?"

"You mean, did I consider moving to Colorado?"

A smile brightened my face. "That wasn't what I meant. I need to look up some things about one of my professors."

"I'm sure you could ask the Witt lady."

I hadn't thought of that. "No, it's not that big of a deal. My faculty advisor wants to recommend me for an internship…"

"Because you don't have enough on your plate?"

My lips formed a straight line. "Because she said it would be good for me." I considered what she'd said. "It would be a good name association. I don't know. I think it's something Bryce said to me that's eating at me."

Patrick plopped down on the sofa and kicked his feet onto the glass coffee table. Faking a full body shiver, he said, "I'd think most anything he said would eat at you. Kind of like a tapeworm, you know, from the inside until nothing was left. Why are you even considering what he'd say?"

"I don't know. I'm confused. Two nights ago, when I came over here, I'd learned something about Nox, something unsettling. I still don't know the details, but it seems that maybe some of Bryce's warnings weren't just hot air."

"You're not second-guessing that handsome man, are you? Not that you can," he added.

"I'm not. But what if there's more that I need to consider? This is about the internship. Bryce warned me that Nox was using me for my name, which is ridiculous since he didn't even know it. Now I'm wondering about this professor. Would a tobacco name like Montague be an asset to his team?"

"That's not something I could even begin to answer."

"Maybe I should ask Bryce?"

Patrick's nose scrunched.

I shook my head. "Or maybe not. I just don't know anymore. Sometimes I think—"

The ringing of my phone, the friend-not-foe tune, redirected my attention. The screen read *CHELSEA*.

A weight I hadn't realized I'd been carrying lifted from my chest. I'd missed my best friend, and soon she'd be with me in New York. I hadn't originally been sure I wanted her here, but after being without her for over a month, I couldn't wait for any little bit of time that we could find to be together.

"Hey! I'm so glad to see your name! When are you getting your butt to New York?"

Her incomprehensible sobs were all I could hear.

I jumped from the couch, clenching my phone in my grasp. "What is it?" I waited. "Chelsea, talk to me. Are you all right? Where are you?"

CHAPTER 22

Present

ADELAIDE

SITTING IN THE dark near the window in the library had become one of my favorite places to be. In the evenings I'd often make my way to the serenity of the solitude there. The velvet chaise near the large leaded-glass panes provided the perfect view. Though it was early autumn, the evening and early nighttime air was still warm. I liked to open the window and enjoy the gentle breeze as it silently fluttered the drapes. The scene below rarely changed. In some ways the moonlit, pristine manicured lawns, various gardens, pool, and lake gave me a sense of immortality.

As I brought my wine to my lips, the thought of immortality made me snicker. Just a little over a week ago, I was ready to test my mortality. My shoulders straightened. That was the past. Now I had a new purpose, a reason to move forward.

Settling against the plush velvet while taking in the never-changing scene a story below, I contemplated something Alexandria had said the last time she was here. She'd said that things at Montague Manor never changed. Even in her youth, she understood what generations before her had known: Montague Manor remained the same.

Throughout my life I'd found a sense of comfort in that. The landscape before me was the same as it had been for my mother and most likely for my grandmother. Even with consistent renovations and updated amenities, the manor and grounds were timeless.

I used to wonder what it all looked like hundreds of years ago, when the tobacco plantation was first settled. I'd ponder if the first Charles Montague knew how far-reaching his investment would take his ancestors or the impact it would have on their lives. Would it have been better to have descended from those who lived in one of the hundreds of tiny homes that once covered this property?

Those were the people who were now free of the burden that came with being a Montague.

Over the years, the peacefulness of the library had become my refuge. I'd long since given up the idea that the bedroom suite I shared with Alton was a place of anything but misery. The physical abuse wasn't constant. It was the mental strain, the constant concern over my husband's state of mind. The only reprieves came in his absence, which were too infrequent for my liking.

I sipped my wine.

If only he liked fast cars the way Russell had.

Since my visit to Hamilton and Porter a week before, my mind had been consumed with the possibilities of my discovery. I'd studied each photograph of each page, the article, and each and every word of the codicil. For days I worried that Alton had been alerted to my visit. I waited for the proverbial shoe to drop.

It never did.

My only conclusion was that Ralph Porter feared Alton Fitzgerald's wrath at allowing me access to my father's last will and testament even more than I was afraid of my husband's reaction to learning of my exploration. That was fine with me. I wasn't ready to announce my findings. I still wasn't sure of their consequences. After all, Alton still professed his desire for Alexandria and Bryce's marriage. He even appeared genuinely concerned when we learned of Alexandria's horrifying experience just yesterday.

According to Article XII, if anything happened to Alexandria prior to her ability to wed Bryce, both Alton and I would be left without access to

Montague assets. I supposed that it was my father's way of protecting his youngest heir.

What I couldn't understand was why Charles Montague II decided to add the codicil and why he did it just before his death. Could my father have known about Alton's mistreatment of me and regretted his earlier decisions and the faith he'd given to my husband?

My father was a proud and determined man who, in a moment of uncertainty about the future of his beloved company and assets, made a deal with the devil, using his daughter and granddaughter as collateral. The mere possibility that in my father's final days he'd decided to right that wrong gave me a new and unusual feeling of empowerment. Just maybe, for once, Charles Montague realized that his daughter and granddaughter were more important than Montague. Perhaps he saw the monster he'd helped create and with a sense of dread at what might happen upon his own demise, Charles II regretted his decision.

My newfound paternal appreciation was muddied with thoughts of his demise.

I held tightly to my wine glass, wrapping both hands around the globe.

The Montague Private Collection chardonnay sloshed within the goblet as I began to tremble. It was after six o'clock, yet since my discovery, I'd avoided my normal reds. The lighter white wine didn't dull my senses the way the red did. With my new knowledge of the codicil, I couldn't afford to slip into my previous preferred state of oblivion. However, as my thoughts volleyed and settled around thoughts of my father, I couldn't seem to control the way I shook. It was as if I were cold, despite my long-sleeved robe and the soft throw over my legs.

I closed my eyes and took a deep breath. No longer seeing the manicured lawns, I worked to calm the theories that vigorously bombarded my mind.

Maybe I should call for a cabernet?

I didn't want to consider the possibility that lingered outside of my consciousness: the idea that my father's death wasn't the result of his age. It wasn't the result of a high level of stress. That maybe—just maybe—there was a more sinister explanation and that explanation was the man who had slept beside me for nearly twenty years.

I'd be hard-pressed to compile a list of my husband's finer qualities, but never had I considered murder. Then again, my father was guilty of the same crime, and Alton had always strived to emulate Charles Montague.

Shaking my head, I lifted the crystal to my lips and enjoyed the unique blend of the Montague chardonnay. With a hint of citrus as well as pear, it went down smoothly, its light flavor teasing my palate but doing little to derail my train of thought.

I took another drink.

I couldn't think about my father's death. Instead, I needed to concentrate on what he'd done during his life—on the codicil. Since leaving Ralph's office, I had more and more questions. I planned to revisit Stephen once Alton left town again. I wanted to know who had viewed the will over the years and when. In all of Stephen's and my exploration, I'd forgotten to take a good look at the ledger. I also wanted to know which judge in Savannah had the fortitude to deny my husband his request to void the codicil. That would be a judge I'd want on my side.

Another question that lingered in my mind was how I could prove Alton's involvement in sabotaging the wedding. I was convinced that Alexandria was purposely persuaded to visit Del Mar the same week as Lennox Demetri was there.

My theory centered around Oren.

Over time, Alton had made innuendos, accusing me of infidelity. While I was certain that it was his own promiscuity that made him suspicious, more than once he'd mentioned Oren Demetri. Thankfully, Alton never had evidence. Our affair was the one endeavor that I managed to successfully conspire to keep under Alton's radar. Our rendezvous were well planned and orchestrated. Whenever the topic reared its ugly head, my obvious defense was Alton's reaction the night in New York after Oren and I had only spoken. Why would I risk my husband's wrath after that?

To Alton's knowledge, I'd never lied to him. In many ways, I believed he thought himself above my deception. What the great Alton Fitzgerald didn't realize was that I'd been taught to deceive by the best.

When I finally broke off my relationship with Oren, it was for one reason: I wanted more of him—his companionship, his adoration, his love. I wanted a life unlike anything I'd ever before known. I wanted it more than I wanted anything else.

Each touch, each kiss, each encounter was but a grain of sand filling the hourglass of my life. With him, I was no longer empty. As the individual grains began to accumulate, the need to be with him was all-consuming.

When we were apart, I thought of him and the way his pale blue eyes scanned my soul. The way he looked at me was more than a scan of my body. Oren Demetri saw inside of me. He knew my innermost thoughts, sometimes even before I did. His voice sent shivers down my spine. Even the memory of his tenor prickled my skin. His touch was like no other I'd ever experienced. A master at his craft, Oren never took, but gave in a way that made me hungry for more.

I'd almost agreed to Oren's requests, leaving Alton, Montague Manor, and everything I'd strived for in my life. He offered me a home and a life—not just me, but Alexandria too. In Oren's arms I no longer cared about my heritage or duties. In his embrace I was simply a woman, in love, being loved.

Such a simple concept and yet one so foreign.

I couldn't fight it any more. It had to stop.

If I'd spent one more second in his grasp, or one more grain of sand would have fallen into the pile at the bottom of my hourglass, the scale would have irrevocably tipped.

It would have pushed me over the edge.

I couldn't do it. My responsibilities screamed at me from the grave, in my father's voice. Generations of Montagues needed me to stay the course. We'd all sacrificed too much to give into emotion.

Yet sometime during those years of deception, I sensed that Alton knew. Not cognitively—he would have beaten me worse than before—but intuitively. That was why I believed he reasoned that Alexandria could possibly be attracted to Lennox. In my mind, it was a last-ditch effort on his part, but as the clock continued to tick, desperate times called for desperate measures.

My theories centered on Alton's belief in the old adage: like mother, like daughter.

His bet paid off.

Now all I had to do was prove his involvement. My next visit to Hamilton and Porter included a private discussion with Natalie, the secretary who'd mentioned Del Mar to Alexandria.

My subsequent sip of chardonnay lodged in my throat, the citrus flavor no longer smooth but coarse, as it refused to go down when accompanied by the bellow of my husband's voice.

"Adelaide!" He repeated my name, softer then louder as he neared the library.

Consciously, I forced the liquid down, struggling to turn off the pictures on my phone and finding my voice. "I'm in here."

"Why in the hell do you sit in here in the damn dark?"

The room filled with light as he hit the switch. As I blinked my eyes at the brightness, I pushed my phone under the throw and stood to meet him. I had no idea what had happened, but as he entered, the library filled with the cloud of rage that accompanied him.

Placing my glass on the nearby table, I seized my own suddenly chilled hands in an attempt to hide that my trembling from earlier had resumed. At the way the hairs stood tall on my arms, I deducted one thing—he knew about my visit to the lawyers. Defiantly, I lifted my chin and tried to recall the rebuttal I'd planned as my excuse. However, thoughts failed me as he continued his tirade.

"I sent the damn maid to find you and she came back empty-handed. Where the fuck have you been?"

Still scrambling with my defense, I stammered, "I-I've been here. I enjoy the view. It's still warm enough to have the windows open—"

"Everything is hitting the fucking fan!"

I stared up at his face, his chest near enough to mine that I felt the heat radiating from him. His normal crimson, the visible flush of his anger, seeped from his collar up his neck and over his cheeks.

"Everything? What are you talking about?"

"Come down to my office now. You need to know what's happened."

My hand fluttered near my neck as I took a step backward. My knees grew weak as I sank to the chaise. "Alexandria? What happened?"

Alton's eyes narrowed. "No, Adelaide, for once it's not your daughter who's trying to ruin everything."

My throat grew dry. I had to know what was in store. "Did I—"

He didn't let me finish. "Not everything is about you!" He scanned my attire. "Get down to my office. Don't worry about getting dressed. It's only Suzy and Bryce. This needs a family conference."

Relief and confusion replaced my initial anxiety.

I shook my head. It was after ten o'clock. Why in the hell were Suzy and Bryce in his office? "What happened?"

He turned abruptly around. "Just shut up and listen. You'll learn everything in a minute. We need to put a fucking stop to this circus."

I stayed rooted to the library floor, the bright lights now obscuring the peaceful view. In the large leaded windows I saw only my own reflection. For a moment, I watched as the woman in the glass straightened her shoulders and secured the ties of her robe.

This was my house. I'd long ago decided not to let my best friend's presence in any situation, even when we were categorized as *family*, intimidate me. If Alton wanted a family conference, I'd take my place as Mrs. Fitzgerald at that damn table and smile smugly at the whore who willingly made my life easier. Maybe when this was done, he'd find a reason to go into town—work perhaps—and I'd have a nice night's sleep.

"Adelaide, now!"

I refilled my glass, emptying the bottle upon the table and followed in the wake of Alton's displeasure.

CHAPTER 23

ADELAIDE

ONLY A FEW steps behind, I entered Alton's office and stepped into his cloud of malcontent. My eyes searched the regal room. Beyond the large windows was only darkness, a contrast to the stark illumination within. The bookcases, filled with treasures that belonged to my father and his father before him, created a colorful addition to the darkness of the wood trim. The air only moments before had been light and freely flowed into my lungs. Now, it was heavy, weighted down with something I didn't understand. No longer did it substantiate life: it suffocated, effectively snuffing out what before it had promoted.

Pressing my lips together, I assessed what had happened. All I'd been told was that the perpetrator of this offense was neither Alexandria nor I, for once. Considering the amount of tension hanging in the air like dark smoke, I was eternally grateful for the reprieve from being the center of yet another mishap. My best friend, Suzanna, stood uncharacteristically quiet, leaning against the far wall, her arms crossed over her breasts and a solemn look upon her face. Her eyes didn't seek to find me. Instead, they stayed set on Alton, pleading some unspoken request.

I'd seen their glances, their silent conversations shared by lovers. Despite everything Alton had done, seeing the way they looked at one another often left me feeling sad and empty. I wasn't my husband's love, his soul mate, or even his partner in life. I was merely his winning lottery ticket, the one he kept crumpled in his pocket. As long as it was there, he was rich beyond his wildest dreams, more powerful than any Fitzgerald before him, and in control of the kingdom bestowed upon him by Charles II.

Tonight was different.

The physical pain I saw in Suzy's eyes made me flinch. Something had happened, something that left her not only uneasy but fearful.

Questions crept into my consciousness—things I'd never allowed myself to think or at least to dwell upon. Had Alton abused her, the way he did me? Had he hurt her, with more than the pain of rejecting her to marry me? Did she know the things he'd done? Had he told her? Had she seen?

As I stared at her grave expression, I felt an unusual twinge of sympathy for my best friend. In her gaze, I read a tale. Perhaps it was the years we'd been friends. Perhaps it was because of what we'd shared. Whatever the cause, I saw it, plain and simple. She was a woman who'd sacrificed her dream of happiness for her son. A woman who'd given away the man she admired and adored to let him achieve his desires.

She was a woman who for the first time had truly seen the monster behind the mask. Suzanna was looking at Alton as if she'd just met him. As if she'd just seen the extremes to which he could and would go to make his dreams come true.

Anguish emanated from her as if she were seeing her dreams dashed for the first time. As if she were looking at the person to whom she'd stupidly given her past, present, and future, only to watch him casually hold it in his grasp, with the ability to crush it with one word.

Her dark eyes shone with a terror that I personally knew too well.

Bryce, on the other hand, was pacing near the far end of the conference table—angry, defiant, a caged lion—as heat radiated from his body. Never before had I noticed the resemblance to his biological father. I'd always allowed myself to associate his coloring with Marcus's. Truly, Suzanna's ex-husband and Alton hadn't been that different in their physical stature. But in this room, Bryce was Alton, complete with red leaching from his neck to his cheeks, and even his ears. The way his chest expanded and contracted with every breath stilled my steps. Though Bryce could be very different, in that second I knew he could also be his father, despite his ignorance of his true parentage.

I said a silent prayer of thanks to God for letting me know about the codicil and for a daughter who stood up not only to me, but also to Alton and—unbeknownst to her—her grandfather's wishes. I'd been wrong about the young man near the end of the table. Bryce wouldn't make Alexandria a good husband any more than Alton had made one for me.

Perhaps I had naïvely hoped that adding love and friendship to the equation would tame the beast within. Looking at Suzy and her current state of devastation, I knew that wasn't true.

Nothing could calm Alton's rage once it was ready to unfurl, and in my heart, I knew Bryce would be no different.

Quietly, unnoticed by the other occupants of the room, I slipped into my chair at the large table with my glass of wine firmly in hand. As if my entrance had opened a valve allowing some of the pressure to release, each participant slowly followed suit: Alton, Suzy, and finally at his father's prompting, Bryce.

I wanted to ask what had happened, what everyone else in the room knew, but I was better trained. I would learn when it was my turn to learn. This was Alton's show, and it would progress on his terms.

"I don't understand—" Bryce began.

"No!"

Suzy and I both sat taller at Alton's reprimand. Though I'd heard that tone directed at both Alexandria and myself, never had I heard him speak to Bryce with it.

Somewhere between a kicked puppy and a stunned shark, Bryce stopped, his gray eyes wide as he stared the length of the table.

Alton ran his hand through his thinning hair and stood, simply unable to contain his anger. His chest expanded and contracted. The sound of his labored breathing filled the office as we sat watching and waiting. I looked again toward Suzy.

Once again, our eyes didn't meet. Hers were downcast as a trail of tears made its way down her pale cheeks.

Confident of my innocence, I considered speaking. Before I could utter a word, Alton poured Cognac from a decanter into a crystal tumbler. One finger, two, he kept pouring. I bit my tongue as he took the glass to his lips and drank. His Adam's apple bobbed as the fiery liquid undoubtedly scorched his throat. He didn't stop.

Once the glass was empty, he turned and threw it into the fireplace. Everyone took a collective breath as shards of crystal fell like snow, littering the hearth. Had there been a fire, the reflections may have been beautiful; instead, they fell to the ashes, their luster extinguished.

"Maybe we should have told them." Alton spoke to the room.

Suzy's eyes met mine for the first time this evening, as they swirled with a combination of sadness and confusion.

No one dared speak.

"I can't even find the fucking words," Alton began as he sat with an exaggerated huff. "Bryce has taken it upon himself to secure a…" He shook his head searching for the right word. "…relationship."

Suzy's chin fell to her chest. No doubt she already knew the information that Alton was sharing with me.

"I-I don't understand," I said.

"He couldn't wait," Alton went on, each phrase louder than the one before. "I told him to wait. I told him to have faith in Alexandria, but he panicked."

Bryce's chin rose rebelliously. "I didn't panic."

Alton crossed his arms over his chest. "You imbecile. You have no idea of the mess you've made."

My thoughts spun. How could what Bryce had done be worse than the mess with Melissa? Yet never had Alton chastised Bryce in front of me during any of that—the accusations of abuse, rape, or even her disappearance.

"What did you do?" I asked Bryce, not confident enough in my innocence to ask Alton.

He shrugged. "Apparently, I fucked everything up. I don't know what *everything* is."

"Bryce, language," Suzanna reprimanded.

We all turned her direction.

Really? Your son has been accused of rape, abuse, kidnapping, and possibly murder and you're going to correct his language?

I didn't say that, but from the look on both Alton's and my face, I was certain we were both thinking the same thing.

"No, Suzy," Alton said, "Bryce's account is accurate. He fucked *everything*. I don't just mean an eighteen-year-old coed or Millie Ashmore or any other willing or unwilling partner. I mean *everything* that we've all strived to achieve."

Bryce leaned back against his chair, his arms crossed to mirror his father's. "Maybe if you'd tell me what everything means."

"It means your marriage with Alexandria."

Bryce's hands came down, slapping his palms against the table. "You don't think I've tried? I have. I tried while she was at Stanford. I went to California. I watched her, waiting for the right time to step back into her life. I asked her—no, begged her—to help me with the Evanston police, the deposition, the charges regarding Melissa.

"She has moved on. She's with Demetri now and won't even talk to me." Bryce stood and resumed pacing. "I can't go into that courtroom without some kind of defense. I need a credible alibi, a reason to disprove everything that Melissa's parents' attorneys throw our way." He turned toward Alton. "It's what the Montague legal team told me to do."

"And I told you that Alexandria was your person." Alton glared. "I told you that people would believe that story. You'd dated for years when you were younger. I said I was working on getting her home."

By doing what? I wanted to ask, but I couldn't interrupt their verbal back and forth.

Bryce shook his head. "Believe me, I'd force Alexandria if I could. But I can't get within fifty feet of her." His eyes narrowed. "And neither can you. So don't act as if this is all my fault. You've been saying she'll be back, but guess what? Melissa is still missing. The case is building. I didn't have anything to do with her disappearance, yet I'm at the top of their list of suspects."

Suzy and I turned back to Alton, our lips held tightly together as if respectfully watching a tennis match.

"How? How did you even learn about this… this business?" Alton asked.

Bryce lifted his brows knowingly. "From Melissa."

"She told you?"

"Yes. She wanted out of it. She said if we were together she could get out."

As the room fell silent, I found my voice. "What business? What are you talking about?"

When neither man spoke, finally Suzy volunteered, "It seems that Bryce purchased a companion."

I opened my eyes wide. "You bought a prostitute?" Then I thought some more. "So what?"

Both Alton and Suzy looked at me.

I went on. "So what? I mean, I'm not happy about it. Alexandria won't be happy, but really, who cares? Compared to abuse, rape, kidnapping… well, soliciting prostitution seems rather unimportant."

"Bryce didn't purchase a woman for a night," Alton explained. "He purchased her for a year."

Suzy nodded as my mouth opened.

"A year?" I asked. "You can do that?"

"It isn't sex, per se," Bryce said. "It's companionship. It's a ready-made relationship with a backstory that will provide the perfect alibi for my defense." He sat back down. "Alexandria would have been ideal, in more ways than one." He turned his gaze on me. "You know how much I've always loved her? But I can't wait, and frankly, I don't think waiting would do any good."

"There are things in the works," Alton said.

"Why?" Bryce asked. "Why is this such a big deal?"

"Bryce," Suzy began, "you know it has always been our dream for our families to unite…"

As she spoke, I stole a glance toward Alton. He was still on the edge of rage, on a warpath. Why? This could be his out. If my theory was correct that he'd intended to sabotage Alexandria and Bryce's wedding, this could be what he was looking for. Why then did he seem so upset?

Thoughts and theories continued to churn. If Alton hadn't been the one to tell Bryce about this company, then I suddenly worried that I wouldn't be able to prove Alton was responsible for the children not fulfilling the terms of my father's will. Could I have been wrong about my theory?

The reason Alton was enraged had to be the codicil.

If Bryce and Alexandria didn't marry, no longer would all of Montague holdings go to Fitzgerald Investments, as per our original agreement. With the codicil they'd go into probate. Alton could lose everything. Bryce would be left with nothing. The rightful heirs would succeed.

I worked to calm my excitement. Our salvation was in sight.

"There's more to this that you should know, Laide," my husband said.

Since he'd used my name, I assumed Suzy was already privy to the additional information. I tried to concentrate. "Okay?"

"Bryce, tell Adelaide the name of your companion."

"Alton," Bryce said, "it makes perfect sense. A relationship with Chelsea Moore justifies my trips to California. I can substantiate that we were together."

Chelsea Moore? What trips to California?

"Though you weren't," Suzy added.

"No, we weren't," Bryce confirmed. "But we can make it look like we were." He shrugged. "She's not bad looking and since she and Alexandria were roommates for four years, we have a plausible reason for not telling anyone about our relationship."

I lifted the wine glass to my lips and drank until every drop was gone. Placing the glass upon the table, I stared Bryce's direction. "That girl? She's a prostitute? My daughter was living with a prostitute?"

"It isn't really prostitution," Suzy said. "It's companionship, a relationship…"

My chest became tight. The answer was right before us, but I couldn't let him do this to my daughter. "No."

Everyone looked my way. "No," I repeated. "Bryce, you can't do that. Not to Alexandria. It'll kill her to think you slept with another of her best friends. Trust me, I know. This isn't right. I don't want my daughter living with that kind of pain."

His eyes shone as his lips fought the unavoidable need to move upward.

The wine in my stomach seemed to curdle as his cruel intentions suddenly became clear. "You little bastard!"

"Laide!" Alton and Suzy said in unison.

"You little piece of shit," I continued, glaring toward Bryce. "That's why you're doing this, isn't it? It isn't just about an alibi. You want to hurt Alexandria. She's with another man and you have your feelings hurt, so instead of manning up, you're hitting her where you know it'll hurt."

A mask of serenity covered what should have been Bryce's smug expression. He was the poster child for innocence. He had always been the boy who never did wrong, but was always wronged. The poor young man who'd been unjustly accused. His continence was perfected.

Maybe he wasn't just like his father. He had his share of his mother inside of him too. She'd taught him well how to wear the mask and only show the world what was intended for them to see.

"Adelaide, that's enough!" Alton bellowed. "We have more important concerns than Alexandria's hurt feelings."

I stood, confident that I didn't give a flying fuck what happened to Bryce. The codicil said that if the wedding didn't occur, all interested parties would have the chance to profess their claim to their rightful share. I was a Montague. My claim was set. If I had anything to say about it, the young man at the end of the table would be the one to suffer—he and his pathetic excuse for a father.

"You're right," I said. "I've done everything I could to follow my father's wishes. I have nothing to fear."

Alton's eyes narrowed. "What the hell? You read the will before we married. You know what'll happen if they don't wed."

My pulse quickened at my misstep. I turned toward my husband. "What I meant was that I have faith in you, dear. You took care of the original charges against Bryce. You'll make all of these other charges go away and then make that dreadful girl follow suit. By the time you do, even Alexandria will no longer care that he'd sought companionship in another of her friends. In the meantime, I'll do my best to convince Alexandria that Bryce's heart is still hers."

"This arrangement can't last a year," Alton said to no one in particular. "Just long enough to convince the lawyers to drop the charges."

"And then her usefulness will be done," I added.

"And then what? I'm here alone?" Bryce asked. "Hell no. I've paid for a year. Besides, I can't have two ex-girlfriends disappear."

"Not disappear, sweetheart," Suzy said. "Paid to go away. It's worked before."

I narrowed my eyes. "Before? Do you care to explain that?"

Marcus? She was talking about paying off Marcus, her ex-husband, I convinced myself.

Right?

CHAPTER 24

NOX

DESPITE OREN'S ARGUMENT to the contrary, my priorities were in line.

My testimony before the Senate committee was complete. I'd emphasized the points I'd set out to highlight. I'd talked with Senator Carroll, tried to get a feel for Severus Davis, and even learned more about the progress he'd hoped to achieve in our negotiations. I'd also introduced myself to Grant Higgins, the senator from the great state of Georgia, as well as the junior senator from Oregon. Now, the Senate Finance Committee's decision was in their hands.

The ruling could come down as early as tomorrow. I'd planned to stay in DC and face the committee as they justified their decision.

I'd like to say that I was confident the committee would call for the rewording of the bill, and that they would back our side—the side of Senator Carroll and others who understood the future ramifications in store in the event of overtaxation of domestic businesses.

I couldn't.

I didn't trust Higgins, Davis, or the swing votes.

Nevertheless, I wasn't willing to sacrifice my time on the chance that my presence in the hearing room would turn the tide.

It may have taken me years and obvious failure, but I had a new priority.

After listening to Charli's voice, full of emotion and confusion, as she told me about her cryptic conversation with Chelsea, I knew my presence in New York was more important.

As she spoke, I heard the distraught voice of Jo. I recalled how my days and nights of traveling upset her. Despite the experience of my childhood, seeing my mother's disappointment and sadness when my father would choose work over her, I'd done the same thing.

I had been responsible for putting the same sadness in my wife's eyes that I'd witnessed as a young child, and naïvely, I hadn't made the connection. At that time, I'd believed my work superseded all else—Demetri Enterprises needed me. Just like the company had needed my father. Unwittingly, I'd fallen into Oren's footsteps, wearing the same shoes and making the same mistakes.

Of course, back then, I hadn't seen my choices as mistakes. After all, I'd been told and conditioned to believe that real men didn't make mistakes. Every action and decision was a conscious choice. Everything had a purpose.

Like he was in so many other things, my father was wrong about that.

Real men did make mistakes. We made decisions for the right reasons, to accomplish the right outcomes, that in the end harmed others—ones we loved. Even though our choices weren't made with malice, that didn't lessen the pain they inflicted.

The real lesson, the one my father forgot to teach me—or maybe one he never learned—was that it wasn't about making mistakes. They were part of life. It was about repeating them. That was where the real men became separated from lesser men.

Character wasn't about perfection. It was about wisdom and the ability to learn and change.

If I were to talk to Oren, my father would tell me to stay in Washington and face the committee as they read the ruling. I could hear his voice echoing in my head. I'd followed that advice in the past. If I chose to do that again, I was the one who hadn't learned. I'd made that mistake before. I didn't intend to make it again.

That was why, late Thursday night—or very early Friday morning—

essentially, a day before I was meant to be back in New York, I was riding the elevator to Patrick's apartment, to the woman I loved. In her voice I heard her pain and holding her in my arms would trump Demetri Enterprises every time.

As I rode upward, my mind drifted to Jocelyn. Since Charli, I found myself thinking of my first wife with more appreciation and less sadness. With each day, the guilt over her death lessened as the gratitude for the time we shared strengthened. Jocelyn and I had both been so young. Fresh out of grad school, we thought we had all the answers when in reality we had much to learn.

I was ambitious and strived to show not only Oren, but also the world what I could accomplish. In that process, I'd neglected her. I'd pushed her to fight for my attention, causing me to do what no husband should do.

I'd reacted instead of responded.

I'd failed her.

Her death would forever be on my hands and my heart, but maybe, with Charli beside me, I could rise above it. Maybe Jo could smile down and wish me the happiness that since her death I'd deemed myself unworthy of having.

In the quiet elevator, I said a silent thank-you. "Thank you, Jo, for showing me the man I should be. You'll always be part of me. I'm sorry that I wasn't that man for you." I hung my head, keeping tears at bay. "I'll always regret the consequences of my decisions." I took a deep breath. "But in the end, because of you, I know that I'll do everything possible not to let that happen again."

As the doors opened, I blinked away the past.

The corridor was quiet since it was after midnight. I had no intention of waking the entire floor; however, I knew that Charli was here. She didn't know I was coming, and since landing, I'd been unable to reach her. That didn't matter. When she didn't answer, I checked the new app Deloris had installed on my phone. The GPS tracker in Charli's new necklace indicated that she was in Patrick's apartment. A quick call to Clayton confirmed her location.

It did my heart and mind good to know that she was still where she'd promised she would be. That was one of the many things I loved about Charli. She was young, but she wasn't immature. She didn't play games. She knew how important it was to me to know that she was safe. Even when she'd walked out of the apartment, she'd gone with Jerrod.

She'd also given me the opportunity to explain. I'd been the one who needed time. I still needed time, and thankfully, being the amazing woman she was, Charli was giving it to me.

If I were completely honest with myself, I understood Charli's desire to be with her cousin. After everything that had happened in the last few days, she didn't want to be alone in our apartment, the place where someone—someone she'd trusted, someone I'd told her she could trust—had betrayed her. Betrayed us. If being with Patrick gave her the comfort she needed, then that was where she should be.

Her choice of location was inconsequential. As long as she was wearing the necklace, Deloris had more than Clayton assuring her safety. After all, her well-being, both physical and emotional, was my goal.

As I neared Patrick's apartment, my arms ached with the desire to be the one to give Charli everything that she needed for her to feel safe.

During our conversation about Chelsea, Charli sounded heartbroken and confused. All I could get was that Chelsea had repeatedly apologized, saying that she'd never meant to hurt her. According to Charli, Chelsea had been nearly incoherent, crying and slurring her words.

Charli didn't get anything else from the conversation. She couldn't even figure out her best friend's location. Was Chelsea in DC? That was why Charli had called. I was there, and she asked if I could find Chelsea.

Unfortunately, it wasn't that easy.

It wasn't like Chelsea wore a GPS necklace.

It was true that I knew more about her friend than I let on, that Chelsea was working for Infidelity, had not been assigned to Severus Davis as we'd planned, and was quite possibly assigned to someone else—I didn't know who or where.

Though I couldn't tell Charli that Deloris was working to unravel the Infidelity web of deceit and free Chelsea. I could say that we were doing our best to find her friend.

Softly, my knuckles rapped on Patrick's door. A moment later, it opened, and Patrick's tired, light brown eyes peered from around the door. "She's asleep," he said as he opened the door wider.

"I figured. Sorry I woke you." I'd called his number after speaking to Clayton.

My gaze scanned Charli's cousin from head to toe. His middle-of-the-night persona didn't match his usual demeanor. Normally, Patrick was the epitome of chic, dressed to the T with a cocky kind of attitude that made you smile in approval and admiration, not turn away in disgust. In the short time I'd known him, I'd come to enjoy his gregariousness. However, in the middle of the night, wearing only an old faded Beatles t-shirt and gym shorts, he looked like any other guy in a dorm, well apart from his receding hairline. That made him obviously older than a coed.

I noticed the way his chest stayed inflated as he scanned me and shut the door.

"Sleep's overrated," Patrick said as he led me into his apartment.

It wasn't the first time I'd been inside his apartment. Charli had brought me here to meet him and Cyrus. The building where they lived was nice, more modern than mine, more so than most in the area. Currently the lights in his living room and entry were low and the windows were covered. During the day, I recalled that the apartment had a great view of the park.

It hadn't taken Deloris long to learn that Cyrus was in investment banking and Patrick was an interior design intern. Between the two of them, they were obviously doing well. I also knew how their relationship began. According to Deloris, they were on their second year of their agreement. I couldn't fault them for their part in Infidelity. Maybe the company did have its benefits.

"Alex was pretty upset about Chelsea," Patrick volunteered. "I have no idea what's going on with her and neither does Alex. After Chelsea called, Alex tried but she couldn't get Chelsea to answer her calls or texts. It's weird. Before Chelsea's call, Alex thought her friend was going to be here, like move to New York, possibly tomorrow…" Patrick shook his head. "…today, I guess. Poor thing, Alex has had a lot thrown at her in the last few months.

Losing her best friend wasn't supposed to be one of them."

I felt more than a pang of guilt. "I'm responsible for most of what's been thrown at her."

Patrick stood taller. "Not the way I see it."

I let out an exaggerated breath. "Well, I don't know how *you* see it." Since Charli was asleep in the other room, I tried to keep my voice down. "The other day she was in the line of gunfire because of me."

"The news said that the victim was the intended target, a domestic thing."

That was what the news said, and I knew how they'd been led in that direction. It was a cover to take the heat off of me, to make Charli's and my presence at the scene fade away as unimportant background information.

"I can still feel responsible," I said, turning to take in the semidark living room and wondering which hallway would lead me to my Charli.

"Yes, sure," Patrick said, bringing my focus back to him, "you can feel responsible. But if you were the cause of more of her heartache…" His tone suddenly became more confident than cocky. "…I wouldn't have let you in."

My eyes widened, amused that this little runt thought he could stop me.

"I wouldn't," Patrick confirmed, as if reading my thoughts. "You don't know half the shit she's put up with in her life. She's a lot stronger than you think."

I didn't know much of her past, but I never doubted her strength. "I think she's strong."

"Yet you ran here to rescue her?" Patrick asked. "So that you could tell her what to do?"

What the hell?

It was my turn to stand tall, at least ten inches taller than him. "I'm not *rescuing* her. I'm not sure what's happening with Chelsea, but I do know Charli cares about her. I don't plan to tell her what to do. I'm here to help her." I wasn't sure why I felt the need to explain my actions to him, but I went on. "I'm here to support your cousin. Help her."

The expression of protective brother that Patrick had been wearing since he opened the door morphed into a smile as he nodded. "Right answer. That's exactly what my little cousin needs. She's had people telling her what to do her entire life."

Oh, I liked telling her what to do, but not about her life or her friends. My demands were more in the directives that included getting her on her knees or lifting her hands so I could bind them. Though that thought sent my blood rushing south, that wasn't what I sought tonight.

Tonight I simply wanted to hold her. I'd also like to know more about what Patrick was saying, more about Charli's life, more about Alexandria Collins. I wanted to know everything. Not because she owed me an explanation or I demanded one, but because I wanted to share everything in her life, present, past and future.

A pang of guilt flitted across my conscience.

If I want to know all about her, then I owe her the same.

"She…" I said, ignoring the inner voice, "…doesn't talk much about her life before Stanford."

"It's not my place to say, but if you ask me, in some ways, Alex started living when she went out west. Unfortunately, what she was doing before—living or merely surviving—is trying to suck her back into its black-hole abyss."

My neck straightened, the hairs on my arms standing to attention with his warning. I could only assume that he was referring to the calls and even the letter telling her to go back to Savannah.

Patrick was right. It wasn't his place to tell me. It was up to Charli. But if it was that serious, then we needed to talk.

"Thanks for taking my call," I said, "and for letting me in. I should take her back to our place and let you get some sleep."

Patrick moved his head back and forth. "No, man, let her rest. I'll show you to her room." His lips quirked to a grin. "And for the record, as I said earlier, if you'd not given me the right answer, I'd be showing you the door out of here."

My brows rose. *You and what army?* That was what I wanted to say, but instead, I smiled.

Patrick was obviously protective of my Charli, and I liked that. I knew from experience I couldn't always be around. I could have Deloris, Isaac, and

Clayton nearby. Charli could wear a GPS necklace that allowed me to see her exact location at the touch of an app, but nothing compared to having someone who loved you looking out for you. If this runt was willing to take me on for her, he was all right in my book.

"Glad I met your approval." This time they were his brows that rose, and I suddenly remembered which way his boat sailed.

"Oh, yes, you do. But since we're both taken, and you bat for the other team, might as well let Alex have the fun."

I just laughed as I followed him down a hallway.

Patrick stopped at a door and inclined his head. "Help her." He flattened his lips to a straight line. "Oh and that thing I mentioned about sleep, about it being underrated? Well, I do have work tomorrow… or today… so keep it down."

I didn't take orders well, but there was something in his voice that caused my smile to grow as I nodded.

He turned and walked away as I reached for the knob and turned it. Pushing the door open, I searched the room, and as my eyes adjusted, I saw small slits of light from the night sky that fell from between the blinds. Illuminated by stripes of moonlight and stretched out on a bed smaller than the one we usually shared was my Charli, her body covered with blankets. Her beautiful hair flowed over the pillow, the auburn waves more brown than red in the semidarkness. As I inched closer, I watched as her chest rose and fell in a quiet rhythm. She was sound asleep. Every muscle of my body ached to lean down and kiss her slightly parted lips, to wake her and explore some of the demands that had skirted across my thoughts just moments ago.

Instead, I pulled my phone from my slacks pocket and pounded out a text message.

Me: "PICK ME UP AT THE FRONT OF PATRICK'S BUILDING AT 6. I'M SPENDING THE REST OF THE NIGHT HERE."

Isaac: "YES, SIR."

Laying my phone on the bedside stand, I eased out of my clothes, leaving them folded on a nearby chair. With only my boxers remaining, I locked the door. Another door was slightly ajar and I found a bathroom. It'd been a long day. The tall shower looked incredibly inviting. It would feel wonderful to get in and wash it all away, but the pull from the woman in the bed was too strong. She was a magnet that I couldn't resist.

After I finished in the bathroom, splashing my face with water and quickly using her toothbrush, I returned to the bedroom. Pulling back the blankets, my cheeks rose. Usually, Charli slept in nothing, or maybe she started in a nightgown but by the time we fell asleep, her warm skin was fully at my disposal. Tonight she was wearing soft shorts and a shiny top with delicate straps that draped over her slender shoulders. Even in the dimness, I saw goose bumps materialize as she shivered at the loss of blankets. Still asleep, she pulled her arms and legs closer to her body.

I eased into the bed, spooning behind her. With my chin above her head as I settled against the soft pillow, my nose wrinkled as her hair tickled it. Flowers and perfume filled my lungs as her round ass fit perfectly against my hips. For the first time since I'd left her in Westchester County, I relaxed, each and every muscle in my body releasing tension as I wrapped her in my arms and she melted against me.

With a deep sigh, I covered us with the blankets.

All at once, Charli gasped and tensed. Then she turned, her small hands moving up my chest and framing my face. In the darkened room, her eyes opened, blinking as if she couldn't comprehend what she was seeing.

"Y-you're here?" Her voice was thick with sleep.

I kissed her forehead and nodded, my kisses raining downward over her nose and finally her lips. "Yes, princess, I'm here."

"But, why? You're in Washington."

"No. I was in Washington. Now I'm here. You are more important than anything there or anywhere."

She shook her head. "You shouldn't have. I don't want to interrupt your work."

I pulled her closer, the soft material of her top doing little to cover the pebbling her earlier chill had brought to her nipples, now against my bare chest. "Never, ever, think anything is more important than you. You were upset."

Charli continued to move her head back and forth. "No, Nox. It's what he said. I don't want to do that to you. I'll be upset. You don't have to take care of me or rescue me."

He said?

"I don't have to," I confirmed. "I want to. I want to be there for you, when you're upset, when you're happy…" My hands roamed down the small of her back and over her round ass. "…and whenever you breathe."

Charli sighed as she melted against me and tilted her head against my chest. "Thank you."

I started to ask her what she was talking about when she said something about it being what *he* said, but by the way her body fit perfectly against mine, the way her breathing steadied, and the way she relaxed in my arms, I let her sleep.

"I love you, princess."

Her unspoken contentedness was all I needed to drift away.

CHAPTER 25

Fifteen years ago

OREN

PEOPLE EASED THEIR way between tables, filling most of the chairs. I watched as some people took more than their fair share of space. For a weeknight, the little restaurant off the beaten path was crowded. It was a local treasure. Tourists liked the flashy new places, but this was where the residents congregated, where the food and drinks never disappointed. From my vantage point, I could see the entire room. It was mostly filled with couples, sipping wine and talking close. That was what couples did: they leaned near one another and shared their space, their breath.

If I were home, I might be doing that. Who was I kidding? More than likely not.

I glanced again at my watch. I was early, waiting for Vincent to arrive. It was one of those meetings that I couldn't or wouldn't miss. Since he'd taken over the family business, my command appearances were required less frequently than they'd been under Carmine's regime. Since Carmine had passed away, somehow Vincent's less frequent requests made them seem more significant, as if each one was of extreme importance.

It didn't matter that it was nearly ten o'clock or that I'd promised Angelina I'd be home early tonight. My marriage and the happiness of it was less of a concern to Angelina's cousin than it had been to her uncle.

Vincent was all about profit, money, and keeping it flowing.

The world was changing and my attempt at legitimate business was the kick-start the Costellos needed and utilized. While his father had been more old-school, Vincent was younger—my age—and saw the promising ways of the future: the new millennium and technology.

No longer did families need bodies on every corner, watching from the shadows. Surveillance technology was the new answer. One man could watch dozens or more places of business. Conversations could be heard, everything up to the dropping of a pen. Secrets were getting harder and harder to conceal, and it was just the way Vincent liked it.

The guys younger than us admired his fortitude as well as his savvy. Vincent was branching out by including other families, ones his father had ignored.

I had to admit that Angelina's cousin was smart. He also had a level head. It was a lethal combination.

The families weren't the only ones with the ability to listen and record. Hell, the feds had done it to them in the eighties. Now it was sleeker and more sophisticated and didn't require the muscle of the old days. Cameras and bugs uncovered dirt—knowledge. As they say, knowledge was power.

Vincent Costello was all about power.

I looked down at the screen of my Blackberry. The little handheld device was revolutionary. I could check email, look up information on my companies, see stocks in real time, and even send messages to my wife.

The problem was with receiving messages from Angelina. She had to send them first.

From my Manhattan office I texted her after I'd received Vincent's call and explained that there wasn't time for me to go home to Westchester and then make it back to Brooklyn. At the most I would have been home for an hour or two.

It made more sense for me to stay at the office and do my daily analysis.

She'd yet to respond.

Some of the different companies, businesses, enterprises—whatever I called them—beneath the Demetri umbrella required constant supervision. Ledgers needed to be watched. In the world of business, I had many qualified employees, vice presidents and CEO's of minor subsidiaries. I didn't trust one of them, not one.

Thankfully, as technology improved so did my ability to oversee. I had daily, weekly, and monthly reports. I had accountants who double-checked the first set of accountants. It was a checks-and-balances system to rival any, and it worked. Demetri Enterprises was growing, buying, and expanding. I'd moved beyond the boroughs, beyond the East Coast.

In the last year, I'd taken Demetri Enterprises international.

London was ripe for everything financial. The time zone alone set it apart.

More and more production was happening in Asia. At the start of business in London, it was the close of business in Japan and by noon, New York was waking. No wonder it was the financial mecca. And the farther I ventured from New York, the more independent Demetri Enterprises became. Of course, it wasn't completely free of family obligation. If it were, I'd be home right now, instead of sipping a watered-down whiskey and waiting for the rest of my party to join me.

I checked my Blackberry again. Nothing from Angelina.

No doubt, she was pissed off.

Again.

I'd promised to be there. Tonight was a dinner with a new family that had moved in down the street. Part of the appeal of Rye for me had been the large parcels of land. It wasn't like the brownstones in Brooklyn, one right on top of the next. In Westchester County we didn't need to know our neighbors. That wasn't my wife's attitude. She thrived on people and community.

I tried, I did. But I didn't have time for backyard barbeques or football games or any of the other thousands of things she wanted to do.

If it weren't for Silvia—Carmine's present for doing my duty nearly five years ago—I'd feel guiltier.

Who would have thought of a person as a gift?

That was essentially what Silvia had been. Five years older than Lennox, Carmine gave her to us. Yes, she was meant to help Angelina around the house, but she'd also become ours to raise. Over the last five years, her role had gone from domestic help to something between a younger sister and daughter for Angelina. At least once she was with us it stopped the talk about another child.

Fifteen years old when she arrived, Silvia was nervous and uneducated. Domestic work was all she'd ever done. Her biological mother basically sold her off as house staff to the Costellos when she was barely a teenager.

It could have been worse for her. Unfortunately, I'd been around enough to see that too. But Angelina wasn't satisfied with a maid: she insisted on more. Silvia became her new obsession. That wasn't to imply that she neglected Lennox—she didn't. With a son and a daughter, Angelina was busy day and night.

Under Angelina's tutelage, Silvia studied, passed her GED, and was now enrolled in college courses. Of course, she also helped take care of the house and was—to my great surprise—an excellent cook. In many ways Silvia had become my wife's best friend. The change in Silvia's demeanor since she arrived was nothing short of phenomenal. She was now confident, a quick learner, and everything that Angelina would want in a daughter. Not to mention she wasn't homely.

When she first came to us, Silvia had been skinny and lanky. That wasn't the case today. Though her heritage wasn't Italian, she'd perfected the behavior. If she were met on the street, no one would know that she wasn't a member of our family or that she'd once been sold off as nothing more than a maid.

The bell on the front door of the restaurant jingled, alerting me that someone was entering or exiting. I recognized the two men walking my direction and stood as Vincent and Jimmy-the-enforcer approached. Jimmy had worked faithfully for Carmine until his death. Vincent obviously appreciated his service. Having Jimmy the man beside the head of the family was one of the few things that hadn't changed.

"Oren," Vincent said with a nod as he sat, the three of us crowding near the far end of the table, back to the wall. Basic survival strategy.

Almost immediately the dark-haired waitress was back to our table. On her tray she had Vincent's and Jimmy's drinks. There wasn't any need to take their order—everyone knew who they were and what they drank. In this part of town, they were regulars. Their table was always ready.

"I'm glad I was in town when you called," I said, "What's this about?"

"Montague."

I almost choked on my whiskey as the name rolled off his tongue. Though I hadn't thought about Russell Collins on a daily basis, the job Carmine had sent me on was the turning point in my life and career. I'd done my best to forget the choices made in California. It had been a risk and not one I wanted to repeat.

More than once I'd thought about the wife and daughter Russell Collins described. I may have even looked them up, taken a small peek into their lives. Perhaps it was a sense of debt that I felt for my part in the price Russell had paid.

"I recall that name," I said nonchalantly. "What about it?"

"I don't know for sure how their paths crossed or why," Vincent began as a prelude to whatever he was about to ask of me. "From what my father told me, there was something about shipping, transporting tobacco up and down the coast. Montagues are best known for their tobacco. High quality.

"Anyway," Vincent continued, "my father was able to reach some remarkable deals with the dockworkers. It was the seventies, the energy crisis. Before the big roundup and sting. Families had more respect. Old man Montague, who wasn't too old then, was grateful.

"Years later Montague helped my father out of financial straits. There was a debt my father owed, one that with accruing interest put more than a few of our family's assets at risk. Exhausting his usual options, my father went to Montague. They were even. Until…"

I didn't need to hear until. I knew *until.* "Yes, I know that part. Now what?"

"The old man wants our help again. The description fits him now. He's getting older and concerned about the future of his name and company."

I stared into the melting ice cubes as I spun them mindlessly in my glass. "Cut to the point, Vinny. I'm not—"

Vincent's large hand fell to the table, loudly and very close to mine. "Oren, careful. We're family, but even family is respectful. Tell me that you're respectful."

"Yes. I'm respectful and thankful for all of the help…"

"Surveillance."

"What?" I asked.

"You know that we have some of the best equipment with some of the best people who watch out for our interests. Talking to Montague made me realize how everyone could benefit from that technology. Under your umbrella, you will form a security company. We'll use our guys. It will look and sound legit."

I clenched my teeth as he continued to describe his plan for a new subsidiary of Demetri Enterprises.

"One of the first jobs," he went on, "and let me say, a lucrative one at that, will be for Montague."

I shook my head. "In his factories? On the dock? In his office buildings? What are we talking about? How many hubs? Round the clock?"

"You get it started. Do what you do. Get other jobs so this one doesn't stand out, but the main goal is his home and corporate office."

His home?

I'd seen it when I checked on Collins's wife and daughter. The thing was a castle. It was just missing the moat.

"Have you seen his home?" I asked.

Vincent's eyes widened. "I have. Why have you?"

"I did my research after… California."

"Then you know he has a daughter and his wife's remarried?"

I shrugged as if I hadn't paid that close of attention to Russell Collins's widow. As if I hadn't watched her more than once in Savannah or seen her and her little girl.

That night, years ago, at the bar, Collins had described his marriage as one from hell with a wife as cold and frigid as a witch's tit. But that wasn't what I'd seen. If I'd allow myself to have any feelings, one way or another, regarding Collins or his widow, I'd admit that I was glad she'd found someone after the death of her husband. She was too young and beautiful to spend the rest of her life alone.

"Yes, I'd heard she had," I replied casually.

"Old man Montague wants to be sure the new husband is the man to keep Montague going. He wants to know without a doubt that when he passes to the afterworld, Alton Fitzgerald will look after the Montague name and legacy."

"And this can't be done with an established company?"

"Not if it's to be kept under wraps. He doesn't want anyone at Montague to be the wiser. No one will know but the old man."

I'd grown cold over the years, but I wasn't dead, not yet. Murder would have been a quicker favor. Nevertheless, I was relieved that it hadn't been the request that he'd made. Setting up a front for some cameras and bugs could be done with a lighter conscience—assuming I still had one.

"Give me a month or two," I said. "It takes time to get the permits and set up the real estate."

"No more than two."

Vincent downed the rest of his drink and slapped the glass on the table. "Tell my cousin I said hello."

"I will." *If she's talking to me.*

"One more thing, how's Lennox doing?"

My chest tightened. Vincent had been the one I'd specifically asked to keep Lennox out of the family business. "Busy. He's in school, playing all kinds of sports. You know Angelina, she wants him involved in everything."

"Everything except the family business?"

"He's only fifteen."

"Do you have any idea what I knew at fifteen?" Vincent asked.

"Two months," I promised, avoiding the subject. "I'll have the security company up and running in two months."

Vincent patted my shoulder. "Luca wants to get the cousins together this summer. New boat."

"Give Angelina a call. She's in charge of our social calendar."

"Until next time."

"Next time," I repeated, as I stayed seated and watched him and Jimmy turn their backs my direction and walk casually toward the exit.

The bell on the door jingled.

CHAPTER 26

CHARLI

WAS THAT A DREAM?

As wake and sleep intermingled and the morning sun eased through the blinds, the question floated through my mind.

Stretching my arms and legs across the mattress, the soft sheets caressed my bare skin as the newly familiar, wonderful ache of contentment settled into my core. Despite my hand only finding an empty bed, I knew the answer to my question: it'd been real.

A smile tugged at the corners of my lips as my fingertips skimmed from my new necklace down to my bare breasts, running circles around my overly sensitive nipples. With a satisfied moan, my hands moved farther down my naked body. When I'd gone to sleep, I'd been wearing pajamas.

Now, I wasn't.

My smile blossomed fuller as I turned my head to inhale the masculine, woodsy scent of Nox's cologne that lingered upon the cool pillow beside me. I'd heard that smell was the strongest of our senses when it came to memories and arousal. With my eyes closed, the unique fragrance transported me to the presidential suite in Del Mar and the first time I'd smelled the remarkable scent. I warmed at the recollection of Nox's jacket as he'd placed it upon my shoulders.

It wasn't a dream.

Nox had been here beside me, with me, and inside of me.

Despite the multiple glasses of wine I'd consumed last night, I'd had trouble falling asleep, distraught and confused over Chelsea. I still didn't understand why she'd been apologizing, why she wouldn't talk, or why I couldn't reach her after her call. After tossing and turning, I'd decided to take the sleeping pill Patrick had offered.

Within minutes, my eyelids grew heavy, and a restless sleep ensued until at some time during the night, a strong arm pulled me against a solid chest. Wrapped in Nox's warm embrace, my world righted. I recalled turning in his arms and facing him, touching his handsome face. In the darkness, his features were hidden, yet under the tips of my fingers I *saw* his prominent cheekbones, scruffy cheeks, and chiseled jaw. I didn't need to see the light blue of his eyes to convince myself that Nox was real. His presence filled not only the bedroom and bed, but also my soul.

With him beside me, I'd drifted into a deeper slumber. Nox's presence hadn't taken away my concern over my best friend, but his presence alone had lessened my burden, allowing me to share my concerns and sleep soundly.

Now, as I started to shift the blankets, I recalled that we'd not only slept, but early this morning as Nox woke, we'd done rather more than that.

Still groggy, I'd awakened to my favorite alarm—the pleasurable probing of Nox's morning erection slowly grinding against the small of my back. As his large fingers splayed over my tummy, pulling me closer and moving downward, my core clenched and more than my consciousness awakened. So had my wanton desires.

In those early hours, I became lost in the sensation that was Nox. My eyes barely fluttered open as my pajamas disappeared, and he stretched and filled me in the most delicious way. As he moved, my back arched in pleasure and his lips found mine. Each breath in and out—warm and heady as our chests heaved skin against skin—gave the other person the air essential for life. It was as if the oxygen and carbon dioxide could only be found in the other. Without our exchange of breaths, I would have ceased to exist. For a time, the world beyond our bubble was forgotten. My every thought was consumed with the man above me, holding me, dominating my world, and making love to me.

His presence satisfied me while his words offered comfort. Declarations of his love and professions of my worth filled a void that my friend's odd behavior had created.

After Nox started my morning with a series of satisfying detonations, he kissed me goodbye and apologized for leaving so early. The last thing he'd said before I drifted back to sleep was that he'd see me tonight at our apartment.

As I recalled the conversation—or his statement and my sleepy acceptance—his parting words may have been more of a dictate, but I didn't care. I wanted to be back in our space. I hadn't been there since I'd walked out on him the night I'd received that letter.

Though that had only been three days ago, with all that had happened, it seemed like a lifetime.

I still didn't know exactly what had happened to Jocelyn, but I knew that I trusted the man who'd surprised me in my bed as I'd slept. I also believed Patrick trusted him. If he didn't, I suspected that my cousin wouldn't have allowed Nox into my room. No matter how dominating Lennox Demetri could be, Patrick was half Fitzgerald. I knew from experience that blood gave Pat more than his fair share of stubbornness.

It wasn't until I woke again over an hour later that I even realized that we'd made love in my cousin's apartment. My cheeks reddened as I imagined meeting Patrick in the kitchen.

Nearly forty minutes later, I did, both of us dressed and ready for our days.

"Little cousin, did your night get better?" Patrick asked as I came into the kitchen.

My shoulder lifted nonchalantly as I unsuccessfully kept a goofy grin from overtaking my face. "I slept better than I expected."

"Hmm."

"What?" I asked.

"Nothing, I'm just making an observation."

I stopped opening the container of Greek yogurt and looked down at myself. After I'd awakened alone, I'd taken a shower and dressed. Despite Nox's approval of my post-sex scent, I'd been sure to cleanse it away. My ballet flats showed from the cuffs of my skinny jeans rolled fashionably above my ankles and my blouse fell to below my waist. My hair was plaited off to one side, lying upon my shoulder in a braid of amber, and my makeup was sparse but fresh.

Pursing my lips, I looked back to Patrick. "What are you observing?"

His cheeks rose. "My beautiful little cousin—happy, and if I'm completely honest, rather satiated, too."

I shook my head as I peeled back the yogurt's lid. "Am I wearing a sign or were we too loud?"

He laughed. "Neither. I just like seeing you happy. Really happy. I'm not sure I've ever seen you glow like that—ever."

"I am," I admitted as I shrugged and lifted the spoon near my lips, "I can't explain it. It's not as if I've forgotten about Chelsea. I haven't. I have no idea what's happening with her. I hope to figure it out, but in the meantime, there's something about Nox that I've never experienced before. He makes me feel…" My breakfast began to blur with welling tears. "…special."

Patrick stepped down from the barstool and came around the counter, wrapping his arm around my shoulder. His cologne filled my senses, making me smile. "Don't cry. You deserve this. It doesn't matter how it happened. Don't think about that. I feel the same way about Cy. We're the lucky ones."

A twinge of guilt settled over me—I hadn't been thinking about Infidelity. Instead of correcting his assumptions, I said, "Damn, Pat, you smell great! I'm surprised Cy doesn't keep that cologne locked up. I mean, it's divine!"

Patrick's brown eyes sparkled. "He's coming home tonight. After the wake-up I heard this morning, I'm not sorry we'll have the place to ourselves."

"You're kicking me out?"

"Never! I assumed that Mr. Good-looking wanted you home."

It was true, he did. But I felt refreshingly playful. "Then you're saying that I cramp your style?"

Pat took a step back and swept his hand over his chest. "Do I look like my style is ever cramped?"

I laughed. "No, not at all. But you're right. I'm going back to our place tonight. Thanks for letting me stay."

"You know that you're always welcome."

"Always? Even when you're wanting *alone* time?" I wiggled my brows.

He kissed my forehead. "Always."

After my breakfast, I packed my few things, called Clayton, and wheeled my luggage with my backpack and purse down to the lobby. No sooner had I stepped from the glass doors that my driver pulled up to the curb.

"After you drop me off at class, can you please take my things back to Mr. Demetri's apartment?"

"Yes, ma'am."

That was the extent of our conversation as we weaved through the morning traffic, moving from the Upper East to the Upper West Side.

AS THE KEY turned in the lock of our apartment door, my chest constricted with an unhealthy sense of trepidation. It had been three days since I'd walked out of here. Three days since I'd read the letter.

Did I know any more than I had that night?

I knew that Nox had implied that he felt a responsibility in Jocelyn's death, but never had he said he'd hurt her. My heart refused to allow that possibility to linger in my thoughts. I took a deep breath. My complicated man wasn't ready to tell me more, and as curious as I was, I respected his privacy as he had mine.

The aroma of heaven in the oven met me as I opened the door. Without hesitation, I dropped my backpack near the door, secured the locks, entered my code on the keypad, and made my way toward the kitchen.

The table near the large windows was set for two, complete with unlit candles. The way the wax beaded along the tall spindles made my tummy flip and lower muscles clench—after our night in Del Mar, I'd never look at candle wax the same way again. Wine glasses were waiting for their contents while plates awaited our meal. A bottle of oil sat near the candles and next to a basket of bread, its crust crisp while the center appeared decadently soft.

On the counter I found a note from Lana and grinned as I read what she wrote:

Miss Collins/Mr. Demetri,

I trust that this won't be another meal that I end up dishing into your trash. I hope you enjoy it. It is the menu you requested.

Happy dining,
Lana

I hadn't requested it. That meant Nox had.

The way my stomach growled told me that I had no intention of letting this meal join the others that had apparently been thrown away. I eased the oven door open. Hot air hit my face warming the chain of my new necklace as a brief burning sensation surrounded my neck. Reaching for the platinum cage holding the pearl, I inhaled the succulent scent. Cheeses bubbled with red sauce in the pan of lasagna. I had the distinct feeling that Lana wouldn't use frozen meatballs if she were to make spaghetti.

I checked my phone to see if I'd received a text from Nox. In the short time we'd lived together, he was pretty good at letting me know if he was to be late.

There was only one text. It was from Jane's phone, but I knew before I read the message that it wasn't from Jane.

Mother: "I'M SORRY YOU DON'T WANT TO COME HOME OR TALK. THIS ISN'T ABOUT WHAT HAPPENED OR YOUR REFUSAL TO COME HOME. THERE IS SO MUCH I SHOULD HAVE TOLD YOU. TIME WAS RUNNING OUT. BUT I'VE SINCE LEARNED MORE.

I NEED TO TELL YOU. I KNOW IF I DO, YOU'LL KNOW WHAT

TO DO. ALEXANDRIA, YOU'RE SO SMART. SO INDEPENDENT. SO MUCH LIKE YOUR FATHER. PLEASE AGREE TO SEE ME. I'LL MEET YOU IN NEW YORK. ALTON WILL BE LEAVING NEXT WEEK. CALL THIS PHONE AND TALK TO JANE. LET HER KNOW WHEN WOULD BE THE BEST TIME.

I'M NOT TRYING TO INTERRUPT YOUR SCHOOLING. BUT THIS NEW INFORMATION IS VITAL TO BOTH OUR FUTURES.

PLEASE, PLEASE, RESPOND.

LOVE, YOUR MOMMA"

I stared down at the screen and wished that it would all go away. I wished that it had never happened, that she'd never married Alton, that my father had never died. I wished for a life of happiness and security.

Slowly, the room around me came back into focus, as well as the table that was set and the uncertain time of my boyfriend's arrival. Suddenly, even that uncertainty made me smile. In Savannah, dinner was always at seven. There were few exceptions to that rule.

Mr. Lennox Demetri and his affinity for rules didn't include mundane things like the time for dinner, and like most other things about Nox, I liked that. I'd found what I'd always sought—a life that was real, happy, and secure with just the right amount of spontaneity.

As I debated the response I'd give my mother, I turned the oven to warm, made my way back to my office with my backpack, and apprehensively reached for the light switch. I'd spoken to both Deloris and Clayton and been reassured that the apartment was secure, but each room held a slight amount of apprehension for me.

Turning on the light, I let out a breath at the order on my desk. The note that had started this chain of events was gone. Everything was as it had been.

Remembering my surprise I'd had for Nox that fateful night, I made my way to our bedroom. The bed was made, pillows covering the headboard. But my attention went to the middle of the bed, the place where I'd left my vibrator. It was gone.

Knots formed in my empty stomach as I imagined Bryce or even Jerrod seeing it. Maybe it was Deloris. My knees grew weak as I sank to the edge of the large king-sized mattress and worked to fight my embarrassment. It wasn't as if they all didn't know what Nox and I did, that we had sex, but that didn't mean I wanted them seeing proof of it.

And then I remembered Jane finding my vibrator in Savannah.

I lay back on the bed and pulled out my phone. Instead of texting, I hit the call button and looked at the clock. It was nearly seven. I hoped that Alton and Mother would be eating or having pre-dinner cocktails. Either way, I thought it might be a time when Jane could talk.

She answered on the second ring. "Child, you called!"

My entire body warmed at the robust sound of her voice through my phone. "Yes, Jane, I did. I wanted to talk."

"Well, you know what time it is. You know your momma is getting ready for dinner."

I nodded, though she couldn't see me. "Yes, I know that things never change in Savannah. I wanted to talk to you."

"To me?" she asked.

"Yes. Since things never change in Savannah or with my momma, I thought maybe if I talked to you…"

Jane's tone slowed in the way it did when she wanted me to listen. "Things do change. Some of it… well, it's kind of slow. But it happens. Don't be so hard on your momma. She's done her best." An edge of excitement came into her voice. "And, well, some of the changes, they're good."

I lifted my head, my elbows supporting my weight. "Tell me."

"It isn't my place to tell. But your momma, she wants to talk to you."

"What? You said *good*. So she isn't ill, is she?" I remembered Bryce telling me that she wasn't well a month ago in California.

"No, nothing like that," Jane said. "Changes. This old place ain't seen changes in, well, in a long time."

I shook my head. "Tell her…" I took a deep breath. "…tell her that I can talk to her."

"Child, I will. She probably call you back on my phone."

"All right. I'll be waiting. But…"

"What is it?"

"I'm staying here. I'm working hard, and I want my dream."

"Alex, honey, that's all anybody wants, they dream. Everybody has them. Your momma, she wanted that too."

My teeth raked my lower lip. "Did she ever get it?"

"It's not too late—it's never too late, not until the good Lord calls us home. I'll tell her you called."

Her answer gave me a little bit of hope and at the same time filled my mind with new questions.

Why had I never thought of my mother as having her own dreams? Or could her dreams have been for me? What had she sacrificed for those dreams? Was Jane right? Was there still time?

"Thank you, Jane."

"You remember?" she asked.

My cheeks rose, just as they had since I was old enough to remember. "Yes, I remember."

"Prettier inside—that's what you are. And on the outside, you's beautiful."

"I love you."

"You know I love you," Jane replied, before the line went dead.

My lungs filled with air just before I collapsed back onto the bed with an exhale. The search for my lost vibrator was forgotten as my brief conversation with Jane replayed in my mind. Unbeknownst to me, tears leaked from the corners of my eyes, emotions I never intended to shed. I hated Savannah, but there were parts, like Jane and even my mother, that continued to call to me, to pull me back.

They were pieces of who I'd been, or maybe they were part of who I was today.

Alexandria? Alex? Or Charli…?

Perhaps it took all three—the scared little girl, the independent young woman, and the woman ready to trust and love—to make me whole. If that were true, then I couldn't leave any one part behind. I needed to face the past and present and recognize that I hadn't done it alone. I'd had help all along.

CHAPTER 27

ADELAIDE

"WHY MUST SHE come here?" I asked as I secured my hair in a French twist. Usually I was completely ready for dinner by the time Alton joined me. Tonight was different. Instead of being down in the parlor or in his study as he usually was when he came home from the office, he was in our suite, briefing me on our upcoming dinner from hell.

"Because, Laide, it's part of the illusion," Alton answered with a tone that suggested I was asking something of common knowledge, like why the sky was blue or the sea was green. "And," he continued, "according to Bryce, she's having trouble with this whole thing. The little whore was willing to take the money, but she never expected it to be from someone who had a history with Alexandria."

I straightened my shoulders as I inspected my hair and makeup. "I never liked her, not when she lived with our daughter. But I-I…" I searched for the right words. "…never thought she was a prostitute."

Alton was watching my response, his eyes narrowing with each of my words.

"I never trusted her," I continued. "Do you think she was using Alexandria for her own benefit, encouraging Alexandria's rebellion for just such an occasion as this?"

Alton tilted his head, thoughtfully, just before throwing back the two fingers of Cognac from the tumbler in his hand. Since the meeting in his office a few nights ago, he'd at least calmed over the whole subject.

He'd attended a few meetings with Bryce's attorneys, the ones working the case about Melissa, and suddenly, Alton Fitzgerald was once again Bryce's biggest advocate. Alton explained that the company from which Bryce had secured Chelsea's companionship—which was just gentlemanly talk for 'bought a whore'—was reputable and secure. The clients were mostly well-known names and the chance of it becoming public that Chelsea was anything other than a sincere girlfriend was minimal to nonexistent. Apparently, in the entire history of the company, there'd never been such a breach.

"Then it all makes sense," he replied to my question. "It works. It all works as a grand plot brewing for years, substantiating Bryce and Chelsea's long-term relationship."

I walked to the highboy in our suite, my high heels sinking into the plush carpet and reached for the already-poured glass of cabernet. Swirling the dark red liquid, I tried to think of the right way to say what I was thinking, a way to question this plan without setting my husband off again. "Will you explain that?"

He huffed as he settled into a plush high-back leather chair and lifted his shoes to the ottoman. "Laide, for Christ's sake, use your head. You just said it yourself. Think like the little slut. She found herself rooming with Alexandria *Montague*. She saw the potential. When Bryce went to California to visit Alexandria, Chelsea ran interference, telling Bryce that Alexandria didn't want to see him and telling Alexandria to stay away from Bryce. She was in the perfect position to cause dissension."

I sipped the thick wine that my husband had poured for me. There was something off about its flavor. I looked at the bottle. It was from our private collection. Maybe it was the year. Maybe it was that I'd been avoiding the cabernets, merlots, and other reds and drinking more whites lately, even more water.

Ever since learning about the codicil, I'd avoided the heavier alcohol, striving to keep sharp. Not only didn't I want to accidentally let on what I knew, I was listening and taking in everything that was said and done around me.

For years—too many—I'd let the world rotate around me, content to stay blissfully dissociated and unaware, but no longer. Time was of the essence and by Alton's reaction to Bryce's plan, there was more happening than I knew. It was time to do as Jane did.

I didn't mean manual labor. Heaven forbid. I meant listen. Jane said that was what she did, how she knew about the codicil. My guess was that she knew a lot more than she let on. I was following her lead.

I nodded in acknowledgment of Alton's explanation.

He went on telling me exactly why I should accept Bryce and Chelsea's cover story, while at the same time analyze her. He wanted to be sure she was believable before they went out into public together, before the vultures began to circle and questions were asked.

I listened as recent events infiltrated my thoughts. During one of Alton's latest trips, I'd met again with Stephen, the young intern. Together, we'd looked closer at the ledger of views for all of my father's documents. It appeared that when Charles was alive, it wasn't uncommon for my father to meet with Ralph Porter and go over issues and legal papers. It wasn't until weeks before my father's death that Charles had met with both Ralph and Alton.

All that Stephen and I could decipher was that they were looking at the structure of Montague Corporation.

Even after digging, we weren't able to pinpoint any specific modifications that were made as a result of the meeting. Most of the documents pertaining to Montague Corporation were held by the board of trustees. Legally, I was a member—the member with the most stock—yet I couldn't exercise my rights, not without alerting my husband. Alton had been named my proxy in all matters Montague. Stephen explained that by legal recourse, I could get my rights back.

The only other time that Alton and Father had visited the firm together was prior to Alton's and my wedding and I'd been with them. It was when we signed the necessary paperwork for the agreement to our marriage. Some may consider it a prenuptial agreement, but in reality it was the fulfillment of Article XII of my father's last will and testament.

I liked Stephen. I was most certain that Ralph had sent him my way in hopes of derailing whatever it was he thought I would find. Perhaps Ralph believed that together Stephen and I would be the blind leading the blind. However, I knew more about the Montague family than I'd ever been allowed to previously voice, and Stephen was extremely well versed in legalese—not only because he was a second-year law student at Savannah Law and an intern in an esteemed law practice, but also because of his undergraduate work where he'd majored in philosophy. Stephen had an uncanny ability to decipher the written word.

"Are you listening?"

I lifted my gaze to my husband's. His gray eyes darkened as he awaited my response.

"I am. I'm concerned that I won't be able to hide my distaste for this entire situation. How can I possibly not let on that I know she's a prostitute?"

"Come now, Adelaide, you're an expert at this."

I stopped my hand with the wine goblet poised at my lips, uncertain if I'd actually received a compliment. "What do you mean?"

"I mean that you can grin and bear it with the best of them."

It wasn't a compliment. "Perhaps you'd like to enlighten me with specific examples."

"No, I'd like you to do as I said and welcome this girl into our home as you would Alexandria's suitor, that Demetri young man."

I took a deep breath. "I haven't met him. But the glaring difference is that Alexandria hasn't paid for his *companionship*." I emphasized the word Bryce had used.

"Not to our knowledge."

I narrowed my gaze. "Alexandria has no access to any of her money. And from what I understand, that *Demetri young man* isn't in need of financial support."

Alton took a step closer. "Really, Adelaide, I thought we were done discussing the attributes of the Demetris. Unless you'd like to reopen old wounds."

I pressed my lips together. If only he knew the extent to which I'd explored Oren Demetri's attributes. In my husband's mind, he was talking about one encounter. Little did he know that it lasted for years. "I believe that you made your opinion of Lennox's father very clear."

Removing the glass from my hand, Alton stared down into my eyes. The intensity was both frightening and exhilarating. I'd trained myself too well to look away, a lesser woman would. But I'd danced this tango too many times. In these situations, my survival mechanism was to become a voyeur. No longer present as a participant, I watched from outside, fascinated by the carnage from the imminent wreck.

With each passing second, my husband's expression hardened. Before I knew what he'd done, his hand was around my throat, causing me to stumble backward until my shoulders collided with the wall. He applied just enough pressure to my neck that I needed to raise my chin to breathe. "This isn't a wise choice of conversation."

"I don't believe it was *I* who brought it up."

The pressure increased but only marginally. "We will have a united front when we dine. Is that clear?"

The telltale taste of copper seeped onto my tongue as I pierced my lip, biting back the response I wanted to say. "Yes, you're very clear."

"For the record, that young man comes from a lineage of criminals, in all meanings of the word. Underhanded business as well as underworld dealings. He will never step foot in my home."

It wasn't a question. I was most certain Alexandria would agree with Alton, though not for the same reasons. "I have not met him," I emphasized what I'd said before.

"But his father…"

My gaze stayed fixed though the pressure on my neck increased. I knew better than to change my expression. Any alteration could be misconstrued.

"You know, Adelaide, not all whores are purchased through a company."

No, some secure their place in your life with their bastard son. I didn't say that.

When I didn't respond, he released me.

I inhaled, allowing my lungs to fully expand. "What about Alexandria?" I asked, rubbing my fingers over my neck and reaching for my glass. The wine felt good as it coated my throat.

"What about her?"

"Her reaction to all of this. I don't know how you think this will get her and Bryce back together."

"Have you told her?"

"No. I haven't spoken to her. She still isn't answering my calls since you used my phone."

Alton shook his head. "That girl needs to be taught manners."

I walked toward the mirror. The skin of my neck was red, though he hadn't squeezed hard enough to leave the markings of his fingers.

Alton went to my dresser and opened two doors revealing multiple drawers filled with jewelry. As he searched, he said, "I was working to get her back here before this change of events. As with everything else, I've given up on your ability to influence her decisions. Besides, I won't allow this Moore girl to change the intended outcome."

Turning from my jewelry, Alton silently handed me a beaded necklace. It was shaped like a large triangle, the design hanging like a scarf secured high on my neck with the point falling just over the neckline of my dress.

It would hide any signs of his recent power play.

Illusion.

Willingly, I took the jewelry, removed the necklace I'd been wearing, and attempted to secure the larger one. But as I did, Alton came up behind me and reached for the clasps. I lowered my hands as he latched the necklace. Next, he leaned toward my ear and brushed the side of my neck with his lips.

"Mrs. Fitzgerald, I suggest that you make your daughter listen." The scent of tobacco and Cognac filled my senses, and his voice rumbled through me, a stark contrast to the menacing meaning of his warning. "This cover story will be just that. The way I see it, it will bring Alexandria to her senses." With the necklace secure, our eyes met in the mirror and his hands cupped my shoulders. "It is in everyone's best interest to keep those people, that family, away from Montague women. I would hate to see anyone get hurt."

He handed me my glass. "Drink up, darling, we have family waiting."

I took the glass, but instead of drinking, I lifted my brow. "Does that mean Suzy is here?"

"Why of course."

I emptied the contents of the glass and left it on the table near the door. To hell with my new pledge to stay alert—some instances were better left forgotten. I was certain that it would take more than one glass of cabernet to make it through this dinner.

Nervous laughter came from the parlor as we descended the grand stairs. We stood at the archway, my arm in the crook of my husband's as the farce played out around us. Bryce was at the far end of the room, an empty tumbler in his hand. No doubt, he'd had the same before-dinner cocktail as his father.

Nothing but the best Cognac for the Fitzgeralds, even the illegitimate ones.

Though I felt no pity for Bryce, I saw through his bravado. The look in his gray eyes as he turned toward Alton and me—he wasn't looking at me. His full attention was on his father, seeking his approval, pleading for a sign that this plan would work out.

I fought the urge to turn to my husband and witness his silent response. Just as I was about to look, my attention went to the two women on the small velvet loveseat. My best friend was absolutely doting over Bryce's new slut.

Though I'd met Chelsea before, in this environment she looked different. No doubt Suzy had helped with the slut's appearance. She wasn't unattractive. With her hair up and her lovely young figure accentuating a stunning black cocktail-length dress, she turned from Suzy to me, her hazel eyes reflecting the same plea I'd just seen in Bryce's.

"Mrs. Fitzgerald," Chelsea said as she stood.

"Adelaide," Suzy offered. "There's no need for formalities."

I took a step forward.

Chelsea extended her hand, but I merely nodded.

"Mrs. Fitzgerald…" I let my stone-cold gaze move from Chelsea to Suzanna and back to Chelsea. "…will work just fine, Miss Moore."

CHAPTER 28

CHARLI

"CHARLI?"

The sound of my name resonated through my dreams, pulling me from my slumber as a warm touch skirted my back, tracing my spine before resting on my shoulder. The connection created a lifeline back to reality. It was one I hadn't realized I needed or even wanted. For so long I'd pretended to be strong. I probably wasn't fooling anyone, except maybe myself. I'd thought that during all of those years in Montague Manor that I'd been alone, but I hadn't.

Jane's voice over the phone, her words, and reassurance—they'd always been there, whenever I needed them. More than that, she'd been the one to constantly remind me that I had my mother's support, even when I couldn't see it. Most of all, Jane had told me that I was loved, was kind, and was beautiful—inside and out.

In the time after the call and before I'd drifted to sleep, I recalled the night years ago, the night before I left for Stanford and my mother's visit to my room. In Montague Manor I'd learned to be strong, but I'd had help—invaluable help. Without Jane's and my mother's encouragement, I may never have been brave enough to start over in California, to become Alex.

My heart ached at the realization. Chelsea had been part of that transition too. She'd been my cheerleader and my rock. She'd helped me close out the shadows of my past and welcome the light of my present and future. I'd never fully confided in her or in anyone, but somehow they knew. Somehow those closest to me knew exactly what I'd needed.

And now I didn't know where Chelsea was. She needed me and I couldn't help her.

"Charli?"

I turned my attention toward the deep velvet voice. Nox's timbre rumbled through the darkened room, its tenor beckoning as his voice overflowed with concern. As he came into focus, his handsome face contorted with uncertainty. His brow furrowed and chiseled jaw clenched. The vein in his neck jumped to life, throbbing with his increased pulse.

"What's the matter?" I asked, reaching up to touch his cheek.

He lifted my shoulders, securing them in his strong hands as he pulled me to a sitting position and held me against his chest. "Princess, I'm sorry."

The haze of sleep left me disoriented and unsure.

Why is he sorry?

"Nox?" It was the only word I could mutter as my cheek smashed against his suit coat and he held me tighter. His cologne filled my senses. Beneath the soft material of his jacket, his hard chest cradled me while his erratic heartbeat troubled me.

"I shouldn't have left you here alone," he said, "not after last time."

I tried to move my head from side to side. "No, it's not… I'm fine. What's upset you?"

"You," Nox replied. "I'm worried about you. Why are you crying?"

My fingers found their way to my face as I pulled away from his embrace. He was right. I hadn't realized I'd been crying, but my cheeks were wet. I blinked my swollen lids and wiped away the evidence.

"I'm fine. I think I fell asleep."

Now at arm's length, Nox's pale blue eyes scanned my features, seeing not only me, but inside of me. Even in the sparse illumination that spilled like golden liquid from the hallway, I saw the navy swirls as he assessed my words and my expression.

"I would've been home sooner," Nox explained, "but just as I was about to leave the office, I got a phone call that I needed to take. I should've called you when it was done."

Still shaking my head, I replied, "Stop, I'm fine. I'm not that fragile."

"Then tell me what happened."

I reached for his hand, still holding my shoulder, turned and lifted his palm to my lips. Giving it a kiss I held it near my cheek and smiled. "I think everything is catching up with me."

As I was about to lace our fingers together, Nox's gaze went to the bed and then to my phone atop it. He dropped my hand, reached for it, and swiped the screen.

Last call: JANE

Nox's eyes moved from the screen to mine. "Tell me who she is and why her call upset you? Does this have anything to do with Chelsea?"

Though his request was more of a demand, I didn't answer; instead, I shrugged. "I'm worried about her. I've tried to call Chelsea, but her phone is off."

"Did this Jane person tell you something?"

"It's nothing. As I said, I think everything has caught up with me. It's been a busy week. I'm just happy it's over and you're home. Thank you for coming last night." I broadened my grin. "And this morning."

Nox wasn't easily distracted, though my mind had drifted to a few of our early morning scenes. "Charli, something upset you. Who is the woman on the call?" This time his question was more persistent than before.

"I'll tell you…" I tried for a more upbeat tone. "… if we can go eat that dinner Lana prepared."

Nox looked toward the clock. "It's almost eight. Why didn't you eat without me?"

My ear met my shoulder as I lifted the corners of my lips. "It appears that I napped instead."

"So you're well rested?" he asked, his brows rising with a hint of a promise that he'd moved on from his earlier concern. As he spoke, he removed his suit jacket, folded it, and placed it onto a nearby chair. "I hope her dinner isn't ruined."

"It smelled great when I peeked at it earlier. I'm pretty sure she doesn't use frozen meatballs."

Nox grinned. "No. That would be cause for immediate dismissal."

"Oh? Should I start looking for a new place to live?"

"No, princess, just let Lana do the cooking. You have different duties."

"Oh, I do?"

The gleam in his eyes and the view he provided as he continued to remove his tie left me momentarily tongue-tied. "Fine," I finally said. "I turned down the heat in the oven. It was my contribution to dinner. It should all be fine."

Nox reached for my hand and helped me stand. "It does smell wonderful," he agreed before his gaze narrowed. "If it didn't, I might decide to keep you in here and skip food."

"Keep me in here?" My tone turned sultry with a touch of innocence. "How would you plan to *keep* me? Tied to the bed?"

One of Nox's brows twitched. "Careful. Food is beginning to lose its appeal."

His innuendo reminded me why I'd entered the bedroom in the first place. "Do you know…?" My question faltered as I searched for the right words and fought the embarrassment brought on by the subject.

My mind told me that it was silly. No one in the world knew me as intimately as Nox Demetri. Simply asking him the location of my vibrator shouldn't make me nervous. Maybe it was because he'd once told me I wasn't allowed to use it. The thing was—I didn't want to be the one in control.

"Do I know… what?" Nox asked, pulling me close, his arm firmly around my waist. "How to tie satin into the perfect knots that keep you exactly where I want you?"

Our hips came crashing together, prompted by his embrace. My breathing hitched as I worked to stay focused on my goal and not allow my thoughts to imagine what he described. With my neck bowed backward, I tilted my head seductively and lowered my lashes. "No, Mr. Demetri. I know the answer to that question. I was wondering if you knew where my vibrator was? Last time I saw it, it was on the bed."

His menacing gaze, which over the last week had been replaced with concern and worry, resurfaced with a vengeance. Its reappearance caused my heart to tremble and body to quake in anticipation.

"Miss Collins, was that the reason for your angst? Were you so horny that you were crying over a lost vibrator, one that I believe I told you was off-limits? Is that what happens when I'm merely an hour late?"

"No!" I said playfully as I pushed against his unmoving chest.

"Really now," he cooed, "I'm certain I can help you with that need and many more. Maybe we should forget dinner?"

"Food, Mr. Demetri. That was where we were going. Lana's note said that some of her meals of late have ended up in the trash. This won't be one of them. Unless you plan to starve me?"

"No. Starving you doesn't sound like fun. Causing you to cry out my name in sexual frustration… now that sounds promising."

My tummy did flip-flops as his grin joined the navy swirls within the light blue of his eyes. It wasn't fair that after a long day he could be so handsome and have the ability to twist my insides with mere words and glances.

"And for the record," Nox continued, "I do know where your vibrator is. And since you've successfully avoided answering my direct questions about the call, I believe our after-dinner activity has been planned. Just wait, Miss Collins, my interrogation technique is very effective." He tugged me closer. "So much so, that if some of my methods weren't considered illegal by the Geneva Convention, Homeland Security would certainly use it to learn secret intelligence."

"I haven't avoided…" I began in my own defense, ignoring the tantalizing cocktail rushing through my blood, the one created by equal measures of anticipation at his promise and the right amount of trepidation at his threat.

Nox bent toward me and kissed my forehead. His deep voice resonated his new warning. "Princess, don't make it worse."

"I'm not. It's just that—"

He shook his head, our noses touching.

"We could just go for sweet and slow," I tried. "This morning was… well, amazing seems woefully insufficient."

Nox smiled at my use of the same words he'd said in Del Mar. "Yes, princess, I agree. But tonight is about learning your secrets, one way or the other. Before this night is over, you'll be telling me what I want to know or suffering the consequences." He tugged my hand, pulling me toward the hallway and kitchen. "Sustenance first, sex coma later."

Trailing a step behind, I bit my lower lip as my mind filled with possibilities and my insides twisted to a pleasurable and painful pitch. If I didn't think I'd need the nutrition, I'd agree to forgo dinner.

CHAPTER 29

CHARLI

SECRETS WEREN'T SECRETS unless they were hidden away. Those things that we shared openly, that we talked, laughed, and even cried about, couldn't hurt us because they were out there for the world to see. It was the things that we kept hidden, that we didn't share, that lurked in the shadows—those held the power to hurt, harm, and even destroy.

Nox and I both had them—secrets we hadn't shared.

Perhaps it wasn't that we didn't want to share. It was that we didn't know how.

After our meal, Nox went to a drawer in our closet and found my missing vibrator. Apparently, it wasn't missing at all, but hidden from possible prying eyes.

"I got the impression that you weren't against voyeurism?" I asked with a smirk.

"Oh, princess, it depends on my mood." He suggestively lifted one brow. "After I have that sexy body perfectly positioned, do you think I should call Isaac?"

"No," I answered too quickly.

As Nox surveyed the items in the drawer, I stepped behind him and wrapped my arms around his waist. I didn't want whatever he had planned filled with confessions. I wanted them out of the way so we could concentrate on other things.

With my cheek against his back, I said, "Jane was my nanny."

He didn't turn, but stood taller. By the way his muscles tensed, I knew I had his full attention.

"Did you call her or did she call you?"

"I called her."

"Why did her call upset you?"

I shrugged against his warmth. "I think it's because she's one of the few parts of my childhood I don't want to forget."

Nox turned and surrounded me with his arms. "Then don't."

He made it sound so simple.

"I love her, as I should love…" I tucked my lips between my teeth, not wanting to cry or ruin the mood he'd been trying to create. "I'm sorry. I wanted to answer your question so we could think about other things." I tilted my head toward his open drawer. Lengths of black satin lay neatly coiled beside the pink case of my vibrator. There were also candles and an accumulation of other toys we'd only begun to enjoy.

Before Nox, I'd never seen most of the *accessories*. Warmth filled my cheeks as I considered my new knowledge. Who would have ever thought a flogger could be so erotic?

Nox reached for my chin, holding it between his thumb and index finger and brought my moist eyes to his. "I've seen your shadows. I want to help rid your golden eyes of them, to make them clear. Your eyes are stunning when they're focused and not filled with concerns from your past. I've seen them shining with wonder as you sit for hours and read about things that would bore most of the world. They've been filled with anticipation as you watch my every move, wondering what I will do next. Those are the eyes I adore. If you talk about the shadows, share them with me, they can't linger in there anymore."

When I tried to look down, he held my face steady. This was a mistake. I shouldn't have answered his question, should have let the evening go where he'd planned. Since I couldn't move my gaze away, my only escape was to close my eyes.

I did, allowing my lashes to lie upon my cheeks.

"No, Charli. Look at me. You brought this up."

I peered upward. "You asked. You said you were going to make me tell you."

"If I thought anything in this drawer could erase that sadness, I wouldn't hesitate, but, princess, you're the only one who can do that." He ran the pad of his thumb over my lips. "I won't *make* you tell me anything. I want you to want to tell me. Do you understand?"

I nodded against his hold.

"I'll ask you questions. Tell me what you can."

His words scared me more than anything in his drawer. The sweet lash of knotted leather would be easier to endure than answering questions, especially if he found the right ones to ask.

Fear at that thought squeezed the muscles of my throat, holding back my answer. Nevertheless, I managed a whispered reply. "I'll try."

Nox shut the drawer, and I let out an exaggerated breath. "I'm sorry. Your plans were better than this."

"Don't be sorry. My plans can wait."

Tenderly, he led me back to the bedroom. "This Jane, do you know where she is now?"

I nodded and took a deep breath. "Yes, she's at my… at my parents' house." The explanation left a sour taste on my tongue.

"It bothers you to say *parents*, doesn't it?" Nox asked.

I nodded again.

"You said you loved her like you should have loved… your mother?"

I lowered my lids. "I do love my mother. But I've hurt her." I shook my head. "I've never meant to cause her pain, but she's been nonetheless hurt because of me. I think I knew it. That was why it was easier to…"

"To leave?" Nox asked.

"Yes. But she keeps begging me to come back. I can't. I can't bear it.

Seeing him makes me physically ill."

"Him? Your stepfather?"

"Yes," I answered quickly. "I don't know what I want to say. I guess I do love my mother, too. I stay away because when I'm around my mother, I say things that upset him. And over the years she's paid for more of my mistakes than I have." My voice trailed to a whisper. "And I paid dearly."

Nox's shoulders tightened as he guided me to the bed. Though we were both fully clothed, he pulled me close and wrapped his arm over my shoulder as we both sat against the headboard.

"Can you tell me what that bastard did?"

The delicious dinner of lasagna and bread that we'd recently consumed churned in my stomach. Maybe it was the wine that had loosened my lips. Even so, my chest ached as if it had been cracked open, the breastbone physically fractured. There was something about the pain that was excruciating yet also liberating. I'd stored so many memories, encased and entombed them. The break freed them. In a few words they'd no longer be shadows but light in our darkened room.

I took a deep breath and closed my eyes. With Nox's arm keeping me safe and giving me strength, I began to explain. "My mother always endured more of his wrath. Now that I'm older and more perceptive, I wonder if she asked for it, took it on intentionally to spare me. All those years I thought she didn't care, thought she didn't see. She'd spend days in her suite, claiming migraines. But now, as I listen to her desperation to see me, to talk to me, and listened to Jane, I wonder if maybe there was more, more that a little girl or a teenager didn't see, couldn't comprehend."

"Your stepfather hurt your mother?"

I nodded.

"Once? Twice?"

"Always. Abuse—mental, emotional, physical. You name it."

"Alex," Nox said, his use of my real name an indication of how serious he was taking this conversation. "What about you? Did he abuse you?"

"Psychologically. Verbally. I was never good enough, at anything. Always an embarrassment. Never the Montague I should be."

"What did he…?"

My tongue darted to my lips, moistening them so that I could continue. "I've never talked about it. Not even to Jane, but she knew. She always knew. She would always find me and do what she could to help." I sighed. "She used to tell me that one day I could leave Montague Manor and I'd find a life that would make me happy."

I placed my hands on Nox's chest, small white buttons ran from his open collar to beneath his pants. Warmth radiated through the thin fabric as his heart pounded a steady rhythm below my touch. "I think," I declared with new determination, "that I have."

"You have?"

"I've found it. I know you have secrets too. I know you have shadows, but in your shadows, mine feel less threatening. For the first time, I feel free to talk about things that I've always kept quiet. I don't want to tell you any of this so that you'll right a wrong or even to make you share your shadows. I want to tell you so that you'll know that I trust you."

I looked back toward the closet and his closed drawer of sex toys. "Not just with my body and safety, but also with my secrets and love. I've never felt that way before, except for Jane."

Nox's eyes squinted as he seemed to consider my comparison.

"Not sexually… not like you. But listening to Jane's voice today, I know I've always loved and been loved by her, because more than anyone at Montague Manor, I trusted her." I swallowed, forcing my emotion down. "You and her. You're the only two people I think I've completely trusted." I shrugged. "Chelsea is close, but I never told her what had happened. And my mother, maybe I owe her more than I've given."

"Did he touch you?" The tension in Nox's expression appeared almost painful.

"Not sexually."

The arm around me loosened.

I went on. "He was a fan of corporal punishment."

Nox's back straightened against the headboard. When I turned, I saw his eyes shut.

"When…" he began, "…I… when you bit my ankle…" He took a deep breath and moved in front of me, so that we were eye to eye. "I thought you were mad, but you were scared… of me? Because of him?"

It seemed so long ago.

"I was…" I admitted, "…both—mad and scared."

"Oh, fuck. Charli, I didn't mean…"

I brushed my lips against his. "You were… different." I felt the crimson fill my cheeks. "Even though you were upset, there wasn't the rage. You made it… I didn't the first time, but since… I guess I like it." Our lips touched again. "Because once I learned your mission for that first time, to teach me a lesson for signing the agreement, I'm pretty sure that harming or degrading me isn't your goal. I trust you not to do that. I trust you to make it right, to take the pain and make it pleasure."

His hand slipped behind my neck, securing my gaze to his. In his pale blue eyes was a mixture of pride and regret, happiness that he held my trust and sadness that he could have lost it.

"Never," he said. "Never would harming or degrading you be my goal. I was upset about the agreement, but everything since and before has been for pleasure." He shook his head. "If I'd known… I never would have…"

I touched his lips, silencing his words. "Nox, I haven't found my hard limit with you, but when—and if—I do, I trust you'll respect it."

"Princess, you'll never have to resort to biting again."

I shrugged. "Maybe I want to."

His lips twitched and his eyes twinkled with traces of his menacing grin. "Then, princess, we may have to revisit some of your more recent likes. Because biting is a punishable offense." His touch skirted my arms, before he tucked me back against his chest. "Thank you for sharing some of your shadows with me. By the way, I'd like to teach your stepfather what happens to men who hurt women and little girls."

"I don't want that. I want to forget it happened, but I can't forget that my mother still lives with it."

"Why? Why doesn't she leave him?"

"To her, divorce is worse. What happens in the halls and shadows of

Montague Manor goes unspoken. To the world, they're a happy couple. It's usually at night. I used to hide in my room as their voices carried. I never knew if I was going to be first or second. I'd stare at my door and pray that it wouldn't open.

"Some children are afraid of the boogeyman. I didn't wonder if he was a myth. I knew he lived down the hall."

The words kept pouring out. "He travels. He always has. My father was killed in an accident while traveling. I was only three, but I remember praying that Alton would meet the same fate. I didn't understand how it could happen to my father, a man who I really can't remember, but it wouldn't happen to a monster like Alton."

Nox stiffened and turned, hovering above me, his arms on both sides of me, like a shield. "You don't have to worry or pray for his demise. Not anymore. I told you before: I'm the only bad I want near you."

Readjusting his weight, Nox reached for the buttons on my blouse and one by one began to undo them. "Princess, I'm feeling a little more like sweet and amazing. We'll save the vibrator for another day."

I didn't argue. After my blouse was gone, Nox unbuttoned his shirt and eased it over his shoulders revealing his muscular chest. As my fingertips grazed his warm skin, he unlatched my bra. Skin to skin, our flesh united. His warmth pinned me to the mattress as his tone turned to velvet, coaxing and soothing, taking my mind from the past and keeping it in the present. Tenderly he filled me with more than hope for shadow-free tomorrows. In his arms I felt safe, as if my secrets were no longer burdens but links connecting and holding us together.

Because in his capable hands, we fit perfectly together with no room for shadows.

CHAPTER 30

Thirteen years ago

OREN

IT WASN'T MY normal gathering. Thirty thousand dollars a plate was steep, no matter how much money Demetri Enterprises was grossing. Nevertheless, I was here, dressed to kill in a custom tuxedo. One simply didn't rent a tuxedo for such an affair.

The convention hall was filled with white lights and Christmas decorations, creating a chic and festive atmosphere. Maybe it was because this was my first Christmas as a divorced man. Maybe it was that Lennox would be staying with his mother for the holidays. No matter the reason, I'd accepted the invitation to this fundraiser. My gift to myself.

Merry fucking Christmas.

When I received the invitation, I decided that attending the fundraiser was my chance to show my success in my own backyard, prove that Demetri belonged among the other names in attendance.

I'd avoided most social gatherings, especially large ones, since my divorce. It wasn't for lack of a companion. I could easily have someone on my arm. It was that I didn't have the energy. My focus was the business. Angelina was better at the social graces. She could mesmerize a table of people with her stories and carry on a conversation with anyone about anything.

In hindsight, I realized it was probably because she was starved for adult conversation. Though Lennox was about to graduate high school and Silvia was somewhere in her early twenties, conversations with them, in my opinion, weren't exactly stimulating. That could be why I avoided those too.

As I glanced at the growing crowd, I wondered with whom I would start. I may not hold a table captive with talk about the latest movie but I could talk business with the best of them. It was all I ever discussed anymore. Stocks and shares. The fluctuations of the market and the impending shitstorm as interest rates continued to fall.

Conversation and networking were why I hadn't brought a companion to this event. I could talk shop with the other men, put a face with the Demetri name, and make my mark in a legitimate business climate away from the chains that bound me in Brooklyn.

I didn't want, nor did I have the energy, to coddle a woman with small talk. I'd grown tired of doing that with Angelina, and I knew her. Indulging a relative stranger, even with the promise of sex afterward, was a nauseating proposition.

The tart champagne constricted the muscles in my throat as I sipped from the tall fluted glass. I'd arrived in time for the cocktail hour. The time before the meal. The time to introduce myself and assess the multitude of opportunities. I scanned the room seeing the usual suspects as well as others I'd never met.

I had a good idea who'd be present. The price tag alone made the guest list elite.

It was then that I saw her.

A vision across the room.

Though it had been years since I'd seen her in Savannah, I immediately recognized Adelaide Montague. Even in my subconscious I avoided the name Collins.

She was stunning, slender and petite, yet despite her small stature, in my eyes she was a glowing pinnacle surrounded by a sea of frivolity. The way she stood, holding herself as the regal lady she unquestionably was—well, it was mesmerizing. I tried to look away, tried to refocus on the crowd, on the business at hand, but I couldn't. There was something about her presence that drew me closer. Overwhelming and enticing, she was beauty and class personified, and yet there was an aura of sadness around her that tore at my heart.

Could I be the cause?

I had to know.

Three strides or was it five? I didn't care, because once they were complete, she was looking directly at me. Blue eyes filled with a sparkle that broke through the sadness. In the eyes of an angel was a ravishing hunger. She captivated me by her complexity before she uttered a word.

I wanted to know more. To know her thoughts and her dreams. To hear her sorrows and share in her joys. Somehow this beautiful lady before me was more complicated than any other woman I'd ever known. I longed to peel back her layers, knowing in my heart that her perfected exterior, as stunning as it was, paled in comparison to what lay beneath.

"Hello." The greeting rolled off my tongue as I reached for her small, soft hand, bowed ever so slightly at the hip, and lifted her delicate fingers to my lips. The faintest scent of perfume graced the air as her pulse beneath my touch thumped in beat with her racing heart. It was floral—jasmine and lavender. The aroma entered my breath, filled my lungs, and marked my memory for eternity.

"I'm Oren, and you are?"

Our gazes held steady. The dance of unfed hunger that swayed and moved beneath the surface of her stare wouldn't allow me to look away. I didn't want to blink, to close my eyes, or lose a millisecond of her presence. I wanted the vision before me etched in my mind forever.

"Adelaide."

Her voice sang to me like a siren calling to a sailor from the depths of the ocean.

With only one word, I knew that like the mythological creatures, this woman was dangerous. First, she was married. If I hadn't known that already, it was glaringly obvious by the gigantic rock on her left hand. Second, I was confident that despite the success of Demetri Enterprises, she was out of my league. I was less than nothing to the likes of a Montague.

Could fate change perceptions?

For the first time in my life, I believed it could.

Years ago, in a California bar, I'd heard the description of a frigid woman who'd made life unbearable. Like other opinions, I now knew that one had been totally erroneous. Adelaide Montague wasn't an ice princess. She couldn't be. During the few seconds that I'd held her hand, the fire that coursed through her veins created a spark that jolted my cold, dark heart back to life.

"A most beautiful name for an even more stunning woman."

I expected her to shake off my compliment, to tell me that she was taken. I expected her tone to be dismissive, addressing me as the lower-class man I was. What I didn't expect was for her cheeks to blush and her breathing to hitch. For a moment I stared, perplexed as to why this woman, who shouldn't even be talking to me, was surprised by my acknowledgment of her obvious beauty.

"Why do you act surprised?" I asked, genuinely curious. "Surely the man who put that ring on your finger tells you that daily? He'd be a fool not to see the gem that he has."

She didn't respond, not directly. Adelaide Montague wasn't the type of woman to bask in flattery. Instead, she asked about me, and what brought me to the event this evening. She spoke in earnest, genuinely interested in someone like me. Before I knew it, I was talking about things I'd only previously thought. I explained that this was my first Christmas as a single man in over twenty years. I talked about the solitude of my New York apartment and how I'd miss spending Christmas morning with my son.

I'd never spoken those words aloud. Yet in the presence of a woman completely out of my league, I babbled on and on. Our conversation wasn't one-sided. It was back and forth as Adelaide too contributed to the discussion. She spoke about her daughter, Alexandria, and how much she'd grown. At ten years old, she was becoming a young lady, not the small girl she used to be.

We laughed about our children's stubbornness. It was a trait I'd never before valued in Lennox that suddenly seemed humorous as she told the tale of Alexandria and a pair of shears. Apparently after an afternoon of refusing a haircut, her daughter had taken it upon herself to create her own style. The result was something so outrageous that Adelaide claimed to have not seen it herself. Instead, a beautician was summoned and now her daughter had a flattering but short hairstyle.

Topics came and went as we chatted. It wasn't until a woman approached and whispered something in Adelaide's ear that I saw the sadness that had been with her earlier return. For a time, she'd been happy. I knew it wasn't just wishful thinking but fact.

Her momentary joy blended with the lavender and jasmine settled into my senses. The intoxicating concoction invigorated me in a way that I hadn't felt in years.

With a return of Adelaide's sadness, the chasm inside of me widened. Though I'd been harboring the void for years, I'd never realized its profound depth until for a brief moment in time it was gone. The money and success. The approval and adoration. All that I'd worked my life to achieve would never fill the emptiness. I knew that now, because for an hour it had been gone.

Turning from the woman back to me, Adelaide was now a shell of the vibrant lady with whom I'd been speaking. Even the melody of her voice had changed, now melancholy and mechanical. "It was a pleasure meeting you," she said. "Thank you for talking to me."

How this lovely lady could thank me was incomprehensible. "Thank you, Adelaide. The pleasure was all mine."

"Fitzgerald," she added, as if I didn't know. "Mrs. Alton Fitzgerald. I must really get back to my husband."

Though her spirit had been taken by the words of the other woman, the departure of her being left me chilled and alone.

For the rest of the evening, every now and then, I'd chance a glance in her direction. Never again did our eyes meet. She was consumed with her task at hand. Never again did she falter as she portrayed the attentive and dutiful wife at her husband's side.

I recalled the relief I'd felt when I'd heard she remarried. After all, even

Collins himself had known they weren't meant to be together. But as I watched Adelaide with Alton Fitzgerald, I looked for anything to indicate that she was better off with him than alone.

I found nothing.

IT WASN'T MY place to intrude in her life.

Throughout my marriage I'd occasionally found solace in the arms of other women, but none of them had been married. Then again, I had been. In the eyes of the church a sin was a sin, yet somehow I'd justified it as warranted.

Adelaide Fitzgerald was different.

For the first time, I wanted another man's wife.

The desire consumed me.

I knew that for me, hell was imminent. My list of sins was not limited to adultery. I fought against the chance of bringing Adelaide with me to the fiery pits… and then I justified my need. Instead of me dragging her to the depths of hell, I saw her as an angel, perhaps capable of granting me salvation on earth before my destiny commenced.

Achieving my deliverance wasn't easy.

She lived in a fortress. Literally.

It was Vincent's favor from two years ago that proved my way in. The cameras that Charles Montague had commissioned were still operational. He'd since passed away and the contract with Demetri's surveillance company no longer existed, but the cameras were still there.

I wasn't a wizard at technology. Finances were my forte, but I knew enough. I could watch from afar and see that Alton Fitzgerald traveled, often leaving his wife and stepdaughter alone with a multitude of servants. Though the cameras were throughout the house, I respected Adelaide too much to intrude. I simply used the information from the downstairs rooms as a way to gauge my approach.

Our first *chance* meeting came the following spring, during one of her husband's trips. I flew to Savannah, making it a point that our paths would cross.

I wanted to see her, to look into her eyes and see the fire that I'd felt when I first held her hand.

After that, the next move was up to her. Absolution was granted not taken. It was my angel's choice if she'd give it to me.

I'd sat across the table from some of the most dangerous men in the country, perhaps the world. I'd watched other men take their last breaths. I'd secured deals that were nefarious at best. And never had I been as nervous as I was waiting at a table in the restaurant that I knew she frequented.

If she ignored me, or worse, pretended she didn't recognize me, I planned to walk away. I'd chalk up our conversation to cosmic fate, a rare occurrence when stars aligned, and accept my damnation.

Rarely did Adelaide's schedule change. Twice a month she met other women for lunch in a private dining room at an upscale tearoom. With a large tip to the right person, I was seated just outside of her destination. She'd need to walk past me to access the room.

Would she be alone, accompanied by friends, or perhaps flanked by a bodyguard?

Doubts swirled through my mind as I sipped sweet tea and waited. Unfortunately, the restaurant didn't serve alcohol. I could have used a stiff drink.

The moment she entered the area where I sat, my lungs seized, hungry for a hint of jasmine and lavender. I couldn't have been more obvious if I'd rented a sign, one of the ones with lights that flashed to indicate an arrow. If I had, the sign would have undoubtedly read, 'heartsick fool' as it pointed to me.

Each step she took was focused, her eyes on the door of the private dining room. She'd almost passed right by me when her steps stuttered and her blue-eyed gaze locked on mine. Suddenly her hand fluttered near her neck and the color drained from her cheeks.

"Oren." My name floated in the air as a whisper, quickly swallowed by the din of the other diners.

Nevertheless, it was the most beautiful thing I'd ever heard. I hadn't allowed myself to admit how devastated I would have been if she'd not remembered me. But she had, and my head was alive with the promise of spring as bees buzzed and birds sang.

"Adelaide." No other words came to mind.

"How? How are you here?" she asked, but just as soon, she stiffened and looked both directions.

"I'm not here to cause you problems."

"Then why?" Her question was again a whisper.

I stood, my hands aching to touch hers. "Because I haven't thought of anyone else since the night we met. Because I've dreamt of seeing you again, talking to you, hearing your voice and laughter."

Tears filled her eyes as she shook her head. "I-I can't. If anyone… If my husb—"

I handed her a piece of paper that I'd kept in the pocket of my pants. "My number. I don't know how this will work, but it's up to you if you call me. I'll be in town for two more days."

Part of me expected her to reject the offer.

I believe there was part of her that knew she should. Her hand trembled as she slowly reached forward, taking the paper and tucking it in her handbag.

"Yes. Mr. Demetri, it was nice to see you again." This time her volume was louder, intentionally audible to those nearby. "I will certainly tell my husband you were in town. Unfortunately, he won't be back for *two more days*."

The final words of her statement seemed to ring in my ears, reverberating off the walls. I smiled and nodded, all the time praying that I was inferring her reply the way she intended.

THEY SAY THAT lightning doesn't strike twice. I disagree.

The next afternoon Adelaide Montague—the last name I chose to use—arrived in a cab and met me at a motel outside of Savannah. The location was her idea, though I doubted she'd ever been to such an establishment.

That was the point.

No one at the motel off of US 95, north of Savannah, would recognize her.

"I-I'm not sure why I came here," she said once she was in the room, her hand again fluttering near her neck.

"I'm not expecting anything, Adelaide. I just wanted to see you again."

The hunger I'd witnessed at the fundraiser was camouflaged behind a shadow of fear. The thought that I was the source of terror tore at my insides. I longed to reassure her. Slowly, I took a step toward her.

"I've never felt an attraction to another woman," I said, "like I do to you. Tell me if it's one-sided. If it is, tell me no and I'll walk away."

"Oren."

My name came out as a heartbreaking tune as it tumbled from her lips.

"Adelaide, tell me no." I inched closer.

I reached for her hand, encasing her fingers in mine, and though they said it wouldn't, lightning struck again. Electricity and energy flowed from her to me, and back. We were a circuit of power spinning wildly out of control. Soon we would combust.

I stepped even closer, my chest just inches from hers. I longed to feel her heartbeat as her breasts heaved and she fought to breathe.

"Last chance, Adelaide. Say no, or I'm going to kiss you."

"Kiss me?" she asked as if the possibility surprised her.

"Yes, I've spent the last months imagining your taste and the feel of your lips against mine. You're so close. I'm losing control. I need to know if my imagination was close to reality. Say no."

Adelaide lifted her chin, bringing her lips a whisper from mine. "I've never wanted to say yes more."

In a seedy motel in Georgia, the world stopped spinning and lightning exploded.

My imagination paled to the reality of Adelaide Montague.

CHAPTER 31

NOX

"IT'S BEEN OVER two weeks," I said, my arms crossed over my chest as I leaned against my desk and stared.

"We need to tell Alex. She's going to find out sooner or later."

I took a deep breath and stared down at Deloris Witt. Perhaps over the years I'd overestimated her abilities. In most things, most instances, she was unstoppable—Superwoman. If that were true, then this assignment, Chelsea Moore and Infidelity, had become her kryptonite.

"I keep hoping you'll have it resolved."

"It isn't that easy," Deloris said. "Chelsea's doing what she's supposed to do. She's integrating into his life."

The thought turned my stomach. "Have you spoken to her?"

"Yes, a couple of times. She understands that the plan didn't go as we'd hoped."

"No shit!" I huffed and walked the length of my downtown office, stopping just before the large windows and turning back around. "Is she… all right?"

"All employees are given a card, a number to call in case of mistreatment."

My mind went to Charli, the day she thought she was an employee, the day I'd frightened her more than I realized. "All employees?"

"Yes," Deloris replied.

"Did Karen Flores give a card to Charli?"

"She did. The first morning I met with Alex, I told her to call me, not Karen."

I wanted to know. I needed to know. "Did she…?"

The sides of Deloris's lips moved downward in a scowl. "Lennox, please don't. I would have told you if she had. I don't want to know why you're even asking. The phone call is only supposed to be made if the employee feels that she is in danger with the client. I realize it was all a setup with Alex, but I'd like to think that I know you, and I'm getting to know Alex well enough to say she has never felt endangered in your presence. Tell me that's the case."

"It's just that some of my…"

Her hand went up. "Too much information. No. Alex never called the number. I've given Chelsea the same option, to call me, if she's unsure about calling her handler, a woman with Infidelity in California. Chelsea hasn't called either number."

I blew out a long breath as I sat behind my desk. "This is bad enough. If she ends up hurt in any way, Charli will be… I can't even come up with a word. I believe irate is a vast understatement."

"I wish I could say for certain that Chelsea is unharmed. I've only spoken with her — it's too much of a risk to see her. I do know that it's taken her a while to come to terms with the entire agreement."

"Then why?" I asked. "I don't understand. Tell her to call the number. Get out."

"It's not that simple. It comes down to dollars and cents—mostly dollars. Since signing with Infidelity, besides the ten thousand we gave her for agreeing to our plan in the first place, the one to be placed with Severus Davis, she's earned twenty-five thousand from Infidelity. That's thirty-five thousand dollars."

"She's Charli's best friend. Surely the money isn't that important."

"Alex was out of Chelsea's league. If they hadn't been roommates, they probably never would have met. It just so happened that they hit it off, but yes, the money is that important. Chelsea attended Stanford for one year on scholarship. After that, she transferred to a state school. She's the first person in her family to graduate from college. You met her sister?"

I nodded, remembering the hospital room in Palo Alto.

"She graduated high school over a year ago and has been working at a store in a local mall. Chelsea now has the money to send her to college. You can only imagine what Chelsea's mother thinks of her daughter's new income."

Her mother. Strange, loud woman.

"But does Mrs. Moore know what Chelsea is doing for that income?"

"No," Deloris replied. "No one can know. It's the way it works. Spencer got her a job at Montague Corporation. It's the perfect cover for why she's in Savannah."

"What about Edward's family and friends?"

"As I said, she's integrating. According to Chelsea, the most difficult part has been facing Alex's mother. Apparently the two never hit it off. She said she'd always had the feeling Alex's mother didn't like her and since she showed up with Mr. Spencer, supposedly having had a secret affair for years behind Alex's back, Mrs. Fitzgerald has been less than pleasant."

"I can't say as though I blame her."

Deloris shrugged. "Chelsea is doing all she can to make this work. The last time we spoke she said she only has forty-nine and a half weeks to go. The young lady is a trouper. I don't see this ending sooner than the length of the agreement. Not without further scandal and to be honest, Edward Spencer can't afford more scandal. He's been called in for questioning on Melissa Summer's disappearance twice."

"What about Melissa's client?" I asked.

"He had an airtight alibi for the night she was assaulted. From everything I've seen and accessed, he isn't a suspect in her disappearance."

"Are there any other suspects?"

"No one who's been questioned."

I leaned back, pushing my chair to recline slightly. "What if they have reason to do more than suspect Spencer? What if they have enough to make a case?"

"It's my understanding that Chelsea is his new alibi. He was in California the week Melissa disappeared."

"Didn't Charli say that Spencer called her the same day we all arrived? That he said he was on his way there?"

Deloris pulled up a file on her iPad. "She didn't tell me that. But you're right: he called her. His number was on her phone. Remember I told you that I deduced that Alex was going to California because other than Isaac, you, and me, all her other calls came from California, including the one from Edward Spencer. I was able to confirm his location with his travel documents. He was in California—he flew into San Francisco on the day before we all traveled out there."

I shook my head. "Maybe I had that wrong. Too many fucked-up things since then."

"Tell her, Lennox. I can pull up an article from a Savannah gossip blog. You can say I showed it to you. Just tell her," Deloris implored.

"It's not going away, is it?"

"No. And Chelsea has resigned herself to that fact. She won't tell anyone that it was me who got her involved in Infidelity. Remember, the company doesn't really exist."

I ran my hand through my hair. "Fuck."

I PULLED MY suit jacket closed, latching the button as I stepped from the car. I wasn't sure if the chill was from the weather or the thought of my impending conversation with Charli.

Without a doubt, autumn was setting its claws into the Northeast. The breeze blowing between the buildings, especially now that the sun had set, contained more than a mild nip. October was almost here, and in New York it wouldn't be long before the snow began to flurry.

As traffic continued to pass, I noticed the small trees bordered by iron fences along the street. They grew in perfect squares of ground surrounded by sidewalk. Even under the streetlights, they were bright with color. Orange and yellow leaves blew in the cold wind as brown ones chased one another in cyclones that danced upon the pavement.

"Seven o'clock?" Isaac asked as he closed the car door behind me.

"Yes. Tomorrow morning."

"Yes, sir."

Another few steps and the glass door opened.

"It's getting colder every night, sir."

One side of my face rose in a lopsided grin. There was something comforting in the predictability of my doorman. "Yes, Hudson, it is."

"Miss Collins hasn't returned. But I do expect her soon."

My steps stuttered. "What? I thought she was home from class hours ago."

"Yes, sir, she was. She left about an hour ago and asked me to let you know that she didn't plan to be gone long."

I pulled my phone from my pocket and swiped the screen. One text message. How had I not seen it?

Charli: "RUNNING WITH PATRICK. WILL BE HOME SOON."

Instinctively I looked back out the windows only to see my own image. The sky was dark, creating a mirror instead of a portal to the world beyond the glass. Dark and cold. The muscles in my neck tightened.

"Was she alone?" I asked Hudson.

"No, Mr. Clayton was with her. I don't think he appreciates Miss Collins's affinity for healthy living."

I smiled at his observation. "Thank you, Hudson."

"Yes, sir. Have a nice night."

As the elevator moved upward, I tapped on Charli's GPS app. Another tap and a tiny map appeared with a moving blue dot. It was ridiculous how much comfort I found in that simple pearl necklace. I could even tap another icon and see that her heart rate was slightly elevated.

Charli didn't usually run in the evenings, but as I walked toward our apartment, the thought of her returning and being in need of a shower had my mind imagining all sorts of possibilities.

A succulent aroma met me at the door. I wasn't sure how much I paid Lana, but the woman needed a raise. No wonder Charli was running. The meals that Lana prepared had become more elaborate since I was no longer eating alone. Consuming them as frequently as we did would require more exercise or soon, a new, bigger-sized wardrobe.

I tossed my keys on the table near the door and flipped the switches to bring the apartment to life. As I did, the lights of the city disappeared and the windows reflected the interior. It wasn't often that I came home to an empty apartment. Though Charli had been living with me for less than two months, I'd grown accustomed to her presence. From her clothes in the closet to her cosmetics in the bathroom, she was part of our home.

I'd never imagined that I'd ever again have someone in my life and never dreamed that another would acclimate to my lifestyle so well. It was as if we belonged together, in every sense of the word. Even minutes without her in our home left a part of me void, creating a space that only she could fill.

I never intended for this to happen. Or imagined that one simple business trip to Del Mar could forever change my life. I chuckled as I took off my suit jacket and went to the kitchen to check out Lana's culinary creation. Who would have thought that a meeting I hadn't even wanted to attend would have brought someone as wonderful as Charli to my life?

"Nox?" Her voice rang through the apartment, accentuated by the sound of the front door closing.

"In the kitchen," I yelled as I waited for her to enter.

Catching her in my arms, I spun her around. She looked too fucking good and too carefree to tell her about Chelsea. Not yet.

"Stop!" Charli said with a giggle. "I'm gross and need a shower before we eat."

"You had me worried." I smoothed back the unruly locks of her auburn hair, strands that had gone rogue during her run. "I'm not used to getting home and finding you gone."

"I sent you a text."

"I know, but I like you here."

"I tried to get back here first. Pat had a rough day and wanted to run…" Her eyes sparkled, forehead shimmered with perspiration, and muscles quivered from her exertion in the cool weather.

I couldn't not voice my assessment. "Damn, you're beautiful."

Charli's face bowed, burrowing into my chest. "I'm disgusting. Give me ten minutes."

"No."

"No?" Her eyes opened wide.

"I just turned our dinner to warm. And well, with you in my arms, I'm feeling a little *dirty* myself." I arched my brows as I emphasized the word dirty.

"Oh." The gold of her eyes shimmered. "In that case. I have some good news."

"You do?"

"Yes," Charli said, taking my hand in hers. "I've got an absurdly large shower off *my* room. Since you don't really have a room anymore, thus no en-suite bath, I'll let you share mine. No sense wasting water."

"Beautiful and a conservationist. How'd I get so lucky?"

"I seem to recall a ridiculous pickup line by a pool…"

CHAPTER 32

ADELAIDE

LIGHT ASSAULTED MY eyes as the beige walls of our bedroom suite swayed, the ornate woodwork no longer present in straight lines but in undulating waves as it bowed against the contrasting color. Slamming my eyes shut, I held tight to the mattress as if it were a life raft capable of jettisoning me into the ocean's depths. Surely that made the most sense. Instead of being on a bed in an old Southern manor, I was being tossed at sea on a succession of whitecaps.

The rocky waters had my stomach reeling and head pounding.

A migraine.

Scrunching my lids tighter, I forced all light from my eyes. The movement caused my face to ache. It didn't matter. I knew from experience that even a smidgen of light could be all it took to send my body into a full-blown revolt. The way I felt, I wasn't sure I could swim to the shore or find the attached bathroom. Everything was too far away. If only I could sink into my pillows as if they were clouds made of fluff, not hard, fiber-filled units.

With attention to my breathing, I exhaled twice for every inhale. Slowly the racing in my veins slowed and my body relaxed just a bit. I tried to listen to the room around me, praying that I was alone.

I hadn't had a headache this bad in years, not since I'd started the preventive medication that I took religiously. I fought to recall the night before. The day before. Anything. It was a fog covered in dark smoke. My memory was a cool, damp spring morning and visibility was zero. I knew the terrain. I'd navigated it for what seemed like forever, but I couldn't find a recognizable marker.

I slowly reached for the bed around me and patted it softly as I confirmed that I was indeed alone.

The breathing had helped.

Inch by inch, I moved toward the edge of the mattress, slowly as to not incite a stampede of hooves that waited upon the plain for the first rock to fall.

With my feet nearing the floor, I attempted to rise, to sit upward.

How could a woman who weighed less than one hundred and twenty pounds have a head that easily exceeded a ton?

It was so heavy, too heavy.

I bit my bottom lip as I pushed off from the bed.

Success.

I was sitting.

Slowly, I tried to open my eyes. Only one at first, allowing just the faintest of light to penetrate my darkened world.

Glaring.

Draperies that covered nearly two walls of our suite were opened, allowing the Georgia sun entrance as it streamed inside, blanketing the room in an assault of illumination.

Morning? Afternoon?

I had no reference other than I was certain it wasn't night.

My phone and a clock were only a few feet away, but I knew that focusing on the little numbers would be that first rock, the one to start the avalanche, the one to incite the stampede through my body. Like Mufasa from the *Lion King*, I would certainly perish.

With my head held securely in my hands and my elbows on my knees, I worked to clear the fog. I recalled taking my medicine yesterday and the day before. I understood how it worked. Missing doses lessened its effect. The medication took nearly a month to reach its effective dose. I would never miss one, not even one.

Last night Alton and I had been to a dinner out near the coast. The eloquent seafood restaurant was refined and catered to Georgia's elite. It had been our first time out in public with Bryce and Chelsea. Not only had she accompanied him to Evanston for another deposition, they'd made more than a few appearances around town. The locals were beginning to talk. Though I knew it was only a matter of time before Alexandria heard the rumors, I couldn't bring myself to be the one to tell her unless it was in person.

That was one of the topics I'd planned to discuss when I visited New York City. My plans had been foiled as I waited for Alton to leave on one of his trips. They normally occurred frequently, yet lately he'd stayed in town. I wasn't sure if it was because of the Chelsea thing, but he'd cancelled his last trip. It was the week I'd hoped to visit Alexandria. Jane had called and asked if we could reschedule.

Two weeks later and I was still waiting for Alton to leave.

It had become the story of my life.

The other thing that had happened since Chelsea had arrived was that my husband had been overly attentive. I assumed it had to do with appearances. Nevertheless, I couldn't manage a one-day trip even if I tried.

Through it all, I'd stayed true to my plan of trying to prove that Alton was somehow involved in orchestrating Alexandria and Lennox's meeting. Though I'd spoken to Natalie about it, nothing seemed to verify my suspicions. If anything, by Alton's reaction to Chelsea, he was growing tired of the continued charade and ready to finalize Bryce and Alexandria's nuptials.

It didn't make sense.

Water was all I drank yesterday prior to dinnertime. I recalled Alton once again coming to our suite instead of staying downstairs, ever dutifully making us both before-dinner cocktails. Mine had been wine. My first glass of the day. And then in the limousine I had a second glass.

The restaurant was simply beautiful. Though she tried to hide it, Chelsea's unease at being out of her element was glaringly obvious. If I didn't hate the entire plan I may have felt a smidgen of pity for the poor girl. It appeared as though she was trying. It also made me wonder if none of Alexandria's refinement had rubbed off on her during their years of living together.

How Chelsea was hired for this position was beyond me.

Looks. Sex.

Apparently she had a brain, but I'd yet to witness it. As the evening progressed, I got the feeling that even Bryce was losing patience with some of her uncouth ways. The looks that I saw exchanged between she and Bryce reinforced my belief that Alexandria should not be married to him.

Many wouldn't recognize the warnings, but I'd lived with them for over twenty years. Chelsea's trepidation was real. Even without the confirmation of physical bruising, I was most certain that Edward Bryce Carmichael Spencer was indeed his father's son.

That was where the night began to fade away. Like a club illuminated by strobe lighting, there were flashes of memory. Nothing stood out. Nothing seemed out of place. The restaurant. Another drink on the veranda overlooking the ocean. A photo opportunity with the four of us. The limousine ride back to the manor. Waking in a shower of sunshine.

Hours were missing. There were large gaping holes.

Two glasses of wine before the restaurant and maybe two during dinner.

It was barely a luncheon's worth of alcohol.

Maybe the memory loss had been caused by the onset of the migraine.

Slowly, I stood and made my way to the bathroom and opened the drawer of my vanity. Through squinted eyes, I caught a glimpse of the woman in the mirror. Surely she wasn't me. Her hair was uncustomarily disheveled. And her eyes… I pushed against the bags that seemed to have grown beneath. Why were they so puffy?

What the hell?

Once this headache was gone, my plastic surgeon would be on speed dial.

It would only take a few of my Vicodin to ease the pain. After all, I hadn't taken any for quite some time. I'd been saving them for another use. And then, Jane found them…

I rummaged around the drawer, pulling bottles out and throwing them onto the counter. The clatter tore at my nerves as one by one, large and small plastic containers littered the vanity. They were the same as any found at a common drugstore. Acetaminophen. Aspirin. Even ibuprofen. There wasn't one prescription bottle, not one amber container with my name printed upon the label.

No Vicodin. No Percocet. Not even any codeine.

Damn Jane!

This was her doing. I knew it.

Not only had she taken the pills I'd had in the glass, she'd come into our suite, my room, my bathroom, and rid the drawers and cabinets of all my narcotics. Hadn't she seen the progress I'd made since that night, since meeting with Stephen?

My body trembled as I imagined calling and yelling at her.

I'd call first and yell later. I wasn't sure my head could take the volume. Even the thought of speaking above a whisper twisted my stomach and increased the throb in my temples.

A knock at the outer door of my suite echoed like a jackhammer off the marble tile of the bathroom.

Thank the sweet Lord. This had to be Jane.

Reaching for the doorjamb, I steadied myself, tightened the robe I'd found hanging near the shower, and made my way toward the outer door of our suite.

This would save me the trouble of calling.

I smoothed my hair as I trekked across the front sitting room.

Another knock.

"Stop," my request was barely audible as I reached unsteadily for the doorknob.

"Jane—" I stopped speaking as Dr. Beck's solemn expression came into focus.

"Adelaide."

My eyes squinted as I tried to make sense of his presence. "Dr. Beck, why are you here?"

He reached for my hand and held it gently in his as he assessed its movement. "Let's get you seated. You're shaking."

I didn't move from the doorway. "Who called you?"

"One of your staff. She said you needed me, and I can see she was right." As he spoke he moved toward me, causing me to step backward until we were both inside the suite. Quietly he shut the door. "How are you?" His words came quietly with an inflection of sympathy.

I reached for my temples. "I have a migraine, and I can't find my medicine. I was about to call Jane. I think she knows where it is."

Dr. Beck's head moved back and forth. "Adelaide, I've prescribed over two months' worth of Vicodin in the last thirty days. I understand that things can be misplaced, but this is getting out of hand."

"Yes, I know. I haven't taken it. I don't need you to give me more. I need Jane to bring me the medicine I have."

"Why would Jane have your medicine?"

"Because… she takes care of me." I straightened my shoulders. "It's her job. Now tell me why you're here."

"I was called and asked to come," he said again. "I was told you needed more medicine. That you weren't waking and with Mr. Fitzgerald out of town, your people were concerned."

Out of town? He hadn't said he was going out of town.

I should call Stephen and see if he's learned any more. I could call Alexandria and go to New York. The thoughts came and went… fleeting moments of cognitive comprehension. I turned to Dr. Beck. "What time is it?"

Dr. Beck looked down at his watch. "It's nearly four."

My eyes opened wide, only to have them close again. Inhale. Exhale. "In the afternoon? No. It can't be four. I have a luncheon at the museum."

Dr. Beck's hand covered mine. "How many Vicodin have you taken?"

"I haven't taken any. I haven't needed them. Not since you prescribed the daily medication. Well, not since it started working. This is the first migraine in months, maybe longer."

"Yet you called the office yourself for more Vicodin only a few weeks ago."

I let out a long breath. "For situations like this. To have it on hand." I shook my head. "Doctor, how did this happen? I-I don't recall last night."

"What do you mean you don't recall?"

"There are gaps, like blackouts."

"I've spoken to you about the side effects of narcotics and alcohol."

"But I haven't taken the narcotics. And…" I spoke louder than I intended, "…my alcohol intake is down."

Dr. Beck looked down at my hand under his. "Adelaide, you're still shaking. I was told you haven't eaten. You need to eat."

The confusion and fog added to my unease. "One Vicodin, please, Dr. Beck. I know you have one. You never come to see me without it."

Dr. Beck opened the bag he'd placed on the floor near his chair. "You haven't taken any today?"

"I just woke. I don't understand what's happening."

He pulled an amber bottle from the bag. The sight was like showing a cookie jar to a toddler. My heart rate increased in anticipation. Dr. Beck turned the childproof cap and sprinkled a palm full of white oblong tablets into his hand.

My mouth watered as I raked my bottom lip between my teeth and swallowed. Those were 5-milligram tablets. I'd recognize them anywhere.

"Doctor, those are only fives. I need two."

Begrudgingly, he pinched two from his hand and poured the rest back into the bottle. "Can I get you a glass of water?"

I pointed toward the highboy across the room. "There's water over there."

Dr. Beck held the pills captive as he went to the highboy, no doubt assessing the bottles of alcohol. It was, after all, the place where as of late Alton had decided to prepare his evening cocktails. After filling a glass with water from a bottle, he lifted a re-corked bottle of Montague Private Collection. "Have you had any of this today?"

"No. I just woke." Exasperation and desperation were evident in my voice.

He returned and handed me the glass of water. I took a sip and then held out my hand for the capsules.

"Adelaide, I think I should run some tests. The memory loss. The sleeping all day. This isn't like you."

The fingers of my hand opened and closed in a silent plea for the pills. After a moment of hesitation, he placed the capsules in my palm. Before I could place them in my mouth, he held my clenched fist.

"Come to my office tomorrow."

It wasn't a request. It didn't matter though. At that moment I'd agree to anything. It could have been the devil himself—I knew him intimately. I would have said yes no matter what the request or command as long as I got the pills.

"Yes."

CHAPTER 33

CHARLI

I SENT CHELSEA another text message. It was my daily routine: each morning before class and each afternoon on my way home. I was beginning to wonder if she'd changed her number. That was the thing with text messages: the sender had no way of knowing if the recipient actually received the message. It wasn't like email that would bounce back a non-receivable message. And it had.

Chelsea's email address, the one she'd had the entire time we were in California, was no longer active.

I scrolled back through my text messages. It had been over three weeks. Not only couldn't I reach Chelsea, but I also couldn't reach her mother. All of my calls to Tina Moore had gone straight to voicemail where her mailbox was full. In desperation, I looked her mother up on the Internet. I didn't know why she wasn't answering my cell phone calls, but maybe she still had a house phone.

My heart leapt with a flicker of hope when I found a number.

With Clayton driving me back to the apartment, I programmed her number and called.

"Hello?" The voice answered.

I recognized Tina Moore immediately. "Mrs. Moore, this is Alex Collins."

"Alex." Her normally gregarious tone dulled. "It's nice to hear from you. I'm surprised you called."

My fingers gripped the phone tighter. "Why would you be surprised?"

"It's that Chelsea told me what happened. I don't blame you for being upset. Sometimes things happen. I was shocked myself."

I shook my head. "I don't know what you're talking about. I've been trying to reach Chelsea for nearly three weeks. Her email is changed, and I'm not even sure she's getting my texts."

"Probably not," Tina said matter-of-factly. "She has a new phone now with her job. I don't think she's using both."

That knowledge made me feel better, in a way. At least Chelsea hadn't been ignoring me, but why hadn't she called? "Her job?" I asked. "The last time we spoke she said she didn't get the job in DC."

"No, not DC. She's in Savannah."

I blinked as Clayton drove us through late-afternoon traffic. "What? She's in Savannah, as in Georgia?"

"Yes, dear. You really should talk with her. This is rather awkward."

Since when did Tina Moore worry about anything being awkward? "I'd love to talk to her. I don't know why she thinks I'm angry. I'm worried. I've been worried sick since our last conversation."

"There's nothing to be worried about. Chelsea's fine. She's working for some large cigarette company in the human resources department. Silly me, I thought a psychology major would go into counseling or something, but apparently it's a good background for HR."

Cigarette? Did she mean tobacco?

I had to be somehow misconstruing. "The company, do you know the name?"

"Yes. Goodness, she's said it a few times. Milburn or Montgate… something like that. You know like the old Shakespeare play everyone reads in high school."

"Montague?" I asked. Acid bubbled from my stomach as I said the name. "Montague Corporation."

"I think that's it!" Tina declared triumphantly.

"Chelsea is working for Montague Corporation?"

"Yes, in their HR department."

I didn't give a shit what department she was in. I was more concerned with why in God's name my best friend would be working for Montague. She had to know it was my family's company. Or did she? I'd purposely avoided all things Montague while at Stanford. Chelsea knew my name was Collins and my parents' last name was Fitzgerald. I couldn't recall if I'd ever mentioned Montague. But without a doubt, she knew I was from Savannah.

"Mrs. Moore," I asked, "why does Chelsea think I'm angry?"

"Well, like I said, you two should talk. Are you still seeing that incredibly handsome gentleman?"

Subject change!

"I am. Please don't change the subject."

"I'm not. That's the point. That's what I told her. Really, you two should talk."

I took a deep breath and held the phone between my shoulder and ear as I unzipped my backpack and searched for a pen and a piece of paper. "Would you please give me her new number?"

"I-I don't know."

"This doesn't make any sense. Why wouldn't you know if you can give me her number? She's my best friend and something isn't right. I can feel it." I was getting more worked up than I'd been before I called.

"You know, I believe in those things."

"What?"

"It's like a sixth sense. I think they're real."

The woman was batshit crazy.

"Her number?" I asked again.

"Alex, dear, I'll tell her we spoke. I'll tell her to give you a call. You really don't sound as upset as she said."

"Not with her," I clarified. "I'm upset that I can't reach her."

"Yes, well, I'll let her know. I need to go now."

"Thank you, Mrs. Moore." *For nothing.*

I held my phone as I peered out the car's window. The skies were gray and a cold rain had been falling off and on throughout day. It was the perfect weather for the way that call made me feel.

What the hell?

Chelsea was working for Montague. Maybe that was why she thought I'd be angry. Maybe she did know it was my family's company, and I knew without a doubt that she knew how I felt about my family. But a job is a job.

If she'd gotten hired solely based on her degree and qualifications, I didn't give a shit. I was happy for her. What concerned me was the rodent of suspicion that began to claw to life in the recesses of my mind: the belief that everything wasn't that simple.

Why would my roommate, Chelsea Moore, whom my mother never seemed to like, be offered a job at Montague?

Someone was up to something and I feared that Chelsea would be the one who'd end up hurt in the process.

Once I was back in our apartment, I went to my office and Googled Montague Corporation. The picture on the website of the CEO made my skin crawl. It was probably taken over ten years ago. Alton's hair still had a hint of blond, but his eyes were just as beady as ever.

It had felt good to be honest with Nox about things from my childhood. I'd been truthful, but not too explicit. Seeing Alton's picture filled me with the dread I used to feel knowing he was home, under the same roof. It wasn't only the corporal punishments or that I was a constant disappointment. It was his need to demean and belittle everything from my choices to my accomplishments. It was as if doing it made him more powerful.

I knew Alton had nothing to do with the daily hire of employees at Montague Corporation. That job was beneath him, unless it was to hire his own assistants. He liked having a part in that. Youth, big breasts, and long legs were the main requirements. I was pretty sure those particular attributes rated more than the ability to read and write.

My stomach churned at the thought of Chelsea working near him. Thank God she was in HR and not in administration.

I scrolled the website until I found an information telephone number.

Deciding if I would use my entire name, I programmed the number into my phone and hit *call*. It took an incessant amount of number-pushing, but I finally reached a real person.

"Montague Corporation, how may I assist your call?"

"I'm trying to reach one of your employees," I replied.

"Ma'am, this is the general information number."

"Then I need the number for your human resources department."

"If this is a job inquiry, we ask that you visit our website at www—"

"No," I said, interrupting the receptionist, "this isn't a job inquiry. I need to speak to an employee who works in HR."

"Do you know the party's extension?"

"I don't," I said incredulously. "That's why I called you."

"I'm sorry—"

"Your name?" I asked, using my most authoritative tone.

"Kate."

"Kate, perhaps you'd like my name?"

"Ma'am, I can't—"

"Alexandria Montague Collins. I will mention your lack of assistance to my father, Alton Fitzgerald, the next time we speak." I spat out the words, not wanting them to remain on my tongue any longer than necessary. Kate didn't need to know I had no intention of speaking to him anytime soon.

"Miss Collins, I'm sorry. May I connect you to human resources? Who is the employee you'd like to reach?"

"Chelsea Moore. I believe she was a recent hire."

"Yes, she'd still be in our directory…"

Suddenly, Kate and I were best friends. She couldn't do enough to help me, other than actually connect me to Chelsea. According to the person who answered in HR, Miss Moore was out of the office, but they would take my message.

As I hung up, I contemplated my new knowledge. At the very least I'd confirmed that Chelsea was all right. She was living in Savannah and employed at Montague Corporation. I couldn't make heads or tails out of why, but that information was more than I knew this morning. I also knew to stop sending text messages to a phone she was no longer using.

I considered calling my mother or Jane and asking them what they knew, but what were the chances that either one of them knew anything about Chelsea? I was most certain that my best friend and mother weren't frequenting the same establishments. I imagined Chelsea with a plastic 'to go' cup on River Street. My mother had never been to River Street after dark, and she'd lived in Savannah her entire life.

I had one last hope.

Since none of it made sense to me, I decided to call the one person who made sense out of everything.

"Deloris," I said when she answered.

"Alex. Is everything all right?"

"Yes, fine." As the words came from my lips, I heard the front door of the apartment open. I stilled and listened, knowing it was too early for Nox.

"Hello?" The friendly female voice came from the living room as the alarm system beeped with the input of a code.

I covered the mouthpiece. "Lana, I'm in my office."

In merely a few seconds, she was stepping through the threshold. Lana was a nice-looking woman in her early forties with shoulder-length brown hair and a fit build. Whenever I saw her, she was dressed casually in blue jeans and Sketchers. I supposed there was no need to dress formally to cook, clean, and do laundry.

"It's just me," she said with a smile. "I'm never sure if anyone is here."

"Only me," I confirmed. "But I'll stay out of your way. Mr. Demetri has made it perfectly clear that your cooking is preferred to mine."

Her cheeks rose as she beamed at the compliment. "I'm sure if you had more time…"

I waved her off. "No. Time won't help my culinary skills." I pointed to my phone.

"Oh, sorry," she said in a whisper. "I'll be in the kitchen."

I nodded as I went back to Deloris. "Sorry, Deloris. Lana just got here."

"What can I do for you?" Deloris asked.

"I just learned that Chelsea has a new job."

"You did?" she asked with more concern in her voice than seemed warranted.

"It's not bad," I reassured. "At least, I hope it isn't."

"It's not?"

"Her mother told me that she's working for Montague Corporation. Do you think that's coincidental or just plain weird?"

"I suppose it could be either."

I tilted my head and stretched out my plea. "I was wondering… if in your spare time… you could do a little research? I just want to know that my family isn't up to something."

"I'll see what I can learn."

A weight lifted from my chest as if I'd passed the baton of concern from me to her. From the little she'd learned about my trust fund, I knew I was passing my distress to capable hands. "Thank you, Deloris. You're the best."

The sound of an incoming call rang through my phone. I looked at the screen.

NOX - PRIVATE NUMBER

I hadn't changed the name he'd entered in Del Mar.

"I need to go. Nox's calling."

"Okay. I'll let you know what I discover," Deloris replied.

"Thanks again."

I swiped the screen.

"Hey," I said with more joy in my voice than I'd felt all afternoon.

"Princess," Nox's deep velvety voice rumbled through me, washing away the last traces of anxiety over Chelsea and filling me with his presence. "Tell me you're home," he demanded.

My fingers instinctively went to my necklace. "I'm sure you can look at your phone and figure out exactly where I am."

"I can," he confirmed. "But I like hearing it from you better."

"I'm home."

"Is Lana there?"

"She just arrived," I said.

"Tell her not to worry about dinner. I'm taking the most gorgeous woman in New York City out to dinner tonight."

"You are? What will I eat while you're out?" I asked with a smirk.

"Have I mentioned how much I love that sassy mouth?"

"Is there a special occasion?" My thoughts volleyed between excitement to be out on a date and the reading assignment that was due on Monday.

"Yes," his voice slowed. "I plan to wine and dine her so I can seduce her later."

My heart fluttered as my cheeks rose. "Mr. Demetri, that sounds intriguing. However, I'd bet any woman would be open to the suggestion of your seduction, even without the wine and dine."

"But you see, I don't want *any* woman. I want the woman who takes my breath away on a daily basis. I want the enamoring and alluring woman who blows my mind with her stubborn, smartass replies. I want the woman who's intelligent beyond my comprehension. I know that she is excessively gifted, because she reads these ridiculously thick law books that would put me to sleep with only one paragraph. And I know she reads those books, because even though she has her own office and I've told her not to, she leaves them lying around the apartment."

My smile grew. "Maybe you should bring that up to her?"

"Yes, princess, reminding her of my rules was part of tonight's plan."

I shifted uncomfortably in my chair. "After the wine and dine?"

"Whenever I say, because let me tell you that right now even the thought of what I have planned is making me uncomfortable. You see, I'm lucky enough to know what it's like to have that gorgeous woman near me, to listen to her sweet voice—her moans and cries."

Fuck!

"I've seen her fine ass reddened and know how tight she is when she's coming apart around me."

"Jesus, Nox." My words were more of a whimper as my ass tingled with phantom redness. I loved that even after my confession of childhood issues, Nox didn't treat me with kid gloves. Instead, he made me feel strong and capable in the midst of his dominance.

"So be a good girl," he said, "and tell Lana to leave, or she may be in for more of a show than she wants."

I nodded, trying to moisten my tongue and lips, but it was quite obvious that my mouth had gone dry, sending all the moisture to another part of my body. "Yes, Mr. Demetri. And when will you be arriving?"

"Six sharp, but you have a delivery coming any minute."

"I do?"

"Your clothes for our evening," he said. "Listen carefully, because I expect to be obeyed. The only items I want added to the ensemble that will arrive are those fuck-me black shoes and your necklace."

My insides torqued at the memory of the shoes he described planted on the dashboard of the Boxster on Highway 101.

"Do as you're told," Nox warned, "and I'll be nice and let you come. I believe it's time to bring your vibrator back to life."

"And if I don't do as you say?" I asked playfully.

Nox laughed. "Sassy and sexy. Don't worry, princess, I have plans for that too."

The line went dead.

I sat unmoving for a minute, my chest rising and falling with exaggerated breaths as I imagined the possibilities for Nox's plans. And then, hearing the sound of pots and pans coming from the kitchen, I stood.

"Lana," I called as I headed her direction.

CHAPTER 34

CHARLI

I STARED NERVOUSLY at the full-length mirror in our dressing room. When I'd opened the large box that had arrived earlier in the day, I gasped, shocked at the dress Nox had ordered. It wasn't the dress itself. It was beautiful: direct from Saks Fifth Avenue with a designer tag. What surprised me was the color.

Red. Bright candy-apple red. Bring-traffic-to-a-screeching-halt red. I had to wonder if it was some kind of play on the skater dress I'd purchased months ago.

If it were, I didn't believe he'd selected this one to make me look like a whore. The red dress I removed from the box was classy and would cover me in all the right places. Nevertheless, I'd searched the box and accompanying bags for a gold armband, like the one I wore that night but found none. As I looked from bag to bag, I also didn't find a bra or panties. There was, however, a black lace garter belt and accompanying lace-top stockings.

Holding Nox's choice of undergarments in my hands, I felt the contrasting sensations of the rough yet soft lace beneath my fingers, and it infused my bloodstream with adrenaline. The hormone flowed and swirled throughout my system until my heart raced and insides clenched.

Once I'd showered and completed my makeup, I secured my hair. With my auburn color, I mostly avoided wearing reds and pinks. Keeping that in mind, I styled it up, sophisticated yet alluring, purposely leaving long curls to dance and bob delicately around my shoulders.

At nearly six o'clock, I eased into the clothes he'd had delivered. Small clasps dangled from the garter belt and linked to the stockings, leaving my thighs and core uncovered. The different sensations from the various materials, or lack thereof, electrified my skin. Soft nylon caressed my legs, the lace of the belt hugged my hips and lower waist, and at the same time, my upper thighs were exposed and vulnerable.

I imagined how the bare skin would tingle as cool autumn air blew under the skirt of the dress and how that same skin would warm as my flesh rubbed together ever so slightly as I took each step. I closed my eyes and allowed one of my hands to cup my own breast as the other drifted lower. Brushing my clit and pinching my nipple, my core tightened. Instinctively, I knew that wind and friction wouldn't be the only elements I'd be exposed to with this choice of undergarments. There would be nothing separating me from Nox's inclinations.

Before my imagination took me too far, I eased the red dress over the lingerie. The fabric fit perfectly in all the right places. Tighter at the breasts, it was strapless with a high-low hem and chic pleats near the trim waist. The hem, even at its highest point was only slightly above my knees. In the back it dropped nearly to my calves. Even if I spun in a small circle and the skirt flared, no one could see what I wore underneath. Only the black nylons and my black Louboutins were visible.

While the ensemble underneath was sexy and flirtatious, it was totally hidden to everyone else. As I continued to peer in the mirror, I recalled something Nox had said. The memory brought a smile to my already-pink cheeks.

He'd said the world would see a princess, but only we would know the truth.

The truth was that Nox's choice of clothing didn't make me feel like the Infidelity whore he'd been alluding to at that time. Not anymore. With Lennox Demetri, whether I wore blue jeans and a t-shirt or scandalous undergarments, he made me feel like the woman he'd met in Del Mar, the princess who enjoyed the thrill of being a secret slut.

"Stunning."

The deep velvet voice thundered throughout the dressing room, pulling me from my imagination-induced trance. I hadn't even heard the beeps of the alarm or the opening and closing of the door. My cheeks blushed brighter, matching my dress, as I imagined Nox arriving only moments earlier and finding me with only the garter belt, stockings, and my own roaming hands.

Before I could spin toward him, Nox's embrace surrounded me from behind, and his cologne settled around me in an intoxicating cloud. With his chin above my shoulder he spoke near my ear, the warmth of his breath prickling my skin.

"You *are* the most gorgeous woman in all of New York City." His lips found my neck, and soft and slow kisses trailed downward over my collarbone. "No," he corrected, "in the world."

My head wobbled as I tried unsuccessfully to stifle a moan.

Nox's eyes met mine in the mirror. "I trust you're wearing everything I sent?"

I nodded, my chest rising and falling, the motion making my new necklace bob against the red material.

"And nothing else?"

"Nothing." The word came out breathlessly, though I was inhaling quicker than I could exhale. "Do you want to see?"

"Oh, I do. I want to do more than see," he promised.

I veiled my eyes at the timbre of his tone.

"Call me a masochist," he went on, "but, princess, for the next few hours I want to imagine what you have under that dress. I will touch it and you, but my eyes will have to wait until I have you back here where I want you." He pulled me closer, my back against his front and my bottom tight against his erection. "Feel what you're doing to me? But I know it'll be worth it, because, fuck, seeing you in our bed, your hands tied, wearing nothing but that garter, stockings, and those sexy shoes will be better than any Christmas morning, ever."

I couldn't stop the whimper as my body clenched with need. "Sadist," I said with a lustful smirk. "That's what you are."

I opened my eyes in time to see his menacing grin.

"That too, princess. That too." He gave me one more kiss, this time chastely on my cheek. "The car is waiting, but I need about five minutes to shower and change."

I reached for his hands, still around my waist. "Don't change. I love you the way you are."

His cheeks rose higher. "More. Five minutes."

And with that, his warmth was gone.

My eyes followed Nox and I bit my lip, watching as he quickly stripped and walked toward the bathroom. His jacket, tie, shirt, belt, and trousers created a trail, like breadcrumbs leading to my pleasure, my ecstasy. With only words and a few kisses, Nox had turned my thighs slick. When the water thundered from the confines of the shower, I considered forgoing our date, stripping out of the dress, and joining him under the warm spray.

However, the masochistic part of me wouldn't allow it. I wanted everything he'd described from dinner on the town to the dessert back at the apartment. Perhaps I had a hint of sadism, too, because the idea of Nox suffering with blue balls while we ate brought an even bigger smile to my face.

As I was about to walk to the bedroom to find the handbag and light sweater that had accompanied the Saks delivery, I noticed the belt Nox had dropped haphazardly to the floor. My fingers covered my freshly painted lips to stifle a gasp.

I would recognize that belt over any of Nox's assortment. What caught my attention was the buckle—very distinctive silver with a swirl. It was the same one I'd found in his closet in Rye, the one he'd told me to use, and the one he'd told me to bring back to the city.

Minutes later, his delicious cologne alerted me to his presence in the living room before anything else. It was when I turned that he took my breath away. It wasn't fair that I'd been getting ready for hours and in five minutes Nox was a walking Adonis. All showered and fresh, his pale blue eyes glowed over the perfect trimmed amount of scruff, while his neck was smooth and freshly shaven. The blue suit he now wore with a silver tie was crisp and clean. However, what caught my attention was the silver swirl of his belt's buckle. He'd put the same one back on.

Nox's lips quirked upward as he followed my gaze and touched the buckle. "Yes, princess, it's definitely become my favorite, but the problem seems to be that you've been too obedient."

I considered confessing my brief stint of self-pleasure, but instead, I squared my shoulders and stepped toward him—this dominant, loving, overprotective dichotomy of a man who towered over me. With mere inches separating us, I lowered my voice and strung out my words, bringing just a hint of my Southern accent back to life. "Oh, Mr. Demetri, give me a chance. I can be *very* bad."

DON'T WISH AWAY your todays thinking about tomorrow.

It was something Jane used to tell me.

As Nox and I rode in the back of the black sedan to a small Italian restaurant, as we walked to a booth with a flickering red candle, one apparently reserved for us, and as my high-heeled shoes clicked on the worn wooden floor, I was doing exactly what Jane had told me not to do. I was thinking about what was to come… yes, literally and figuratively.

While my sexy lingerie and Nox's teasing touches in the car had me wound tighter than a drum, the dimly lit room and the tantalizing aroma of garlic, awakened a new hunger. The growling of my stomach as we sat, alerted the man holding my hand to my newfound desire. With simply a glint in his light blue eyes, I saw his thoughts.

Princess, you'd better eat. You'll need your strength.

Nox hadn't said the words, but my two cravings—him and food—converged into one insatiable hunger. I was on the brink of sexual as well as nutritional starvation and my only source of gratification was the man with the knowing gleam.

Standing back, Nox allowed me to enter the booth. As I sat, he surprised me by scooting in next to me. "What?" I asked.

"I don't like having my back toward the door," he replied nonchalantly. "This way we can both see the entire restaurant."

His explanation sounded plausible. After all, he was right. Other than the kitchen, from our vantage point we could see the entire place. I'd never eaten at this restaurant, but with one glance I knew it was one of the establishments that the locals loved—a diamond in the rough hidden from tourists.

"Have you eaten here before?" I asked.

"Many times. Next to my mother's and Silvia's, Antonio makes the best lasagna on the planet."

"I thought Lana's was amazing."

Nox's large hand splayed over my thigh, revealing the real reason for our seating arrangement. I sucked in a deep breath as his fingers slowly moved, lifting the hem of my dress.

"Wait until you taste this," he said enthusiastically, making no reference to his wandering hand. "It's like heaven on your tongue."

As his fingers inched upward, an older man with a chef's apron and a thick mustache appeared. "Mr. Demetri, so good to have you here. It's been too long."

I swallowed as Nox's hand stilled, staying hidden beneath the red fabric.

"Antonio." Nox nodded at the man. "What have I said? Oren is Mr. Demetri. I'm Lennox." He turned my direction. "And this is my beautiful girl friend, Alexandria."

"Alexandria," Antonio said, lifting his hand toward me palm up.

I managed to free my right hand from behind Nox's arm as his fingers stayed fused to my thigh.

Taking my hand, Antonio bowed at the waist and kissed my knuckles. "A beautiful name for an even lovelier woman."

I grinned. "Thank you."

"So," Antonio asked, "what are you doing with Lennox?"

My head sprang back in surprise. "I-I…"

As I fought for words, Antonio went on, "My wife, she die two years ago." He motioned dramatically toward his chest. "I'm available." He gestured around the room. "All this could be yours. Say the word."

My smile grew. "That's quite the offer, Antonio." I leaned slightly forward. "Maybe you and I should talk when Lennox isn't around."

Nox's fingers inched upward, staking his claim as well as making it difficult for me to keep my concentration on Antonio.

Antonio winked and nudged Nox's shoulder. "I like her. You hold on to this one." He lowered his tone. "If he doesn't…" Antonio was speaking to me. "…you call me."

I placed my hand over Nox's to stop its ascension. "I will keep that in mind."

"Dolcetto?" Antonio asked Nox.

"*Sì.*"

It was only one simple word, yet the way the Italian rolled from Nox's lips, caused me to turn and look at him anew.

"*Subito*," Antonio replied with a grin and turned away.

"You speak Italian?" I asked with more than a bit of awe to my voice.

"Princess, we've yet to explore my large array of talents. Speaking of which…" Nox's fingers grazed the lace top of one of the stockings and a low murmur resonated from his throat. Just as he began to move his fingers higher, Antonio reappeared, a bottle of wine in his hand and two glasses. Next to Antonio was a young woman carrying a large plate with antipasto—meats, olives, mushrooms, anchovies, artichoke hearts and a variety of cheeses and two smaller plates.

While Antonio spoke, uncorked the bottle, and poured a small amount of wine into one of the glasses, the pad of Nox's finger moved back and forth over the clasp connecting the garter belt with the stockings. As Antonio handed Nox the glass, Nox unsnapped the clasp and moved his hand to secure the goblet offered. The small elastic strap sprang from the stockings, causing me to jump with an embarrassing, audible gasp.

Pink flooded my cheeks as Antonio asked, "*Signorina*, you no like *vino*?"

"I do." My response came too fast as Nox's pale eyes danced with navy. Mischief filled his expression as he took a sip of the wine and drank in my embarrassment.

"Perfect," Nox announced, before lifting the same glass to my lips.

Obediently, I sipped the medium-bodied red wine, allowing it to linger on my tongue. It wasn't nearly as thick as a cabernet and had a slightly tangy flavor. After swallowing, I nodded in agreement. "Delicious."

"The *primo*?" Antonio asked.

"Antonio," Nox said with a shake of his head. "Nothing but the lasagna. You know it's my favorite."

"*Si*," he said, and again he was gone.

Nox's eyes sparkled with the reflection of the flickering candle as he poured wine into both glasses. "You seem a little jumpy, princess?"

I shook my head. "Dick," I muttered under my breath.

Nox leaned closer. "Keep begging, beautiful. You'll have it."

Young ladies came and went, bringing glasses and water as well as clearing away the antipasto. Next, the lasagna arrived. Visually it was as appealing as Nox had promised, but it was the aroma that had my mouth watering. When I reached for my fork, Nox shook his head.

Unsure what he'd meant, I pulled my hands back to my lap. Nox took his fork and cut off a corner of our second course. Before offering me a bite, he reached for my water glass. Lifting it to my lips he said, "Drink."

My tummy fluttered with butterfly wings as I did as he said.

"Cleansing the palate," he explained.

Pouting his full lips, Nox blew gently on the combination of warm noodles, cheeses, and sauces, and then he directed the fork toward me. "Close your eyes and open your mouth."

Such a simple request, yet his words made the butterflies in my tummy turn to bats as both of my hungers screamed for fulfillment. Dutifully I lowered my lids and opened my lips.

The lasagna was heaven, just as Nox had said. It enticed my tongue just before I swallowed, and the deliciousness made its way toward my stomach to feed and hopefully calm the ravenous bats. When I was certain I couldn't eat another bite, the young ladies returned, one with a platter of chicken and fish and the other with an assortment of vegetables.

I shook my head after they walked away. "Are you trying to make me fat?"

"No, princess. I'm making sure you have the sustenance to endure all that I have planned for the evening."

My breath caught in my lungs as I lifted my fork piled with broccoli and zucchini. "I'm not sure I can anymore. After all of this food, I may be sleeping."

Nox leaned closer, his hand back on my thigh. His fingers splayed. "I'm most confident I can keep you awake."

When the tray of cannolis, tiramisu, biscuits, and slivers of cheesecake arrived, I helplessly shook my head. "No, I can't."

Nox graciously declined the *dolce*—the sweet ending to our meal—explaining that we were too full to eat another bite. It was Antonio who insisted that he box them up and we take them home.

Moments later we were back in the sedan with a Styrofoam box of delectable delights.

With his eyes fixed only on me, Nox moved the small white container from my lap to the floor. His hand moved shamelessly under my dress. I'd long since given up the idea that Isaac and even Clayton wouldn't witness some of their boss's advances. Nox simply didn't seem to care that they were present.

I gasped.

At the brush of his fingers on my bare skin, my blood forgot its assignment. Digesting my food was no longer a priority. My circulatory system accelerated its functions with a vengeance, tightening my core.

"N-Nox," I panted as I leaned toward him.

"My patience has expired," Nox said, lifting my skirt and exposing the top of the stockings.

The sound he expelled was somewhere between a growl and a hiss as he tenderly refastened the small clasp from the garter belt to the top lace of the stockings.

"Is that really necessary?" I asked. "I mean, won't you be unhooking that soon?"

Nox's grin broadened as his fingers moved higher. "Not until I have you begging for relief."

Begging? I was ready to start before we ever made it to the apartment.

Hours? Days? Weeks? Later…

More likely only minutes…

We were in our apartment. Nox placed the food container on the kitchen counter and tugged my hand toward the bedroom. Only briefly did I consider that the pastries should be refrigerated.

Maybe less than briefly.

The sweets were forgotten as Nox spun me around and slowly lowered the zipper on the back of my dress. Breathlessly, he stood back and watched as the red material puddled at my feet, leaving my breasts exposed with only the garter belt, stockings, and shoes remaining.

"Not even fucking close," Nox exclaimed. "My imagination… you are so damn sexy." His pale eyes raked over me from my Louboutins to my auburn hair, burning my skin as his gaze scorched everything in its path.

While the air in our room filled with electricity, the ions and neutrons pulsed faster and faster. I found it hard to believe that this man staring at me had just eaten a four-course meal. Everything about him emanated an air of starvation.

My flesh tingled with goose bumps as I realized that I was his next meal.

"Up on the bed, princess."

I looked down questioningly at my shoes and back to Nox.

Silently, he shook his head before adding, "No, I want you just like you are."

As I turned toward the bed, his large hand landed loudly upon my bare ass, the sting sending vibrations to my core and reminding me of the silver buckle.

"I-I forgot," I confessed as I scooted up the mattress to the headboard. "I wanted to misbehave."

When I turned back around, my lungs fought to inhale. Surprise. Uncertainty. Anticipation. Excitement. My mind swirled with emotions as Nox walked from the dressing room, his expression contracting my insides to a painful pitch. In his hands he held a pink case and a coil of satin.

He really is going to awaken my vibrator.

"It's a good thing you didn't…" he said and after a pause added, "…misbehave."

"It is?"

Nox opened the case to my purple vibrator. "Because, princess, tonight's punishment wouldn't be my belt, though as I said, the one I'm wearing is now my favorite. I told you on the phone how I'd punish you. Do you remember?"

My exposed breasts rose and fell as my nipples tightened. "By not letting me come?" I asked, my voice softening as my thighs came together and lip disappeared behind my teeth. I could barely recall his question as my mind fully focused on the man before me. With the pink case and satin placed on the edge of the bed, Nox removed his clothes piece by piece until each one had disappeared, falling messily to the floor surrounding our bed.

Once he was naked, his broad chest turned my direction, and rock-hard erection sprung forward, pointing toward the ceiling. "Only good girls get to come," he said as reached for the coil of black satin and crawled across the mattress toward me.

I wanted to reach out and touch him, to take his length in my grasp and stroke the solid rod covered with his velvety smooth, stretched skin. But I couldn't. I couldn't move or speak. I couldn't do anything but watch with wide eyes as Nox's defined muscles flexed and he inched closer. Each movement reminded me of a panther slowly approaching its prey.

I was the prey.

The warmth of Nox's body covered mine, his flesh a spark to my kindling. Heat surged as he moved upward and lifted my hands.

"Do you trust me?"

It was the same question he always asked, and each time the answer came with less hesitation. "I do."

Carefully, Nox bound my wrists before securing them to the headboard. I tugged against the restraints as he ran the tips of his fingers from the inside of my wrist, along my exposed breasts, all the way down to my waist. His chest inflated as he teased the edge of the garter belt. His hands continued their exploration as he ran lower, moving my legs to his desired position. When Nox was done, my knees were bent, the high heels were against the sheets, and my core was fully exposed.

Lowering his lips he kissed the inside of my thigh just above the stocking—but not as high as I wanted—and deeply inhaled. "You're fucking perfect." His deep tone sent ripples through my body causing my insides to quiver. Glancing up at me with navy swirling in his light blue eyes, Nox added, "I was wrong earlier at the restaurant."

"You were?"

"That lasagna wasn't heaven on my tongue." He lowered his head and ran his tongue along the seam of my folds.

"N-Nox!" I writhed against the restraints as his strong, unyielding grip held my hips in place.

He teased my core, my clit, and lapped at my essence. Mercilessly, he set off flares as the kindling of my flesh scorched from his searing touch. I longed to weave my fingers through his dark hair, to push him harder against me; instead, he taunted, igniting sparks but not allowing them to fully combust.

As I moaned in both agony and ecstasy, Nox sat back and reached for the vibrator. With a flip of a switch, the room filled with the combination of its echoing hum and my mindless whimpers of unmet need.

Nox's brow lengthened as he moved closer. In his hand wasn't the vibrator that I'd expected. In his grasp was a black blindfold, one that I'd never before seen. Without a word, he eased the elastic over my head, darkening my world.

With the loss of vision, the vibrator's hum was amplified. Each movement made as Nox shifted upon the bed was more pronounced. Even the scent of our impending union was heightened. I flinched as Nox sucked one of my nipples, his teeth grazing the hardened nub. Anticipation covered my skin, leaving chills as well as a sheen of perspiration in its wake. My breathing hitched and my heartbeat hastened as I waited, blind to his next move.

Then all at once, Nox's thunderous voice reverberated against the walls, his question echoing in my ears. "Tell me, princess, you didn't really want to misbehave, did you?"

CHAPTER 35

Ten years ago

OREN

"RESPECT," VINCENT SAID through the phone. "It seems that you haven't taught your son to respect the family. It's time he learned."

My throat clenched at his threat. "I have. He's young. What are you talking about?"

"Young? Lennox is twenty years old. He's an old man in our world."

"He's not in *our* world."

"And whose fault is that?" Vincent asked.

"Mine. It was my choice. We had an agreement. I don't know what you're doing, but do it to me instead."

"It's too late."

My knees gave out as I sunk to my chair behind my desk. The office where I sat disappeared, as did the view from the windows overlooking the financial district. Nothing mattered. "I have respect. I pay my dues. Do you want more? I can do that. I will, because we're family. Family, Vincent. Lennox is family."

"Newark."

It was his only response before the line went dead.

Newark. What the hell?

And then I knew. I remembered Lennox's ridiculous hobby. I'd told him to stop—more than once. I'd told him that he shouldn't be spending so much time in New Jersey. Brooklyn was where his family was. New York was his home as he attended NYU.

I pushed the button on my desk phone. "Michelle?"

"Yes, Mr. Demetri?"

"Have my car brought up from the garage. I need to leave."

"Sir, you have one more meeting."

"Cancel it."

"But, sir, Judge Walters is already here."

Joseph Walters had already been helpful in a few court rulings over the years through his influence in not only New York, but also his connections elsewhere. Not only was he moving up in the circuit courts, he had tenure at Columbia.

"Michelle, send him in and call for my car."

"Yes, sir."

"Judge," I said, rounding the desk as Michelle led him into my office. "I apologize. I just received an urgent call. I'm afraid I'll need to cut this meeting short."

Joseph nodded. "I understand, Oren. Things happen. I just wanted to let you know that I see the wheels turning. I don't like where it's going."

"Marijuana?" I asked.

"Yes. Legalization will upset many people. Many groups who have a vested interest in it remaining, shall I say, untethered by legal restraints and regulations."

The Costello family had never dealt in drugs of any kind. It was a hard, fast rule of Carmine's, and Vincent had stood strong on the same belief. It wasn't that the Costellos were against making money in illegal endeavors. It was that there were others who specialized in the drug trade. Others who knew to pay their dues. Everything from marijuana to cocaine, meth, and crack. Most recently the news reported increased heroin usage, especially across the bridge.

In Newark.

"Judge, I really need to go. What can I do to stop the trend for legalization?"

"I know you have connections."

Yes, quid pro quo.

"Ones that wouldn't be appropriate for me to speak to directly," he continued. "I can help with writing the legislation. I need to know more, to learn details. If you can help me with that, I can help you. I recently saw an emissions bill that could end up costing Demetri Enterprises a fortune in government penalties or refinery alterations to avoid them."

"You tell me who and what," I said, looking at my watch. "I appreciate the heads-up on the emissions. Next week?"

"Yes," Joseph Walters agreed as we exited my office together.

"Michelle," I called toward her desk. "Lock up my office. I'll be back in the morning."

"Have a good evening, Mr. Demetri."

Good wasn't the description I had in store for me.

As we stepped into the elevator, Walters lowered his voice to a whisper. "I was thinking about the Bonettis."

I nodded my understanding and acceptance of his request. Yes, the Bonettis were the center of the drug cartels in Newark.

"Thank you, Oren. I'm sure we can make this mutually beneficial."

I found the warehouse off South Street in the Ironbound district, and the irony wasn't lost on me. This was Bonetti territory, the same people Joseph Walters had just asked me to contact. That wasn't my goal for tonight.

It wasn't my first time at this particular warehouse. I'd been here a time or two to watch Lennox do what he did. I didn't like it. Hell, I'd spent most of my life keeping him away from shit like this, but even I had to admit he was good.

I made my way through the crowd as the stench of sweat and something worse assaulted my nose. In my thousand-dollar suit and Italian loafers, I wasn't exactly dressed for a fight club, but it didn't seem to matter. People were screaming and calling out Lennox's name. Not Lennox, but *Nox*, some asinine stage name he'd assumed.

Elbowing through the mass of people who'd come to watch at ten dollars a head, I made my way toward the tall chain-linked ring. It took a while before I got close enough to see, but when I did, my feet stilled, the roar of the crowd silenced, and the scene blurred.

Bruised and battered, wearing a bloody white wife-beater and track pants, my son wobbled on the balls of his feet, his fists clenched and eyes focused on his cousin, Luca Costello.

Both of their faces had begun to swell as blood and spit splattered the first rows of spectators. It was there, ringside, that I saw Vincent Costello. Within seconds, I was there, pushing Jimmy out of the way and moving beside Angelina's cousin.

"Tell me what you want and make this stop," I pleaded. "They're going to kill each other and then what do we have? We both lose our sons. Is that what you want?"

My stomach heaved as the crunch of cartilage and bone forced us both to turn toward the ring. This time it was Luca who'd taken the hit. He spat blood onto the floor.

"Ten percent on all," Vincent said.

"All?" I asked. I paid the Costellos ten percent of all earnings in New York, but Demetri Enterprises had grown globally.

"All."

"Fine. Make it stop. You're nearly killing our sons over money?"

"Respect," Vincent said. "I stop this. You pay. Lennox, he's good. He has talent. It's time he uses it in an honorable way—for the family."

"I'll pay," I confirmed. "Stop this now." Both young men were looking as though they might fall helplessly to the mat.

Vincent turned to Jimmy and nodded. Immediately, a referee or announcer, I didn't know who he was, stepped into the ring and the vise that had been crushing my chest loosened a bit.

I stood, my new focus on getting to Lennox, when Vincent grabbed my arm. "We'll talk."

It wasn't a request but a summons. "Yes, Vincent. We'll talk."

Lennox's left eye was nearly eclipsed by the red and purple swelling. I supported his weight as he draped an arm over my shoulder. The crowd parted as I helped—carried—Lennox, my over six-foot-tall son, and Vincent did the same for Luca.

"Brooklyn," Vincent said, his way of telling me to take Lennox somewhere else. Luca would be going to seek medical treatment in Brooklyn. Both of the boys couldn't be at the same hospital or it would be questioned.

I nodded and assessed my son. Was he well enough to tolerate the drive to Westchester? "Lennox, do you hear me?"

"H-he… a hit?"

"Do you hear me?"

"I'm alive."

He was. He was alive.

If I got him to Rye, Angelina would be close. She'd be better for him during his recovery than I.

"We're going to the hospital in Rye," I said after I had us both in the car. Though I had him belted in and his seat reclined, he continued to jerk his head forward and mumble things I couldn't make out.

"WHY WON'T THEY tell us more? It's been hours," Angelina said as she stood again. Up and down, back and forth. It was as if she needed to keep moving.

"Because he's an adult." I didn't like the answer any more than she did, and obviously he hadn't acted like an adult, but nevertheless, according to his age, it was the truth. It was the hospital's policy. It didn't matter who brought him here or who was paying the damn bill. Fucking regulations.

My ex-wife finally spun toward me.

"I want you to be honest with me."

"About?" I'd fallen into that trap too many times to count.

"About tonight. It doesn't make sense," Angelina said, wringing her hands as she again paced the small waiting area.

Sitting back in an orange vinyl-covered chair, I stretched out my legs. There were red droplets on the leather of my shoes. I'd washed Lennox's blood from my hands, but my suit and maybe my shoes were probably ruined.

"I don't understand," she said, her blue eyes darkening. "What did you *do*?"

"Me? I saved our son's life."

"We're family, Vincent and I. He wouldn't do this if he didn't have a reason."

"He said he was teaching Lennox respect."

Angelina lowered her tone. "Lennox or you? Why'd he call you and not me?"

I stood and tried to keep my volume low. "I don't know. Maybe he didn't want his princess cousin to show up in the warehouse district and watch her son beaten to death."

"You promised something, didn't you?"

I shrugged. "Money. He wants more."

Her lip disappeared between her teeth like it did when she was thinking. "Money doesn't show respect. He wants more." She straightened her neck. "Tell me."

"He wants Lennox to work for the family."

Angelina's blue eyes widened in panic. "Tell me you didn't agree. Please, Oren, tell me you said no."

"Fuck, have you ever said no to Vincent?"

"Yes," she said matter-of-factly.

"I didn't answer. I purposely left it unanswered."

"Then I will."

I spun like a caged animal, unable to move more than a few feet in any direction, and ran my hand through my hair. "No. It's not a woman's—"

"It's a mother's place," she declared.

"How does it look when Lennox's mother is the one who faces Vincent, fights his battles?"

"It's not his battle yet. I'll talk to Vincent before it gets to Lennox. And I'll tell you how it looks. It looks like we're still a family…" She motioned between the two of us. "…like we still talk, and that we both still care about our son's future. It looks like *the princess* finally decided to take control of her reign."

"Excuse me, Mr. and Mrs. Demetri?" the small woman in light green scrubs asked.

We both turned and answered in unison. "Yes."

"You can see your son now."

I reached for Angelina's hand. "I'll talk to Vincent if you want me to. I'd never ask you—"

She squeezed my fingers and smiled. "No. You didn't ask. Let me do it. It'll go better. I'm certain."

She was right. It probably would.

"The money is his," I confirmed. "I don't give a fuck."

"You do. You care and not just about the money. I guess I always knew that. I was just too hurt and lonely to see it. We'll do this. Lennox deserves more than what we had."

I couldn't take my eyes off of my ex-wife. Sometime during the last twenty years she'd become more, or had it just been since our divorce? "Angelina," I began.

She squeezed my hand again. "Oren, stop. This is about our son. We'll make it right."

"I'm just…" I searched for the right word. "…awed."

"Don't be," Angelina said. "It took me being me—seeing the world alone—to finally figure it all out. I'm sorry I couldn't have done it when we were married."

"I never…"

She smiled a sad, knowing smile. "We both did what we know. Whether Lennox ever admits it or not, he needs both of us."

He did. Lennox needed us, and he deserved more than his mother and I had. I'd never be the hands-on baseball dad who cheered my son on from the stands, but I would do what I could to ensure that he had the chance for a future without all of the strings that had been attached to mine.

I was a hard man. Life had made me that way. My heart was shielded, a fortress that was accessible to few people. The woman beside me would always have her place. We'd shared too much to let something like divorce also serve as an eviction notice. The young man down the hall was part of me. His place was secure. The only other person who resided in my cold heart belonged to someone else.

While I didn't see the last changing although I'd sell what was left of my soul to make it happen, Adelaide still was part of me and among the three people who would forever be my priority. Whatever I had to do, I would do. Whether it was from the sidelines or in their face. Having only three people to care about allowed me to stay focused when the world around me became unclear.

I let go of Angelina's hand and we walked to Lennox's hospital room.

CHAPTER 36

CHARLI

I SETTLED AT my desk in my office, moving my mouse and summoning my computer to wake. Water dripped from my freshly washed hair as I wrapped the sweater around my shoulders, relishing its warmth. The apartment was tepid and lonely. It had been a couple of weeks since Nox took me out on our date, and over that time I'd developed a love/hate relationship with what had been my purple friend. I loved what Nox could do with it while I hated how much I craved the things he did.

It was as if my body operated with a series of switches that only he could flip.

Low.

Medium.

High.

Out of this world.

I was addicted to everything about Nox.

That was all right when we were together, but for the last two nights, he'd been out of town. Thankfully, he was due back this afternoon. I tried for other relief.

Glancing out the window, I decided that the blue sky was deceiving.

Earlier this Saturday morning, I'd gone out running with Patrick. When I did, I'd nearly frozen my fingers. Late October weather in New York was as diverse as any I'd ever known. No doubt that in Savannah, as well as Palo Alto, the mornings were without frost. Here, the afternoons could warm to a pleasant temperature, but the mornings resembled a scene from Disney's *Frozen*. Thankfully, the skies hadn't decided to snow, but by the way I stood under the shower's spray for longer than normal this morning, trying to return warmth to my extremities, I doubted it would be long.

My legal methods paper had been turned in and the next writing project was started. The outline was growing as I found more and more references. Sometimes I wondered if there would be more to law than reading, researching, and writing.

Over the last few weeks, I'd decided not to apply for the internship that Dr. Renaud had suggested. I would have tried for it in California at Stanford. I knew I would have. But life was less complicated there. Though my faculty counselor seemed disappointed in my decision, I had my reasons, none of which I felt compelled to share.

Although Patrick sometimes referred to me as a rich, spoiled princess, I wasn't narcissistic or self-centered enough to believe that my life was more complicated than those of my classmates. Yet I knew my limits—well, some that didn't involve a certain blue-eyed, sexy-as-hell man.

I knew how important school and success in my classes were to my future. I also knew that the internship would open doors and look great on my résumé. Nevertheless, I was only capable of focusing on so many things at one time.

I adored the man whose bed I shared—Lennox Demetri was a force of nature, the centrifugal force that steadied my world's rotation. His presence cemented the tilt. It overwhelmed me while at the same time bestowing gifts. Equal measures came and went that were forever fluid—giving and taking.

His strong, steady commands brought a sense of balance, grounding me with an anchor of love and support. Never did an evening pass that he didn't ask about my day—classes, concerns and even my family and friends.

Through the weeks and months, we'd had ups and downs. He'd had business successes and disappointments. There was something happening in California with Senator Carroll that had dominated more of his time than he'd wanted.

Often he'd ask if I could travel with him. Only a day or two at a stretch, but with law school, I couldn't.

The necklace that Deloris had made for me may have bothered me before the shooting in Central Park. Now, I found it comforting that there were people who cared about me and my safety. It was nice that the information was limited and not available to everyone as it was with the GPS on my phone.

Though my mother and I had scheduled a few meetings, they'd never occurred. Something had always superseded her plans. I was tiring of the anticipation.

I didn't want to visit Savannah, but with each week, my mother's messages were more evasive and cryptic. I spoke often to Jane, but I couldn't get a real feel for what was happening at Montague Manor. The last time we were supposed to get together, Jane called to let me know that instead of coming to New York, my mother had decided to travel with Alton out west.

She decided? I found that hard to believe.

It had been nearly a month since I'd spoken to Tina Moore, yet I'd only received one voicemail from Chelsea. The number on the phone she used was blocked, so I couldn't call back.

I'd replayed her message over and over, searching for a clue. I'd listened so many times that I had it memorized.

"Girl, Mom said you called. Things have been hectic. You know what we said? Life throws us curves, but we learn to swerve."

What the hell?

I knew the song, but we'd never said it to one another. The next line said: 'Me, I swung and I missed and the next thing you know, I'm reminiscing… '

I had no idea what she was trying to tell me or why she couldn't just say it.

Had she tried something that didn't work? Was she reminiscing?

I missed her humor and her smile, the way she'd cut through the bullshit and tell it like it was. I missed my friend. The apartment by Columbia was sitting empty.

As I tried to concentrate on my paper, I saw the notification for unopened emails. Mostly I avoided them. Maybe it was the cool morning, my uncertainty about my mother, or the quiet apartment. Maybe it was my way of avoiding my paper that I had to write, but for whatever reason I decided to skim the subject lines and senders.

One name jumped from the screen: *Millie Ashmore.*

Why would Millie be emailing me? Wasn't she busy with her wedding plans?

I shook my head, wondering if I should open the email, wondering if she would actually have the nerve to send me something as ridiculous as an invitation to a wedding shower or worse, expect me to help plan it.

With better judgment on hiatus, I clicked open the email.

To: Alexandria Collins
From: Millie Ashmore

I'm so sorry you couldn't help plan it, but I would just die if you didn't come. My bridal shower is going to be the Friday after Thanksgiving. I had Leslie schedule it when we thought you would be in town.

I understand that you might feel uncomfortable with Chelsea there, but you shouldn't. You know we're here for you.

Love and Kisses,
Millie

What the hell?

I stared at the screen in disbelief. Not only had she had the audacity to think I wanted to be at her shower, but Chelsea was going to be there?

I did what I'd sworn not to do.

Being sure my location was turned off on my computer, I logged into Facebook.

First, I searched *Chelsea Moore.* The last posting she'd made was late August. It was a picture of her in the hospital bed with thumbs up and said that she was well.

With a feeling of impending dread, I searched *Millie Ashmore.* Her page was full of posts and pictures. There were wedding dresses and wedding cakes. The picture that caught my eye and turned my stomach was of Millie and several other women in a booth at a bar. I recognized the location as one of the bars on River Street. Most of the women were laughing and holding drinks. And on the end, looking scared and reserved—two adjectives I never thought I'd use for my best friend—was Chelsea.

I clicked the picture and made it bigger.

Chelsea's hair, which over the years had been every color from fuchsia to green, was a rich amber, pulled back in a low twist. Her royal blue dress was formfitting yet modest. As I stared, I had a flashback of standing with her at a full-length mirror in Del Mar, talking about how we could be sisters. For the first time, I saw the resemblance.

She looked like me.

She could be me.

My good sense told me to exit out and forget what I saw.

I didn't listen.

My hand had a mind of its own as I scrolled Millie's page. The magnitude of information was a wealth of Savannah's twenty-somethings' social life, all compiled in one place. As I rolled my mouse, it all played out before my eyes: people with whom I'd attended academy living the high life in clubs and mansions, by pools as well as in rooms with chandeliers. It was the life where I was raised, and in picture after picture over the last month, Chelsea was present.

And then my breath caught in my chest, painfully stagnant, unable to flow in or out of my lungs. The screen blurred with tears as beside my best friend, with his arm draped over her shoulder, was Bryce.

I thought he'd given up on me, finally freeing me from his plans.

But that wasn't what had happened. I wiped the warm, salty droplets away from my cheeks with the back of my hand. I wasn't shedding tears for Bryce, but for Chelsea.

Sometime while I'd been preoccupied, she'd stepped into my life. Granted, it was the one I hadn't wanted, the one I'd rejected, but that didn't lessen the pain. My best friend had become me.

Time passed as my work on my paper was forgotten, and I searched the Internet for clues that could help me understand.

It was only a shred of self-control that stopped me from dialing Bryce's number and asking to speak to Chelsea. Would she be with him? Why?

It was the photo in the news article that opened my eyes.

The picture showed Bryce and Chelsea walking into the courthouse in Evanston, Illinois, hand in hand. They were both named in the caption and following Chelsea's name was the descriptor: longtime girlfriend. The article pertained to Bryce's most recent depositions. Though the Evanston police were promising that they were close to issuing an arrest warrant for Edward Carmichael Spencer for his involvement in the disappearance of Melissa Summers, the defense claimed insufficient evidence. Supporting Bryce's claim of innocence was his own testimony as well as Chelsea Moore's. Mr. Spencer claimed to have been in California visiting Miss Moore at the time of Miss Summers's disappearance. Miss Moore's statement, as well as Mr. Spencer's travel records, substantiated his claim.

Visiting *her*?

Do I feel jealous?

No.

Dazed and confused was more like it.

Bryce hadn't been visiting Chelsea. Then I remembered that she'd said he'd been to her hospital room. She'd said that she barely knew who he was, certainly not that they were involved.

Had she lied to me? Had he been at the hospital to see her and not me?

My head ached as I tried to unweave truth from fiction. The two were twisted too tightly to unravel.

The sound of the front door knocked at my consciousness, the beeps of the alarm pulling me to the present. The clock on the corner of my screen read nearly five in the evening. I'd been sitting there since before noon and none of my work had been accomplished.

"Charli," Nox's deep voice resonated through the apartment.

Mindlessly, I realized that my hair had dried in unruly ringlets, and I was without makeup. I wiped my cheeks and nose with a Kleenex as I peered up to the doorway.

He instantly recognized my angst. I didn't try to hide it. I couldn't hide anything from Lennox Demetri even if I wanted to. He knew me better than I knew myself.

"Charli, what's going on?"

I shook my head. "Y-you're home?"

He came toward me, and I drank him in: his long legs covered in jeans, white v-neck t-shirt that hugged his chest, showing enough definition to make me want to reach out and touch it, and the wool suit coat that emanated the sexy aroma of his cologne.

Nox reached for my hand and pulled me to his muscular chest. "Is it your mother?"

He knew I'd been concerned about her.

I shook my head. "I-I don't understand."

I didn't know how to explain what I'd learned. Would Nox misconstrue my feelings as jealousy? I wasn't jealous. I had him. I didn't want Bryce, but I didn't understand how Chelsea was with him, living my life. Had she set me up all along? Had our friendship ever been real?

"What, princess?"

"It's Chelsea."

His body tensed. "Is she all right?"

I narrowed my eyes as I leaned back to scan his features. Emotions ricocheted through his pale eyes. Concern was present, but it wasn't alone. Something was off.

"You knew," I said.

His tone, smooth as velvet, tried to lull me to think otherwise, but it was his body's reaction to her name that convinced me he had previous knowledge—more than he wanted to admit.

"You knew about her," I accused. "When I told you that she was in

Savannah, you already knew, didn't you?"

"I wasn't sure…"

I took a step back. "You lied to me?"

Nox reached for my arms, gently holding me by my shoulders. "I've never lied to you."

"Have you always told me the truth?"

"Yes."

"All of the truth?"

His neck straightened as his chin jettisoned outward. "I told you from the beginning that I'd never lie to you. I also told you that I'd share things when I was ready."

"When *you* were ready?" My volume increased with each word. "This wasn't about you. This wasn't about your past or your secrets. I've remained content to take what you've given me, even though I've shared more with you. Lennox, this was about *my* best friend. I was worried about her and you knew that she was in Savannah being me?"

His features scrunched in obvious confusion. "Being you?"

CHAPTER 37

ADELAIDE

"HAMILTON AND PORTER, Natalie speaking. How may I help you?"

My hand trembled uncontrollably as I held tightly to the phone. "Natalie, this is Mrs. Fitzgerald." I took a deep breath. "I want to speak to Stephen."

"Mrs. Fitzgerald, it's nice to hear from you."

I closed my eyes in frustration; chatting wasn't my intention. I needed to talk to Stephen. The last time we spoke he was checking on Montague Corporation assets. It had occurred to me that after all of this time, I had no idea how much money everything was worth.

If the codicil were about to go into effect, what would it mean? What was I willing to fight for?

"Natalie, I'm not feeling well. Stephen, please?"

"Ma'am, Stephen is no longer with Hamilton and Porter. Perhaps Mr. Porter can help you?"

"What?" I asked in confusion. "We had a meeting scheduled."

"Ma'am, he left rather suddenly. Mr. Porter would be happy to meet with you."

I fell back against the plush sofa in my suite. I was still wearing my dressing gown and it was after noon. Ever since the horrible migraine that I'd had nearly a month ago, everything seemed off. My appetite was nonexistent and my sleep patterns were shot to hell.

Even wine had lost its appeal. The only thing keeping me going was hoping that soon I'd figure out a way to make my father's codicil go into effect. It was the first thing I thought about when I woke and the last before I went to sleep.

Alton claimed that my behavior was so unusual that he didn't want to leave me home alone. He told me to travel with him. I didn't know why. It wasn't like I was any help. Most of the time I didn't attend his dinners with investors or clients. The new medication Dr. Beck had given me to prevent the migraines had me too out of sorts.

Today was the first time in months that he'd left town without me. He would only be gone for the day, but I'd hoped to meet briefly with Stephen.

Though I hadn't been happy about the Chelsea thing, Alton said it had helped in weakening the prosecutor's case against Bryce. The last conversation I'd overheard was that Montague Manor was going to settle the civil lawsuit with Melissa's parents. According to the attorneys at Montague, it was the respectful thing to do, in light of her disappearance.

From what I'd observed, Chelsea was getting better at fitting in with Bryce's friends. There was something almost familiar about the way she now dressed and spoke. I couldn't put my finger on it, but she was worlds away from the young lady I'd met during Alexandria's first year of college.

"Mrs. Fitzgerald? Are you still there?"

"Yes, Natalie," I said, concentrating on the phone call. "I'm just… disappointed. Do you have a number where I can reach Stephen? He was such a great help to me."

"No, ma'am," Natalie said. "Mr. Porter is available this afternoon at two-thirty. Will that work for you?"

I sighed once again. That would mean not only getting dressed, but also showering. "Yes, tell Ralph that I believe I can make it."

"Wonderful. Mr. Porter will see you then."

I disconnected the call and stood, bracing myself on the arm of the sofa.

Dr. Beck had run a few tests, one he called a metals test. The results took months, not days. I didn't care what he did, as long as he figured out what was happening. I hadn't had another excruciating migraine since the one he'd witnessed, but I knew things weren't right.

I dialed Jane's number, and like the reliable person she was, she answered on the first ring.

An hour later, with her help, I was presentable and walking out the door.

"Mrs. Fitzgerald," Jane said. "Brantley's with Mr. Fitzgerald. Are you sure you can drive yourself?" Her big dark eyes begged me to say no.

"Nonsense. I've been driving myself around for years. I can do it today."

"Ma'am, I need to go to town. I can drive you. My errand won't be long."

I shook my head. The shower had helped me feel better. "I'm not a child. Just because Mr. Fitzgerald likes to be driven doesn't mean that I do."

She nodded. "Yes. Could you call me…?"

"I'll be home before dinner. Don't you worry. Is the car out front?"

"Yes, ma'am."

I couldn't understand what had happened to Stephen and why he'd left his internship so abruptly. By the time I reached Hamilton and Porter, my hands were back to trembling. The ostentatious office, established largely through the exorbitant billings of corporations and families like the Montagues and Fitzgeralds, was regally positioned in a historic district in downtown Savannah. It made for a beautifully constructed building with ornate craftsmanship but one terrible for parking. As I'd searched and searched for a space along the street, my nerves stretched beyond their already frayed state.

The autumn sun shone with new intensity, keeping the Georgia temperature pleasant while continuing its assault on my eyes.

"Mrs. Fitzgerald," Natalie greeted as I entered the main lobby and she looked up at the opening of the glass front door. "Are you all right?" she added with obvious concern as she rushed around her large reception desk toward me.

I steadied myself on a nearby chair my fingers sinking into the fabric. I stood taller, feigning the strength I wanted to possess as the room around me tilted. The polished oak floor was a fast-moving river, flowing beneath my precarious footing. I pulled my hand back. The furnishings were liquid and the walls alive. Rationally, I knew that wasn't true, but their movement both fascinated and terrified me as I took off my sunglasses and blinked away the illusion.

Only seconds later, the wild carousel I'd been riding slowed, the music softening as Natalie's words finally held meaning. "Yes, Natalie. I'm fine. Is Ralph ready to see me?"

I took another step, cautious to avoid the raging torrents.

"Yes, may I help you?"

I narrowed my gaze. "Help me? I'm perfectly capable of walking to Ralph's office."

"Yes, ma'am. Ice water?"

"I'm not sure," I admitted, checking the river below my feet again. Was it icy or warm? Thankfully, rocks created a path that kept me dry.

When I looked up from my steps, Natalie's eyes were narrowed.

"Sure, Natalie, ice water." My answer seemed to bring her some relief. Maybe she'd been wondering the same thing too.

The office seemed uncharacteristically quiet as we rode the old elevator to the second floor. I breathed a sigh of relief as the iron scissor gate, which she manually pulled shut, stopped the flowing floor.

Isn't there usually someone else who mans the antique elevator?

Ralph stood as I entered his office. It was exactly the same as it had always been. No liquid floors or moving chairs. Quickly, Natalie closed the door and left Ralph and me alone.

After shaking hands, I sat on the edge of the chair facing his desk. It didn't seem that long ago that I'd done the same thing, demanding to see my father's will. In reality, that had been nearly two months ago.

"Adelaide, you're looking well."

"Thank you, Ralph," I replied. "Please tell me about Stephen."

"Stephen?" he asked with a questionable inflection.

"The intern from Savannah Law. The young man you had help me."

Ralph shook his head. "Help you? I don't understand. The last time you were in here, *I* helped you." He laughed. "You know, we used to utilize interns, but found it was more problem than it was worth. As you can only imagine, we have confidential information within our walls…"

My stomach knotted as I stared at Ralph's features. His lips moved like a movie out of sync, the sound of his words reaching me after the movement of his mouth. It was as if everything he said was delayed in a time continuum. Natalie entered, handing me a stemmed glass with water and just as quickly exited, leaving us alone.

"As I told you weeks ago…" he continued, "…I'm not able to share the documents of your father's will with you."

I moved my gaze beyond his face to his desk and tried to concentrate. "Ralph, we settled this. I was here. I've been here multiple times. My name is on the ledger for my father's documents. I've seen them. I've seen the will and the codicil."

His brow furrowed. "Adelaide, can I get you something stronger than that water? Maybe something to settle your nerves… like whiskey? I know…" he said triumphantly, "…I have wine. A nice bottle of Montague Private Collection. It was a Christmas gift last year."

"I don't want wine. I have an entire cellar of Montague wine. I'm Adelaide Montague." I stood as my volume rose.

Ralph came around his desk and reached for my hand, his lowered tone of voice no doubt attempting to pacify me. "Laide, it's all right. I know who you are."

"Of course you do! Get the ledger. Get the papers." I pulled my hand away. "I know all about it. I've reread Article XII. Why are you looking at me as if I'm crazy?"

"You're getting yourself agitated."

"No," I said convincingly. "I'm not getting myself anything. I want to see the ledger for my father's papers, for his last will and testament."

"All right. Have a seat. Let me pull it up on my computer."

I sat back down as my heart beat in time with the keys of his computer, too fast, as he clicked and searched for the file.

"Laide," he said, turning a large screen my direction. "Here it is. You see the last person to access the documents was your husband over five years ago."

I shook my head. "That's not true. I watched Stephen enter our names every time I was here."

Ralph pursed his lips. "Perhaps I should call Alton? Do you have a driver?"

"Stop it!" I declared. "I was here."

"Yes, of course. Now, you aren't driving, are you?"

I narrowed my gaze. "Ralph Porter, I don't know what you're trying to do or to pull, but I want you to access those papers. I want to see them this afternoon."

"They're in storage and haven't seen the light of day as I said, for years. It would take one of the paralegals at least a day to locate them."

I clamped my lips together. "I'm not leaving."

His head tilted apologetically to the side. "Laide, I would if I could. You don't have access."

"What do you mean, I don't have access? I'm Adelaide Montague Fitzgerald. I'm joint heir to Charles Montague II with my daughter, Alexandria."

"Dear, we've established who you are."

"As I said two months ago, you will show me those papers or I'll take Montague's business somewhere else…" I tried to recall the name of the new firm in town. Surely they'd be happy to gain the Montague business. "Preston, Madden, and Owen."

Ralph tapped again on his computer and the screen changed. I narrowed my eyes as I made out the top of the page. It was obviously a scan of a paper document. The first line read: Power of Attorney.

"What?" I asked again.

"Laide, this is why you don't have access."

"I don't understand."

"I know. We all know. Do as the doctors say. When you're better—in a better frame of mind—I'm sure we can have the order reversed."

"My state of mind is fine!"

Ralph touched a button on his phone and Natalie's voice filled the room.

"Yes, Mr. Porter?"

"Natalie, could you please call Mrs. Fitzgerald a cab? And then I'll drive her car. I can't in good conscience allow her to drive."

I stood again, clenching my purse to my stomach. "No, that won't be necessary. I'm going."

"Adelaide, I really must insist."

When he stepped toward me, I backed away. "Do not touch me, Ralph. If you do I'll leave here and go directly to that new firm and sue your ass for sexual assault."

He lifted his hands, palms toward me. "I'm trying to help you."

"Help me? How did you make that document without my signature? I'd never give up my rights."

Ralph leaned over the desk and reached for his mouse. Scrolling down the document, two maybe three pages later, he pointed. There it was—my signature. "You did. On this document and on the medical power of attorney. You understood that your husband is in a better state to make your decisions." He took another step toward me. "Just as you did twenty years ago when you signed over your voting rights on the Board of Trustees of Montague Corporation. It's what Charles wanted. He wanted someone to take care of you.

"Are you sure I can't call Alton?"

My mind spun in confusion. "No." I was less convincing than earlier. "Ralph, I'm perfectly capable of driving."

"I don't want to have to defend a DUI lawsuit where you're deemed incapable of driving."

"DUI?" I asked. "I'm not under the influence. I have *not* had a drink all day."

His eyes went over to the conference table. My breath stuttered as I followed his gaze. On the table was an open bottle of wine. I recognized the label without reading it: Montague Private Collection. The bottle was open with two glasses sitting near, one empty but obviously used with my shade of lipstick on the rim. The other glass was nearly full.

"I understand that this is difficult on you," Ralph said. "You know that we're here for you?"

I shook my head slowly, but the tempo increased as I held tighter to my purse. "No! I didn't have a drink. I didn't."

"Mr. Porter," Natalie said from the doorway. "I'd be happy to drive Mrs. Fitzgerald, and then you can drive her car?"

I turned to Natalie. "Do you remember our conversation about Del Mar?"

She smiled, sweet and sad. "I'm sorry, no. But it is a lovely place. Have you been?"

"Adelaide," Ralph said, "please give me your keys and we won't need to mention this to Alton."

I swallowed as I looked from Ralph to Natalie.

Alton. He'd be mortified that I'd made a scene, even if I didn't remember making it. Also, he'd question why I was here and possibly learn that I knew about the codicil.

Looking back to Ralph, I said, "Please, please don't say anything." I handed him my keys.

Natalie reached for my elbow. "Mrs. Fitzgerald, I'm parked out back. I can take you so no one else sees us leave."

I nodded as I took one last look at the table. The wine in the glass was red. It wasn't six o'clock.

CHAPTER 38

NOX

CHARLI WAS RIGHT. Not only did I know about Chelsea being in Savannah when she told me, but I knew a lot more. I also knew that my amazing girlfriend had shared more about her past than I had about mine. When Charli simply stared, I asked, "What the hell do you mean?"

"About which part?" she asked, bristling, "About Chelsea being me or your not telling me… anything?"

"Her being you," I confirmed.

Charli's lips formed a straight line as she stared at me.

I couldn't help that I wasn't ready to delve into my shadows. I hadn't, not since that terrible night. As long as she was content with what I gave her, why would I want to relive what happened—what I'd done. And if I did open that door and shed light on that past, what would Charli do with that knowledge? What would she do when she knew the monster that I had been?

"I mean," Charli said, "Chelsea's living my old life." She spun from my arms toward the computer. "Here, let me show you some pictures."

What the hell?

"Chelsea sent you pictures?"

"No. I went to Facebook. I'm almost never on there, but after Millie's weird email, I had to see."

She was dropping names like bombs in a war zone. "Charli, calm down. Who's Millie?"

"She used to be a friend."

Used to be?

Charli's large golden eyes peered up at me as her sexy body leaned over the desk and keyboard. In that instant, I noticed how sensual yet sweet she looked. Though I knew she'd been upset, she'd calmed. Her hair was different with lots of long curls, and her face was clear of makeup. For only a second, I wondered why she normally wore it. She didn't need it. I reached out to touch the auburn curls.

She pulled her head away. "Stop it. I never dried my hair. It looks awful."

"You could never look awful." I tried a grin as I pulled gently on one of the spring-like curls wondering if it would bounce. It did. "I like it."

"Look here," she said, ignoring my attempt to lighten the mood and pointing to the computer screen.

The picture was of a group of women about Charli's age, seated in a semicircular booth. I narrowed my gaze as I scanned across the women. By their clothes and the background, it appeared as though they were clubbing. The one on the end caught my eye.

I pointed. "Chelsea?"

"Look at her! She's never worn a dress like that or done her hair that way. She's being me!"

I tugged Charli's hand and pulled her back to me. "No one can be you. There's only one you, and I'm lucky enough to have you all to myself." I touched her hair again, petting the ringlets. "And she doesn't look like you. I mean, look at you. You're all fun and curly, and she's all pinned back and stuffy."

The corner of Charli's lips moved upward as she took an exaggerated breath. "We've switched. I'm living the bracelet, doing what Chelsea would do, and she's doing what I did."

The bracelet?

She was talking in riddles.

"No, princess. I've seen you all straitlaced and proper. I know she's your friend, but she doesn't come close to having your flair or class." I cupped her cheeks. "I remember the first time I saw you all sophisticated. I'd seen you sexy as hell in Del Mar as well as bent over a sink in a roadside gas station." Pink returned to her cheeks. "It wasn't until you walked into that restaurant in San Francisco to have lunch with Senator Carroll and me that I saw the sophisticate from Savannah. My God, I almost forgot my own name." I lifted her face toward mine. "Princess, you are you. Chelsea could never be anything more than a cheap imitation. And I don't see her trying to do that. Do you?"

I released her cheeks as my hands slid to her slender shoulders.

"I don't know," she said as she released her breath and collapsed against my chest.

Allowing my hands to move lower, I wrapped my arms around her sensual body and held her close. Slowly, her muscles relaxed, melting into me.

"And you're not her," I went on. "She's the one who hasn't called. You're too caring for that. You'd never do that."

"God," Charli said, now holding on to my waist, her hands locked behind my back under my jacket. "Next thing you know she'll be married to him and pregnant."

My jaw clenched at the word. I tilted Charli's chin toward me. "Why would you even say that?"

"Because that's what my mother has been telling me to do forever. Get married… to Bryce…" She spoke with an exaggerated Southern accent. "…and have babies. Hurry up, you're not getting any younger."

"You just turned twenty-four."

"I know." Her golden eyes were veiled by thick lashes. "I don't know how to feel. I don't give a damn that Bryce's attention has moved away from me. Actually, I'm thrilled." Her face tilted ever so slightly to the side. "I have my hands full with you."

"So you're not wanting a threesome?"

This time she smiled. "Mr. Demetri, you're definitely enough man for me. Besides, I thought you said you didn't share."

"I don't. I just wanted to be sure you were satisfied."

She wrinkled her nose. "Do you really need to wonder?"

I shrugged. "I've been gone. It's been a few days since I've heard the sexy, satisfied noises you make." I widened my gaze. "But I'm free right now. We could take care of that?"

Her smile dimmed. "I-I'm confused. Right now, I don't know what to feel. Chelsea was my best friend, and I can't help but wonder if any of it was real. Was everything really just a big scam, a way to move herself up the social ladder?"

"What's your heart telling you?" I asked, praying she'd have faith in Chelsea.

"It says Chelsea was never interested in social status and this is out of character. My eyes tell me something totally different. I'm not sure if I can believe my heart."

"What does it say about me?"

She tucked her head back against my chest. "It says that I love you." Her head sprang back up. "But you knew, didn't you?"

"That Chelsea was in Savannah and working for your family's business? You told me. About her being you? I had no idea." Those were all true statements.

"My heart," she went on, "is telling me that something isn't right. I don't like it. I don't want her with Bryce, not because I'm jealous but because…" Her lip disappeared between her teeth. "…I don't believe him about Melissa Summers, that college freshman. I don't know if he had anything to do with her disappearance, but I do think he was the one who hurt her. I hate myself for saying that. I know how important his mother is to mine, but I can't shake the feeling. Sometimes he can be nice and remind me of my childhood friend. Other times, there's a look or action and he reminds me of Alton. That's not a compliment."

"I didn't think it was." I leaned back. "Do you have more work to do or do you want to go grab some dinner?"

"Is it that late?" Charli asked. "I wasted my whole day on this. Tomorrow I need to work on my paper."

"Then tonight, my lady, you are mine. Dinner and then I get to hear those satisfied moans."

"It could be like that old movie Jane loved and we used to watch: *When Harry Met Sally*. I could just make noises while we eat."

"Princess, I've never seen it, but the noises you're going to make won't be faked. I'll have the real ones."

"You seem pretty sure of yourself, Mr. Demetri?"

Instead of answering, I kissed her lips lightly, letting mine skirt across hers. As she began to pull away, I moved my hand to her neck, winding her beautiful hair around my fingers and moving her head to the side. With her neck exposed, I kissed the sensitive skin behind her ear, painstakingly slow, each touch of my lips lingering longer as I moved down her neck. By the time I reached her collarbone, her flesh was sprinkled with goose bumps. When I nipped her skin, a soft moan escaped her open lips.

With a grin, I said, "Yes, I'm very sure of myself."

Later that night, after I'd elicited not one, but a chorus of sounds, some I'd never heard, Charli cuddled close. Her soft curves fit perfectly against my chest as I wrapped an arm around her shoulder. For only a few moments, she traced the ridges of my torso before her fingers splayed and breathing evened.

As she drifted off to sleep, I thought again about what she'd said, how I hadn't shared with her like she had with me. Since the first time she told me about her childhood, she'd shared more. Each story solidified my hatred for Alton Fitzgerald while at the same time caused my love and admiration for Charli to grow. She was so strong to have survived—not only survived, but to have become the marvelous woman she was today.

I also recalled what she'd said that her mother had wanted her to do: marry and have babies—with Edward Spencer.

I wasn't proud of how Chelsea ended up in Savannah, and it was never intended. But if her being there, making the money she wanted, and being Edward's alibi, kept Charli away from that prick, it was worth it. I may be damned to hell for subjecting Chelsea to whatever was happening there, but I had no hard limits when it came to the extremes I'd go to save my Charli.

She deserved more than my protection. After all she'd given me, Charli deserved to know the truth.

My eyes squeezed closed. I hadn't allowed myself to think of that night in detail—in living color. No. That was such an erroneous term for that night. The color wasn't living. It was dying.

Moisture stayed trapped behind my lids as I remembered the blood, the stickiness as it covered my hands. Having Jo's blood on me wasn't at all like it had been when I fought in the MMA octagon. Then, I'd enjoyed the sensation, the destruction and carnage. That night was different. As panic overtook me and I shook her lifeless body, a part of my soul died.

How could I share that with Charli? If she knew what I was capable of doing, she'd never trust me again.

"Nox?" Her sleepy voice broke through my memories. "What's the matter?"

CHAPTER 39

CHARLI

THE VIBRATION OF Nox's chest awakened me from my sleep. At first, I wasn't sure what I was hearing or feeling. My senses were spent, overwhelmed by his mastery and sexual proclivity. I'd fallen into the beginning of my favorite comatose state when he began to stir. The darkness of our room and softness of our bed shielded me from what was happening until slowly the sadness that emanated from his every pore filled our space, wrapping me in his misery. His breathing became ragged as his chest tensed and body trembled.

"Nox?" I asked again.

"Go to sleep, princess." He choked on the words.

I lifted my head. Unable to see clearly through the dark, I reached toward him. He captured my hand before it touched his cheek.

"Please let me touch you."

Nox cleared his throat. "It's my hard limit."

"Touching you?" I asked, trying to understand.

"No…" His tone returned to the velvety rumble that I adored. "…something you said earlier today."

I shook my head, my hand still captive in his grasp. I didn't try to remove it, but relaxed as he held it in the dark. Then no longer captured, our fingers intertwined. "I don't remember what I said. I said a lot of things."

"You said that your mother wanted you to marry Spencer and have babies."

I scoffed. "I think that plan's been blown all to hell."

"It's not the Spencer part. I want to know how you feel about children."

I sat taller and pulled the sheets over my breasts. All the while his grip of my hand stayed true, as if he couldn't let me go, as if for once, I was his lifeline. "I don't know… I think I'm too young." I shrugged. "I guess my mom had me when she was about my age, but I want other things first."

"But eventually?"

"I suppose," I admitted.

Nox let go of my hand. "I don't."

His declaration sounded final as if debate wasn't an option. Those two words drilled a small hole into my unspoken dreams. I'd never expended much energy on the subject, but I also didn't think I could totally write it off. "I think this conversation is premature."

He sat up now too, meeting me against the headboard, both of us staring into the darkness. "Jocelyn died because of me."

My breath stilled, fearing that if I reacted in any way he wouldn't continue talking.

"That letter was right," he went on. "If it weren't for me, she'd be alive. I killed her."

I turned toward him. My eyes had adjusted to the darkness enough that I could make out his profile: his protruding brow and straight nose. I couldn't see his high cheekbones, but I knew they were there. Even in the shadows I saw the movement, the way his chiseled jaw flexed as he clenched and contemplated his next words.

"Her family," Nox went on, "has been suing me for years, a civil suit. It's a matter of public record. My people have worked to bury it, but it's there. I'm not sure why your stepfather or Edward Spencer thought it needed to come out, other than to show you the monster I am. But the letter was also wrong—I didn't stop her parents from seeing her. They didn't come. I know you hate your stepfather, and you should. But I'd never wish the separation Jo had with her family on anyone."

His head bowed as his chin fell to his chest.

Through the darkness, I reached toward him, finding his large hand, the one that had been holding mine, and again laced our fingers together. "I don't believe you'd hurt the person you loved. And I know you loved her. I'm okay with that. Nox, you wore your wedding ring until Del Mar. I don't know what you think you did, but you didn't kill her."

"I did. Her blood was on my hands."

I wasn't sure where the bravery was coming from. I was lying naked, next to a man who was confessing murder, yet I refused to believe it. "You don't mean literally."

He turned toward me and lifted both of his hands, releasing mine. Holding them in the air, he said, "I. Mean. Literally."

"Stop it. Now you're the one trying to scare me and it won't work."

"I'm not trying to scare you. I'm trying to tell you the truth."

I reached for his face. "What does this have to do with your hard limits? Security? Babies? Somehow they're connected."

"She was impulsive… liked to go here and there. I was gone a lot. My father had a terrible time when the markets crashed in '09. It was around the same time my mother had died. I'd recently gotten out of grad school and understood the financial climate better than he did. Things had changed since he started Demetri Enterprises. I worked nonstop and traveled, more than I do now. I knew Jocelyn didn't like it but I just kept promising her that one day we'd have more time."

Releasing his cheeks, I kissed one, and wrapped my arms around his chest with my head lying on his torso. I wanted to comfort him and be close. I wanted to support my strong boyfriend as he finally freed some of his shadows.

Nox sighed and returned his arm to my shoulders as his words vibrated from his chest. "Deloris began working for Jocelyn and me. She understood that some of the deals Oren had made could come back on us. I told Jo constantly to be careful, to keep me informed. Sometimes I think she'd upset me so that I'd notice her. It was this sick dance we did.

"I'd be consumed with work and she'd do something to piss me off. We'd fight and make up. But the thing was, I did notice her. I was just obsessed with Demetri Enterprises and proving that I was capable of continuing what Oren had begun."

"What happened?" I asked, my head still on his chest.

"We didn't have time for children. We both knew that. I insisted that she do something to prevent it from happening. She had one of those things, an IUD, inserted."

"It didn't work?"

I could feel his head shake. "It did and didn't."

"Jo had just figured it out. She hadn't told anyone, even me. No one except Deloris." He took a deep breath. "I didn't know. If I'd known, I never…"

"Nox."

"She left our apartment. Not here. I moved… after. Anyway, she went to Rye. It was mine—ours—since my mom was gone. Jocelyn wanted to surprise me. I was supposed to be there after work. I didn't know," he repeated. "She wanted us to be alone, make the announcement special. She made everyone leave the property, even Silvia.

"I continually told her to stay safe. She promised."

Dread filled my body like a weight in the pit of my stomach as his words came thick, dripping with pain and regret.

"I ended up working late," Nox went on, "like I always did. When I got to the house, the kitchen was bright, table was set, and on my plate was an envelope. Inside was a card with a date. At first I didn't understand. Then I realized it was in the future, a little under eight months away. When I flipped it over it said, boy or girl?

"I should have been happy, but I wasn't. I was livid. How could she do this? We'd talked about it. I'd said not yet. Part of me thought maybe this was just another cry for attention. My emotions were all over the place."

My heart beat faster as his story came quicker.

"I screamed her name. Except for the kitchen and dining room, the house was dark. I kept yelling but she didn't answer."

His head bowed as emotion ripped through him. "God, Charli, there was so much blood."

I sat up. "What happened? Did someone break in? Is that why you don't go to Rye?"

"The light was on beside the bed. She was lying on her side with her knees drawn up. At first I thought she was sleeping, but then I noticed how pale she looked. Not pale, white. It was her lips. The color was wrong. I called her name again, screamed it, but she didn't move. When I pulled back the blankets, there was blood, so much blood."

Nox was on a roll. His eyes were open, but he wasn't seeing me. He was seeing her.

"I couldn't stop myself. I shook her. If I could just wake her…."

"She didn't wake?"

"The coroner said she'd hemorrhaged. He called it an ectopic pregnancy. The IUD didn't allow the egg to implant where it was supposed to, so it implanted in her fallopian tube. They estimated she was only about seven weeks along."

"Nox, you didn't kill her. You aren't responsible."

He threw back the covers and stood. His gorgeous nude body paced beside the bed. "Did you listen to what I said? I've never told this whole story—maybe ever."

"I did listen. It was an accident. It wasn't your fault."

"She had the IUD because of me. She was pregnant because of me. If I'd gotten home when I said I would, I could have gotten her to the hospital in time. Fuck, Charli, there are so many ifs. It's all on me. I should just pay her parents and be done with it. But I know she wouldn't want that. She wouldn't want them to have a dime because of her. I never told them exactly how she died."

"Deloris knows?"

Nox nodded. "The media speculated all sorts of things. They said everything from my murdering her to a hit. Deloris was the only one thinking straight. She had the foresight to have everyone, from the EMTs to the coroner, sign a do-not-disclose statement. Records were sealed. I don't know how she does what she does, but Deloris handled it all."

He sat back on the edge of the bed with his back toward me.

I crawled close and draped my arms over his broad shoulders, burying my cheek against his back.

"The coroner said that it happens," Nox said. His voice now filled with defeat. "He said she was probably having abdominal pain and that was why she'd lain down." He reached up and rubbed my arm. "Charli, when you asked, I couldn't tell you that I didn't do it, because I did. I don't lie. I won't." He tugged my hand, bringing my face in front of his. "I don't want to let you go, but if now that you know the truth, you don't want to be here, I won't stop you."

As I stared into his eyes, for the first time I truly understood his obsessions. I was looking not only at a man who loved with all of his heart, but a man who needed control and needed to keep those he cared about safe. I saw pain and guilt that he'd held onto for far too long. Swirling in his pale eyes I also saw fear, a weakness he didn't want to admit.

It was the dread of losing his new chance at love, his new chance at life, something that up until recently he'd given up on ever feeling again. And that was the one answer I could give him. I couldn't take away his pain or his loss, but I could offer to spend the rest of my life trying to fill that void.

"I don't want to go anywhere," I said. "I love you more than I did an hour ago. I'll do everything in my power to keep her promises if you'll let me."

"Her promises?" Nox asked.

"To love you and do my best to stay safe."

His warm palm caressed my cheek. "I don't want to ever lose you."

"Then hold on tight. I'm not going anywhere."

IT HAD BEEN nearly a week since Nox's confession and neither of us had brought it up again. We didn't need to. I was more than satisfied with his honesty and had no desire to hear or see again the pain I'd witnessed that night. Instead, I wanted to see the light blue of his gaze, the menacing gleam, and the grin that told me he was up to something. I wanted to wake in his arms and fall asleep listening to him breathe.

I adored the way he always found me the first thing after entering the apartment. It didn't matter where I was—my office studying, the kitchen getting Lana's meal ready, or even soaking in a tub after a long day. It was as if I wore a tracker. Well, I did, but he didn't use his phone. He followed his heart and his need to confirm that I was present and safe, just as I'd promised.

When Nox found me, the first words from his lips were always, *How was your day?* Though they didn't vary, I never felt that they were said with anything less than genuine interest. Of all the things he did and said, it was close to my favorite.

There was this thing that he did when my hands were bound that topped the list, but I couldn't think about that too much or I wouldn't accomplish anything else.

I had just finished my lunch on campus when I saw the text. I didn't recognize the number, but I didn't need to. She told me who she was.

Unknown number:

"ALEX, IT'S CHELSEA. I KNOW YOU PROBABLY HATE ME AND I'M NOT SUPPOSED TO CALL YOU. DOES TEXTING COUNT? I THINK IT DOES. I THOUGHT YOU SHOULD KNOW THAT YOUR MOM IS SICK. SHE'S GETTING WORSE AND NOW THEY'RE TALKING ABOUT PUTTING HER IN A HOSPITAL. EVEN THOUGH I DON'T HAVE THE RIGHT TO SAY IT, I THINK YOU SHOULD BE HERE.

PLEASE DON'T TELL ANYONE, ESPECIALLY BRYCE, THAT I CONTACTED YOU.
I'M DELETING THIS TEXT FROM MY PHONE AS SOON AS I SEND.

I AM SORRY. PLEASE DON'T CALL ME BACK."

CHAPTER 40

CHARLI

I STARED IN disbelief at the screen of my phone. I may have doubted that Chelsea had really been the one to send the text had it not been for the one line: *does texting count?* That was definitely Chelsea, the one to find the loophole in every agreement.

I couldn't think about why she knew what was happening at Montague Manor and I didn't, or why she wasn't supposed to contact me, or a million other concerns. I needed to concentrate on the most important one.

My mother.

I picked up what remained of my lunch and threw it in a trash bin as I looked around the cafe. Clayton was sitting at a table near a window, looking at both his iPad and occasionally my direction. Having him tag along seemed extreme, but since I knew Nox's reasoning, I didn't argue.

Bryce had said my mother was sick once and it wasn't true. I held onto that hope as I scrolled my contacts and called the one person who would tell me what was really happening.

Jane answered on the third ring.

"Hello?"

Didn't my name come up?

I immediately stood taller, my nerves on alert.

"Jane, it's Alex."

"Yes, I understand."

I lowered my voice. "You can't talk right now?"

"That's right."

"Can you just tell me how Momma is?"

"So sad," she said. "I wish with all my heart it was different."

Tears filled my eyes as the world lost focus. "Do I need to be there?"

"I can't say. But it'd be the answer to my prayers. Bye, now. I needs to go."

"Why didn't you call me?" Though I asked my question, Jane didn't hear. The line had gone dead.

My stomach dropped to the ground as a million questions ran through my mind, all vying for voice. What was wrong with my mother? Why couldn't Jane speak to me? Why wasn't anyone telling me what was happening? How long had it been going on?

My hands trembled as I found a chair, sat, and called Nox's phone. It was rare for me to bother him during the day. I'd probably only done it less than a half dozen times. He respected my school and my time, and I respected his.

After four rings, his cell phone went to voicemail and my head fell forward, my chin to my chest as I waited to leave a message.

"Nox." I whispered his name, "I'm sorry to bother you." With each phrase, emotion rained over me. What started as a gentle shower quickly became a torrent, drowning me in a rapid river of regret.

Why hadn't I called her? Why hadn't I gone to see her when she couldn't come to me?

"I-it's my mother. I don't know what's happened." My voice cracked, leaving space for the tears that now cascaded down my cheeks. "She's sick." I gulped air, my chest suddenly tight. "Very sick. I need to get to Savannah."

I didn't ask. I told him what I needed to do. There was no doubt that I was going.

I disconnected the call and called Deloris. Thankfully, she answered right away.

"Alex. What can I do for you?"

I wiped my nose with the back of my hand and licked my salty lips. My mouth was suddenly dry as I worked to keep the tears silent. "I need to get to Savannah."

"What?" she asked.

I stood, and with the phone to my ear, I paced small circles in the cafe. "My mother's ill. I just found out. I don't know any details, but I know I need to get there. Something's wrong, terribly wrong."

"Clayton and I'll go with you," Deloris volunteered.

I nodded. "Thank you. I called Nox, but he didn't answer." One hand went to my necklace. "I'm not running as I did when Chelsea was hurt, but I need to go now."

"Tell Clayton to take you to the airport. I'll have a plane ready. Lennox will surely want to come when he finds out."

My chest ached as my regrets grew. "Deloris, I've said some things to my mother over the years… but I love her."

"Of course you do."

"I-I'm not sure if Alton… I don't know about staying at the manor. If Nox…" I'd never had a man stay with me in Savannah. I'd never had one who I wanted to have stay with me. All I knew was that if my mother was ill, the choice would be up to Alton, and I doubted he'd be as accommodating as Oren had been in Westchester County.

"I'll book a suite for the two of you in Savannah. Unless you want to stay at your home."

I let out the breath I'd been holding. "A suite would be wonderful. No, I don't want to stay there. My home is here in New York. That's just a house." A house of horrors was what Patrick called it. "A suite would be perfect."

"Alex, go tell Clayton. Let me get everything else settled."

"Thank you," I said with relief as I turned, my eyes meeting Clayton's.

We met halfway across the cafe. No doubt he could see my wordless plea. "Ma'am?"

"I just spoke to Deloris. I need to get to Savannah. She said to have you take me to the airport." I shook my head. "But she didn't say which one."

"I'm sure she meant the private hangars, but I'll call and check. Give me five minutes, and I'll have the car out front on 116th Street."

I nodded and waved him away as my phone vibrated.

NOX - PRIVATE NUMBER

"Nox," I answered.

"Princess, wait for me. I can leave in a couple of hours."

I shook my head. "No."

"No?"

"It's over a two-hour flight. Deloris is getting it set up," I explained, more composed than I'd been only minutes earlier. "I don't want to wait any longer than necessary. I don't know what's happening. The way Jane sounded, it's not good."

"I don't want you walking in there alone."

I reached for my necklace. "I'm not alone. You're always with me."

"Charli."

I closed my eyes. "I have to do this for my momma." I choked on the word. "Please understand. Deloris will be there, and she said she'd get us a suite in Savannah. I won't stay at the manor. Hopefully, I can find out where my mother is, and I won't even need to go to the manor."

"Princess," he implored, "a couple of hours."

"I love you, Nox. I'll be safe. I promise, and I'll see you tonight. Text me as soon as you land in Savannah."

"You text me. Let me know what's happening. No matter what, Charli, I'm there for you."

I nodded. "I know. I love you."

"I love you, too."

Clayton had been right about the private hangar. Lennox didn't own his own plane, but Demetri Enterprises had some kind of leasing contract to ensure that one was always available, whether for him, Oren, or any other high-ranking member of their company.

"Are you sure this is okay?" I asked Deloris. "I mean this is a business contract. This isn't business."

She patted my hand as the plane taxied on the runway and we waited for our turn to take off. "Yes, it's fine. You have an in with one of the CEO's. He said you could."

My cheeks rose. "Thank you for helping me. I'm scared."

"What do you know?"

"Nothing."

"How'd you learn about this?"

"Chelsea," I replied, not thinking about anything but what could be happening in Savannah.

"Chelsea?"

Deloris's reaction reminded me of Chelsea's plea for anonymity. "I'm not supposed to tell anyone it was her."

"She called you?"

"Text," I said as I found my phone in my purse and swiped the screen. Seconds later I handed it to her. "See. She doesn't want anyone to know. I don't understand why I wasn't called before now if my mother's so ill."

After reading the text, Deloris turned on her iPad. "Chelsea said some hospital. Let me do a search of hospitals in the area and see what I can find."

I nodded as I laid my head back against the leather seat and the small plane ascended. Over the next two hours, Deloris searched the patient records of all of the major hospitals and came up empty. Nothing. No Adelaide Fitzgerald was registered anywhere.

"Alex," she asked as we neared Savannah, "have you heard of Mongolia Woods?"

"No."

"It's a private facility west of Savannah that specializes in rehab for alcohol and drug addiction."

"What? Are you serious? My mother is going to dry out?"

"Does she drink?"

"Yes, but not… well, it's never been a problem."

She turned the screen of her iPad toward me. The old Southern estate looked similar to Montague Manor with giant oak trees draped with Spanish moss along a driveway. She swiped the screen and the next picture was of a lovely old home, large, but not as large as the manor.

"That's where she is?" I asked. "So she's not dying. It's not cancer or something?"

Deloris nodded. "That's where she is. She was admitted a few hours ago. But her records aren't fully updated. I don't know exactly why she's there. I'd venture to guess that it's not a life-threatening diagnosis; however, alcohol and drug abuse can lead to death."

"She's always drank, but I've never known anyone who could handle it better than her. But drugs? My mother would never take drugs." I handed Deloris back her iPad. "How do you do that? Is it public record?"

"No. I have ways. The thing is, this place is fully subsidized through private funds. What little information that I can gather, your mother has a strict no-visitor status for the first forty-eight hours."

"That's ridiculous," I said. "I'm her daughter. They'll let me see her."

"We'll do our best."

MY FINGERS DRUMMED on the inside of the window of the large black SUV that Deloris had secured for our use in Savannah. Clayton sat at the steering wheel while I sat alone in the backseat. It had been over fifteen minutes since Deloris had disappeared into the front entrance of Mongolia Woods. I'd wanted to go with her, to plead my own case, but she thought she would have better success on my behalf.

Click, click, my nails tapped on the glass as time stood still and I impatiently waited.

Beyond the windows, the Georgia sun reminded me that warm weather still existed in late October, even if New York had surrendered to the impending winter.

I pushed my sunglasses onto my head as my purse vibrated in my lap.

NOX - PRIVATE NUMBER

I sighed, wishing he were beside me instead of back in the frigid North.

Nox: "ANY WORD"?

Me: "NOT YET. DELORIS IS STILL INSIDE."

Nox: "I'M LEAVING IN A FEW MINUTES. THE BATPLANE IS FUELED AND READY. I'LL BE THERE IN STEALTH SPEED."

Me: "BRING YOUR CAPE. I THINK I SHOULD HAVE SEEN THAT BY NOW."

Nox: "SEE YOU SOON."

Me: "LOVE YOU."

Nox: "MORE."

I took a deep breath, realizing that for the first time since Chelsea's text, I was actually smiling. My brief reprieve quickly dimmed at the sound of Clayton's words.

"Ma'am, Mrs. Witt is coming."

I lifted my eyes from my phone toward the facility. Deloris was descending the large concrete steps. Her lips pursed tight as she navigated the unfamiliar terrain. She looked our way. There was nothing encouraging in her expression.

A moment later she was in the backseat beside me, speaking. Her tone was placating and calm. "I learned that she is stable, but they won't allow anyone to see her."

Disappointment gutted me as hope faded away. "No. Let me go in. Let me talk to them. She's my mother!"

"Alex, they know who you are. The problem…"

Deloris's words dimmed as rage bubbled from my toes, engulfing my entire body with scorching heat. I knew the problem. I saw the problem. Alton Fitzgerald was the problem.

My mother's husband buttoned his suit coat as he exited the same door that Deloris had just used.

Without thinking, I opened the door of the SUV.

"Alex…"

I didn't hear Deloris's warning or Clayton's door open as blood coursed noisily through my ears. Adjusting my sunglasses, I stepped quickly toward my stepfather.

"Let me see my mother."

CHAPTER 41

CHARLI

SIGNATURE CRIMSON FLOWED upward from the starched white collar of his shirt as Alton Fitzgerald stopped midstep and turned my direction. "It appears as though the prodigal daughter has returned."

I didn't stop walking until I was right before him. "I want to see her."

"You'll have to understand that I have no intentions of slaying a fatted calf on this occasion simply because you've decided to grace us with your presence."

"What happened?" I asked.

He looked over my shoulder toward the SUV as a limousine pulled past it and up to the edge of the walkway.

I turned back to see both Clayton and Deloris standing beside the SUV looking as though they were both ready to run in my direction.

"Come home and we'll discuss this. *Alone*," he emphasized the last word.

"Discuss it now. I don't want to go back to the manor. I want to see my mother."

Alton's tone lowered. "You see, Alexandria, that's the problem. For too long you've been coddled. Your days of getting what you want are over. It's time you acquiesced to your future, the same way Laide did."

I shook my head. "I don't know what you're talking about."

"Of course you don't. You've been too wrapped up in your own frivolities to worry about what's important. Perhaps if you hadn't been off in New York, you would have been able to help your mother. Now her fate is in my hands."

"What the hell does that mean?"

I cringed as he reached toward me and placed a hand on my shoulder. My stomach turned as he inclined his face closer to mine and his warm, putrid breath filled my nose.

"Turn around, Alexandria."

I did, not because I wanted to obey him, but because I needed to breathe fresh air. Brantley was standing near the open door to the limousine.

Alton spoke near my ear, his hand still holding my shoulder. "If you want to see your mother, or if she has a chance of ever being released from this facility, you will get in that car and do as you're told."

I looked back toward Deloris and Clayton.

"Alexandria, I won't ask again."

My eyes closed, blocking out the afternoon sun as I clenched my teeth and shook his hand away. With a deep breath, I took one step and then another. As I walked the plank to my own death, I said goodbye to Charli.

Alexandria nodded to Brantley and climbed into the backseat of the limousine.

Before the door was shut, encasing us in the cool, dim interior, my phone vibrated with an incoming call.

"Give me your purse," Alton said with his hand extended.

I lifted my sunglasses to the top of my head and stared. "What? No."

Tears prickled my eyes and I turned quickly as my face stung from the slap of his palm against my cheek.

What the hell?

I sent daggers flying from my eyes as I blinked away the moisture.

"Your mother is no longer a factor. Listen to me the first time and I won't need to be sure of your attention." Alton extended his hand again. "I don't repeat myself."

When I didn't move, he reached for my purse, his glare daring me to stop him.

Stupid! Why did I get into this car?

With the scenery moving beyond the tinted windows and the limousine in motion, I sat statuesque trying to contemplate my next move.

Alton removed my phone and gave me back my purse.

I held my tongue, as I'd been taught to do, as he turned off its power and placed it in his pocket. Though my thoughts were filled with too many things to register, Chelsea's text message came to mind. I hadn't erased it. If Alton turned on the phone, he'd see it.

"Alton," I tried for my most respectful tone. "Please tell me about my mother."

He leaned back against the seat, seemingly composing his response. "Your time in New York is done. Your mother wanted a Christmas wedding. I think if Suzy gets started on the plans, it can still be accomplished. The only variable will be if Adelaide is well enough to attend." Alton sighed, cocked his head to the side. With a straight-lipped grin, he added, "I suppose that's up to you.

"Welcome home, Alexandria."

The end of DECEPTION…

Find out what happens next in ENTRAPMENT

ENTRAPMENT

CHARLI & NOX

Coming September 13, 2016, the continuing story of Charli and Nox, the Montagues and Demetris. Deals and agreements loom like shadows in Montague Manor. What will happen as promises are broken and choices are lost?

Can and will love survive ENTRAPMENT?

Book #4 of the five-book Infidelity series,
ENTRAPMENT, by Aleatha Romig.

WHAT TO DO NOW...

LEND IT: Did you enjoy Deception? Do you have a friend who'd enjoy Deception? Deception may be lent one time. Sharing is caring!

RECOMMEND IT: Do you have multiple friends who'd enjoy Deception? Tell them about it! Call, text, post, tweet… your recommendation is the nicest gift you can give to an author!

REVIEW IT: Tell the world. Please go to the retailer where you purchased this book, as well as Goodreads, and write a review. Please share your thoughts about DECEPTION on:

STAY CONNECTED WITH ALEATHA

Do you love Aleatha's writing? Do you want to know the latest about Infidelity? Consequences? Tales From the Dark Side? and Aleatha's new series coming in 2016 from Thomas and Mercer?

Do you like EXCLUSIVE content (never released scenes, never released excerpts, and more)? Would you like the monthly chance to win prizes (signed books and gift cards)? Then sign up today for Aleatha's monthly newsletter and stay informed on all things Aleatha Romig.

Sign up for Aleatha's NEWSLETTER: http://bit.ly/1PYLjZW
(recipients receive exclusive material and offers)

You can also find Aleatha@

Check out her website: http://aleatharomig.wix.com/aleatha
Facebook: https://www.facebook.com/AleathaRomig
Twitter: https://twitter.com/AleathaRomig
Goodreads: www.goodreads.com/author/show/5131072.Aleatha_Romig
Instagram: http://instagram.com/aleatharomig
Email Aleatha: aleatharomig@gmail.com

You may also listen Aleatha Romig books on Audible.

BOOKS BY NEW YORK TIMES BESTSELLING AUTHOR ALEATHA ROMIG

INFIDELITY SERIES:

BETRAYAL

Book #1

(October 2015)

CUNNING

Book #2

(January 2016)

DECEPTION

Book #3

(May 2016)

ENTRAPMENT

Book #4

(September2016)

FIDELITY

Book #5

(TBA)

THE CONSEQUENCES SERIES:

CONSEQUENCES

(Book #1)

Released August 2011

TRUTH

(Book #2)

Released October 2012

CONVICTED

(Book #3)

Released October 2013

REVEALED

(Book #4)

Previously titled: Behind His Eyes Convicted: The Missing Years

Re-released June 2014

BEYOND THE CONSEQUENCES

(Book #5)

Released January 2015

COMPANION READS:

BEHIND HIS EYES—CONSEQUENCES

(Book #1.5)

Released January 2014

BEHIND HIS EYES—TRUTH

(Book #2.5)

Released March 2014

TALES FROM THE DARK SIDE SERIES:

INSIDIOUS

(All books in this series are stand-alone erotic thrillers)

Released October 2014

DUPLICITY

(Completely unrelated to book #1)

Release TBA

THE LIGHT SERIES:

Published through Thomas and Mercer

INTO THE LIGHT

To be released June 14, 2016

AWAY FROM THE DARK

(October 2016)

ALEATHA ROMIG

Aleatha Romig is a New York Times and USA Today bestselling author who lives in Indiana. She grew up in Mishawaka, graduated from Indiana University, and is currently living south of Indianapolis. Aleatha has raised three children with her high school sweetheart and husband of nearly thirty years. Before she became a full-time author, she worked days as a dental hygienist and spent her nights writing. Now, when she's not imagining mind-blowing twists and turns, she likes to spend her time with her family and friends. Her other pastimes include reading and creating heroes/anti-heroes who haunt your dreams!

Aleatha released her first novel, CONSEQUENCES, in August of 2011. CONSEQUENCES became a bestselling series with five novels and two companions released from 2011 through 2015. The compelling and epic story of Anthony and Claire Rawlings has graced more than half a million e-readers. Aleatha released the first of her series TALES FROM THE DARK SIDE, INSIDIOUS, in the fall of 2014. These stand-alone thrillers continue Aleatha's twisted style with an increase in heat. In the fall of 2015, Aleatha will move headfirst into the world of dark romance with the release of BETRAYAL, the first of her five-novel INFIDELITY series. Aleatha has entered the traditional world of publishing with Thomas and Mercer with her LIGHT series. The first of that series, INTO THE LIGHT, will be published in the summer of 2016.

Aleatha is a "Published Author's Network" member of the Romance Writers of America and represented by Danielle Egan-Miller of Browne & Miller Literary Associates.

Made in the USA
Columbia, SC
18 October 2017